PRAISE FOR
DAUGHTER OF A PROMISE

"Blasberg aces it again with her masterful handling of a Biblical tale transposed into our modern world with her captivating new novel. *Daughter of a Promise* is a rich and engaging coming-of-age tale of a young woman who gains her confidence slowly but surely as she casts off conventional wisdom and proffered advice and learns to listen to the deeper—and more timeless—voice that guides her. This is a novel that will remind you to be brave enough to listen to your own inner voice."

—DEBORAH GOODRICH ROYCE, author of
Reef Road, Ruby Falls, and *Finding Mrs. Ford*

"I defy you to place the characters in this novel into any neat category based on ethnicity, gender, wealth, age, or professional status. In this retelling of an ancient story—with gleaming office towers and stately mansions as its backdrop—Blasberg stands current cultural tropes on their head and masterfully invites us to examine the only power that really matters: our human capacity to learn, grow, nurture, and forgive. Bets is a heroine for our times. I loved this book."

—KATHERINE A. SHERBROOKE, author of
Leaving Coy's Hill and *The Hidden Life of Aster Kelly*

"Biblical narratives speak truths of the human condition. Jeanne Blasberg has unearthed these ancient truths and allowed them to blossom into a modern milieu. The intrigue and the drama remain with all the emotion and turmoil that touches the reader's soul. Blasberg launches us into a journey of discovery in this beautifully written novel, taken out of the pages of the Bible and given new life through the artistry of her magnificent storytelling."
—RABBI ELAINE ZECHER, senior rabbi
of Temple Israel, Boston

"Blasberg's *Daughter of a Promise* is an engrossing literary novel that defines the start of an era—the COVID-19 pandemic—much as Jay McInerney characterized the downtown Manhattan scene in 1984 with *Bright Lights, Big City* and as Michael Lewis's *Liar's Poker* gave us a vision of the wild conduct of Wall Street traders in the 1980s. This is a novel worth savoring . . . and coming back to read again and again."
—DAVID HIRSHBERG, author of
My Mother's Son and *Jacobo's Rainbow*

"This novel captures the intense pulls of love, ambition, and friendship for a young woman starting out in the world."
—MARJAN KAMALI, author of *The Stationary Shop*

"Jeanne Blasberg writes like a dream, and *Daughter of a Promise* feels like the lovely braiding of a real life rendered and the culmination of a prophecy. All of which to say it is nothing less than biblical in its ambition while it remains entirely grounded in the real. This is a book about love and money, and how both make the world go 'round. I loved every page."
—SCOTT CHESIRE, author of *High as the Horses' Bridles*

DAUGHTER OF A PROMISE

Also by Jeanne McWilliams Blasberg

Eden
The Nine

DAUGHTER
OF A
PROMISE

A NOVEL

JEANNE McWILLIAMS BLASBERG

SHE WRITES PRESS

Published 2024
Printed in the United States of America
Print ISBN: 978-1-64742-608-8
E-ISBN: 978-1-64742-609-5
Library of Congress Control Number: 2023915539

For information, address:
She Writes Press
1569 Solano Ave #546
Berkeley, CA 94707

Interior Design by Tabitha Lahr

She Writes Press is a division of SparkPoint Studio, LLC.

For John

"The most common way people give up their power is by thinking they don't have any."

—ALICE WALKER

Late one afternoon, David rose from his couch and strolled on the roof of the royal palace; and from the roof he saw a woman bathing. The woman was very beautiful, and the king sent someone to make inquiries about the woman. He reported, "She is Bathsheba daughter of Eliam and wife of Uriah the Hittite." David sent messengers to fetch her, she came to him and he lay with her—she had just purified herself after her period—and she went back home. The woman conceived, and she sent word to David, "I am pregnant."

2 SAMUEL 11:2-5

PART I

CHAPTER ONE

I f Yaya was alive, she'd say doctors have no idea, that babies come when they are good and ready. Although her wisdom is my guiding light, I've circled your due date on the calendar nonetheless. I've counted down seven months and then four, and then weeks, and now days with your grandmother, Gloria, calling every morning, warning me not to worry. "It's not good for the baby," she says. I tell her to be quiet, she's the one who keeps calling, as if our relationship was built on daily contact—exchanging trivial happenings, updates on Tía Julia's health or maybe a storm heading toward Miami—when it's obvious she's only listening for anxiety in my voice.

She forgets I'm a trained actress with control over things like tone and volume and resonance, that I'm used to performing for an audience. When the nerves do take hold, writing to you has been good medicine. With your arrival right around the corner, I've learned to breathe through my tightening chest. Nighttime, however, is a different story. That's when I'm hounded by the recurring dream of Doctor Hernandez placing my feet high in metal stirrups, fastening on a headlamp, and peering between my thighs. She reaches in deeper and deeper but can't find you, can't find anything for that matter. I wake in a sweat, pressing a hand to my stomach to make sure you're still there.

1

Yaya told me the pain of childbirth is readily forgotten other-wise we'd live in a world of only children. Forgotten is not the right word. Women don't forget anything, rather we rid ourselves of certain memories with pain being the first to go. It's a biological adaptation to ensure the survival of our species, not to mention a key ingredient for things like forgiveness and moving on.

I haven't told anybody, but I plan on naming you Sol after the most fiery star in the sky. I've written this story for you, to be read when you are a grown man, because above all else I aspire for you to be a principled man, a virtuous man, a man who is good and fair and behaves decently. I have also written it for myself, in the here and now, to get the details down before they fade any further, to clarify the line between what was real and what were dreams or memories. More than anything to dissolve the shame shrouding it all. I've written it because there are people who think they know what happened and while I may romanticize and be out of focus, I need my own version out in the world.

I am not seeking your approval, not yours nor any man's. I'm only asking that you take my story as a series of choices, some smart, some not as smart. Yaya always encouraged me to gather expe-riences, and while these were seasoned with dreams and desire, taking place while the world tipped on its side, she often said painful events bring clarity. "Betsabé, life is a mysterious journey of the soul. Let it take you through meadows as well as deep valleys."

You might be naturally inclined to heed your father's disci-pline, but please, don't ignore my teachings. With these words, I hope to weave a wreath of wisdom upon your head. Not cleverness nor threats of splitting babies, but true wisdom, the kind that might repair the widening chasm between people, the kind that might remind us how to compromise and reinforce the power of love.

Withhold judgment as you read, and maybe you'll glean something. I know that sounds self-important, as if a year in my life holds the key to anything, let alone understanding. But it was quite a year and I have spent a great deal of time turning events over in my mind, making meaning and becoming stronger.

I've vowed to cherish these final days with you tucked into a ball, floating about inside me. My rational mind says there is no reason to worry. My body has been nothing but nurturing for the past nine months to the point where I've gained forty pounds and each night after dinner, you tell me you are perfectly healthy with punches and kicks to the wall of my stomach.

Your father says, "What did you expect from the grandson of an Olympic boxer?" But if you are a prize fighter, it stems from having two parents who love you. People greet me with a grin these days, saying, "Any day now," and I picture your arrival into the spotlight of the delivery room, and my heart beats wildly with love and excitement and, I can't lie, a tinge of fear. It is my hope you disregard the fear and carry only love with you into the world, and that this story may serve as a guide in securing a wise and discerning heart.

———◆———

It's not a nice, clean calendar year of which I write, but the twelve months spanning June 2019 to June 2020, beginning the day I started at First Provident. I start with this day not because my analyst position at an investment bank was a big deal (it was), but because it was the day I first laid eyes on David. I try many times throughout this telling to explain the effect he had on me. It was as if he'd cast a spell, or more accurately, as if he found me at the precise moment I was longing for a spell to be cast. Meeting him was all wrapped up in the thrill of the new job, the magic of New York, everything charged con tanta ilusión, with so much hope. I'd moved into a studio apartment with Rae days after our college graduation and when I wasn't exploring the East Village, I was putting together the right outfit or practicing my commute, the best strategy for the morning rush. From riding the subway to savoring spicy mustard atop a salted pretzel, I thrived on the pulse of the city which pounded in my inner ear like the heartbeat of the universe.

It's possible David and I crossed paths by chance just as I was inhabiting every movie and song about New York's propulsive quality, convinced my destiny waited around the next corner, but when our lives did collide it was as if I recognized him or recognized something about him. That intangible something at the core of every fantasy, with the lights on Broadway as a backdrop or the snow falling in Central Park. And in every version of that dream, I was on my way to becoming glamorous and strong, a confident woman who thought nothing of darting into midtown traffic to flag down a yellow cab.

No taxis that first morning, however. I was just as happy to cram onto the F train at Second Avenue, transferring at Lafayette to the Six uptown. I finally felt relevant, an honest-to-god member of the adult population, having checked my bag for phone, keys, wallet before hurrying out the door to make things happen. Disembarking at Fifty-First and Lex, I paused on the stuffy underground platform to freshen my lipstick, using the same tube Rae once dubbed backstage as "my red-hot shot of confidence." I ascended the stairs and caught sight of a corner bodega and a man dousing white plastic tubs full of tulips with a hose. It was another wonder of the city that freshly cut flowers showed up each morning on street corners of wet concrete, fresh, damp, and ready for the stampede.

My fellow pedestrians were glued to their phones or balancing trays of coffee as they waited for the walk signal, but I gripped the shoulder straps of my new leather satchel, gaped at the towering skyscrapers, as the current of humanity carried me along until it deposited me in front of First Provident headquarters on Fifty-Second between Park and Madison.

"I barely recognized you," I whispered to Ethan. He sat at the end of a long folding table wearing a dark blue suit with hair cut much shorter than the lax bro look he'd fashioned at Lyle College.

"My new look," he said, running his fingers across his scalp.

"Coffee any good?"

We'd been mere acquaintances in college. He was one of those jocks who wore the name of a fancy boarding school across his chest. Born and bred in New England, Ethan was a lacrosse star at our small college whereas I came from the country's southernmost tip and was part of the theatre crowd.

"It'll do," he said.

First Provident prided itself on its two-month boot camp, claiming its methods were proven to convert even the most humanities-centric liberal arts major into an investment banker, or, at a minimum, into somebody who could crunch it out for two years. Despite the sour energy of the fifteenth floor, it provided a familiar classroom-like setting, an intermediate step before being assigned to one of the floors above.

I took a moment to survey the room. It couldn't have been more different than the rich environment where I'd been interviewed and welcomed back on "sell day." The training floor had no well-appointed offices, no panoramic views of the skyline, no windows at all, for that matter. It was 100 percent utilitarian with a drop panel ceiling, beige soundproof walls, and industrial carpeting punctured at regular intervals with electrical outlets. I'd later learn it had been home to the now defunct sales & trading department, disbanded rather abruptly in 2008 after a calamitous proprietary trade.

I won't lie. I was pretty nervous about my lack of finance experience. I'd been reading the *Wall Street Journal* in my college library all spring and I'd always been good at math, but I'd only taken one econ class at Lyle. I was a double major in theatre and psych and found comfort in my advisor's postulation that in the end "success comes down to acting and psychology."

"Go ahead, apply," she had shrugged. "Why not? It's the only white shoe firm that recruits on campus." I had no idea what that meant, but it sounded rebellious, like trying on the glass slipper an evil stepmother was keeping from me. I also liked the idea of detouring off my expected path and doing something more cerebral because for as long as I could remember, adults had been telling me, "With that height and that face, you'll be famous." Besides, once you heard about the serious coin people banked in those two-year analyst programs, it made the idea of scraping by on tips between auditions seem sort of silly.

I filled a mug with coffee and sat down, grateful for the respite from my heels. I didn't mind if Ethan saw me wince because we were in this together, outliers hired due to the bank's chairman, Theodore Johnstone, being an alumnus of Lyle College. He'd mandated two graduating seniors from his alma mater be extended offers each year along with recruited talent from the nation's top campuses. He'd likened Lyle to small top-tier New England colleges, the Amherst and Williams of the world, which Ethan and I both knew it wasn't. Chairman Johnstone was either out of touch or chose to ignore Lyle's evolving reputation as a safety school for rich kids, with a student body of twenty-two hundred, tucked away in a frozen pocket of upstate New York where partying and bad behavior were overlooked byproducts of extreme isolation.

We would be dubbed "Lyle hires" by the other analysts, but Ethan would never feel it as much as me. He was a white male with a degree in economics whereas I was not white, had a name people had a hard time pronouncing, and hadn't yet deciphered the instructions for my HP 12c. I tucked my hands under my thighs and reminded myself that this firm had hired me. I inhaled deeply and turned my attention to the woman at the front of the room, wondering if anybody else was pinching themselves.

Her name was Helen and she said she headed up HR. Standing at the podium, she cleared her throat. "Now, the pace of the summer will be fast. The equivalent of a four-year finance degree condensed into ten weeks. We don't have a minute to spare." Her underlings made their way around the room, issuing First Provident email accounts, cell phones, laptops, credit cards, and paperwork for our 401(k)s. When a young woman got around to the table I shared with Ethan, I said, "Hey, I'm Bets Ruiz." The woman scanned her clipboard, her harried expression turning into a frown.

"Oh dear, there must be a mistake," she said.

"No, you've got it right," I said, pointing to my name on her list. "I'm Betsabé, but people call me Bets for short."

My first-grade teacher had even gone so far as to suggest, "We'll call you Betsy." So, in the same way I dutifully dressed in an itchy plaid jumper, I wore that nickname for a few weeks too. That is, until my mother found out. She marched into the classroom, dragging me by the wrist, and corrected the teacher. "Her name is Betsabé Isabella Ruiz." And even though Betsabé rolled off the tongues of our clan in Miami like music, it was not a name you'd often hear, as in I'd never met another Betsabé. The literal meaning was "daughter of a promise" or in my case, a broken one.

Helen started up again from the front of the room, asking us to remove tax forms from our manila envelopes, and the "first day of the rest of my life" excitement began to fizzle out. Paperwork can do that to you. I'd been looking forward to this day for so long, too . . . could clearly recall the afternoon back in October when I'd called my mother to tell her I got the job.

"A bank?" asked Gloria.

"Yes."

I wasn't going to explain the difference between an investment bank and the branch where she cashed her checks, but I didn't want her thinking I'd be stationed behind bulletproof glass at a teller's window.

"You got a desk, then?"

"Yes, in a high rise on Park Avenue!"

"Wait, Wall Street or Park Avenue? You're confusing me."

"Mami, it's New York City!"

7

"Well aren't you something! But the school year's just begun, aren't you going to get that diploma?" Although her question smacked of sarcasm, it was justified. Classes had barely begun but investment banks had locked in their new hires for the following spring.

"I'll start at First Provident right after graduation."

"So next year?" She harrumphed as if anything might happen between now and then.

"They gave me a signing bonus, so I'm coming home for break!" The VP who made my offer said it was to cover moving expenses, but I purchased plane tickets to Miami for Thanksgiving and Christmas. I was done crashing on couches and imposing on friends.

"So expensive!" she said, albeit with minimal protest.

I'd never divulge what a First Provident starting salary was to my mother. My classmates at Lyle, however, knew exactly what I was making. Compensation was the first thing to leak each fall, inevitably working its way into conversations. And even though the most talented and creative kids in my senior class were going into banking, consulting, or insurance, people had the gall to ask, "How can you sell your soul to the devil when you might actually do something impactful in the world?"

Oh, how I hated the word impactful. To my mind, doing good for Betsabé Isabella Ruiz was doing good for the world. I owed it to myself and my family to take the money and take the job and show up at the First Provident offices in all my glory. I'd show them impactful, hiring a car for the drive to the airport at Thanksgiving instead of taking the chartered bus. I'd dress the part too, throwing away the stained down jacket I'd purchased freshman year and splurging on a chic wool coat. It felt good to be bankrolling myself and moving on to a stage in life where it didn't matter if I had hovering helicopter parents.

CHAPTER TWO

Even in college I had the bad habit of daydreaming during lectures, imagining my future, but also refashioning the past. You'll run across people who take medication for it, Sol, but I don't necessarily think a wandering mind is a bad thing. I guess that depends on whether you can pull it together when you need to. Anyway, when I turned back to Helen and her tax forms, a tall dark-haired man had taken over the lectern. He didn't apologize for interrupting either, leaving Helen to step aside and smile dumbly, her rouged cheeks extra wide and shiny.

"Good morning," he boomed. I pushed my glasses up the bridge of my nose to get a better look. He was at least six foot four with a voice to match. "I'm Robert David, Managing Director in Mergers and Acquisitions."

The first word that came to mind was distinguished, his pink button-down with white cuffs and collar on top of gray pants suggested an ease with fashion. He was older, maybe mid-fifties, but emitted something undeniably playful. His white teeth were set off against taut, suntanned skin, and his slicked-back hair curled around his ears. His face revealed the lines of a man who smiled often, reminding me of the fathers I'd seen during Lyle's Parents Weekends, wearing Barbour jackets to tailgates with a confidence that said they possessed all the right clothes as well as the occasions on which to wear them.

"Shit, that's him!" Ethan whispered as if spotting a movie star. "You can call me David," the man continued. "I came down to welcome you all to First Provident." He shrugged at our dungeon-like way station, as if doing time on the fifteenth floor was a rite of passage. "And you are to be congratulated. I'm told we received twenty thousand resumés this year for your forty spots. You, it seems, are the best and the brightest. Leaders of tomorrow. This summer we will mold you into wizards of finance, indoctrinating you in accounting, financial modeling, corporate finance, as well as FP's culture. You've likely heard of our work hard, play hard ethos and you may have friends from college who opted for more 'balanced' lifestyles," and he smirked, using air quotes around the word balanced as if it was code for lazy. "Soon you'll be giving us your evenings and weekends. Best to binge on whatever fun you can now. But don't have too much fun," and there he paused, allowing the nervous laughter to die down. "Keep your heads down and your eyes open. You'll have assessment tests every Friday, and by summer's end we will have enough data with which to make your two-year assignment."

And with that he nodded farewell, the sheen of his hair reflecting the fluorescent light above, and if I remember correctly, I think he actually saluted. He did not offer to take questions, nor did he make eye contact with anyone in particular, despite those in the front row squirming at the chance to be noticed. He simply did an about-face and retreated to the elevators. The enrapt silence in the room broke into a buzz, and my heart raced despite thinking the man was a little full of himself. Ethan was wiping his forehead with a napkin.

"Who *was* that?" I asked.

"Fucking David!"

"But?"

"Oh, c'mon Bets. Really? He's like the king of Wall Street. He may not have made the papers recently, but he's a legend. He built the M&A practice which drives the profits here; everyone knows it's the place to be."

Back in the fall, when we'd attended sell day, old Theodore Johnstone made welcoming remarks after lunch, and I just assumed the title of chairman meant he was the big boss. And so, it seemed I would have to stick close to Ethan if only for the ways he might clue me in.

———

After David left, Helen announced a fifteen-minute break. I made my way to the elevator where another girl was pressing the call button insistently. "That guy was like too much," she said under her breath. I nodded even though I was still picturing the way David's cotton shirt strained against his chest muscles and was like, hot damn, maybe he has reason to be. She crossed her arms as we waited. She was a little high-strung and thin, probably an anorexic overdue for a vape. I'd never smoked on account of my singing voice, but I remember envying her bad habit that morning, wanting something, anything, to tamp down the nerves rising in my throat.

She introduced herself as Sandra but as soon as the elevator doors opened into the lobby, I lost her among the hectic crowd crisscrossing the floor. The sunlight was disorienting too, refracting in a million directions across the marble floor like a shattered rainbow. The revolving door sucked me into a vacuum and then spat me out onto the sidewalk where I spotted Sandra tucked into a delivery ramp cutout.

I'd had my eye on an espresso kiosk and a halal food truck on the corner but stopped by her side. She surprised me by lighting up a good old-fashioned cigarette. I stood next to her like a zombie in the heat, inhaling a putrid combination of steam billowing up from a manhole cover and car exhaust. The din of voices and engines punctuated by a car horn every few seconds contributed to sensory overload. I closed my eyes, reminding myself this chaos was the reason I'd come to Manhattan. It wasn't to "do deals," but to be part of that "if you can make it there, you can make it anywhere" mystique.

After a few moments, Sandra tapped my shoulder and pointed to her watch. "Back to the lion's den for us," she said, wiping her forehead. It seemed neither of us was entirely sure what we'd gotten ourselves into, and sometimes, Sol, that's all it takes to make a friend.

After Helen finished with the housekeeping items, a first-year associate began a review of "basic accounting." It may have been "basic" for all the business majors in the room, but I had a hard time balancing a balance sheet. And at the end of the first week, when our assessments were returned, Ethan spied the red ink all over mine and offered to be my tutor. I told him to mind his own business. So, while he became the self-appointed social director of our training class, spearheading evenings to the bar of the moment or weekend excursions to the Hamptons, I opened the windows of my fifth-floor walk-up, changed into a T-shirt and shorts, and sidled up to the kitchen table to study.

Thank God for YouTube. I became a self-taught expert on net present value, valuations, and internal rates of return. I crammed at that table in front of the window as the sky went from blue to black. I ordered tacos from Café Habana, letting Styrofoam containers pile up among graphs, pencils, and packets of case studies. I never described my ghastly existence to Yaya when we spoke on the phone each Sunday, leading her to believe I was taking in the sights and even splurging on theatre tickets.

I mastered the functions on my new calculator, even if the reverse Polish notation messed me up on occasion. I started with simple interest rate and amortization problems and soon was solving for compounded annual growth rates. Ethan said my obsession with the calculator was a waste because Excel spreadsheets did everything faster. But he hadn't read the instruction packet thoroughly, the part that said our calculators were the only tools allowed on assessment tests, and on week three, there were only about a dozen of us able to turn in our tests on time. After that, I was the one offering to be Ethan's tutor.

Despite a string of minor successes, I tossed around at night, sweating from the heat but also from dreams in which Helen from HR asked me to lunch to say, "Recruitment isn't an exact science. There are always a couple new analysts we need to let go." And then she'd extend her palm, expecting me to repay the signing bonus. There were also dreams where I was trapped inside Excel, unable to climb the columns of numbers to get out, crisscrossing a landscape of error landmines, #N/a or #REF, ready to trip up and explode like a high-stakes version of Tetris.

One evening, I opted to cook for myself with a glass of wine, something along the lines of pork, rice, and yuca with mojo like Yaya used to make. I stopped at the market and bought the meat and the spices, but when I turned the electric coil of the efficiency stove on high, oil spattered everywhere and all I could think about was the care with which Rae had arranged the kitchen with matching salt and pepper grinders, a tin canister for sugar, glass cruets for oil and vinegar. The skillet smoked and I threw it in the sink, meat and all, turning on the faucet and opening the windows wide. The last thing I needed was to set off the fire alarm. There had already been a situation with the landlord, something about my name not being on the lease and his unwillingness to provide a second set of keys. I didn't want to be known as Rae Stern's screw-up roommate.

I settled for a bowl of rice, mixing in salsa from a jar and melting cheese on top in the microwave. I sat on Rae's futon, chewing slowly and staring at her art posters. She was spending the remainder of the summer at her family's home in Rhode Island before starting work after Labor Day. I fluffed her throw pillows before getting back to work because it always felt like the walls had eyes and she knew what I was up to.

———

Rae and I had become friends in Lyle's theatre department, working on Les Mis our freshman year and then several other productions throughout college. When I introduced her to my mother on graduation weekend, she was standing with her own mother, Sarah Stern, who happened to be one of my advisors as well as Lyle's dean of students. After a few minutes of polite chitchat, we walked away with Gloria scrunching her face. "She's so little. How old is she anyway?"

"Rae was homeschooled, Mami," I said. "Started college young. But she's alright." Rae had delicate features, beautiful in a porcelain sort of way. Despite having hazel eyes that popped against her creamy complexion, everyone at Lyle knew her for her bright orange hair. One look at Dean Stern told you ginger ran in the family, but Rae had set her curly tresses ablaze with a chemical concoction that turned it borderline neon.

Still, Gloria zeroed in on her size. As far as my mother was concerned, being plump made women trustworthy. Hueso puro is what she called those fussy matriarchs Yaya worked for over the years. Skin and bones. So, for the two days spanning baccalaureate and graduation, while helping break down my dorm room, my mother would refer to Rae as "that skinny, little gringa."

I hadn't attempted to explain that she made it possible for me to live in the East Village. Even though I'd be pulling in a great salary and could afford my half of the rent, landlords expected people with no credit history to have somebody cosign the lease. Don't get me started on how messed up that is, but fortunately for me, Rae's trust fund would serve as our financial guarantee.

We were an unlikely pair, with me agreeing to the arrangement somewhat out of necessity, and Rae because she saw us on the road to best friendship. Ethan coined us the odd couple, with her on the petite end of the feminine beauty spectrum and me standing five foot nine with a figure that took up space. Another difference between us was that my idea of New York centered on theatre and a club scene, while she wanted to hang out in cafés with hipster menus and write in her journal. Taking her American coffee with as much milk as she did, well, I was afraid she'd come across as a neophyte.

I liked Rae well enough, but in college I could go hot and cold. In truth, I could go hot and cold on a lot of people, especially senior year as classmates paired up to hunt for apartments. Even though I was one of the first in my class to land a job in New York, none of the entitled assholes thought to ask me to live with them. So, when Rae brought up the idea right after spring break, I was relieved to say the least.

Back at the kitchen table, I stared at a case study about a buyout financed with a private bank offering, later to be replaced by a bond offering. I was supposed to solve for the order in which subordinated debt got paid back after the refinancing. I flipped between our text and something I'd found online but was happily distracted when my phone buzzed with a text from Rae. *Hey roomie, do we need a bathmat?* She'd be returning soon, and I vacillated between craving her company and dreading it. For the majority of the summer it had been just my food in the fridge, my dirty clothes on the floor, my makeup on the edge of the pedestal sink. She'd been so particular on move-in day, never apologizing for showing up late after the tussle with the landlord. All the time waiting had cost me a $150 parking ticket and a late fee when I returned the rental car, which she hadn't even offered to split.

I got over it when she helped carry my luggage up the five flights of stairs, however. The fact that the space was jaw dropping didn't hurt either. Her grandmother was friends with someone at the management company, so we didn't need to pay a broker fee. "Ay, this is nice!" I cooed, shimmying through the doorway. It was a really large studio, occupying half the fifth floor of the building. The wall facing the street was made up of mullioned windowpanes, casting a pattern of rectangular shadows across the hardwood floor. Rae had described it as an atelier, a space created for an actual artist back in the day with lots of natural light. It had a clawfoot tub in the tiny bathroom and somewhere along the line had been equipped with an efficiency kitchen.

I spun around on the ball of my foot, taking it all in. The glass panes may have been cloudy with cigarettes crumpled in an ashtray on the sill, but I didn't care. I sent Yaya and Gloria pictures of the exterior and interior with plenty of exclamation points and thumbs-up emojis. I'd explain that there was a Murphy bed for me, and Rae slept on the futon, the subtext being Gloria shouldn't show up in New York expecting a place to crash. Later that afternoon, Rae's grandmother, Rachel, arrived with a U-Haul filled with furniture. I wasn't sure about their family cast-offs, but I'd been living with standard college-issue for four years and was in no position to be picky.

———

Rae burst through the door a few nights later with a healthy, sun-kissed glow, full of energy and ready to start her job at the publishing house. "Helloo!" she sang, and I stood up, pushing aside my cold dinner. I actually brightened at the sight of her, someone who knew nothing about spreadsheets, the markets, or internal rates of return.

"Rae!" I said, making a move to help with her bags, but she must have seen the circles under my eyes, the exhaustion in my posture, a combination of the training program and sleeping in an overheated walk-up all summer.

"Oh, Bets, sit down, I've got it." The least I could do was slide her bags across the floor. "Looks like you've been killing yourself. I'll have to get you up to Rhode Island while the weather's still nice."

"Sure," I said, the likelihood of such a thing seeming slim to none.

With her bags inside, I tidied my papers and watched her unpack. It quickly became evident my belongings had crept farther afield than she liked. I began stuffing clothes into drawers and hiding dirty laundry in a garbage bag on the closet floor. I pushed my dresses to one end of the closet, but she seemed a little put out.

I turned on music and suggested we open a bottle of wine to toast her return.

She agreed, kneeling on the floor folding sweaters onto stackable shelves. After her clothes were put away, the wine bottle emptied, and our glasses in the sink, we took turns in the bathroom. Before slipping under the covers, Rae turned out the overhead lights and lit a large gardenia-scented candle on the coffee table.

"Want to hear the latest?"

"On?"

"The coywolves, what else?"

"Really?" It was like discovering a bonus episode of my favorite series had dropped. They were the animals that had been terrorizing our college campus for the past year. A cross between Eastern coyotes and wolves, and I was one of the first to have a close encounter. I'd been stumbling home from a party with some friends, not paying attention or expecting anything to be on the path in front of us. We screamed, practically running into the creature and attracting campus security, who assumed there had been a sexual assault.

Rae described how her mother was now caught in the middle of the mess. Students were afraid to walk across campus in the evening and parents were calling up in arms. It seemed President Addington was making her the scapegoat, pointing to mismanagement of dining hall waste in an effort to appease the community.

The irony was that Dean Stern was the faculty advisor to the Sustainable Food Initiative, or SUFI, which I chaired my senior year. I had joined the organization as a freshman after witnessing all the waste in the dining hall. Yaya had taught me "no comer con los ojos," to take no more than my share, but at Lyle kids tossed full plates of uneaten food onto the bussing conveyor. What's worse, instead of creating compost from discarded food, like Yaya always had, kitchen workers threw it in dumpsters behind the building, practically luring the frightful creatures out of the woods. Dean Stern and I had been working tirelessly to change all that.

"Somebody started a Facebook group called Concerned Citizens of Lyle," Rae said. "A place to post exact times and locations of coywolf sightings. They gathered enough data to map their daily migrations and pinpoint where they're feeding and where their dens are."

"Wow." I pictured a college administration previously obsessed with binge drinking and sexual violence declaring war on coywolves.

"Now it's open season."

"And that's making people happy?"

"You would think, but turns out Addington was the one behind the Facebook group, giving data to the hunters and paying a big bounty for each carcass."

"You are kidding me."

"So, instead of working on the campaign against food waste, my mom is now spending all her time fending off PETA."

For some reason, while everyone was trying to get rid of the animals, I had secretly taken their side. I appreciated their brazenness, the way they showed up where they weren't wanted, disrupting everything. Or maybe I was just partial to the big bad wolf archetype. As a little girl, my favorite fairy tale had been La Capurcita Roja. I even once dressed up as Little Red Riding Hood for Halloween, Gloria lending me her reddest lipstick to match the cape Yaya had sewn. Each time Yaya read me the tale before bedtime, she did the most dramatic voices. I loved to mimic back, "Pero, what big eyes you have, Yaya."

Who knows, it may have been her animated storytelling that inspired my acting career, but it also romanticized the notion of a brave little girl heading off into a dark forest to deliver a meal to her sick grandmother. Never mind the moral of the story being attractive young ladies should never talk to strangers lest they become a wolf's tender morsel, or that in the end it was the luck of a hunter passing by who cut open the belly of the wolf to save both Little Red Riding Hood and her grandmother, my takeaway was a little girl's capacity to be brave.

Rehashing the saga before falling asleep had me dreaming of anthropomorphized canines who were well-dressed in tweed, standing on furry hind legs. They wore spectacles and smoked pipes to fool sweet young things traversing the forest. I was relieved the next morning to wake up in the safety of New York City, where you didn't have to worry about dark forests or fanged animals lying in wait.

CHAPTER THREE

The next morning, I hugged Rae before we headed our separate ways. It was an impulsive gesture that surprised me, but the night before had shone a light on my lonely existence and how nice it was to have a friend. Sol, as much as you might be anticipating a tale of unconventional love in these pages, trust me, it's coming. But this is a story about a blossoming friendship as well, which is its own sort of love and arguably the most important kind.

"Good luck on your first day!" I said. Rae responded with exaggerated fright across her face and fidgeted with her messenger bag. Even though I was the actress and she was the director, her facial expressions had me laughing the entire walk to the subway. After a crowded ride and a steamy walk down Lex, I turned left on 53rd Street and ran into Sandra. "Happy Judgment Day," she said before pushing through the revolving door.

"Oh jeez, that's right." One bottle of wine and some bedtime chatter with Rae and I'd totally forgotten permanent assignments were being doled out that afternoon. A prickly heat ran across my chest. It was the same feeling I got waiting for callbacks after an audition. Everyone knew which were the major roles and which were the duds with no lines at all.

Once upstairs, I popped a couple Tylenol and Ethan placed a steaming cup of coffee in front of me. He was like a puppy who couldn't stop thumping his tail, raising his eyebrows and quickly texting everyone the name of a bar. "Bets," he whispered, "people are going out for drinks tonight to celebrate the end of training. You down?" Sometimes I thought he'd committed *The Wolf of Wall Street* to memory, as if his career hinged as much on what happened outside the office as what happened within.

"Is Rae back in the city? Maybe she'd want to come?" He'd been bugging me to join the group all summer, and delivering Rae, the girl he'd had a crush on since sophomore year, would certainly make him happy.

"Possibly," I said, "but I feel sick to my stomach." Heads were huddled in speculation, and nervous energy filled the room.

"I'm not too bullish on my prospects either." Ethan jerked his neck in what I'd come to recognize as his nervous tic, a morning crack, first one side and then the next. He tugged on his shirt collar as if it was a size too small and straightened his tie. "I had lunch with a guy in the real estate department last week. He was putting on the sell. I guess I'd be happy there."

I put my hands on my hips. "Wait, what? People are getting recruited? What the hell!" A few heads turned at my outburst, and Ethan placed his hand on my shoulder.

"I wouldn't worry about it. You'll be fine," he whispered.

His tone pissed me off. It was the same one he'd used after the accounting disaster. Typically, I'd throw my hair behind one shoulder and sit up tall in the face of irritation, but in that moment next to Ethan, a few hours from being handed my fate, I shrank. I took slow breaths and asked myself, What do I care? I had taken the job because it was a ticket to New York, and it paid well, well enough to save up for the day when I would follow my real dream, even if I hadn't exactly figured out what that was yet. The problem was that over the course of the summer, I'd begun wanting what everyone around me wanted. It had been the same with college admissions, rushing a sorority, casting calls, and job interviews. Half my life's ambitions seemed thrust upon me because they matched what everyone else was after.

Helen flicked the overhead lights on, our cue to stop talking. I swatted Ethan's hand from my shoulder and sucked in my cheeks, turning my attention to a guy at the front of the room who was focusing his PowerPoint. I put on my glasses, assessing his fair skin and light hair, his genuine smile. He was about my height with the build of a farm boy, and his happy demeanor took my mind off the fact the day was headed toward a lackluster conclusion.

"Good morning," he said. "My name is Grant Schafer and I once sat where you are. After graduating from Yale, I spent three years as an analyst at First Provident before B-school at Columbia. Now I'm a second-year associate in M&A."

He pronounced the acronym like a word in its own right: EMINAY and *B-school? Please.* And I didn't need any further reminder that M&A was where the action was, where the money was, that an assignment there was the equivalent of your name on the marquis. Grant listed the skills needed to do well in any practice area, a review of what we'd heard all summer as well as a pep talk before being sent into battle. *Attention to detail.* I was increasingly frightened by that phrase as if one typo or miscalculation would see my head rolling. "For the fees we take, there can be no errors. Our clients have zero tolerance for mistakes."

He went on to describe how due diligence was conducted, the firewalls that were in place, the strict confidentiality required on deals, and the consequences if insider trading was ever suspected. He admitted that it was easy to get flummoxed by all the rules and regulations. "In the end, if you have a question or are unsure of anything, you need to ask; err on the side of caution. You won't be shot for asking a question." Only in a crowd of know-it-alls, raised on the fear of being less than perfect, would there be constant reminders that asking questions was okay.

"Associates are here to help you succeed. Practice humility, we've all been there." So instead of sending down some cocksure egomaniac, M&A surprised us with Grant Schafer, an all-American boy, glowing like the setting sun on a field of wheat. Based on the way he rattled off his resumé, I had been prepared to hate him, but he was growing increasingly likeable. The fact that he'd survived the life we were about to embark on gave him an aura. Not only had he survived, he oozed a casual comfort with the way it all worked.

The other analysts in the room may as well have been drooling, so desirous of his life were they. Sure, there was a contingent who assumed any associate who hadn't yet jumped ship for the high pay offered at a hedge fund was likely second rate, but rumor had it Robert David compensated his people extravagantly, and so who was to say? Ethan had once told me he'd cut his balls off for the chance to work in M&A.

I pulled my phone from my bag to see if Rae had texted about her first day at the publishing house. Maybe we'd split another bottle that night and commiserate.

I texted her: *How's it going?*

I coughed into my fist and accidentally knocked my calculator onto the floor, and everybody turned to look for the source of the clatter, including Grant. We momentarily locked eyes and I mouthed "sorry," and he flashed a forgiving smile before finishing his presentation. When he was done, he made his way to the table I shared with Ethan.

"I don't mean to be forward," he said. "But are you Betsabé Ruiz?"

"That's me." I nodded, impressed by his flawless pronunciation.

"Ethan Pierce," said Ethan, standing up and extending his hand.

Grant turned as if he hadn't noticed the person next to me.

"Hello, um, anyway Betsabé. I wanted to be the first to say congratulations and welcome. We're excited for you to join the team." His eyes glistened, his smile broadened.

"Wait, what? Me?" I asked, unable to mask my surprise over what must have been a very big mistake. Ethan's jaw dropped and several of the analysts around us turned as if they couldn't believe what they were overhearing.

"The list doesn't go up until after lunch," Ethan said as if this guy didn't know what he was talking about.

"David always gets first dibs," Grant said. I raised an eyebrow in disbelief, remembering the man's intimidating welcome speech. "You must have aced training. But hey, speaking of lunch, text me when you're wrapping up and I'll meet you by the elevator. We have a big table on Fridays."

"Sure," I said, standing my full height while Grant jotted down his number before taking long purposeful strides toward the exit.

"What the fuck was that?" Ethan whispered.

"I guess I'm a hot commodity," I said, elbowing him in the ribs. The prospect of M&A was terrifying, but it was obviously a huge victory. "C'mon Ethan. A win for team Lyle."

He sighed. "I don't know how you do it," he said. "But maybe some of your magic will rub off on me."

———

I met Grant a few hours later at the elevators, which attracted plenty of stares. We descended to the lobby to gain access to the executive elevators with access to the top floors of the building. He swiped his pass card on a scanner below the buttons, an option that didn't even exist in the "local" bank of elevators I'd been relegated to all summer. That's another thing to be aware of, hierarchy exhibits itself in a million ways in life such as a preferred class of elevator. Sometimes, Sol, life is easier when you just don't know.

When the doors glided open on the sixtieth floor, I was struck by the light. M&A had abandoned the firm's traditional wood paneling for a futuristic brand of its own. It gave off the sensation of floating on a cloud high above the canyon where I'd taken morning breaks with Sandra, above the fluorescent lighting and forced air of the training floor, not to mention every other department at the firm.

Offices on sixty were demarcated with glass partitions, and administrative staff was positioned at ample workstations. Equally pristine desks were scattered throughout the open floor plan for analysts and associates. The overall impression was of sleek, abundant space. In a city that measured success over a denominator of square feet, it was the ultimate luxury.

"This is your bullpen," Grant said, pointing to a grouping of six desks. "David likes an unobstructed view." He nodded toward a large corner office and the man whose back was turned but whose dark hair I recognized. He was on the phone, gesturing in the air, his leather shoes propped on his desk.

"He watches us?" I asked.

"The minute he stops watching," Grant said, "is when you need to worry. And I'm right there," he said, pointing to a desk between the bullpen and David's office with a smile that implied proximity meant everything. I pushed a strand of hair behind one ear and gazed over the floor, but I couldn't help turning back to David. He was running his hand over his hair. Accessibility was one thing but sitting so close seemed exhausting.

Grant led me down a long corridor lined with colorful modern art. When we arrived in M&A's private dining room, I gasped at the view. Growing up in Florida, the Manhattan skyline was an icon on a postcard, representing the best our country had to offer. Finding myself suddenly atop all these buildings was intense, like arriving at the nexus of everything that mattered.

"Everyone, this is Bets, one of our new analysts."

My introduction was met with a whine of "welcome," and "congratulations," and an array of sympathetic smiles, with those sitting closest shaking my hand. There was no chance I would remember names, with the exception of Marnye, the only other woman at the table, an associate in Grant's class. "No guys joining us?" she asked. "Why'd you only invite the woman, Grant?"

"There's no winning with you, Marnye," Grant said, shaking his head. The rest of the table chuckled at their sparring as if it was commonplace. "And yes, three other analysts will be starting Monday, all male. But I was not asked to mentor them, therefore I did not go out of my way to invite them to lunch."

"Aaah," said Marnye with a sarcastic grin. "So, do you think I'll be asked to mentor the young men?" she asked.

"God help them if you are," Grant said, eliciting chuckles from the table. My advisor at Lyle had suggested I seek out a mentor. Having no idea how to go about such a thing, it was nice to hear that it had already been taken care of. A server appeared at my side and asked for my order, but without any idea of the choices I looked around to see what the others were having. "Chicken salad?"

"Sure, and to drink?" She asked as if nothing was out of the realm of possibility in a dining room in the sky.

"Water's fine."

———

I picked at my chicken salad and asked Grant for directions to the restroom. I needed to freshen up but also to catch my breath, as the events of the day were making my head spin. I stood at the sink for a moment after washing my hands and a woman entered, catching my eye in the mirror. I had seen her earlier near my soon-to-be bullpen, occupying the large desk outside David's office.

"Welcome," she said. I supposed she was about forty. Her blond hair was swept back in a twist and she was made up subtly and effectively. She wore a navy suit and cream blouse.

"I'm Lenore, David's assistant."

"Oh hi. I'm Bets, a new analyst. Nice to meet you."

"We'll get to know each other soon enough." She smiled.

I wasn't exactly sure how and wondered if the ladies' room was an appropriate place to discuss it. Office politics had not been covered during the summer's training, and although Lenore appeared friendly and kind, I missed having Ethan's advice. "Well, I'll certainly look to you for guidance. I'm excited to get started."

She wasn't shy about giving me the once-over. "Nice to see a young woman in heels. Watch out for Marnye, she'll try to change your tune." She winked as she opened the door, and I intuited her approval was important. Growing up, Gloria had modeled one version of how to be a girl, how to wear jewelry, makeup, and flattering clothes. However, it was becoming increasingly clear I'd benefit from having a female role model here, not just in New York but right here.

After lunch, I mentioned to Grant that I'd met Lenore.

"Your classic gatekeeper. Skim lattes in the afternoon go a long way."

I laughed. "And Marnye?" The jibing at the table had raised a red flag but given that she was one of the few female professionals on the floor, I was eager to befriend her too.

"Yeah," Grant said, looking over his shoulder. "Have coffee with her when you start, but otherwise best to keep your distance." So much for solidarity.

CHAPTER FOUR

Monday morning, I must have changed outfits a dozen times before settling on a white pencil skirt, a yellow blouse, and the navy blazer a Bloomingdale's saleswoman had passed through the curtain in a dressing room. "If you're working at a bank, you can't go wrong with this," she'd said, which ended up being good advice. Sol, don't let anyone tell you clothes don't matter, they absolutely do, especially if you're trying to break into an old-school profession without an Ivy League pedigree. Wearing the right brands implies you can not only be trusted with clients but also that you "get it" in general. Ignoring the dress code is a foolish mistake unless, of course, you're a successful man who's earned the privilege to wear a T-shirt and jeans. Young adults and women, I'm afraid, will never get away with looking sloppy.

———◆———

I also arrived early that morning. It was something Yaya had drilled into me. I ventured into the M&A dining room for a cup of coffee, then paused in front of Lenore's desk with a cheerful "Good morning."

"Nice scarf," she said.

"Thanks. Nice weekend?"

"My ex took our boys to the ball game. Everybody was a winner," she said with a smile.

I caught her checking out David as he paced his office. He was pounding a fist into the palm of his hand, and Lenore rolled her eyes like it was going to be another one of those days. I was just about to return to the bullpen when I sensed him staring at us. I froze at the sound of him tapping on the glass.

"Ooh," Lenore said with a grin, "lucky you."

"Oh, what? Really?" I said, gripping the edge of her desk.

"Easy," she said. "He won't bite."

"Okay then," I said, sucking in my stomach and swinging my hair behind my back. I proceeded toward his door, afraid my clacking heels could be heard across the floor. He waited in his threshold with kind eyes and a firm handshake.

"Betsabé Ruiz from Miami, Florida," he said, as if I was a much-anticipated guest.

"That's me," I said, my mouth suddenly parched.

He made a sweeping gesture. "Have a seat," he said with a welcoming smile. I crossed his sparse office and perched on a black leather couch while he returned to his desk. There was a round glass conference table with two matching leather chairs, a desktop adorned with a handful of Lucite deal toys, and his reclining high-back desk chair on wheels. On a console behind his desk sat a massive monitor as well as a can of Diet Coke.

From the back of the training room that first day, it had been impossible to discern his green eyes and aquiline nose, but sitting close, I was hungry for more details of his face. Something about him evoked a memory I couldn't quite place, as if his image was already imprinted on my brain. It wasn't just his features, but his gestures and his friendly smile that struck me as familiar. It slowly began to dawn on me David reminded me of Mr. Levine, Yaya's landlord, of all people. He hung around a lot when I was a little girl, my grandmother saying it was because he was lonely. He was a kind and gentle man that Yaya trusted, probably the reason she became partial to Jews, insisting they made the best doctors, dentists, and lawyers.

David cleared his throat and smiled. "So, Cubana, no?" he asked, stretching back in his chair and cradling his head in his hands.

"Sí," I said, smiling affirmatively even though the question seemed out of bounds. Ever since coming north for college, people had been lumping me into a Latin American hodgepodge, seemingly unaware of the status enjoyed by an American-born Cuban in Miami. I was surprised my classmates weren't more aware of the influence we wielded in Florida politics, the fact that Cubans in South Florida weren't considered Latino but a variant of white. So, even though questioning my ethnicity was taboo, David made me feel seen rather than uncomfortable.

"My grandparents retired to South Beach, back before it was South Beach," he said. "I visited them every winter. Watched a lot of shuffleboard." It meant something that he was familiar with the worlds I straddled, as if he might be offering his hand to a novice gymnast crossing the balance beam.

"I was impressed with your training scores."

"Really? I didn't get off to the greatest start."

"You showed steady improvement and finished with the highest marks in your class." I sat up a little taller. I hadn't realized. "That's what I need in M&A," he continued. "Scrappiness, people who don't give up. So many kids come through here exuding ambition but it's not the same." Who knew my accounting failure would turn out to be a blessing in disguise?

"Besides, you're a legend." He chuckled. "Rumor has it your last interview was sensational." Heat rose in my face. Back in the fall, when a VP had asked why I'd devoted so much time to musical theatre, I wasn't sure how to respond. I was deep into rehearsals as Maria in Lyle's production of *West Side Story*, so I broke out into a few verses of "America."

"Oh, jeez."

"No, no, that took guts. Anyway, I called you in to take notes on a call. But first, I'm curious, how did Betsabé Ruiz from Miami wind up in Lyle, New York?"

30

I was still naïve to all the ways in which Lyle and First Provident were intertwined. Not only did First Provident hire two analysts each year, but it turned out the college's president, Rick Addington, had been the head of corporate finance, all stemming from the fact that Chairman Johnstone, class of 1965, was the college's greatest patron.

I fidgeted. "You really want to know?"

"I certainly do." He settled back in his chair, crossing an ankle over his knee, ignoring the fact Lenore was putting his calls on hold.

"An admissions representative visited my high school and singled me out because of my grades. So, I did my research and learned Lyle College was in New York, had a football team, a campus of brick buildings, bell towers, steeples. The pictures looked idyllic. My mother said the guidance counselor was loco, but my grandmother listened."

"And your father?" Another question that seemed inappropriate.

"My father didn't live with us."

"Oh."

"Anyway, I almost declined the scholarship, but my grandmother told me the story for the thousandth time of fleeing Havana when she was nine years old in 1961. She hadn't spoken a word of English, so what did I have to be afraid of?"

What I didn't say was that it meant boarding a plane for the first time, my stomach heaving during takeoff and landing. I didn't tell him how I found baggage claim and the chartered bus to campus, nor how stupid I felt as the scenery turned from urban to suburban to rural to the middle of nowhere as it dawned on me that New York was a very big state.

"Sports?" he asked.

"Just theatre."

"Any sports just for fun?"

I shook my head even more emphatically. "Nope, but . . ."

"But?"

"Well my father was an Olympic boxer, and the high school basketball coach begged me to come out for the team." For some reason I felt compelled to vouch for my athletic genes.

"No kidding? What's his name?"

"Edmundo Cardon. Cuba's bronze medal middleweight in 1996." The only thing I'd inherited from my father, as far as I could tell, was skin a shade darker than my mother's side of the family. David cast his eyes at the ceiling, as if searching his memory or storing that data away for some future date.

"Okay," he said, resuming a serious posture. "You've arrived at an interesting time. Let's make that call. Roland McGee, CEO of AgriGlobal, old buddy of mine. We played tennis at Michigan. You see, Bets, the secret to success in this business is basic sales. If you want to sit in this office someday, keep in touch with people, listen to people, help them find solutions. CEOs always have somebody breathing down their necks."

He dialed the landline on his desk, and I moved to a chair closer, pad and pen at the ready. David cleared his throat and ran his hands over his hair, waiting for McGee's assistant to put him through. When Roland came on the line with a pleasurable tone, David's eyes shone with satisfaction. The conversation began with inquiries into the family, recent vacations, eventually transitioning to "a restless market . . . some noise about a weak third quarter . . . a strategic merger could be viewed positively."

David played to Roland's insecurities. He gestured for my benefit, as if human nature was so predictable. It was hard not to be mesmerized by the rapport he established, so much so that whenever Roland said something revealing, David had to point to my pad. My job, after all, was to capture information so that he could converse naturally, but I could tell he also enjoyed having an audience.

After the call ended, David's tone was urgent, such a contrast from the way he welcomed me into his office. It wouldn't be the last time I witnessed the competing forces in his personality, his insistence we all work nonstop on the one hand, and the luxury of having all the time in the world on the other. He could be both generous, probing into my life's story with genuine interest before the call, then letting insecurity take hold afterward, as if his best days were behind him and his plate was less than full. Nobody on sixty would dare refer to David as "over-the-hill," but looking back now, I understand that's probably what he was afraid of.

He asked me to take a crack at the target list, assemble potential buyers and sellers in the agriculture space, and to do a competitor analysis as well. "Pull everything publicly available on AgriGlobal, its products, its divisions, and its employees so that I sound smart when we call Roland back." He nodded toward the bullpen as if there wasn't a second to waste. "You don't need Grant's help on this, do you?"

"No," I said.

"Good." He smiled and turned back to his computer monitor.

I returned to my desk and took a deep breath. Our training had been thorough on how to access First Provident's database, and I'd remembered the mantra to distill all analysis down to earnings per share; that one simple ratio was all CEOs cared about. Wall Street analysts and boards of directors didn't remember much beyond the current quarter, and CEOs operated with a short-term scoreboard, requiring results every three months. If Roland could not make his numbers the old-fashioned way, mixing in an acquisition or selling off a division was a tried-and-true strategy to muddy the waters.

But before beginning my research on AgriGlobal, I couldn't help digging up all there was to know about Robert David. His Wikipedia page outlined a modest upbringing, the youngest in a family of boys with a mother who died when he was very young. I read an interview in *Time* in which he was quoted, "Growing up, I was on my own most of the time." It was in response to a question about the source of his creativity. As an only child, I related to the imagination one develops, not to mention the time one has for extra-credit projects, while waiting for your adults to come home from work.

Based on his graduation year from college and taking into account his years in the military, I figured him to be in his mid-fifties. Google images revealed a 1985 wedding announcement in The New York Times to a Michelle Berenson whose father had been First Provident's managing partner. Then there was a brief marriage to Marcella Gesher, and most recently to Abigail Kramer. There were allusions to his many children, various sons but only one daughter. His wedding announcement to Abigail was followed by a profile of them as a power couple who graced the society pages for over a decade. I found images showing them attending philanthropic gatherings at The Met and MOMA. A profile in Town and Country described Abigail as "a natural peacekeeper, the perfect complement to David's warrior inclinations." The articles became increasingly sad after Abigail was diagnosed with pancreatic cancer. David flew her around the globe for experimental treatments, even joining forces with Steve Jobs at one point.

Thinking back on it now, it was a year post funeral and a perfect example of timing being everything. David was at a turning point in his grieving, pain having transitioned to loneliness. I would get the impression he didn't like what it was doing to him, that living behind a wall in order to honor Abigail's memory wasn't doing anyone any good. The creases around his eyes, along with the wrinkles at the corners of his mouth, the ones I had first attributed to laughter, turned out to be remnants of grief. The connection between David and Mr. Levine was becoming increasingly vivid. "That's what loneliness looks like," I remembered Yaya saying.

Later, when I asked Grant about it, he said David had taken a month off after his wife died, and since returning he'd barely come up for air—that burying himself in deals (and making a boatload of money for his younger team members) was how he coped with the loss. That seemed even more sad to me. So, although rakishly handsome, the David I met that day was a faded version of the original legend.

At the next Friday round table lunch, I mentioned I was preparing the pitch deck for AgriGlobal. I was especially excited because based on what I'd already learned about the company, working with them would be incredibly relevant to my work on SUFI. At Lyle, I stood at the bussing station, asking people to put their scraps of lettuce, cucumbers, and tomatoes into the compost bucket. Working with David, I'd be studying the industry on a grander scale, maybe identifying opportunities to make a real difference.

Marnye barely listened, as if it would be the first of a million pitches I'd have to scramble together on account of David's batting average not being so hot lately.

"Marnye," I said. "I wanted to ask you about an invitation to a working mother's group?"

"Oh, you can opt out of those."

"Isn't it odd I received the email?"

"They wouldn't want to exclude a potential member of the club." Even to a newcomer it was apparent how few investment bankers at First Provident were also mothers.

"But still."

"You'll see," she said. "Women like to categorize each other based on their fertility."

"What are you talking about?"

"There are those who already have children, those who still might, and those who never will." I was curious which category she put herself in but asking would only play into the stereotype of women categorizing other women. "Whether people say it aloud or not, everyone has a point of view on your uterus," she said. It was a classic Marnye comment that cast a pall over the table, but looking back on it, I'm struck by her prescience.

"Have you noticed?" she asked, changing the subject and directing her question to the table at large. "David's more agitated than usual."

"He committed a lot of the firm's capital to that deal in Hong Kong and I heard things are heading south," said a second-year analyst.

"Pacificorp is certainly part of it, but I think it's also his daughter," said Grant.

"Tamara?" I learned her name from Lenore, who was tasked with reviewing the credit card bills of all David's dependents.

"Shhh." Grant pressed his finger against his thin lips. Nobody could afford getting caught gossiping about David's personal life. "She wants to go to some boarding school in Europe."

"So?" I asked, matching his quiet volume.

"Her mother won't hear of it," said Marnye. "But David can't say no to his daughter. It's like he's perpetually running for Father of the Year."

"Here she goes again," Grant said.

"You'll see, Betsabé," she said, continuing a performative tirade. "These men put their wives and daughters on pedestals while they load companies with debt, putting thousands of jobs in jeopardy to strike a deal. Do they even think about the families they crush?"

"Jesus, Marnye," Grant said. "Why do you even work here?"

"Change can only happen from within," she said.

"Oh, okay, so you're in it for the movement? I call massive bullshit on that too." People were getting up from the table.

"I'll admit," Marnye said, "I want to make money. But more for the sake of breaking barriers, tackling the patriarchy at its core."

"Oh, my God, you two," I said. "Enough." Their rivalry was good-natured for the most part, but I noticed how Marnye filed every perceived inequity away. They compared assignments and watched closely as David walked the floor every afternoon. If it hadn't been in poor taste, they would have compared bonuses as well. It explained why neither went home before the cleaning crew began buffing the marble floor. The thing was, even though Grant was my mentor, I couldn't help rooting for Marnye to keep pushing back.

CHAPTER FIVE

David asked me to join him on the follow-up call with Roland. I took notes but also sat back and watched the way he worked. His ability to shape the man's imagination made a big impression on me. "You'll be creating a better company," he challenged. "That's what any good CEO wants. Am I right?" Roland responded with an agreeable tone that sounded like it stemmed more from a desire to associate with the legendary Robert David than expecting a positive outcome for AgriGlobal. By the end of the call, Roland had agreed to explore the options, and as soon as we hung up David clapped his hands and asked Lenore to set up a billing number with accounting, as in there would finally be a client to cover our dinners and cars home at night.

David pulled Grant onto the team. I'd be building the model that would back up the transaction's merits for AgriGlobal's board, and Grant would be supervising. My fellow first-year analysts, Joseph, Thomas, and Alan, however, were still waiting to be staffed and were updating boilerplate marketing materials. I'd expected the four of us would look out for one another the same way Ethan and I had during the months of summer training, but the vibe in our bullpen was one of keeping tabs. There was this undercurrent of suspicion whenever Grant helped me with the model, as if he was passing on secret intel. Alan kept mentioning he'd heard there would be scant promotions to third year analysts, and Joseph said David was known to write very few B-school recommendations. How sick I was of the term "*B-school.*" So, even though we'd landed at the top of the heap, a scarcity mentality had already entered our midst.

"Look at this," Thomas said, "we've been invited to a party." The same message sat unread in our inboxes from a VP across the floor. "Sorry for the short notice but I'm hosting a department-wide barbecue. BTW maybe you can arrive a little early in case my wife needs help." It was a request couched as an invitation that had me feeling like a pledge in a sorority all over again. My fellow analysts seemed eager to attend but I was curious what Grant had to say. He looked up from his keyboard and smiled as I approached his desk.

"Have a sec?" I asked.

"Sure thing."

I pointed to a silver-framed photograph of him arm in arm with a blond woman prominently displayed by his phone.

"Your sister?"

"No." His cheeks flared red.

"Girlfriend?"

"Wrong again." He looked at me with impatience.

"I'm going to send you a new version of the model, but what's up with this barbecue?" I asked.

"Ugh, who even knows if we'll have Saturday free?" It seemed he didn't care for the host, which I deduced had something to do with his recent promotion.

"Do people socialize outside of work often?" I asked, curious if Grant had any friends on the floor.

"Uh, no," he said, "and we don't do morale boosters either. David says your paycheck is your morale booster." He said the party was this guy's attempt at altering his asshole reputation, but I sensed a tinge of competitiveness. So, I'd reply "yes," tightroping the polite manners Yaya espoused and Grant's prescribed skepticism.

If I was going to sign away my weekends to First Provident, better to spend a beautiful Saturday in somebody's backyard than chained to my desk. I boarded a commuter train at Grand Central for this rarified town many a snooty classmate from Lyle had called home. To catch myself physically there, witnessing the late afternoon light filter through a canopy of linden trees on Main Street, had me laughing inside. I snapped a few pictures, thinking of the text I might send Rae, but grabbed a coffee and called an Uber instead.

Arriving at the address on the invitation, I paused before getting out of the car. If this was what motivated these Wall Street bankers, I wanted to soak it in. Was it the long circular driveway? The traditional colonial architecture? Was it the lime-washed brick? The massive lantern hanging over the front door? Never underestimate, Sol, the je ne sais quoi, the effortless charm. It was something I couldn't pinpoint back then. All I remember thinking was the town seemed very remote, and definitely not what I'd work hundred-hour weeks for.

It did smell nice, however. It wasn't Lyle, New York, pine needles and freshwater lakes, but recently cut grass and red-barked mulch raked about the begonias, the scent of suburbia. I followed voices to the back terrace where Thomas and Joseph were playing ping-pong with the VP's kids. I introduced myself to the hostess, who looked me up and down before asking if I was Thomas's date.

"No. I'm a new analyst." I smiled.

"I'm sorry. Ron invites people without telling me."

"No problem," I said, appreciating Grant's disdain. "Thanks for having me."

———◆———

Once Alan arrived, the VP shooed his kids into the house and suggested the four of us kick off the drinking games. It appeared he was counting on us to be the entertainment, to remind the guests of the fun they used to have. It could have been that competitive drinking was simply how my fellow analysts were conditioned, but

I sensed they suspected our social skills to be put on display and were looking forward to getting me in an arena where they assumed an advantage. I thought back to the prior fall, when as a senior at Lyle, I'd watched Brett Kavanaugh's confirmation hearings with my roommates. "I like beer," was the quote everyone joked about later. Standing on that terrace with Alan, Joseph, and Thomas was like getting a glimpse of Kavanaugh as a young lawyer and it made me cringe.

I snapped a picture of the red Solo cups arranged in a Christmas tree pattern on the table and texted it to Ethan with the caption: *A Saturday in M&A*

He texted back: *you suck*

I wrote: *haha*

He ended with: *Make Lyle proud. Pong is what we do.*

I summoned his positive energy every time the ball bounced my way. Despite my fellow analysts playing by slightly different rules, I could sink a ball with the best of them. I vowed, however, that after the game ended, beer from plastic cups would never again touch my lips. Nothing but cocktails made with top-shelf liquor for me. As the third round began, I was surprised by the crowd that had gathered to cheer Alan and me to victory.

Win or lose, day-drinking was not a good idea. Luckily Grant appeared, taking the paddle out of my hand so I could make my way to a tub of soft drinks sitting on the kitchen counter. Searching for a seltzer, I overheard the VP and his wife arguing in the pantry.

"What did you expect?" he whispered harshly.

"That you would be more helpful?"

"That's what I'm paying the caterer for."

I exited quickly, heading down the long slope of cool grass toward the swimming pool. A cluster of people had gathered around the deep end, and I slipped out of my sandals and sat on the edge, dipping my ankles in the mild water.

The invitation had billed the afternoon as an '80s party, an optimistic nod to Wall Street's go-go era, two crashes before I was born. It was another thing Grant had snickered about, the host's obnoxious Trump-bump, "happy days are here again" attitude. Although First Provident had weathered the 2007 financial crisis better than most, no firm was immune from the next one. "The arrogance," Grant said.

When Joseph, Thomas, and Alan speculated as to whether there'd ever be a return to the obscene bonuses of the past, I shrugged indifference. If this had been the high-flying, no-rules environment of the '80s, I likely would never have been hired. Even if First Provident made only a superficial show of valuing diversity, at least they'd hired Helen in HR to execute new policies. My presence at the firm was a testament to a modern era where the recruitment and retention of women and people of color was their attempt at creating a workforce more representative of the world at large.

Swirling my legs in the water, I alternated between sipping the seltzer and covering my mouth, quietly belching up the carbonation from the beer. From behind my sunglasses, I took in the richness of it all, the perfect lawn lit by a fading sun, but *how long did I need to stay?* This job had already swallowed up all my free time.

Earlier in the month, Grant had taken me and Ethan to the recruiting presentation at Lyle. A car there and back in one night. It was exhausting, but Grant was in his element, impressing the crowd with statements like, "The capital markets are the closest thing to a meritocracy the world has to offer. First Provident doesn't care what you look like or where you come from, we only care about results." When he finished, Ethan and I stepped away from the shrimp cocktail to answer questions, dazzling people with our Clark Kent–like transformations from Lyle seniors into Wall Street bankers practically overnight.

Dean Stern was in the audience, not because she cared about the First Provident analyst training program, but presumably to say hello. We'd become fairly close working on SUFI, and I was her daughter's roommate after all. I was half expecting her to slip me a care package to take back to Rae. She stood against a wall, flashing a smile of pride that said I was a valued alumna. Not long after I spied President Addington making his way to her side, and my stomach dropped. So much for my opportunity to ask how it was going with the coywolves.

I'd never met President Addington while attending Lyle, as he was often on the road fundraising or visiting his wife who had fled the cold for Palm Beach. But when I approached Dean Stern to say hello, he was the one who reached out to shake my hand.

"Rick, do you know Betsabé Ruiz?" Dean Stern asked.

"I don't think we've met," he said, sizing me up. Something about him said he hadn't anticipated the likes of me representing his old firm.

"Bets and I worked together on SUFI." He looked slightly puzzled.

"The Sustainable Food Initiative," I said.

"Aah. Let me guess, you're one of those kids who liked to protest in College Hall and now that you've graduated, you're a capitalist!" His sarcasm made me hate him more.

"She's also Rae's roommate in the city," said Dean Stern, further explaining our relationship.

"Aah," he said, visibly uncomfortable at the mention of Rae's name. "Did you know I used to head up corporate finance at First Provident?" he asked proudly.

"I'd heard that. I'm working in M&A."

He cocked his chin in surprise. He'd never gained admittance to David's universe on sixty. Regardless, he asked Dean Stern to take a picture of the two of us. I envisioned him holding it up at future fundraisers, taking credit not only for my scholarship, but for my landing a job at First Provident as well.

————

Thinking about Addington turned my stomach even more than the beer. But gazing toward the house, it seemed the hostess's careful chignon was straying from its clip and I couldn't help but chuckle. The associates had hacked her playlist, errant ping-pong balls were landing on her buffet, and it was becoming clear this huge effort, this coming-out party meant to mark her arrival as the wife of a VP, was boiling down to nothing more than higher-ups checking their watches and yawning, while people she cared nothing about worked their way through her wine cellar. Having an attractive family and living in a beautiful home didn't quite seem like a consolation prize, but it was beginning to dawn on me all she might have given up. I wondered where she'd worked before getting parked out here in the middle of nowhere with two kids and a dog. I wondered if she was happy.

I'd promised Rae I'd be back in the city for dinner. It was likely our last night on the town before AgriGlobal heated up. I Googled the train schedule. I was well-positioned to slip out through the yard and meet an Uber in the driveway. But as I began to rise, a set of hands grabbed me by the armpits and my phone fell in the grass. Before I knew what was happening, Thomas grabbed my legs at the knees. I screamed, drawing the attention of everyone at the party as my fellow analysts dangled me over the edge of the pool.

"They're really going to do it!" somebody shouted from the terrace.

"Stop!" I said.

"One, two . . ."

Joseph couldn't stop laughing. He was shit-faced.

"Goddamn it, Thomas. I will kill you." I tried to kick free. But they shouted "three" in unison and hurled me into the water. I sank to the bottom. And in those seconds before surfacing, myriad thoughts streamed through my head, not the least of which was that I was wearing a white blouse. I held my breath and opened my eyes underwater as my hair swirled about my face in slow motion, weirdly reminiscent of the times my cousins and I had underwater tea parties as kids. I flashed back to Gloria teaching me to swim in the waves. "You have to dive under them!" she had said as I shrieked.

It sounded completely illogical. "They crash but they also return you to shore." Even at that young age, I doubted she understood the hazards—the rip currents and the undertow.

Never mind the pool water being crystal clear, my lungs burned in a way that recalled the force of those waves pulling me down. I wondered what Helen in HR might have to say about this, and whether hazing was illegal outside of college, and how I would continue to share a bullpen with my fellow analysts. Had it been the VP who dared them to do it because his stupid party was getting dull? And then I thought about Ethan and how, if he'd been thrown in a pool, he'd spin it, and that my demeanor upon emerging would define me. I could come up in a fury like Marnye may have, or I could reserve all that for later. The most important thing, I decided, was to maintain some dignity. I felt for my sunglasses and was grateful to have something to shield my eyes.

When I pushed my feet against the bottom and came up for air, the sounds of the party were gone. "Is she okay?" asked a woman's voice from afar.

I crouched at the shallow end, careful to keep my chest out of view, and peered toward the house. Joseph and Thomas were jogging up the hill, bent forward in laughter. I scanned the faces on the terrace and then noticed a man on the roof, his silhouette holding a wine glass, a hand shading his eyes, and I recognized the unmistakable curl of David's hair.

—◆—

There are many things I want to tell you about how to treat a woman, Sol, and although I can't imagine a child of mine behaving as immaturely as Thomas or Joseph did that afternoon, there is a mean streak men feel permitted to direct toward women, and I am determined for you to condemn it. Those young men made me want to sink to the bottom and never come up, but Grant was different. He crouched by the edge, holding a large towel like he was beckoning a little kid from the bathtub. I wrapped it about my torso, held my head high and my shoulders back. I laughed as if I was in on the joke, even bowing to the audience who let out a collective sigh before going back to fill their plates with food.

Grant escorted me across the lawn to the house. "Those fuckers."

We entered the kitchen through a sliding glass door where an air-conditioning vent in the floor was blowing up such a chill, goose flesh immediately erupted on my arms and made my nipples go hard. The hostess frowned at the water pooling around my feet on her hardwood floor.

"I have your sandals and your phone," Grant said, gripping my elbow protectively.

My teeth began to chatter. "I was just about to call for a ride back to the city."

"There's a car waiting outside," he said. "I'll take you home."

My knight in shining armor with a chariot no less. I began to shiver ferociously and bit down hard on my bottom lip to keep from crying.

"No need for goodbyes," he said, grabbing two more of the hostess's monogrammed towels for the ride. Although I avoided most of the stares on our way out, the one face I did connect with was Marnye's. Her squinting eyes said she shared my pain.

Safely in the back seat of a black Mercedes, I asked Grant, "How did you get a car so quickly?"

"It's David's," he said. I pulled a dry towel tightly around my shoulders, getting a clearer picture of how these men worked in tandem. David was the one who conceived the plans and Grant was expected to execute.

———

Monday morning, Marnye stood at my desk, hands on her hips in a power pose. "I think our coffee is long overdue." I followed her obediently to the private dining room and a table by the window. Typically, I would have taken an espresso to go, but she was determined to sit and talk. I just wanted to forget the whole thing. She stirred cream into her coffee before looking into my eyes.

"You can file an incident report and probably get them fired," she said with the same indignation Rae had expressed when I'd told her why I'd arrived home soaking wet Saturday night.

"Marnye. I don't know."

"Bets, look. I'm sure you are a very smart girl. But you need to make it clear you won't take that shit."

"I know."

"Plus, I think you should tone it down a little."

"What do you mean?"

"Your makeup, your nails, maybe wear your hair up instead of down, throw in a cardigan sweater, flat shoes."

I was not expecting fashion advice from a stocky woman in a brown pantsuit. "I guess whether people say it or not, everyone has a point of view not only on my uterus but on my appearance as well?"

Her eyes popped and she sat back in her chair. "Anyway, they served you up a softball. This is our chance."

"Our chance?"

"We women need to stick together." As far as I was concerned, gender was all we had in common. Whereas Gloria had taught me to take care with my looks, even if I was just going to the corner for a carton of milk, Marnye wanted me to join her in deliberate dowdiness. "I'm pretty impressed David sent Joseph and Thomas down to the generalist pool. Helen will rake them over the coals," she said. "She'll probably be calling you for more details."

I sipped my coffee slowly. She wanted me to be her fellow insurgent, but the truth was I bonded with women like Lenore more naturally. We made easy conversation over Netflix favorites or the occasional recipe, eventually gossiping about Tamara blowing through her credit limit. She'd been commuting into Manhattan on the Staten Island ferry for over a decade, coming to work each morning having summoned the energy I'd witnessed in Gloria and

Yaya over the years, doing their jobs mainly to create opportunities for their children.

Marnye, on the other hand, had cut her teeth on Lean In by Sheryl Sandberg. Certain her smarts and her pedigree guaranteed her place at the firm, she operated with the assuredness First Provident needed to retain women professionals. "My friends from college," she said, "don't see the need for change. They love their doorman buildings too much. They love their Soul Cycle and their Sweetgreen salads. They've been co-opted. I'm just saying, don't let the paycheck go to your head. Take the opportunity to stand for something."

I couldn't help wondering whether her female-empowerment-in-the-workplace mantra extended to a class of people who couldn't afford to speak up and didn't have a Helen in HR to go running to every time something offended them.

"Marnye," I said, rising from the table. "I do want to pave the way for other women like me, but I just don't think getting two guys fired my first month on the job is how to go about it."

CHAPTER SIX

It was a clear morning in early October, and Grant and I were sitting at David's conference table going over various assumptions in the AgriGlobal model. "You've been doing excellent work," David said. "And excellent work breeds results. Look what just arrived." He broke into a smile, waving Roland's signed engagement letter overhead.

Up until it arrived, David had been wearing a path in his office, pacing back and forth and stirring up anxiety across the floor. I had been keeping my head down, gathering market data and industry multiples, running scenarios that showed what a bigger company might be able to spew off in earnings driven by cost savings. I graphed the outcomes of any number of transactional structures including the implications to Roland's stock option package. Depending on how David wanted to sell it, bigger was better or leaner was better; I prepared slides that made an argument for either case.

The long hours meant I often got home after Rae was asleep. I'd scroll through Instagram in the back of a town car, her posts providing insight into what I was missing. She tried to make me feel better in the morning, saying, "It would have been more fun if you'd been there." And then there were Ethan's posts, selfies with other analysts holding up cocktails, neon lights in the background. Despite the fact I'd turned down their invitations all summer, I couldn't help feeling left out.

When I first saw a picture of Ethan in a bar with his arm around Rae, I was like, wow. Shouldn't I have been the first to know they were a couple? The idea of everyone else my age having a social life sent an ache through my chest especially since the pool incident had the other analysts on the floor keeping their distance. And the sight of Marnye and Grant each night with their stern, ghostly lit faces gave me no reason to believe this lifestyle was going to improve anytime soon.

All that is to say, after forty-five days on the sixtieth floor, I was desperate for some time off. David said, "Why don't the three of us take Columbus Day weekend?" I was pretty sure people had begun calling it Indigenous Peoples' Day, but I didn't want to spoil the moment. Lenore mentioned Tamara was asking for David to take her to a horse show in Florida that weekend, but his confirming the break was a godsend. "There are a few loose ends we'll leave for Marnye, but the three of us should recharge. This acquisition is going to have us flat out until year end."

If I remember correctly, Grant's jaw actually dropped. I wasn't sure if this was because David's offer of respite was so uncharacteristic, or because he had no idea how to spend a free weekend. As soon as I returned to my desk, I texted him: *I have an idea.* It was a bold move, but I was overcome by an impulse to reclaim some fun. Maybe I also wanted to prove to Rae and Ethan that I was also making friends.

A few minutes later, Grant positioned himself behind my chair as if to check a number on my screen. "Do tell," he whispered.

I looked around to make sure nobody could hear. "So, my roommate's family has a beach house in Rhode Island," I said. "She's invited some friends up for the long weekend to celebrate her birthday. There's plenty of room if you want to join."

Heading back to his desk, he looked over his shoulder and flashed a smile along with a thumbs-up.

That's how I found myself riding a northbound Amtrak with Rae, Ethan, and Grant on Friday evening. What first seemed like a pipe dream was crystalizing into reality, and I was struck by the incongruity of mixing characters from different parts of my life, how it lent a quality of playacting to the outing. Inviting Grant meant I wouldn't be a third wheel, but this guy who dressed so well for work didn't seem to do casual with the same refinement. I assumed the gaps in his wardrobe said something about the gaps in his life, the reason why the woman in the framed photo couldn't take it any longer.

When the train pulled into Kingston, Rhode Island, Ethan stretched his arms overhead and gathered the wrappers and empty bottles from the dinner we'd consumed on the ride up from the city. Grant retrieved our luggage from the rack above.

"Constance left a car at the station," Rae said, fishing around in her jacket pocket for a key.

While Rae searched for the car, Ethan did that silly thing with his eyebrows implying something might happen between me and Grant, and I would have hit him if I hadn't been seized with shyness.

I returned to the anticipation of seeing Rae's ancestral roots, a home sporting a name of its own, "Eden." It was one of those old Yankee summer cottages situated on a rocky peninsula that was claimed by the white upper crust at the beginning of the twentieth century. Photos of its barrier beach lined the bookshelves in our apartment. I had my heart set on a crisp New England weekend with bulky sweaters and rolled-up jeans, maybe a bonfire in the sand with blankets wrapped across our laps.

"Just hit unlock on the fob," Ethan said. "We'll listen for the beep and look out for the blinking lights." He had all the life hacks. He may have been crushing on Rae since our sophomore year at Lyle, but it did not appear to be scattering his brain.

I, on the other hand, had the jitters. I rolled down the window as we pulled away from the station and let the briny air waft through the back seat. The sight of tiny Rae behind the wheel was a little comical. Ethan asked if she needed a booster seat, which resulted in a teasing smack. A buzzing sound vibrated through Grant's pocket.

"Aah, turn it off!" said Ethan.

I shot Grant a worried glance.

"It's probably Marnye," he said. We agreed that as far as people on sixty were concerned, nobody should know we were away together, and the mere idea of her calling made me nervous. I prayed Grant had remembered to disable his GeoMarkers.

Ethan spun the radio dial, and landing on a song we all knew, he began to dance in his seat. Thank God for Ethan. I joined in on the singing, sitting tall and swaying back and forth. Despite the fact we were all tired, I hoped we would rally for a festive night. We were in our early twenties and it was the beginning of a long weekend, and I would be damned if I was going to cave to my exhaustion. I wanted to fall into bed drunk rather than soberly march off to our bedrooms. It was for Ethan's sake as well, as he had no idea what Rae had in store.

A few nights earlier she was waiting up for me to go over the train schedule. As we lay in bed with the candle flickering, she confessed, "I'm tired of being a virgin. At this point it's embarrassing even."

"No, it isn't," I said, even though I didn't think I had any other friends who were still virgins.

"I like him, and he's liked me for a long time." A siren wailed outside our window.

"Holy crap," I said, shifting on my pillow. I hadn't been expecting that. "I'm sure Ethan will be honored."

"He's a nice guy, right?" said Rae.

"Nobody nicer."

As Rae drove on under a black sky, I closed my eyes and listened to the wind. My mind drifted to Miami, palm trees, white sand, and glimpses of turquoise water. I knew that in the light of day, Rhode Island would shine a different palette, but the Atlantic Ocean was the Atlantic Ocean, the same body of water that washed up on my home's shore. When the car turned off the main road, passing through a divide in the hedges, it looked like we were heading into one of those gated communities in Coral Gables. But there was no guard house, and it became apparent the entire tree-lined stretch was their driveway. *What the hell?* The car's tires crunched on white shells glistening in the moonlight.

Grant peered through the car window at the enormous house. It was impossible to tell where it began and where it ended. *Nice, Rae.* I began grinding my back molars. I never dreamed of something so huge. Why was she shopping at secondhand stores? And expecting me to split bar bills and hassling me for my share of the utilities? The way she downplayed her money suddenly bordered on offensive.

Grant seemed to have a different reaction. Any skepticism he may have harbored over spending a weekend with recent college graduates was instantly replaced by an eagerness to plunge into the abundance and forget the city we'd left behind.

Ethan shined a light on the kitchen door while Rae dug the key out from its hiding place. I helped Grant unload the luggage, shuttling it to the spot where Ethan and Rae were fidgeting with the lock. A light was on and when we entered the kitchen, two standard poodles lunged toward us, barking excitedly. I jumped.

"We're dog-sitting, remember?" She turned to face me. "They're the reason we're here."

Rae opened the refrigerator with the ease of a family member, grabbing four long-necked green bottles and handing one to each of us.

"Ethan, want to take the dogs for a walk with me?"

Grant and I followed but got waylaid in the dunes. Looking up at a black sky sprinkled with stars and the moon glistening light on the water, I was a little self-conscious, as stargazing was a cliché preamble to romance. "God, it's been so long since I've seen stars. You almost forget they're up there," I said. Forget the stars, I hadn't seen an expanse of sky since graduating from Lyle College.

We sipped our beers as he pointed to Orion and I found the Big Dipper, the easiest constellations to identify. I wished I'd remembered more of Yaya's stories based on the night sky, even though I'm not sure I would have felt comfortable sharing them with Grant at that point anyway. Our familiarity had been born in an office where we breathed recirculated air and felt sunlight only through sixty's massive windows. It was better than nothing but created a hothouse effect where everything seemed accelerated.

The sound of waves crashing against a backdrop of silence was so incredibly soothing, it made me emotional realizing how I'd once taken the natural world for granted. Even though Yaya's casita wasn't on the beach and Miami didn't boast the same kinds of dunes or sea grass, I'd felt the ocean's pull since I was little. I was raised on salt, sunshine, and tropical downpours which Yaya claimed was the reason I'd grown so tall. She liked to say people from the Caribbean were used to oppressive humidity, readying us for hard work and giving us an appreciation for sweat instead of fearing it.

Grant may have been basking in the natural stimulants as well, but I sensed his smile had more to do with the two days miraculously given to us by David. He'd sacrificed his youth not to mention a fiancée to work on Wall Street, and it was dawning on me that if I was going to contribute to the AgriGlobal deal in a meaningful way, I'd need to do the same.

We talked long after our beers were empty, sitting cross-legged in the dunes. He must have noticed when I began to shiver because he stood and pulled me to my feet. "Do you think the deed has been done?" he asked, and I immediately regretted betraying Rae's confidence.

I changed the topic away from my friend's sexual goals for her birthday weekend and filled him in on what I knew of her family as we walked back to the kitchen door. Her great-great-grandfather was named Bunny Meister, a man from Pittsburgh, a rags-to-riches success story who made his money in the railroad industry and built the summer home in the early twentieth century. I told him about the long-lost sister coming around, a midwife who actually delivered Rae in one of the bedrooms upstairs. "Yuck," he'd said.

"I know, right? But she's sworn everything's been remodeled. Her cousin swooped in and saved the day when her great-grandmother's money ran out. They were all grateful to keep the house in the family even if he and his wife changed up all the furniture and dug a swimming pool."

———◆———

When we got upstairs, I thought, again, he might make a move. I was in the midst of a six-month dry spell and sort of dying to be touched. Even if a physical relationship with my mentor was an incredibly stupid idea, it would have been easier to deal with than navigating my feelings around Rae's money and that house. Eden was the kind of place I'd only seen from the outside. Even the homes in which Yaya worked were nothing like this. The moon and the ocean belonged to everyone, but the grand staircase and my massive bedroom made me feel foolish.

Later, alone in a four-poster bed, I dreamt like crazy. I was half girl and half mermaid, pumping my tail as hard as I could into the depths of the sea. And as I pumped, I felt a longing in my pelvis and then a beautiful sensation and release before floating atop the waves, into the moonlight, glowing silver on the water.

———◆———

"So, I take it, last night went well?" I asked Rae in the kitchen the next morning. She spun around in her slippers, her pink terry robe catching the air like a hibiscus. She twirled to the toaster where two pieces of bread sprang up with a ping. Her cheeks were flushed, and hair was pulled atop her head in a way that revealed her natural coloring at the roots.

"It did indeed." She scurried back and forth from the coffee maker to the stove where she scrambled eggs, showing off her domestic acumen. "Help yourself to anything in the fridge, there's juice and cereal too." I poured a mug of coffee with the intention of taking it back upstairs, but Ethan appeared in the doorway in sweatpants and a T-shirt, his hair standing straight up on the crown of his head and sleep still in his eyes.

He said, "I thought I'd gone to heaven; it smells so good."

I had to agree, this home had awakened my senses. Pushing the curtains aside that morning revealed a crescent beach and endless ocean stretching out over the horizon. It was beyond anything I could have imagined. When I left my bedroom, I tiptoed toward the scent of coffee and lingered on the back staircase lined with black-and-white photographs. The most prominent one was of a man standing proudly with a golf club over his shoulder. I got it in my head it was Bunny Meister, Rae's great-great-whatever. She liked to go on about how he was the self-made son of immigrants. I told her we had the American Dream in South Florida too, but seeing his picture, I could tell there was something about him. With his slicked-back hair, strong, tall build, and dark complexion, I was struck by his resemblance to David. If nothing else, he was around David's age when the picture was taken, and he smiled with the same benevolent spirit. I pictured the two men commanding opposite ends of a banquet table, napkins tucked into their collars, feasting on life's bounty.

"Morning Ethan," I said with a playful grin.

"Morning yourself, sunshine."

I joined them at the kitchen table. Condensation on the window created a dappled glow over their eggs.

"Did you sleep well?" Rae asked. On the train ride up, we'd all agreed good sleep was priority number one.

"Yeah," I said. "But I could doze off again. No sign of Grant?"

"Hmm" was all Ethan could say, possibly wishing a lazy morning had been in the cards for him too. I was all too familiar with the way Rae bounced out of bed. We shared amused expressions watching her energy mount.

"With this weather there are so many possibilities!"

I scrunched my shoulders and sipped some coffee.

"We can walk the dogs on the beach, then take the bikes out. If Grant wants to jog, I can give him a great route. Ethan and I can go shop for something to grill while you guys get dressed." She was certainly in her element, and I caught Ethan basking in her happiness. It was contagious, something I hadn't seen since college when we met during Lyle's production of Les Mis.

Grant came down while we were still at the table. We may have been adulting for a while, but there was something about that big house on the beach that made us children again. Just like the dogs in our care, we wanted to roll in the leaves and play fetch in the sand. Once the poodles were sufficiently tired, we took four bikes out of the garage and pumped up the tires.

Rae guided us through the village, past touristy shops and a harbor emptied of boats. We rode past the lighthouse and a large Victorian hotel with a massive portico decorated with bales of hay, pumpkins, gourds, and chrysanthemums. We rode along the ocean side of town and a country club with a golf course.

"Do you belong?" I asked.

"My mother never joined." Rae made sure we all knew it wasn't her thing. It was all just so beautiful, made even more gorgeous by the foliage and the clean, crisp air.

Ethan wanted her to take us past the Crandalls' property.

"Who are the Crandalls?" I asked, getting a quick glimpse of another mansion behind some privet.

"Justin Crandall went to Dunning Academy. He was at the center of this scandal."

Despite the birds having migrated south by that time of year, Rae rode us past her favorite osprey nest. She was delighted to discover a lone bald eagle up on the high wooden perch, nestled among the straw and sticks. We rode past the docks and came upon a big stack of wire boxes. "What are those for?" I asked.

"Lobster pots, silly," Rae replied. "Have you ever eaten a lobster?"

"Caribbean ones," I admitted quietly.

"Oh, we need to fix that! New England is the only place for lobster," Ethan said.

Rae biked on, ignoring the huge houses and pointing out the jetty where she used to fish for crabs and the rocks on which the seals sunned themselves. Sol, I can't emphasize enough how, beginning with that weekend, each of my interactions with Rae's family affected me. On the surface, they were nothing but kind but there was something underneath that rankled me. Privilege isn't the right word, it's an oversimplification, a buzzword that seems to be thrown about too often. It was something else about their clan, their established trek back and forth between the city and the sea. You might call it entitlement, which I'd learned plenty about at Lyle, but that wasn't the best description either. They possessed this guilt-ridden state of dumb luck, as if embarrassed by everything that had landed at their feet with no idea what to do with it all.

CHAPTER SEVEN

After returning the bicycles to the garage, Ethan turned on college football and Rae, who seemed to love playing hostess, snuck off to the kitchen. She returned with an oversized bowl of popcorn, and when that was devoured, Grant and Ethan grilled burgers. Rae made a trip to the fish market and returned with four lobsters.

Grant said he didn't mind eating them, but he couldn't be the one to drop them in boiling water. He uncorked the red wine, and we laughed at Rae's instructions on how to use the special utensils for getting the meat out of the shell and the legs. Luckily, we also had the burgers, because I was hungry and the whole episode with the lobsters was a mess, more like an opportunity for Monty Python humor than for us to get fed. Rae seemed used to raucous gatherings, saying, "We'll get it all cleaned up in the morning."

If I felt out of place when we arrived Friday night, Saturday night was an entirely different story. We capped off Rae's birthday with a bonfire on the beach, just like the one I'd dreamt of, complete with roasting marshmallows and hot chocolate. She was extremely gracious, encouraging me to help myself to whatever I wanted, but it was hard to accept her largesse. I hated feeling more beholden than I already was.

It hit me that evening that with the exception of the burgers and the lobsters, how much seemed to always be on hand . . . staples in the pantry, wine in the cellar, beer in the fridge, books on the bookcase, towels in the linen closet. The abundance was one thing, but so was Rae's certainty it was hers for the taking. It was similar to the way she had no doubt, despite several minutes of searching, that the family car would be waiting for us at the station.

Growing up, my inclination had been to assume things wouldn't be there, that Gloria would have forgotten, wouldn't have shopped, or would have had to work late at the last minute. That night in my inebriated state, I wondered how growing up in a different family, in a place like Eden, would have made me a different person altogether. It was maddening because I didn't want to covet what Rae had, but I couldn't deny a spark of envy for that view when you rose out of bed in the morning and the oversized bath towels. Sol, I promised myself that whenever I made my money, I would know how to spend it.

I fell into bed drunk on the wine but also on the entire day, which had been close to perfect. I needn't have worried about fooling around with Grant because he was snoring in front of late-night television. The next morning, everyone slept late except for me. I had a headache and dry mouth and was thirsty for a glass of sparkling water with plenty of ice cubes.

I crept out of bed and walked down the long hallway, peeking into rooms I hadn't yet seen. I spent some more time in front of the grainy black-and-white photo of Bunny Meister as if it might reveal the answer as to how a second-generation immigrant from Germany amassed such a fortune. I took in his dark, persistent eyes and almost felt his ghost. Even though most of Rae's stories were about the women in her family, the mystery of this man was what I couldn't let go.

Something about him made me want to return to the dunes. I found a down jacket on a hook with the dog leashes. I sat on the sand and looked out at the waves, remembering Yaya's bedtime stories about Yemayá, queen of the oceans who wore a rainbow for her crown. After Gloria's futile attempt at getting me to dive through the waves, Yaya had tried to reason. "Make friends with the sea, Betsabé," she said. "It's the origin of all life and the tomb of all death." Although her words had meant to comfort, as a child, they made that endless stretch of deep water even more terrifying.

I was grateful for that time alone because when I returned to the kitchen, all fun had come to a screeching halt. Rae was scanning the mess on the countertops and Ethan was taking orders, putting out the recycling and running loads of sheets and towels in the laundry. I could tell Grant had begun worrying about what awaited at the office. Although he had promised not to, David was already sending texts.

The combination of a hangover, David's messages, and the prospect of a crowded train ride back to Manhattan twisted my stomach. Grant went upstairs to pack and charge his laptop, and I began cleaning lobster shells off the kitchen floor. Down on my hands and knees under the table, I felt the need to say a few things aloud.

"So, Rae. Between us girls," I said, ignoring Ethan's bustling about. "I knew you came from money, but you are like richer than God."

Rae turned off the faucet. "Eden belongs to my second cousin. I'm just the dog-sitter."

"Jesus, Rae," said Ethan. "It's not like you need to apologize."

"Well, Bets is making me feel like I do. I am not rich."

"And so what if you are?" asked Ethan.

Rae shook her head and turned toward the window.

"Rae," I said. "It doesn't matter who has title to this house. You know where they hide the key and you can help yourself to whatever is in the refrigerator. In New York you try to downplay your trust fund, but you are so busted." And then I chuckled, sensing a need to diffuse the grenade I'd just lobbed.

Ethan closed a cabinet gingerly as if any sudden movement might set off the explosion. He looked back and forth between us. Rae stared at him for backup, but he shrugged. This lifestyle was as foreign to him as it was to me.

"I may have been born into a certain family," she said. "But it's not like I wake up every morning and get a free pass because my great-great-grandfather made a lot of money."

"You don't get it," I said, getting out from under the table. And for some reason I continued lunging at this girl who only wanted to be my friend. But I couldn't let her have it both ways, sharing this estate with me for the weekend, while claiming it wasn't hers. And it wasn't just the house, but the fact that she'd inherited a trust fund from her father, the fact that her mother was a dean at Lyle, the fact that her whole life was sugarcoated while I had to double-check my direct deposit had landed before paying her my share of the rent every month.

Was I angry with Grant or Ethan for appearing to be at ease in this mansion? No, it was something about Rae, about us both being female, only children, both "Gen Z," both our fathers disappearing, that gave me that "Trading Places" feeling where I'd gotten the shit end of the stick.

"Hey, I know what you're earning, Bets," said Ethan. "And David is known for doling out huge bonuses."

"Please," I said. "That's not what I'm talking about."

"Ah come on, you got a great education, a great job, you got a spot in M&A." Ethan lifted his arms as if to say, *who can argue with that?*

"Which you don't think I deservedly earned?"

"I didn't say that."

"It's what you're thinking."

"Why are you so sensitive?"

"Oh, fuck you, Ethan. Who had to show you how to use your calculator?"

"Hey, hey, hey, calm down," said Rae. "Both of you."

In a matter of minutes, I had picked fights with my two closest friends. To this day, I can still blow up like that, although I don't do it as often. It's just that when I get swarmed with confusing emotions, anger rises to the top. But looking back, I understand it was shock more than anger, as if Rae should have warned me before we got there, as if true friendship requires all the backstory. It was also the general dread of returning to work and insecurity over everyone having fun without me. It was the stress of getting the numbers right on a billion-dollar deal, the acrimony in my bullpen, the late nights, the loneliness.

So, there I was, letting my emotions get the better of me and ruining everything. It did feel good to say what was on my mind, but it was like puking after you drink too much; you feel better, but you feel like shit too. "I'm sorry. I just wasn't expecting this house to have such an effect on me," I said. "And I really don't want to go to work tomorrow." On my way up the stairs, I froze in front of Bunny Meister's likeness again, wondering if it was still possible in this day and age to make something out of nothing.

Dust from our confrontation clouded the entire ride home. Grant was oblivious because he hadn't witnessed it firsthand and also because he'd already turned his attention to David's mounting requests, but Ethan and Rae were uncomfortably silent more or less the whole way. We hailed three cabs outside Penn Station and when Rae and I pulled up in front of our building, I had a twenty out ready to pay the driver.

We lugged our bags upstairs. Besides the tiny bathroom, there were no doors, no boundaries. We had two choices, either to make up or ignore what had happened. Retreating to separate rooms was not an option.

Rae opened the refrigerator. "You hungry?" she asked.

I didn't want to be. I felt like all we did was eat all weekend and I wanted to be sated, I wanted to be just fine without anything else entering my stomach. I wanted to be superior in the way Sandra was, disciplined enough or self-depriving enough to wave off stupid things like food. Sometimes it felt like you couldn't be a true woman if you had a big appetite, like eating was something men did, and women were supposed to have more self-control.

"Yeah, I'm starving," I said.

"Should we order in?"

"My treat," I said.

"No, you don't have to."

"I want to. Consider it a thank you for the weekend."

"I'm sorry about this morning, whatever got you so upset."

"I'm sorry too. Let's just forget it."

"Are you sure?"

"Yeah. Let's forget it." It was a Sunday night and we were both tired, so forgetting it seemed like the best idea although I wasn't sure we could. The thing with friendships, Sol, is that it doesn't take energy to talk about conflicts, it takes courage. That night, we chose not to deal with it, to order dinner instead. Rae ordered Mexican, which was her favorite but also irritating because everyone knows Mexican in New York is the worst, and she'd get these oversized burritos which she'd take a few bites of and then keep in our refrigerator for days, while I got pork, rice, and beans from Café Habana.

When the food arrived, we unwrapped the foil and dug in with abandon. I was halfway done before sitting back in my chair and stretching my arms overhead. My phone was buzzing with requests from Grant and Marnye, but I turned it upside down and then off completely to keep from getting indigestion.

Takeout also meant easy cleanup. When we cooked, Rae got a little OCD with spraying down the counters and the stovetop. She could never sit still, in constant battle with the ants. I was rarely home in the daylight and so I didn't see things like ants. Besides, I was used to insects, living with Yaya who just accepted our coexistence with nature in South Florida, refusing to use pesticides inside or out.

We took turns in the bathroom and by the time I was done, Rae had the beds pulled down, the lights turned out, and the candle lit. I breathed a sigh of relief that things might get back to normal.

"Grant is such a nice guy," she said. "Do you like him?"

"I don't think he's into me in that way. Besides it would really complicate things at work."

"Did you see how he looks at you?" The intensity of his stare was hard to miss.

"Well, all he did was look," I said. "So, tell me, how did it go with Ethan?"

"Good, I guess, I mean I don't really have anything to compare it to. It certainly wasn't like the movies. I mean, he kept his socks on." I laughed, picturing striped athletic socks stretched about Ethan's muscular calves. The media had certainly warped our idea of what sex was supposed to be like. I had a boyfriend at Lyle with whom I lost my virginity, a guy who I found attractive, in part because he found me so attractive. In all honesty, my biggest crush at Lyle had been on my psychology professor. I always felt more aligned with the adults on campus, probably where I got the impression older men could teach me about myself.

There were two other guys I slept with in college, but in the end, I chalked dissatisfying sex up to my partners' lack of experience, their not knowing how my anatomy worked, or caring about it for that matter. My mother once told me I'd have to kiss a lot of toads before I met my Prince Charming, but I had started to doubt whether there was a man alive who got me.

I felt the need to pry a few more details out of Rae before she fell asleep, as if hearing more about her romantic interlude might satisfy the part of my twenty-three-year-old brain wired to propagate the species. "But it was good?"

"I mean he told me he's been in love with me since college, which was really sweet. But I couldn't tell him I loved him back. And there I was, naked and waiting. So, I sort of felt like I was using him."

"He must be over the moon."

"Yeah, I think he is."

"And what now?"

"He thinks we're like, a couple."

"And are you?"

"I guess." Her ambivalence was palpable, and I dreaded what it might mean for my friendship with Ethan.

"Do you want to hear my prediction about you and Grant?" she asked.

"Not really," I said, opting to fall into a dreamworld, one that quite surprisingly starred Bunny Meister. The setting was cinematic, black and white, crackly more like a silent movie from the '20s. Bunny looked just like Clarke Gable, dressed in a white dinner jacket. I wore a long flowing gown, and he carried me across the bedroom at Eden. I got lost in the down, and the silkiness of the sheets. He kissed me and there were no words, just the weight of his body on mine.

CHAPTER EIGHT

Despite it ending with a blowup, that weekend was probably the highlight of my autumn. Because upon returning to sixty, Sol, the days blended together, my lack of sleep lending a foggy quality to every memory. I was going home basically to shower and put on fresh clothes and had to sneak naps on the cot in the copier room. I pounded coffee and applied gobs of concealer to cover the dark rings under my eyes, becoming a poster child for the long hours that made M&A famous. Maybe the lack of REM sleep did something to my brain. Studies have proven making good decisions when you are awake requires adequate time to dream.

Grant, Marnye, and I worked with David on AgriGlobal with a shared sense of deprivation and bunkering down. Atypical to most teams, I was the only analyst and David kept me close like his external hard drive, storing the scenarios and assumptions contained in the model. Lenore made me part of the inner circle, memorizing my coffee order and bouncing questions off me when David was busy. When I'd return to the bullpen, Allen would roll his eyes and make comments under his breath. "Why don't you just move your desk in there?"

My phone rang one afternoon, and my first thought was that it was Gloria or Yaya wondering if I was still alive, but it was Rae speaking in a burst of excitement as if I might not have thirty seconds to spare. "Rachel wanted me to invite you to Thanksgiving dinner."

I wasn't even sure how many days until the holiday. "Oh."

"So, can I tell her you'll join us?"

"Absolutely." It would be nice to have a place to go even if Thanksgiving was lost on me. Growing up, Yaya and my mother elected to work on Thanksgiving so that they might secure days off around Christmas. My mother worked in the nursing home and Yaya served the meal and cleaned up after her employers' families. They'd both come home exhausted, wondering aloud what people saw in beige food topped with brown gravy.

"I should warn you though," she said, "the estrogen level will be running high. It's our first Thanksgiving without my great-grand-mother." If I remembered correctly, her name was Becca and she was Bunny Meister's only daughter.

Grant had no plans to fly home. He painted his family's tradi-tion in Ohio as the epitome of boredom, his mother's cooking and cheering on football games with his brothers as something he'd outgrown. "Besides, the market is open on Black Friday," he said. I'd heard the term Black Friday before in relation to the first shop-ping day of the Christmas season, but the way he described Wall Street traders making bets on American consumerism introduced me to a cynical view of the world, Sol, one that's taken the fun out of holiday shopping ever since.

———

When Thanksgiving arrived, Rae gave me the rundown on who would be at dinner while we got dressed and walked over. Her grandmother, Rachel, of course, and her mother, Sarah. And I would have the added treat of meeting her long-lost great-aunt Lee, the midwife who reappeared just before Rae was born. "Oh, and I can't forget Lee's partner, Beverly," Rae said, ticking the women off on one hand. Given her mother was an academic, I assumed the table conversation would be loftier than what I'd grown up with even if I did see parallels between Rae's grand-mother and mine.

Rachel was your quintessential New York liberal, sporting a free-spirit seventies vibe. She typified blue-state politics while my yaya was decidedly red, listening to Spanish radio stations that disseminated information to Miami's exilio. My yaya voted Republican, was indebted to conservatives and their professed protection of democracy, and would rather die than cast a vote for the party of JFK, whereas Rachel was a stalwart viewer of CNN and took the Trump presidency as a personal affront. Rae said her grandmother had a "hard time holding it together" since the 2016 election. The nation's toxic state had gotten under her skin, contributing to her frazzled appearance and dwindling work productivity. So, besides our families' obvious cultural and economic differences, there was a deep political divide as well, but I knew better than to raise any of that with Rae or her family.

As we approached her grandmother's building, Rae's expression was anxious. I was grateful to be carrying a bag of Macintosh apples to offset any be-on-your-best-behavior and don't-show-up-empty-handed worries of my own. But she seemed more tense as the door to the building buzzed open and we boarded a compact lift, forced its accordion door shut, and slowly ascended.

"Hello girls!!" Her mother was waiting for us in the corridor and her presence had Rae go rigid. After prying the rickety gate open, Dean Stern reached in to hug her daughter.

Rae said, "Wow, Mom, careful," straightening her jean jacket and squeezing out of the ancient elevator past her mother. After the jerky ride up, I was relieved to be on solid ground.

"Bets, I'm glad you could join us," said Dean Stern.

"Thanks for having me."

The corridor was warm, but not as warm as the inside of the apartment. Smaller than I'd expected and crowded with furniture, it made Rae's claim that the family's money had dried up more believable. I paused in the dim light. I was acquainted with the anxiety of not having enough money, but I began to imagine what it must feel like to watch it slip away.

Carrying the scent of onions, Rachel emerged from the kitchen with an apron cinched around her middle and her skin glistening. The stretched neckline of her black T-shirt gave off the air of line cook rather than a matriarch hosting Thanksgiving. "Girls! Take off your coats!" she said, waving a wooden spoon in the air. "I'm basting!" I had liked Rachel ever since move-in day when she showed up with a U-Haul full of furniture as well as a practical housewarming gift in the form of a potted succulent.

A white-haired version of Rachel sat in the living room, her silky braids gathered at the back of her head in a loose bun. She went straight to Rae and hugged her.

"This is Lee!" Rae said once she broke free.

"So nice to meet you," I said, shaking her hand.

"And that is my partner, Beverly," Lee said, pointing to an aged woman clutching a cane in a lounge chair across the floor.

"Will there be room in the oven for the pie?" Rae called into the kitchen.

"I thought you were going to bake it at your place," said Sarah.

Rae looked like she might cry. "Mom, we always . . ."

"It's okay, I brought a pumpkin pie," said Lee.

I, for one, was relieved. Attempting to recreate the great grandmother's apple pie seemed like a setup for failure. I'd take the apples home and eat them for breakfast.

After the introductions, Lee returned to Beverly's side and Sarah unfolded the legs of two card tables, setting them up end to end in the open area between the living room and the foyer.

"Can I help with those?" I asked, removing my sweater.

"Sure." Sarah nodded toward a white linen tablecloth folded over the back of the sofa while Rae went into the kitchen. We each took hold of two embroidered corners, billowing it above the stained gray vinyl. Sarah smoothed the wrinkles and tested that the legs were stable. She placed a bowl of yellow and orange gourds in the center of the combined tables, flanking it on each side with brass candlesticks, which anchored the wobbly legs into the worn beige carpet.

"But before we set the table," Sarah said, "there's something we need to do." She laid a half dozen small velvet pouches across the tablecloth and grabbed a bottle of wine from the sideboard.

Rachel poked her head out of the kitchen, a strand of hair pasted across her forehead. "Do you really want to get into this now, Sarah?"

"Mom, we talked about this. When else will we all be together?"

Rae's eyes darted back and forth between her mother and grandmother. She didn't seem to know what was going on either.

"We need to take advantage of Lee being here," Sarah continued. At the mention of her name, Lee left Beverly's side and huddled with Rae and her mother next to the card tables.

I pretended not to mind being edged out of the conversation and walked to the living room where Beverly was seated. She gazed out at the darkening sky, the fire escapes, cracked terra cotta pots sprouting weeds, and bird-shit stained air-conditioning units. I wondered if it might be acceptable for me to crack a window.

"Hello, I'm Bets," I said to Beverly.

She looked up at me, surprised. "And what kind of name is that?"

"It's short for Betsabé."

Beverly may have been coarse and slightly offensive, but there was something refreshing about people with no filter. Her short gray hair was in a kinky perm and there was a crop of white whiskers sprouting from her chin.

"You and Rae live together?" Beverly asked.

"Yes, roommates since the end of August."

"I see she's still wearing her hair like Bozo the Clown."

I couldn't help laughing.

"You like the city?" she asked with monotone blandness.

"Yeah," I said. Of course, it wasn't as simple as all that, but beaming optimism seemed like the most polite thing to do.

"I can't stand it," Beverly said and pointed at the television. I realized she was watching something with the sound turned down. "That damned parade," Beverly said. "The traffic."

"Where did you drive in from?"

Beverly turned toward me with a surprised expression. "Took the train from Mystic. Make me a cheese and cracker, will you?"

I handed her a Triscuit covered with cheddar then pulled the table closer to her chair. I made one for myself while trying to decipher what the huddle at the other end of the room was all about. I overheard Rae say, "Bets won't mind," and then Lee say, "and Bev is glued to the television."

Rachel poked her head out from the kitchen again. "Well then get on with it, will you? I want to eat while the food is still warm. And I have a guest arriving!"

"Can I help in the kitchen?" I asked.

"Oh, Bets, you are a dear. Thank you," Rachel said, making room for me to enter. As I passed by the card tables, I saw what the commotion was all about. A mound of jewelry. A couple dozen rings, various strands of gold and pearls, broaches and chunky bracelets that must have come out of those velvet pouches, all glittering like pirate's booty.

"I've already set aside some pieces for Lilly, Ruth, Constance, and her girls," Sarah said.

"What's all that?" I whispered in Rachel's ear.

"My mother's jewelry," Rachel said, untying her apron and joining the others at the table. Even though we wouldn't be eating her apple pie, the grand dame had found a way in after all.

"*Our* mother, Rachel," said Lee, correcting her.

"Right," said Rachel. "Our mother." She caressed a gold chain between her thumb and index finger.

"Oh, Mom, since when did you care about jewelry?" Sarah wiped her nose with a tissue.

Rachel cast a warning glance at her daughter then trained her eyes on the cache in the center of the table. "Stop making assumptions about me," Rachel said, pulling her chair closer to the pile. Rae combed her fingers through strands of pearls as if she was separating strings of pasta. Lee held a diamond ring up to the light. Sarah examined a broach, a red ruby cat with an onyx top hat. "Nobody pins jewelry to their clothes anymore," she said.

"I remember the Christmas Daddy gave that one to her," Rachel said. "Mom searched all the drawers of his desk for the receipt. She was desperate to return it."

"Have you ever thought about selling some of it?" I asked.

"These are family heirlooms, Betsabé," Sarah said, as if I couldn't relate.

"Maybe Bets has a point," said Rachel. "We could sell some of the less meaningful pieces." The subtext being everybody could use a little cash.

"Ooh, but not these," Rae said, holding a choker length of pearls against her sweater.

"Chica," I said. "I could see those on you, so retro." I tugged on the pendants hanging from a gold chain around my neck, un regalo por mis quince, a cross and a ceramic medallion of the Virgin Mary draped in blue and white from Yaya. Not many people up north understood she was a stand-in for Yemayá.

"How long is this going to take?" Rachel asked.

"Oh, Mom," Sarah said. "Don't take all the fun out of it. These are our last remnants of Sadie and Bunny." I perked up at the mention of his name, recalling the photo in the back staircase at Eden, not to mention my romantic fantasy.

"Why would Gran have a pin in the shape of an O?" Rae asked, holding up a round broach encrusted with diamonds.

"It's a circle pin," said Lee.

"Young ladies wore them when they had a steady boyfriend," said Rachel in a mocking tone.

"Like an engagement ring?" I asked from my spot in the kitchen.

"No," Rachel said. "It came before the engagement ring but didn't need to be given by a suitor. A woman could just decide to wear one when she was ready."

This family was fascinating, but I was grateful to have chores in the kitchen. If reconciling the plentitude of Eden with Rae's protestations that the money was all gone had proved a challenge, so did that hot, tiny apartment with its mound of jewels spilling across the table. Still, listening to the importance they vested in these objects and their holding onto the lore of Bunny and Sadie reminded me of Yaya waxing poetic about the Havana of her childhood.

"Wrap the rolls in foil and pop them in the oven," Rachel called to me.

"Sure," I said, a little puzzled I was the one putting finishing touches on the dinner. I closed the oven door and looked back at the table.

"Rae will end up with all of it, so what does it matter?" Rachel asked.

"Someday she will," said Sarah. "But someday is not today and until someday, we should decide who gets what." She smiled at Lee in a way that gave me the feeling they'd prearranged this activity. My heart swelled with allegiance to Rachel.

"Whatcha all doing?" Beverly called from her place near the television. I needn't have worried about playing the outsider at this gathering, because Beverly had a lock on that role. She was slicing the last bit of cheddar and sandwiching it between two crackers.

"Just going through some of Becca's things," Lee called to her without turning around. Rae cooed, "Look, a note card embossed *Goldstock Jewelers, Pittsburgh*. It says, 'Darling, I couldn't help myself. Forever yours, Bunny.'"

"Oh, I just think it's all so romantic," Sarah gushed, clasping her hands against her heart. I was increasingly transfixed by the idea of Bunny Meister, how the women in his family had been shaped by his benevolence. He would never seek a marked-down, good-enough present for his wife or daughter. I pictured him passing storefronts and impulsively purchasing every shiny bauble that caught his eye.

My grandfather had returned to Cuba before I was born, and my father certainly hadn't shown my mother much generosity. My mother defined a good man not in terms of what he gave, but in the absence of a negative. As in he didn't drink too much, he didn't gamble away all his money, he didn't hit her. As if women dare not ask for more. And although Yaya described Abuelo as a "good man," she never explained why he left her behind in Florida with a pregnant daughter. And when he died, it went without saying there would be no inheritance.

"Would you take a look at this?" It was a tennis bracelet dripping with diamonds. Sarah pointed to each stone, using words like "marquis, baguette, and full cut," before reading the faded script off a slip of paper tucked in the long velvet box. "'July 15, 1920. A gift from Bunny in honor of Robert's birth.'"

"It's like Sadie cared more about marking the milestones than wearing any of it," said Rae.

"My finger's too fat for this one," Rachel said, trying to squeeze a platinum band with a mass of inlaid diamonds over the knuckle of her ring finger.

"And it's huge on me," said Rae as she spun a diamond and sapphire anniversary band around hers. "Here, you try it on, Bets." Before I could protest Rae slipped the ring on my middle finger.

Wouldn't you know, it fit just right.

I held up my hand to admire it and time stopped. In addition to the brilliance of the sapphires and diamonds, the ring had some heft, the sort of weight I'd never before felt in a piece of jewelry. It was the type of ring I'd seen on girls at Lyle, gifts for graduating from prep school or coming out as debutantes, worn loosely on a finger or hanging from gold chains as they played tennis or rode horses.

"Ooh that looks good on you," Rae said, turning the awkward moment into dress-up fun, diluting the assertion that this would all be hers someday, as if she was happy to share. She liked to emphasize her one-off luck: a freak inheritance from her father, a second cousin who welcomed her home at Eden, and now, it turned out, a treasure trove of gems.

"If truth be told," said Lee, "I'd really like that ruby broach in the shape of a cat."

"That's it?" asked Rae, prompting an eye roll from Rachel. "Lee, you should have one of Becca's rings too."

Lee had been admiring a cocktail ring with a large rectangular amethyst.

"That one came from my great-grandmother's family, the vault of Helene Thompson herself," Rachel said with a tone that implied it was off limits to half-siblings. Rachel glanced sideways at me as if I would understand this had nothing to do with materialism and everything to do with the fact that she would never consider Lee a real sister.

"That settles it then," said Lee. "Why don't I just take this amethyst and the broach."

Rachel stood up in a huff. "Fine. I need to change. Harvey will be here soon." She twisted her mouth while stuffing all the jewelry back into the velvet pouches. Sarah tapped my shoulder and held out her hand and smiled as if I would forget to remove the diamond and sapphire band and give it back.

CHAPTER NINE

hile Rachel stowed the jewels away, I remained stationed
by the oven, determined that nothing burn on my watch. I
kept opening the door, peeking in, and when the foil pouch began to
steam, I transferred the rolls into a wire basket lined with a napkin.
The cranberry sauce was already scooped into a dish with a small
silver ladle by its side. There were platters and bowls with Post-it
notes affixed indicating "stuffing" and "potatoes," and Sarah began
putting food in its rightful dish.

"Ugh, somebody open a window," Sarah said, wiping her
forehead with a paper towel. She looked different than she had in
September when I'd returned to campus for the First Provident
information session, her hair down around her shoulders and her
skin paler and more chapped than I'd remembered.

"I'll do it," said Rae.

"And then, girls," Sarah said, clapping her hands. "Will you
please set the table?" It was ironic because back when we were
undergrads and she was our dean, she would have never gotten
away with calling us girls. We were young women, period.

The doorbell rang.

"And Rae, grab the extra chair from Rachel's bedroom," Sarah
said on her way to the door. "Harvey, come on in!"

Rachel's guest was a bald, elderly gentleman, thin and dressed smartly in a light blue button-down and tweed sports coat, carrying a bouquet of flowers he seemed unwilling to hand over to Sarah.

"Harvey!" Rachel said as she emerged from the bedroom in a charcoal dress, her hair in a bun, and wearing dark lipstick. "You shouldn't have." She took the flowers and kissed him on the cheek, exuding a sweetness I hadn't thought possible.

"Is that you, my Shefala, cooking up this feast?"

"It is, it is," she said.

Rae and I exchanged smiles. It was nice to see affection never got old. Rachel ushered Harvey to the living area with Lee and Bev while Sarah, Rae, and I set the table and the platters out on the buffet.

We assembled around the makeshift dining table, waiting for some direction, and I gripped the back of a plastic folding chair. I didn't know if it was the heat or the wine, but I was dizzy.

"What? Do you think I made up place cards? Just sit!" Rachel said.

She took the head of the table where Harvey was pulling out her chair. He sat to her right. Sarah took the other end. Everyone else filled in and I sat next to Rae with my knees knocking into a table leg. It definitely wasn't Norman Rockwell, but it was the closest I'd ever been.

Rachel raised a wine glass filled with Diet Coke. "Well, isn't this nice?" she said as a form of welcome, and she went around making eye contact with everyone. She held my gaze for what seemed like an extra beat.

"Are those Gran's candlesticks?" Rae asked as if noticing them for the first time.

"They are," Sarah said, her eyes welling up with tears.

"You'll have to excuse the nostalgia," Rachel said, turning to Harvey. She pointed her knife across the table at Sarah. "First Thanksgiving without my mother."

Harvey smiled sagely, as if grief was a sentiment he understood well. He took a spoonful of stuffing as the dishes came around, and Beverly poured gravy over her turkey and mashed potatoes. I sipped my wine and wondered if I might volunteer to open the window even wider. Whatever cool air was coming in had triggered the thermostat and the radiators were now throwing off more dry heat behind me. I couldn't fathom how everyone was standing it. Beverly still had her sweater on and Harvey his sports coat. I took minimal amounts from the platters that were passed around.

"No turkey?" Rachel asked Rae, spying her empty plate.

"You keep forgetting I'm vegetarian."

I swallowed the last of the tap water in my glass before reaching for the wine. It wasn't exactly nausea I was feeling, but an unsettledness, possibly the onset of menstrual cramps. I took deep breaths while the conversation swirled about. By the time I focused on what was being said, Rae was clanking her utensils against her clean plate, her cheeks bright red.

"Oh my God," she said. "You are moving back to the city?"

"I thought you'd be pleased," said Sarah, looking toward me for approval. We had gotten somewhat close during the SUFI campaign, but if there were sides to be taken, I was with Rae.

"Why did you let it get so out of hand? You could never stand up to him," Rae hissed.

"Why can't we have a conversation without dragging Rick into it?"

Watching the interaction between Rae and her mother was startling. I had never seen my peace-loving roommate so mad. Rachel provided background to the rest of the table. "These coywolves invaded Lyle and the whole town blames Sarah." I sensed it wasn't just the wolves, but the rumored affair between Sarah and Rick Addington was true and had possibly soured. *Yikes.*

"That's enough," Sarah said, and I had this vision of her as the older woman someday, commanding the head of the table and insisting on polite conversation. Yaya once joked about everything her wealthy clients used to sweep under the rug, and all she had to suck up in the vacuum as a result.

"We can talk politics if you prefer," said Rachel.

"Will you excuse me," I said, standing up as the room began to spin. "The bathroom?"

"Through my bedroom," Rachel said, pointing to the closed door behind her before changing the topic to an emergency meeting she'd attended recently at the Planned Parenthood Manhattan Clinic.

———

I made my way to the toilet, trying to breathe through the discomfort. Passing Rachel's dresser, I noticed a silver tray loaded with perfume bottles and a framed black-and-white photo of a couple, presumably her parents. It was too dark to inspect the photograph, but the velvet pouches of jewelry were right next to it. Even though Sarah made it clear treasures weren't meted out at every family gathering, I was struck by the casual way in which they were tossed aside. I grazed my index finger across the surface of the dresser, lingering on a green velvet bag with its contents practically spilling out. I gave it a little jiggle and the sapphire and diamond ring slid up against a picture frame. I took it into Rachel's mauve bathroom, wanting to try it on one more time just for fun.

By the time I returned to the table, Rae was clearing the dishes. I went to the kitchen to help her serve pumpkin pie. While everyone finished dessert, I stood at the sink, alternating between loading plates in the dishwasher and holding my wrists under cool water. I was definitely feverish. My phone buzzed in my pocket with a text notification.

Grant: *Done eating?*

I checked my watch. I had expected a few more hours of peace before being summoned back into the office.

I wrote back: *Yeah.* Even though I was looking forward to curling up later with some brown rice.

Grant: *What r u up to?*

Was this a work request, or was this something different? Maybe his own loneliness poking through. He'd professed wanting to catch up on sleep and work out on his day off.

"I'm sending you home with leftovers," Rachel said, lifting two large plastic containers in the air. I still wasn't sure how to respond to Grant.

"Rachel," I said. "I can't thank you enough for including me."

"I just wish you girls weren't such picky eaters. I made too much food!"

I turned toward Rae, "Um, I just got a text."

She scowled.

"It's work."

"What, now?" Rachel asked, looking appalled.

"Oh, you wouldn't believe the hours she keeps," Rae said, sounding wounded.

"Yeah, the team needs to do a check-in because we have a really full weekend."

"My Lord, I have never heard of such a thing," Rachel said, putting her hands on her hips.

I said my goodbyes to Harvey, to Lee and to Beverly, who were also making moves toward the coat closet, and then to Sarah.

"I guess we'll be seeing more of you, then?" I asked, but before she could reply, Rae pulled me into the hallway.

"Hey," she said, giving me an unexpectedly warm hug. "Thanks for being here."

I squeezed her back. "See you later tonight?"

"We're driving up to Rhode Island, remember?"

I hadn't remembered, but it didn't matter as I was planning on being in the office for the next seventy-two hours straight.

"Okay, then Sunday night?"

"Yeah," Rae said, her eyes downcast.

"Ah, c'mon you'll be okay," I said. "It's only a long weekend." But I could understand why she was upset. I wouldn't want my mother descending on my turf just as I was sprouting wings either.

Down on the sidewalk, I responded to Grant: *Heading home.* It had rained at some point during our meal and cool moisture hung in the air, coating the asphalt which now gleamed black under the streetlights.

Grant: *Come out for a bit?*

As a fellow member of the lonely banker's club, I felt compelled to rescue him. *Go ahead, Betsabé, it could be fun.* Besides, there would be plenty of people my age who, released from family obligations, would be out on the town. So, I agreed to meet him at a tavern located on a midtown block between the First Provident tower and his apartment. Maybe we'd reconstruct reality, pretending after a few drinks it was pure coincidence we'd shown up there at the same time.

After the dry heat of Rachel's radiator and the moist night air, the breathy smells inside the bar were an affront to my senses. I didn't know how long I'd last; besides I was wearing an outfit better suited for a friend's grandmother's house than going out to a bar. I was used to attracting looks, but this outfit gave off the modern-day vibe of a circle pin. Plus, what had first passed as indigestion was now unmistakably PMS.

I spotted Grant's shiny blond hair and wide shoulders hunched over a bottle of beer and felt pity. Always a gentleman, he stood when he saw me coming.

"It's gotten busy. Here, take my seat."

"Thanks, you okay?"

"Forget what I said, spending Thanksgiving alone sucks." Again, with that penetrating stare.

"What did you do last year?"

"Christine, my fiancée, my ex-fiancée was here."

"Ugh, sorry."

"Yeah she hated New York to begin with so my long absences pushed her over the edge." He took a long swig of his beer as if saying her name put a nail through his heart. I thought about all the places I would have visited with limitless time alone in the city if I had been the fiancée. My mind brought up images of Times Square lit up in neon, and street saxophonists playing *New York, New York.*

He ordered me a glass of red wine. "Thanks for coming out." I was thinking one drink, then home and straight to bed.

"Being alone is hard, but families are hard too."

He nodded.

I relaxed against the bar. "I was at Rae's grandmother's. I think they were about to break out the board games."

He laughed.

"No, but really, before dinner they had all this jewelry out on the table trying to decide who was inheriting what."

"Jeez."

The bar was filling with people our age shedding winter coats and heading to the back where there were pool tables and dart boards. The front windows facing Second Avenue were fogged over. The televisions behind the bar played football games on mute while the rock music got gradually louder, making it necessary for Grant to shout in my ear. I avoided looking him in the eye because if I turned my cheek, I would have brushed his chin.

"Seen any good movies lately?" he asked. His small talk teetered on corny.

"When would I have a minute to do that?"

"It's just my family usually goes to the movies after Thanksgiving dinner."

"Traditions." I shrugged. I didn't explain how in my neighborhood, men dug pits to roast whole pigs, and everyone sat around late into the night eating roast pork and lighting fireworks as if Thanksgiving was a dress rehearsal for Christmas Eve.

"There's a ten o'clock showing at the Cinépolis. What do you think?"

He was a goof. "Sure. Why not?" I loved popcorn and couldn't remember the last time I'd been to an actual theatre. He pulled out his phone to read the listings. "Charlie's Angels or Hustlers?"

"Seriously?"

"Well there's also a car racing movie or a movie about Mr. Roger's Neighborhood. I figured you'd like something about female empowerment."

Grant slapped two twenties on the bar. We buttoned our coats by the door before returning to the fresh air. We chose Hustlers, a movie that ended up being about strippers who drugged and stole from mid-level Wall Street stockbrokers. It starred Jennifer Lopez, and her opening scene was nothing less than a provocative pole dance. It may have been my hair, or my figure, but guys in college had often compared me to JLo despite the fact she was Puerto Rican and I was Cuban. It seemed in upstate New York nobody knew the difference, just as the theatre director at Lyle said I'd be perfect for the role of Maria in West Side Story. I said, "Thank you, but you do know I am Cuban and not Puerto Rican." He didn't seem to hear me or at least he didn't respond.

Anyway, I sat horrified, in the same way I could never watch a sexy movie with Yaya. It could have been an innocent mistake, in that movies featuring half-naked women were hard to avoid, but I squirmed in my seat and Grant kept crossing and uncrossing his legs. Poor straightlaced Grant, this was probably the closest he'd ever get to a real strip club. This will make you uncomfortable, Sol, but the truth was the movie got me slightly aroused.

Emerging from the theatre and onto the cold sidewalk, we strode in silence with bright windows lighting our way. Our heads were tucked down against the wind, facing the ground instead of taking in the displays decorated for the biggest shopping day of the year. "My apartment's not far," he said, jamming his hands into the front pockets of his jeans. It was neither an explicit invitation nor a request to walk him home, more like something to fill the silence, and I was unsure how to frame a response that would come out right.

My eyes were tearing from the cold as he unlocked the front door and still as he unlocked the door to his apartment. I was thinking of the last line in the movie when JLo said, "The whole city, the whole country is like a strip club. Some people throw the money, and some people just do the dance." Such a bad movie but I'd have that line stuck in my head for a long time.

Grant turned on the light. "Want a beer?" he asked.

"No thanks, I'm done for the night." Before I could say good bye, he took me by the shoulders, bore right into my eyes and said, "Oh God, Bets, I really need to kiss you."

I'd sensed it coming, not his asking permission, although I did appreciate that. I sensed him wanting to kiss me the whole walk home, and I stared back at him, knowing the only way to put the sexual tension behind us was to walk through it. "So, do it," I said.

It wasn't just any kiss; it was long and deliberate. We were in his entryway, avoiding the part where we separated and had to look into each other's eyes, deciding whether or not to carry on any further. It was ironic because I would have been into hooking up with him six weeks earlier at Eden, but since then Grant had turned into more of a big brother to me. If I was going to break the cardinal rule of not messing around with coworkers, there were plenty of anonymous guys I'd noticed in the elevator. I hated that Grant had interpreted my showing up at a bar and sharing a large bucket of popcorn as an invitation for sex. Or maybe it's possible he'd misread what I'd intended as sympathy for his loneliness as something else.

He was leading me down the hall, but I pulled back. "Are we really doing this?"

"Oh, Bets, is it okay? I want you so badly." I knew he did, and although I appreciated his desire, my heart sank. Why did friendships with guys always hit this wall? Ethan was the one exception only because he was dating my roommate.

He asked again, "Is it okay?" He had likely been through countless Title IX trainings and was following the most important rule, but our generation's barrage of consent education in its binary simplicity could make sex feel like a legal transaction. He was checking the first box, but this would definitely complicate our relationship at work. Backtracking at that point, however, felt like it would create even more stress on sixty. At some point along the way I'd internalized the idea that men can't handle rejection. That's what I told myself, at least. It wouldn't take long to realize, Sol, that not wanting to disappoint Grant was in no way worth what would come next.

So, I said, "Yeah, I want it too," removing my cardigan and following him into the bedroom. Whether he was a neat guy who made his bed every morning or had anticipated a visitor, I didn't ask, but as we lay together on top of his bedspread my breath quickened. My anxiety built as we kissed, and I tried to pull myself together when he got up to retrieve a condom. Dear Sol, you may be feeling angst about what comes next. I'm afraid it's a scene that will make you uncomfortable, but it is important I convey everything. You need it for context. Perhaps it would help if you detached from the story. Think of Bets as a character instead of your mother.

———◆———

When Grant joined me under the covers, the sensation of our bare skin touching was surprisingly arousing. I closed my eyes and tried to access one of my dreams so as not to get too freaked out by the fact it was him. I convinced myself that what we had was a modern form of love. It was, even though we shouldn't have been having sex. I should never have gone to his apartment. No matter how cold it was, I should have waited for a cab outside the theatre. The smallest decisions can turn everything upside down, or the compounding effect of a series of small decisions, but if I had just gone home that night, I might never have needed to write this story.

Nevertheless, I was in Grant's bed, my head sinking into his plush pillow as I squeezed my eyes shut, surrendering to my exhaustion as well as the softness of his mattress. I fell back into my fantasy of Bunny Meister, an exquisitely dressed man who adorned his wife with jewelry. Grant was tender, moving slowly on top of me, giving me plenty of time to conjure up my dark-haired romantic. Bunny morphed into Clark Gable, black-and-white blurry images of dark hair, dark skin, dark eyes. It seemed Grant was getting close to climaxing, and as the intensity built, he buried his head in the nape of my neck. I wrapped my arms around his strong back and another dark-haired man's face flashed through my mind. "Oh, my God!" I screamed, and Grant seemed pleased at my rapture, although I was nowhere close to orgasm. I was screaming because the face flashing through my mind no longer belonged to Bunny Meister. It had turned into David's.

We lay still for a moment before Grant's phone buzzed on the bedside table. "Weird, it's my brother, I should take this." He rolled out of bed and sat up straight.

"Oh shit," he said into the phone, rubbing his eyes. He walked across the room, leaving me alone to search for my clothes.

There was a long silence and then he said, "No, yeah, absolutely. Don't worry, I'll catch the first flight in the morning." I was fully dressed by the time the conversation ended.

He sat down next to me and I caressed his back. "My grandfather," he choked on the last words, "passed away."

"Oh, Grant," I said. "I'm so sorry."

"I've got to get home," he said. I felt for him, it was the same call I dreaded receiving.

"You know I'll do whatever I can to cover for you on this end."

"Thanks."

"You should get some sleep," I said. "I'll call an Uber." I kissed his cheek and stood up to leave. I left him naked and frozen on the edge of the bed, turning his phone over in his hands.

CHAPTER TEN

I was grateful Rae wasn't home because she would have noticed something immediately, the way I went directly to the bathroom to shower and then turned on her kettle to make some tea. I burned my hand on the stovetop as I was going for the sugar, and despite rooting around all our cabinets and drawers I couldn't find any bandages or cream. I sent myself a text: *Buy first aid kit.*

I set my alarm for eight in order to get to the office by nine. It was almost two and I was overtired, but also biting my lip over what I'd done with Grant. I had no idea what time it was when I actually fell asleep, but it seemed like my alarm went off minutes later.

The streets were deserted, but passing Macy's on my way uptown I saw lines stretching around the block. Grant was right about Black Friday. He had warned that once the Christmas tree in Rockefeller Plaza was lit, we'd be suffering five weeks of crowds making it impossible to move above ground freely, and that we'd be relegated to the subway with the rats.

Marnye did a bad job concealing her opportunism around Grant's family emergency. Not that I wished ill on anyone, but after what we'd done the night before, I was relieved I didn't have to face him either. She and I devised a work plan before David arrived and I fired up the model. I'd recently made a concession to life at the keyboard, a simpler manicure, nails cut short and polished pearl. Marnye gave the new look a stamp of approval as it was more professional and didn't show as much when it chipped. My nails had actually been a matter of discussion with Rae one night before bed. She got away with black polish at work. "They don't mind orange hair," she joked. "And nobody gets close enough to see my nail polish anyway."

I'd picked up blue light glasses a few weeks earlier as Agri-Global had escalated my screen time twofold and Marnye lent me a bolster pillow to support my low back. I didn't have a cure for the twitching muscles around my eyelids, however, except to look away from the screen every ten minutes or so. I alternated glances between David on the phone, Marnye at her desk, and Grant's empty chair, wondering if I'd ever be able to handle him looking at the screen over my shoulder again.

I turned to the stacks of publicly available documents I'd collected both on AgriGlobal and its competition. Marnye suggested I get better organized in general, and culling through the documents for what could be shredded would be a mindless exercise that would give my eyes a longer rest.

A major player in agribusiness and factory farming, Agri-Global was headquartered outside Minneapolis. Early in the deal, I'd really gotten lost in the research. I was interested in their products, where they were located, the people they employed. It was easy to view everything quantitatively, but the company had thousands of workers influencing the food we ate. Google satellite imagery made their offices three-dimensional and helped me imagine the humans running the operations.

I set aside the annual reports, 10-Ks, and offering documents, keeping the articles on mega-agricultural businesses who were notorious for over-tilling farmland, leading to the erosion of the nation's topsoil. Desertification from an overdependency on fertilizers and pesticides was a major contributor to climate change. Whereas I was originally excited to be working on a deal that was so relevant to farming and food, the research also gave me a sickening insider's view of all the ways our world was going to shit.

David ultimately sold Roland on an acquisition to solve his earnings problems, and even though it wasn't going to improve the company's carbon footprint, I held out hope the merger might launch them toward greener initiatives. Marnye had a good laugh when I suggested we include slides that addressed the unquantifiable opportunities that came with the merger, as in the human and environmental consequences of the transaction.

"Uh, Bets, we only deal in what is quantifiable, that's what they hire us for."

"But I wonder . . ."

"Look, they have consultants to figure that stuff out. We've been hired to get the deal done. Period."

"But Roland didn't even know he wanted a deal until David talked him into one."

"He knew he needed something."

It boggled my mind that the genesis of this billion-dollar transaction affecting thousands of people was a well-timed call by David. Once he had Roland doubting his business, David's next step was to make sure he didn't "wimp out." He said it was easiest for a CEO and his board to do nothing.

In coming up with a target list, I'd considered each company's position on the value chain, where they were located, as well as their key product lines. Despite focusing on the rows and columns on my monitor, I couldn't stop picturing the dust released into the atmosphere during tilling season and Gloria's inability to afford produce from the organic aisle at the grocery store. In the end, David suggested AgriGlobal acquire two seed breeders who created genetically modified seeds designed to withstand soil that was fertilized with nitrate and sprayed with chemicals. The photographs in the annual reports spoke of sun-soaked fields and the efficient manner with which these companies fed the world, but it couldn't have been more different than the way Yaya tended her garden back home.

I got up from my desk and went to the ladies' room and just as I suspected, the previous night's cramps were the precursor to my period. I felt lousy, but blood was also a welcome sight after spontaneous sex with Grant. I helped myself to the feminine hygiene products in baskets on the counter. I'd once considered that supply of pads and tampons a generous convenience made available by First Provident, similar to the free food and drink in the dining room. I was coming to realize, however, the bagels, the coffee, even the tampons were the firm's way of keeping me from ever going outside.

I tucked my chin into my chest to get a whiff of my underarms, although Gloria once told me it was impossible to smell yourself. I brushed my hair, swallowed a couple complimentary acetaminophen, and returned to the bullpen.

After another long stretch glued to my screen, I got up to ask Marnye some questions but as I approached her desk, she was in a heated conversation. "I can't predict exactly," she said into her phone. "I told you, I have no idea!"

I tried to back away, pretending I hadn't heard a thing, but she had already seen me and put her hand over the mouthpiece. "Hey, Bets, order our lunch and I'll be over in a bit."

She joined me in the bullpen ten minutes later and attempted to help me find the root of an error message in the model while we waited for the food. "I was never the best at this," she admitted in a rare moment of weakness. Her eyes were unmistakably red and her hands a little shaky. I searched each embedded formula and eventually discovered the problem myself.

"See, you know what you're doing. You should be more assertive. Assertive men are called leaders, but assertive women are called difficult." And there she went again, preaching the ways of the world. The truth was, Marnye's statements contradicted her actions all the time. She could be so critical of David while complying with everything he asked.

Security called when the food arrived and based on the number of delivery bags lined up in the lobby, it appeared plenty of us were working over the holiday weekend. When I returned with our lunch containers, I found Nathan Goldstein, First Provident's

Chief Counsel, reclining at one of the empty desks in the bull-pen, presumably waiting for David to get off the phone. He wore casual attire, dark jeans and a fisherman's sweater, and with his ruddy pink complexion and bushy gray eyebrows, he looked like he was heading out on a fishing expedition instead of working in midtown Manhattan.

"So, how's he holding up?"

I turned around slowly, not entirely sure he was talking to me.

"Oh, fine I guess," I said.

"Just wondering, with all that's going on in Hong Kong." I didn't know anything about the deal in Hong Kong.

"He has you on AgriGlobal?"

I nodded, slightly alarmed he was saying it aloud. We were now using the code name "Tough Corn" in order to keep it confidential.

"Sorry, I haven't introduced myself. Nathan Goldstein," he said, reaching across the empty desk and stacks of annual reports to shake my hand.

"Betsabé Ruiz."

"Oh, I know who you are." He smirked. Then again, I knew who he was too. He strolled across the sixtieth floor often, always around five o'clock, looking more or less disheveled. Lenore explained he and David had a standing date for a workout and dinner ever since Abigail died. Their body language telegraphed a friendship that went back a long way, apparently extending to the squash court.

"So, how's sixty treating you?" he asked.

"Survived my first three months." He gave a thumbs-up as if survival was all one could hope for.

"You a baseball fan?" he asked out of the blue. I'd barely lived in New York one season, but it was long enough to understand the Yankees were a religion with investment bankers, fellow pinstriped masters of the universe, boasting inflated payrolls and valuing a win at any cost.

"Not really but I guess I've absorbed some." I recalled think-ing it was a weird thing to bring up as the season had been over for months. Then he asked what I knew about the recent agreement between Major League Baseball and the Cuban Baseball Federation. He assumed that because my family was Cuban, I knew players from Cuba were being allowed to join the majors without having to defect. There had been some talk among my cousins, but I couldn't offer him much.

"Take Yasiel Puig, for example," he continued. "Awful things happen to a lot of people, but when a baseball star tells his story, everyone takes notice." Puig had been trying to leave Cuba for nearly a year, and on his fifth attempt to flee, Mexican smugglers held him hostage in a motel on the Yucatan Peninsula, demanding ransom from the MLB. "Going through Mexico," he said, shaking his head. I may not have heard of the baseball player, but I was well aware of the story. I tried to maintain a straight face; Nathan couldn't have known my father tried the same thing. "Why wouldn't he take advantage of the wet foot, dry foot policy and venture the ninety miles by sea to Florida?" I shrugged. I had no idea. But hearing him talk about it made it easier to forgive my father, and my grandfather for that matter.

I was distracted by a window-washing crew hanging on scaffolding outside. It was a terrifying sight in the November cold. "Would you like half of my sandwich?" I asked, my eyes glued to a harnessed man holding an oversized squeegee.

He turned to see what I was looking at. "Ah, no thanks," he said. Then he glanced at his watch. "Hey, I've got a train to catch. Can you ask David to give me a call?"

What was it about their generation? Couldn't he just text or leave a voicemail like a normal person? His request confused me, like there was an ulterior motive to his visit. I couldn't stop wondering what was going on in Hong Kong and the insinuation David wasn't holding up well.

I delivered David his lunch while he continued on the phone. I took his scrunched eyebrows to mean I'd messed up his order, or maybe that he'd spotted the window washers and was as concerned about them as I was, but turning to follow his gaze, I saw Tamara crossing the floor. Her cheeks glowed a healthy pink and she wore the type of boxy fur hat I'd only seen before on fashion models.

"Hi, Tamara," I said, exiting her father's office.

"Hi!" she said with extra enthusiasm, making up for the fact she'd forgotten my name.

"It's Bets."

"Right, Bets. I just need a sec with my dad."

He was off the phone and standing in wait.

"There's my girl. To what do I owe this surprise, princess?"

"I need to talk to you, Daddy," she said, pushing him into his office and pulling the door shut.

I turned to find Marnye in the bullpen giving me a grand eye roll. "She is such a spoiled brat. Has him wrapped around her finger." Back then, I still considered their closeness endearing, especially the way David made himself available no matter what, the way his face softened in her presence. It actually made me feel fortunate to be under his wing.

"She probably maxed out her credit card." Marnye despised everything about Tamara, a teenager dressed in thigh-high boots and leather pants, long blond hair cascading down her back. Although she didn't share David's coloring, they were the same height, spoke with the same authority, and had similar mannerisms. Lenore told me they talked on the phone every day which, in my opinion, put him even further in the camp of Bunny Meister, who I imagined reserving big chunks of his inner life for his offspring. When I asked if David spoke with his sons just as often, Lenore emphasized that even though Tamara had many brothers, she'd been the one to console their father during Abigail's illness and after she died.

I hated being a voyeur, but it was hard to turn away from the glass, the two of them talking seriously one moment and breaking into laughter the next. It was like an instructional video on how fathers and daughters were supposed to interact, a glimpse into what my life had been missing. If it was the job of the mother to teach you how to be a girl, I decided, it was a father's job to tell you whether you'd gotten it right. I had never appreciated, until seeing David and Tamara together, how my father's approval might have changed my personality, imperceptibly boosted my confidence. I shifted uncomfortably in my seat, remembering the image of David's face that had flashed through my mind the night before, lying in Grant's bed.

CHAPTER ELEVEN

Weekends in the office had a way of passing more quickly than weekdays, and when I next looked up, it was dark, Tamara was gone, and David was standing by the door to his office holding a red-lined document. "Marnye, I've done all I can on this term sheet. Why don't you go home and get some rest? We'll review this with the lawyers in the morning."

He likely intended her release as a kind gesture, but Marnye frowned at the suggestion she didn't manage her own time.

She protested, "Bets and I are still—"

But he cut her off. "I'll go over the model with Bets. We'll all be getting out of here pretty soon."

"Okay," Marnye said, eyeing him carefully. She closed a binder and carried it back to her desk. "See you tomorrow."

I stared at my computer as her footsteps faded toward the bank of elevators, the emergency exit lights shining red across the white marble floor. It was my first time alone on sixty with David. "Bets, let's go over the numbers at my table," he said.

I carried a set of slides through the door. He sat down and I found myself marveling at his clean-shaven skin even late in the day. It was something guys my age had given up on entirely. I caught a whiff of his aftershave and at the same time wondered how many people might still be working on the floors below and if, in the event of an emergency, somebody would know where we were. I organized the PowerPoint slides and various models in neat piles on his table.

"So, in this first version," I began.

He rubbed his eyes. "I'm sorry Bets, I've lost my concentration. Tamara has a way of throwing me off balance."

"No problem," I said. "We've got eight different versions here."

"I knew this day would come sooner or later, but I'm just not ready." I wasn't sure I wanted to be the one hearing this, but presumed, as with the rest of us, David had few friendships outside of work. He had a tribe of children and ex-wives, but it probably felt natural to share his thoughts with his colleagues.

"Okay," he said, picking up the top page. "What's this assumption?"

"It's a variable I came up with," I said. "I call it the regen factor. As more farm acreage transitions to regenerative farming, less water is required, and the heirloom seeds do better." Grant focused on synergies we'd achieve through centralization, basically laying off employees, but I'd been eager to identify positive levers. The market valuations didn't yet take into account the drought out west, rising temperatures, or the increasing number of diseases affecting crops.

"Hmmm," David said. "And what's this one?"

"I call this one the climate factor. We can manipulate average temperature assumptions." When AgriGlobal's fertilizer mixed with the target company's engineered seeds, the economics improved with rising temperatures.

"I like it," he said grinning. "Really good. We'll use it to show Roland even higher valuations."

"Becoming a leader in regenerative farming would have benefits too."

"A warmer climate seems more likely," he said. "Did Grant help you with this?"

"No," I said quietly.

"You know, I watch the two of you working together. You seem to really enjoy each other's company."

"Oh, he's been a great mentor."

"And you went away for a weekend together, I'm told?" I probably turned beet red as a surge of heat rushed through my body and perspiration beaded on the back of my neck. "Don't be embarrassed. I know better than anyone how hard it is to meet people outside of work." His knee bumped into mine under the table. "Whoops, sorry," he said, patting my arm in apology. "My lord, what happened to your hand?" The place where I'd burned it on the stove the night before had blistered white.

"Just a burn."

"Looks painful."

"It's fine," I said, trying to laugh it off but I let out a yawn instead.

"You're exhausted," he said.

I nodded. "I am." I didn't mention that I was also hungover and suffering the worst menstrual cramps of my life. I worried once more about what kinds of odor I was giving off. There wasn't enough deodorant in the world to mask all that was going on in my body.

"I'm a little distracted too. Tamara's mother. She's so protective. My daughter is acting out, you know? She wants more independence. She applied to some study abroad program. I don't know. I'm caught in the middle."

"Oh, wow."

He stared into my eyes. "I'm sorry, I shouldn't be unloading my personal problems on you."

"No, it's fine. I mean it must be hard."

Even sitting, David was a good six inches taller than me. He held my hand in order to get a closer look at the burn. "I think Lenore has a first aid kit in the copier room."

"Really, it's fine. My grandmother says it's better to expose burns to the air."

"Okay then." He smiled. "Well, we've made good progress. Let's call it a night."

I often felt like I was just treading water at First Provident, so David's praise meant a lot. Designing environmental variables in the model intrigued me, and I was confident I could dig up some socially redeemable ones to show Roland in the coming days as well.

"Have you been getting enough to eat?" he asked.

"Yeah. I'm just tired."

"You've been killing yourself today."

"Without Grant, it's a lot." I shivered. Mentioning his name was like inviting him into the room. Going to bed with him the night before could be reduced to lust after a sexy movie, but the goosebumps rising on my flesh in David's presence rocked me. He was powerful, successful, worldly, intelligent. It was hard to know whether I was feeling an attraction or whether it was all in my imagination.

He leaned against the table and started talking about his daughter again. She had begged him to intervene with his ex-wife. "Which believe you me is fraught with complications." It was unclear to David whether Tamara's motivation to study abroad was purely academic or whether there was a young man in the picture. He may have been reckless when it came to stripping corporate assets, but as a father, he was the picture of conservatism, as if safekeeping Tamara's virginity was his most pressing responsibility.

He ran his hand atop his hair. "But the truth is, I'll miss her," he said, coughing into his fist as if to drive back emotion. Maybe it was the late hour that added to the sadness in his eyes, but he didn't seem embarrassed. He had just lost a wife and he would miss his daughter. A few tears welled in his eyes, but he didn't wipe them away.

He held my gaze, but I wasn't sure how to comfort him. I had a strong point of view on what it was like to be a young woman in this day and age, how society made it hard for us to grow into strong, healthy humans, but that's not what he needed to hear.

"I'm sure she'll miss you too," I said. He smiled and nodded. "I mean, I know my mom worried when I left for Lyle that it was goodbye forever, but Tamara will be back." As the words left my mouth, I realized I had rarely returned to Miami and it was possible my mother missed me too.

He took my hand and examined the burn more closely. Looking back, I don't think he intended it to be suggestive, but his hand holding mine started something. It could have been a paternal gesture, or flirting, but in the moment, I tried to shrug it off as generational, the closeness between two people who had been working hard for fourteen hours straight when most were on holiday. Down deep, I took his touch to be a question. If I was okay with being thrown into a swimming pool, then how about his holding my hand? And if I was willing to spend a weekend with Grant, then how about the two of us alone in his office? And when I dared to look at him with a bold expression of my own, his eyes twinkled. *Well then.*

The truth is I could have easily pulled my hand away, but I chose not to. The energy volleying back and forth between us was dangerously exciting. He never looked more handsome, but it was also his ability to pace things, the interplay of personal and professional conversation. He was a master of suspense, and I was drawn as much to the art of his seduction as I was to his person.

"You should get some rest," he said.

Heat rose in my cheeks. "I'll call a car," I said.

"I think I'll walk home," he said. "You should take mine."

When I reached the street, there was David's Mercedes. "Ms. Ruiz?" His driver's sympathetic smile suggested he remembered the drenched girl he'd ferried home from Connecticut back in September. His friendly eyes reflected in the rearview mirror as he pulled away from the curb, asking, "Are you warm enough?"

"Yes, thank you," I said, while cataloging the belongings David kept at hand in the back seat: reading glasses, newspapers folded in a rear pocket, and a pack of Trident cinnamon gum. There was a fairy godmother's carriage-like quality to this car, appearing at the stroke of midnight before something irreversible might take place. Trash collectors were working overtime after the holiday, and coffee shops glowed neon offering breakfast all day. I reclined into the luxuriously soft leather and helped myself to the small green bottle of Pellegrino in the cupholder, letting its effervescence tickle my nose.

———

Saturday morning, I arrived on sixty to find it unexpectedly quiet. Marnye arrived a few minutes later carrying a white paper sack in one hand and a large Styrofoam cup of coffee in the other. The private dining room was closed on weekends and we had to fend for ourselves.

David arrived while Marnye was giving me marching orders. He sat inside his office as I crossed the floor back to the bullpen. He had this way of looking up and catching my stare. I imagined it was nothing he paid much attention to, that it was a "gotcha" game only in my mind, my magnetic will, causing him to look up and sometimes chuckle. I swung my hair behind a shoulder and sat down. I looked at the list of things Marnye had given me, knowing Grant wouldn't have cared about half of them. When my internal phone line rang, the loud sound took me by surprise. David's name appeared on the screen and I stared at him through the glass as I picked up.

"Come in here a moment?"

I placed the receiver back in its cradle and walked into his office, holding a yellow pad to my chest.

"I have something for you," he said, pulling a white envelope from the pencil drawer of his desk. I took it, all the while looking at him with slight confusion. "Tamara asked me to get them, but she forgot and made other plans. They're for the three o'clock matinee. You have just enough time to invite a friend and be on your way."

What was he talking about? Where was he sending me? I opened the crisp envelope and two theatre tickets spilled out. They were to Hamilton.

"What? Oh my God, really?!"

"You've probably seen it."

"No! I mean thank you. I am so appreciative." He smiled broadly at my reaction. My instinct was to hug him, but there was no way I could do that. "Thank you so much."

I looked at my watch. One thirty. Rae wasn't back in the city yet. Grant was in Ohio. Sandra? I thought about asking Ethan, but in a way, I sort of wanted to go alone. I didn't know if anybody would be able to share my excitement. I was the last person on earth to see this hit show and I wanted to be the geek who sang along about not giving away my shot, and I wanted to be able to dance in my seat without anybody making fun of me.

Marnye gave me the evil eye as I approached her desk with my coat over one arm. "I'm sorry, but David insisted I not let these tickets go to waste."

"What?"

"Ask him yourself."

I proceeded to the elevator without waiting for her response. I called Yaya as soon as I was down on the sidewalk to tell her where I was headed. The Richard Rodgers Theatre wasn't far. I found my seat in the orchestra, five rows back. I gripped the red velvet armrests and took in the gilded gold decor as streams of tourists filed into the seats around me. A holiday weekend, the best musical on Broadway, the aisles were clogged with family groups, inching their way to their seats and wedging winter coats onto their laps. I devoured every word in the Playbill about this quintessentially New York show. Alexander Hamilton was the man who turned New York into the world's financial capital.

I couldn't remember the last time I'd felt so right, so at home. A theatre. It was Broadway, not the Johnstone Performing Arts Center at Lyle College, but with the lights and the stage and the costumes, the singing and the dancing, it was my world. After the last number concluded, tears streamed down my cheeks. I had an iota of the talent on that stage, but there had to be a way I could find my way back.

———◆———

There was no way I could return to sixty after the theatre. I walked home slowly that evening, arriving just as Rae was returning from Rhode Island, a day early. We were both in need of a good night's sleep, but our friendship was based on bedtime talk, which meant forfeiting rest.

"Guess who went to a matinee of Hamilton today?" I asked, stashing away the fact that Grant and I had consummated our flirtation, not to mention the sparks flying between David and me the night before in his office. She lit the candle on the coffee table, its warm glow creating a teenage sleepover atmosphere.

"Really?" She was excited for me and we carried on about the score, the Schuyler sisters, which one I would have played. "Angelica!" we sang in unison.

"How was Rhode Island?" I eventually asked, snuggling down under my covers.

"Ah, you know. I love being at Eden. I love Constance and Joseph and the family all together. But I had to share a bedroom with my mother."

"And?"

"Yeah, I never realized how dicey the situation was at Lyle. She put on a good face at Thanksgiving, but once we were alone, she kind of lost it."

"What happened?" I knew it was wrong to want the juicy details behind Dean Stern's demise. Despite our regular interactions on SUFI, she had always been a bit of a mystery.

"It's crazy. The board of trustees holds my mother responsible for the failings of the sustainability task force which resulted in the coywolf infestation."

"What? That's insane. It was College Hall that kept shooting our ideas down! That's totally unfair."

"Yeah, but I think we both know there's more to it." President Addington's name didn't need mentioning.

"Hey, Rae. Do you mind if I ask you something?"

She laughed, because when I was curious, my question was coming regardless of whether she minded.

"What about your father? If he never married your mother, and wasn't around, why did he leave you a sick trust fund?"

"Well, when I was twelve, I found his number on my mother's phone, so I called him. I suggested an outing to the Natural History Museum. After that, getting together became a weekly thing. I'm pretty sure it's why my mother moved us upstate."

Yeah, Sarah Stern was hard to figure out. It wasn't like Rae's father was a deadbeat or violent, he was an esteemed academic, and from the looks of the pictures on Rae's dresser, attractive and in a way reminiscent of my psychology professor.

"And I kept calling him after we moved," said Rae. "Because he was an interesting guy, but also to get under my mother's skin. Before I could graduate from college and move back, he went and died." The size of her inheritance seemed disproportionate to the depth of their relationship, and maybe the reason Rae felt conflicted about the money.

"Well, at least you had him for a little while," I said. Unlike Rae, I'd completely lost touch with my father. Edmundo Cardon was Cuba's great hope in middleweight boxing at the 1996 Atlanta Olympics. He came up short, winning only the bronze, but made headlines nonetheless when he defected along with eleven baseball players. My mother met him later that year after he'd settled in Miami and began coaching at a famous boxing academy.

I remembered the day he moved Gloria and me into Yaya's casita. It was supposed to be temporary while he went to Mexico City for altitude training and then on to the Dominican Republic to coach team Mexico in the 2003 Pan American Games. Before leaving, he scooped me up in the air and wrapped me in his steel-like arms. I squealed as he blew raspberries into the nape of my neck. He masked his emotions well, undoubtedly understanding the risks he was taking by leaving the country. I was too caught up in his attention to notice my mother's tears. He placed me on the floor and took a boxer's stance, bouncing on his toes. He lifted his fists, one at his chin, the other poised to jab and said, "Protege tu cara bonita, Betsabé." Protect that pretty face. I giggled while mimicking his darting and dancing across Yaya's porch before feeding the next line back to him, "Papi, noquéalo!" Go for the KO!

Nobody ever explained to me why he didn't return as planned. There was crying and shouting and desperate phone calls and Yaya taking me into the bedroom so my mother could explain to some authority that her hombre was missing. More than a year passed before we heard from him. Yaya answered the phone, speaking to him in a soft voice for several moments before passing the receiver to Gloria. My mother crumpled to the floor. Her prayers had been answered. My father was alive in Monterey and was trying to return, but there were complications. He called from Mexico regularly and Gloria would put me on the line, but my father never came back to Miami. Gradually, he faded from our lives until all that was left was a picture on the wall and stale gossip in the neighborhood. Gloria said I was lucky my papi and abuelo were gone. Latin men didn't like their women too independent, she said, and neither of them would have allowed me to travel north for college.

"My mother considered the inheritance an insult," Rae said. "She expected me to turn it down. Give Alistair one last fuck you, but Rachel said, 'Now what good would that do? The man's dead, Rae should take the money.'" It had resulted in her having a bigger bank account than either her mother or grandmother. I clenched my teeth at her problem, too much money.

"To be continued," I said with irritation bubbling up in my throat. I needed to end the conversation out of fear I might say something I'd regret. I reminded myself my annual take-home pay was four times what she earned in publishing. For an industry concentrated in a city as expensive as New York, its entry involved unpaid internships, making trust fund babies like Rae the only ones who could afford to take them. Even though she teased me and Ethan for working on Wall Street, at least it wasn't self-selecting from a population of wealthy white girls. Yes, remembering my professional accomplishments put everything back in balance.

And then there was David's attention. I'd doze off remembering his concern for my burn, his twinkling green eyes, those theatre tickets. Were they leftover fatherly residuals I was feeling, or did he think about me romantically too? Imagining him smiling at his desk made my insides stir, and I had to count backward from one hundred to fall asleep.

CHAPTER TWELVE

Monday morning, I received a message from Grant saying his grandfather's funeral was that afternoon. Arrangements were pulled together quickly to take advantage of the siblings already in town for Thanksgiving. I made a note to send flowers and called him as I walked to the subway.

"You doing okay?"

"Yeah, I'll be back tomorrow night."

"Quick turnaround," I said, sort of surprised. Whenever we lost an elder in Miami, especially someone close, observances lasted days. I winced at Grant shortchanging his grieving because it was an inconvenient time at work. If that was the case, I actually sympathized with the fiancée.

"Dinner tomorrow night?"

"Don't we always have dinner?" referring to the takeout we shared around the conference table.

"Not in the office. I want to take you somewhere."

I thought about asking him to forget it ever happened, but his grandfather had just passed away and I was afraid of coming across as mean. "Okay, sure."

After hanging up, I spent the subway ride scrolling through the requests Marnye had sent while normal humans slept. Shit like that happened all the time with her and I just shook my head at the image of her fuming, messaging me orders like she had something to prove. Never mind playing second fiddle to Grant, now she was getting competitive with me because David seemed to be favoring me. She tried to bury me for the next thirty-six hours: an entirely revised model, new scenarios that would align with a new term sheet, proofing whether her redlines made it into the new docs from the legal team, and following up on requests from First Provident's legal department.

Afternoon turned to evening and I checked my watch, willing Nathan to pick up David. He made his way down the hall right on time. "Our court's at six," he announced.

"Good luck with that," Lenore said, her face up lit by the unflattering glow of her monitor.

"He has to let his people eat," Nathan said, flashing a smile toward the bullpen.

We were fortunate David took fitness so seriously. Whether it was vanity or health consciousness, we could count on him leaving for a couple of hours most evenings. When I asked Lenore about their health club, she was quick to correct me. It was nothing open to the public but one of those old-world, male bastions nestled on Central Park South. I pictured David and Nathan dressed in white, running around a small court and then having a bite of dinner or nibbling on a nut mix, maybe sipping scotch in front of a fire in the men's locker room. The scene had them wrapped in towels around their waists, rolling dice and pushing pieces around a backgammon board. Because Lenore told me David's one vice was the occasional cigar, it also included plumes of smoke twirling about their heads.

"Okay, I'm coming," David said, grabbing his overcoat. On his way to the elevator, he said something to Lenore that got her laughing and she shut down her computer. I messaged Marnye there was a personal matter I needed to attend to and would be back in a bit. I acted as if it was unexpected and annoying, feigning exasperation before darting into the ladies room to freshen up. I straightened my blouse and brushed my hair out of its messy bun before buttoning my coat and heading to the elevator.

Grant's face lit up when he spotted me in the lobby.

"Hey, how are you doing?" I asked, thankful I could lead with sympathy.

"Better now. You look great," he said, turning his gaze toward the asphalt.

"Guess what? David gave me tickets to the Saturday matinee of Hamilton. It was amazing!"

"Cool," he said, although nowhere near matching my enthusiasm.

"So, what's the occasion?"

Looking straight ahead, he said, "We need to talk."

There were policies at First Provident against intraoffice romance, but flings among the analyst class were common enough and overlooked. They took it seriously, however, when analysts got involved with senior bankers. There weren't many whistleblowers at First Provident, so Helen and her staff were often chasing rumors. Fooling around had been a mistake on both of our parts. He was my mentor for God's sake. I hoped he'd come to his senses while away, and this dinner was his way of letting me down easy. I didn't want to tell him if anyone needed to be let down easy, it was him. He was the one closing in on thirty, the one who'd been anticipating marriage as the next step, but if he thought I needed a letdown dinner, then, well, whatever.

Once we were a safe distance from the office, he took my hand in his. Sweet but awkward. He stopped in front of a restaurant I had heard Lenore say was David's favorite for lunching with clients.

"Nice," I said.

"It's quiet."

"Sorry," I said. "I can't be away too long." I checked the time as the maître d' led us to our table. "David's asked for a dozen scenarios using the new climate factor I came up with. He really likes that angle," I said, assuming the air of someone momentarily more in the know on AgriGlobal than he was.

"We'll order right away," he said, gesturing for the waiter's attention.

"You're coming back to sixty, aren't you?"

He clasped his hands atop his menu and stared into my eyes in a way that made my stomach flip. I got a text from Marnye: *When will you be back?*

While I texted back *Give me thirty minutes,* Grant ordered two mojitos.

Text bubbles appeared on the screen and then her follow-up: *David wants slides on his desk when he returns*

As soon as I looked up at Grant, he said, "Look, I need to apologize. After the movie. Back in my apartment, I never . . ."

I looked away.

"I never got a chance to say it, but I really care about you."

"Grant, I care about you too."

"Wait, let me finish. This is really hard."

"I know, you just went through a big breakup, don't worry. You don't need to explain."

"What I've learned over the past year is that I need to be with someone who can appreciate the hours I keep, not somebody who gets jealous of my work. I actually like being in the office because you're there. And on my flight home, I admitted to myself just how strong my feelings are for you."

"Oh, Grant." I held my breath.

"But I need to tell you, well, I'm transferring to the Hong Kong office."

"What?" I leaned across the table gobsmacked.

"First, let me just say that ever since we, well, Thursday night, working together would be pure torture. I'll put in a few years in the Hong Kong office, by the time I return, your stint as an analyst will be over and I know this might sound really out of the blue, but I'm hoping we'll be able to pick things up where they left off. I could see us together, you know?"

"Oh, Grant." I flashed back to the VP's wife at the barbecue and Marnye bitching about women raised on fairy-tale endings. "When is this happening?"

"In two days."

"Holy shit! Two days? How long have you known about this?"

"David called me yesterday."

"What?"

"It's because of the Pacificorp deal. David committed five hundred million of the firm's capital. Also, First Provident is growing its presence in Asia and I'll be promoted to VP as part of the transfer." He could hardly contain himself, as if a fast-track promotion justified a move across the globe.

I leaned back in my chair. "Let me get this straight, David offered you this job yesterday and you are leaving in two days?"

"He's counting on me to salvage this deal."

I shook my head at the bizarre timing, not to mention the unlikelihood of an associate single-handedly salvaging anything. "Unbelievable."

"Look, Bets. I know you're disappointed, but this will put me way ahead of Marnye and everyone else in my class. Plus, there's the international experience, and a raise and huge bonus potential. I'll be back in the New York office before you know it. Will you wait for me?"

Since I couldn't give him the answer he was hoping for, I asked, "Is it safe?" I'd been reading the news all summer. In June a million demonstrators took to the streets to protest a proposed law that would allow extradition to China, and a week later two million people marched. Violence had continued for months, the police using tear gas and rubber bullets and protesters retaliating with petrol bombs. Police had recently lay siege to two universities. My family knew all too well what happened to vulnerable democracies on small islands.

"Last week's elections were promising," he said. "Carrie Lam said she was humbled and possibly swayed by public opinion."

"Jeez. Okay. So, congratulations, I guess." I raised my glass. I hated for him to disappear completely, but it would certainly cool things off. Two years was a long time, and anything could happen.

Considering how thoughtful and caring he was by nature, I'm not terribly proud of where my mind went next. Grant sat across the table, filled with a yearning I'd never seen before, and all I could think was that a girl could do a hell of a lot worse. The word "optionality" came to mind, investment banking jargon that drove copy editors like Rae nuts. I put Grant's offer in my back pocket as if it was a get-out-of-jail-free card in the game of life. I tell you this now, about all the insecure places my mind could go, Sol, because it helps to explain what happened later on.

So, without committing to anything, I mirrored his smile and took his hand in mine. Our fingers intertwined against the white tablecloth, amplifying the disparity in our skin tones, and I wondered if we ever did have a future together what his Midwestern family would think of me.

"I'm so glad you agree," he said, holding my hand gently. "I'll buy you a plane ticket to come visit."

He acted as if going to Asia was no different than a jaunt to Rhode Island. If I visited him, I'd finally get my passport stamped. It was still a stiff laminate blue and at that point in my life had only been used as proof of citizenship. So, even if my interest in a future with Grant was halfhearted, the fast-paced life and the travel were very appealing.

I rose from the table but needed to ask one more time: "Are you sure about this, not me, but whether you'll like living in Hong Kong?" I had no idea about its jutting hills and tropical vegetation, only saw it as a drawing on a map, a tiny bastion of democracy surrounded by communism, the polar opposite of Cuba, a tiny island of communism surrounded by democracy. It was as if the cosmos had mixed up the pieces on a world map jigsaw puzzle. Yaya used to describe the paranoia that came with living on an island. Cuba was an island, Hong Kong was an island, Manhattan was an island, which got me thinking maybe a life back in Ohio wasn't such a bad idea.

"I'm sure. It's only a few years. I'll be fine."

DAUGHTER OF A PROMISE

Grant didn't know anything more about Hong Kong than I did, but we both knew he was getting sick of New York. He made fun of everything on my wish list. I'd mention museum exhibits, galleries, and store openings, and he'd say, "Impossible to get into, lines around the block. Don't bother. And forget trying to get a restaurant reservation." At first, I thought it was sour grapes because he was the straight white guy all the bouncers ignored. But over late-night takeout in the office, he'd grumble about the city in a way that implied deeper disappointment— the exploding rents, new construction of luxury housing, all bought up by Russians and Chinese. Or it would be the consumerism, the next wave of college grads, or the holiday tourists clogging midtown sidewalks.

He didn't have the grit of a real New Yorker. It didn't have anything to do with where you were born, it was in your blood manifesting in the way Rachel knew where to find the best bagels or the way Rae wore her nose piercing and Doc Martens. Wall Street was Darwinian, with those succeeding naturally circumspect and thick-skinned. New York was no place for friendly farm boys who made direct eye contact and greeted passersby on the sidewalk.

I kissed him on the cheek. "Congratulations. It sounds amazing. And, yes, I would love to visit." I pointed to my phone. "Marnye is going crazy. I gotta go."

"I'll be in tomorrow to pack my things," he said. "But really, Bets, I'm going to book you a first-class ticket as soon as I set up my apartment. And we can Skype all the time. A twelve-hour time difference actually makes it easy."

I didn't get that logic, still naïve back then to the consequence of time zones, but my phone buzzed again. I texted: *I'm coming!*

"Sorry, I've got to run." I dared a light kiss on his lips before striding back and flashing my ID at security to gain access to the express elevator. When I stepped off on sixty and turned the corner, David was leaning against my desk.

"I assume you were with Grant?"

"Hong Kong?"

"I need him there," he said in all seriousness. "The international experience will do him good, a tour of duty long overdue."

———

Marnye had obviously heard the news because she was in quite a mood. "You can't just disappear like that." I regretted not eating anything at the restaurant because the private dining room was closed by the time I returned. I took a few packets of oyster crackers back to my desk and sucked off the salt one by one while making the changes she wanted to the model. Flashes of heat swept through my chest whenever I got the variables confused or forgot which version was saved under which name. All this extraneous work was her way of punishing me, but I was determined to show her I could get it done before going home. In the hours after midnight, however, I got increasingly flustered.

I didn't leave the office until close to three in the morning and in the privacy of the town car, I put my fingers to my temples and started to cry. All that had transpired in the past week was overwhelming, from having sex with Grant on Thanksgiving night, to being in David's office on Friday night, to my first Broadway show, and Grant telling me he wanted to be forever mine after a quick two-year stopover on the opposite side of the planet. It's possible my heightened emotions were the result of my period, my uterus and hormones having their way with me, but in retrospect, it would have been a lot under any circumstances.

All my friends in college were on the pill, even Rae was now for God's sake, which they said flattened their mood swings and made their monthly cycles more manageable, even kept their skin from breaking out. I had never considered such a thing, not because the Catholic Church forbade it, but because Yaya was habitually cursing the way Big Pharma interfered with Yemayá's grand design. If I had another monthly flow like the one I was having, however, I was going to reconsider.

It was a weird coincidence that the bleeding stopped the morning Grant's flight took off. I woke up feeling like a new woman, the bloating gone along with the cramps. I took a long shower and tore open the shrink-wrap on a fresh parcel of laundry, choosing a crisp white blouse to wear with a plaid wool skirt and black leather boots I had recently splurged on, a professional version of ones Tamara wore. I felt pretty, lighter, clean.

I told myself to forget the previous week and focus on the new season in the air . . . Fifth Avenue windows decorated for the holidays, and midtown extravagantly festooned with Christmas lights. Festive and bursting with possibility, the city was electric and fun and the place to be. *Focus on that.* With just four weeks until Christmas, my visit home to Miami felt like something I could start looking forward to as well.

Lenore had overseen tasteful holiday decorating on sixty, some candy canes and silver balls in glass vases, and there was a preparty buzz among the support staff. They'd return from lunch hours loaded with shopping bags while Lenore was busy with stacks of envelopes and labels, David's holiday cards. He acted as if they were a silly custom, but I noticed the pleasure in his smile when I commented on the photo. "What a beautiful family," I said. The picture had been taken on a beach, with him surrounded by his adult children. His sons were also handsome, hinting at what he must have looked like several decades earlier.

The VP who hosted the barbecue hung a tuxedo on the back of his office door. It was the beginning of black-tie season, but I felt like Cinderella, working by the glow of a computer screen while the sky around me turned black. Winter dark was its own kind of dark, blacker than the deep blue evenings in the fall when I began. The interior lights on the surrounding buildings burst with clarity, and I wondered what the First Provident tower looked like to neighboring office workers, the sixtieth floor glowing like the tip of an upright cigarette, with me enmeshed in its ash.

CHAPTER THIRTEEN

One evening the following week, David returned to sixty all pink-skinned and fresh, what I imagined were the aftereffects of a massage or maybe a sauna, ready to start the evening push. I looked up at one point to find him standing in front of my desk.

He shuffled through the hard copy of slides I'd been working on. "These are good," he said. "But if I'm going to use them with Roland's board, I need you to add the EPS from the scenarios you ran for me yesterday."

"Sure thing," I said.

"You miss Grant, don't you?"

"Working with Marnye is fine."

"I mean it was just so apparent, what was going on. I don't know, I could feel it between the two of you."

My face prickled with heat.

"Don't be embarrassed," David continued. "I was sort of jealous," he said quietly. "And damned impressed with Grant." The comment stopped me in my tracks. If he was going to be inappropriate, then I would be too.

"Is he really getting promoted?" I asked.

David raised an eyebrow and turned all business again as if there were Christmas parties he wasn't attending and shopping he wasn't getting done. "Enough about Grant. Let's finish up the presentation and get home." Closing this acquisition required non-stop back-and-forth between the two management teams and their lawyers, and every revised term required another iteration of my model and a new set of slides. I brought revised pages into his office and sat down at the conference table while he put on his reading glasses and began flipping through them.

"You're good at this," he said. "I know you counted on Grant, but you're good enough to fly solo. Roland loved this climate change angle you came up with. Said it really helped convince his board."

"Thanks," I said, his praise once again feeding my spirit.

"You don't need him anymore. Bets, I'm always here." I was rattled by his continued mention of Grant and adding "I'm always here" set me back even further. He could have meant he would look out for me at First Provident, but I wondered if he meant it in a larger sense, as if he'd look out for me everywhere, as if someday I'd be invited to join the huddle of young adults in the Christmas photo. He put his hand on my shoulder, sending an electric current through my body. I inhaled deeply and closed my eyes.

"You are one of the most talented analysts I've ever worked with." Compliments from David, well, it's hard to describe, but they made me feel deserving in a way I never had before.

"I mean there have been plenty of analysts who worked all hours, completing every task asked of them, but you really add value."

"Thank you," I said. I was trembling inside and wondered if Marnye was watching.

And when it comes to this part, I might not be remembering things correctly, Sol, but instead of thinking about work, I was fantasizing and possibly preparing myself for his hand taking mine again. I remember wanting him to. However, when I looked up, he was removing his coat from the hanger on the back of his door, pulling his arms through the sleeves, and wrapping a scarf around his neck. "Run one more scenario with the higher purchase price and print it out for me," he said, "and then, oh, there's this." He placed an envelope on top of the stack of slides. More theatre tickets? He picked up his briefcase and I watched him disappear toward the elevator.

After he was gone, I returned to my desk. I thought about the miles of stairwell between me and the sidewalk. I breathed deeply and regarded my reflection in the glass. My phone buzzed. It was Grant wanting to FaceTime while he ate breakfast. I declined the call and opened David's envelope instead. No theatre tickets, only a handwritten note folded in two. I needed to press out the crease in the paper to decipher his scratchy handwriting. I read it a second time to make sure I'd gotten it right. *Come to my place for a drink? Lance is waiting downstairs.*

That was it, Sol. The invitation that, if I chose to accept, would change everything. Not a small decision, a place to get out of the cold, but a big decision. No middle ground. I could carry that note to Helen in HR as evidence of impropriety or I could show up at David's apartment, an unequivocal act of consent. It was one thing or another, white or black. It was one of those moments after which nothing would ever be the same. You'll have those moments too, and I hope you recognize when they are upon you. I certainly did at the time, closing my eyes and praying for an answer. I knew what I wanted to do, but I prayed for a surge of prudence. When I closed my eyes, what did I see? A picture of Bunny, looking across the horizon at the unending sea and Sadie's sapphire and diamond ring on my finger. I saw the way David looked at Tamara, smiling with pride when she surprised him at work.

I closed my laptop, surveying the bullpen, the random mementos and juvenile detritus other analysts collected: Mardi Gras beads draped across a desk lamp, coasters from local bars, a pair of pink flamingo sunglasses. I looked around for Marnye. She was nowhere to be seen.

I texted Rae: *Working late, probably an all-nighter. Don't want you to worry.* A bubble appeared right away, and I waited for her reply.

Rae: *Are you okay?*
Me: *Yes*
Rae: *Are you sure?*
Me: *Yes*
Rae: *Okay, blowing out the candle.*

———

Rae and I spent plenty of time before bed talking about our mothers, but most recently we had been talking about our fathers, or more accurately, the absence of our fathers. One of those conversations led to us reminiscing about Lyle's run of Les Mis. "It's always the same story, Bets," Rae said. "Rich father or poor father, it's the unwed mother whose life is forever changed." She'd been compelled by Victor Hugo's feminist themes and wanted my character, Fantine, a poor, young, orphaned woman in Paris impregnated by a rich student, to outshine Jean Valjean. I'd fallen in love with the score growing up, as Yaya played the soundtrack often, reminding me each time that Victor Hugo had been a champion of Cuba's revolution against Spanish colonial rule.

I told Rae, "My father never married my mom. He disappeared after the Pan Am games and ended up in Mexico. He said he was trying to return to Florida, but my mother concluded he never tried too hard. He married a woman in Mexico and started a new family." Even though my father was barely in my life, I would think of him at the weirdest times, while holding that note from David, for example.

Descending the escalator to the lower lobby, I still wasn't sure what to do. I stood in front of a ten-foot display of conical Christmas trees coated with glittering confectioners' sugar. I'd been trudging past them for weeks, but this was the first time I'd looked up and taken notice. They were not trees you would see in nature, festooned with gold and silver balls, and they made me think of Gloria in that combination of artificial minimalism and glittery bling she'd have loved to pose in front of for a holiday selfie.

I recalled my Christmases as a child with Yaya and Gloria and maybe a call from my father late in the afternoon. He once sent me a package, which was exciting in its own right, but the stuffed animal inside made it painfully clear he had no idea how old I was or what my interests were. I'd once felt it necessary to feign excitement over a pink unicorn, my mother rolling her eyes from the couch and Yaya going into the kitchen to stir her soup.

Spinning through First Provident's revolving door and stepping out onto the sidewalk, I spotted Lance in the driver's seat of David's Mercedes, the engine running. I heard my father's voice: Go for the KO, Betsabé. *Go for the KO.* I took a deep breath and entered the back seat, its plush leather upholstery all the reassurance I needed that I was making the right decision. And Sol, that was that.

As the car made its way uptown, the first snowflakes of the season were falling with unnatural slowness, giving me the sensation of being inside a snow globe. I focused on the gentle beauty outside the window because I wasn't sure what I was doing. Was I attempting to crawl into my father's lap? Sol, that's what can happen when a parent is taken away too soon, when a parent is never there in the first place.

A doorman decked out with gold-tasseled epaulets and a gendarme cap met me in front of a fortress of a building. He ushered me across the broad sidewalk and through the awning-covered entry. The brim of his hat masked all expression and I surmised from the gold watch gleaming from the margin between his wool coat and leather glove that he was handsomely paid for discretion. Eventually I'd learn his name was Marcel.

He escorted me to the elevator, turned a key and pushed a button, and I began to rise. I trembled in those seconds before the door opened, knowing the threshold of David's apartment presented yet another line to cross. But as the door slid open, I was shocked to see I'd not been delivered into a corridor, but into the foyer of David's apartment. I'd yet to learn, Sol, that some elevators open inside actual apartments, and I felt a bit tricked as if denied my last breath in private, one last chance to change my mind. David stood before me in stocking feet, his necktie removed and the top buttons of his shirt undone. He placed a glass of dark liquor on a side table and reached his hand toward me, urging me to make that final step. I inhaled deeply, my shoulders back, shook out my hair, and walked onto the parquet.

"You're here. I didn't think you would come." I'm not sure why he said that as Lance surely had given him a heads up. But it got me rethinking whether the idea of meeting up for a drink had been mine. I'd already done something irreversible to Grant and now it seemed I was having the same effect on David. Maybe I'd be held to blame, like Eve in the garden, for bringing down a great man.

He took my bag off my shoulder and I unbuttoned my coat. He then led me down the hall to a wood-paneled room where crystal decanters lined the surface of an antique chest of drawers. "What can I get you?" he asked.

"Whatever you're having," I said, sitting on a loveseat. "This room is beautiful." Obviously, his study. Amber light glowed from the fireplace. He handed me a weighty cut crystal glass then sat down. Our hips touched, igniting a flutter in my pelvis.

"Hmm, the fire smells good," I said, becoming aware of the origin of all his scents, the cigars, the fireplace, the cologne.

"I love this room," he said. "I've fallen asleep here many a night."

I had never sipped scotch before, but this was a night of firsts and I nursed the smoky liquor, letting it burn the back of my throat. Was this the equivalent of ending a collegiate night of partying in a tattoo parlor, a lapse in judgment that couldn't be undone? Or was this the actual first day of the rest of my life? I was scared as much as I was excited, the two sensations swirling together like the ice cubes in my glass, a current of arousal, dangerous but also appealing.

"The colors in here, everything is so warm." I clung to the small talk, commenting on the décor as some sense of propriety. It was laughable given my mounting desire and what was about to happen.

"The cedar paneling is fairly unusual, but the effect in the evening is wonderful." He smiled into my eyes and then leaned forward to kiss me. I didn't resist. He put his drink down and pushed the hair from my face as our tongues met. His kiss was slow and tasted of scotch. His hand wandered from my cheek to my breast to my leg.

"I'm nervous," I said, although what I was feeling was hard to put a name to. With other men I always had to summon the desire, but with David I was having a hard time tamping it down.

"I'm so sorry, Bets. Do you want to leave?" Before I could answer he said, "Believe me, I'm more nervous than you are." He rested his chin on my shoulder so I could no longer see his face. "I can barely remember what comes next." Lenore was always boasting about the women who sent him dinner invitations, making the idea of his being out of practice a little ludicrous.

"My God, you are sensational," he said. "But really. I don't want this to get out of hand. I just wanted for us to get to know each other outside of work."

"It's okay," I whispered, telling myself that pursuing what I wanted was an expression of independence, possibly even a feminist act.

"Really, because I have been wanting you for so long." There was that same phrase that Grant used before undressing me. The idea I really wasn't the best analyst he had ever worked with made me go stiff.

"I'm not sure I should stay," I said, crossing my arms in front of my chest.

"Do you want to leave?"

"I'm not sure."

He held me close, breathing me in. Sitting in his embrace, we were just two bodies, about the same size, and I relaxed as our differences evaporated. Gloria used to say Anglos lacked passion, in both the way they loved and in the way they argued. But David's heart seemed enormous and also a little unpredictable, and I told myself that if I was brave enough to keep going, I might be rewarded with the connection I'd been searching for.

"I know." He kissed me again. "Look, It's late. Lance is waiting downstairs. He can take you home, or . . ." he said, and then he kissed the tip of my nose. "Or, we can let him wait."

I was amused by his coyness. I sensed he wanted me to see him like this, fine either way, perfectly able to restrain himself. It was the way he wanted to see himself as well. I slid off the love seat and onto the rug in front of the fire. That was my answer. Once again, Sol, just pretend it was Bets the character beckoning David down on the floor next to the fire and not the mother who rocked you in her arms and read you bedtime stories.

David and I kissed again and I felt him hard against my leg. He removed my blouse button by button and unclipped my bra, the heat from the fire warming my skin. Once I was completely bare, lying naked beside him, he propped himself up on one elbow and surveyed my body hungrily. It was a little weird with him still mostly clothed, and fear crept over me again, giving me a moment to worry about what all this would mean. I sat up.

"What's wrong?" he asked.

"If this is going any further, we need protection," I said, as if that might slow things down, giving us a moment to return to our senses. Because what was about to happen was pure madness, like jumping off a cliff.

"Do you want it to go further?"

Despite the insanity, I did. I wanted my life to careen with excitement, to inch up to the apex of a rollercoaster track where we could throw our arms in the air and get carried away by the sensation of dropping, maybe a few loop de loops along the way. I wanted to close my eyes and scream and not be sure which way was up. I found it hard to form the word yes, so nodded instead.

He went to his desk and opened a drawer. "I got these," he

said, holding a package of condoms. "Just in case. I don't want you to think . . ."

"Shhh, it's okay."

"I never needed them with Abigail, she . . ."

"It's okay." I wanted him to stop talking and get back down on the rug before I changed my mind again. He undressed and lay with me, and a moan worked its way from my throat as he touched me. He made me feel beautiful, electric. I held my breath and he entered me. He did so cautiously, as if acclimating to the sensation, wanting to experience my body completely. We sighed at the same time. There was something glorious happening.

The fire was warm and the rug under my back incredibly soft, and for a moment I felt as if I was a spectator floating across the ceiling. I turned toward the fire's red embers. His kisses moved across my neck and chest and his gentle rocking became forceful. It wasn't exactly a cry, more like a loud whimper which he tried to hold back before shuddering, "Oh God."

He rolled onto his back, sweaty and spent, the mess of the condom already in his palm. We lay side by side, naked, a glow of perspiration coating our skin.

"Oh, Bets," he said. I couldn't speak. There was the implication of what had just happened, but also the way my body responded.

"Are you okay?" he asked.

"Yes," I whispered.

"Oh, Bets, don't regret this. It was inevitable," he said.

"What do you mean?"

"It had to happen. Some relationships are sexual before the first touch," he said, and in a rush to explain, "I fell in love with you the first time I looked into those big brown eyes. And then the vision of you rising out of Ron's swimming pool. You were a Venus." So, in the same way my terrible score on the accounting assessment made a positive impression on him, being thrown in the swimming pool had been an attraction.

"The pool?" I shivered at the memory.

"After our call with Roland, I had to find ways for us to be together, so I could get to know you. And there hasn't been a day since when I didn't believe you were the most thoughtful person in the room. And there has never been an analyst as creative. Most people are afraid of taking risks, afraid of looking stupid." He spoke so fast as if he'd been holding the words in for a long time.

I sat up and began collecting my clothes.

"Can't you stay?" he asked.

I touched his cheek with my palm. "No. I want to shower and change before work."

He kissed my hand. "I understand. Get some rest. There will be time for us in the future."

"After AgriGlobal closes?" I asked, as if everything was on hold until then.

"Yes, in the new year." He laughed. "I won't be assigning you to any more of my deals." That was reasonable, but he had to know it wouldn't come close to satisfying company policy.

I nodded, happy he was talking about a future. The new year was weeks away. He walked me to the elevator, wrapping my coat over my shoulders. "Until tomorrow," he said, handing me my bag and kissing me one last time.

PART II

CHAPTER FOURTEEN

I can imagine you pausing here, Sol, putting this book down, not at all sure what to think. I am asking quite a lot, to have you read about your parents in this way, but by the time you are an adult, David will be an old man. It may be perverse, but I want you to see him as I did in 2019. I want to portray David's charm, not that he was "charmed," as many would accuse, but that his charisma was one I wanted to be around. He was an original and he made me feel one of a kind as well. Grant was attracted and Marnye was too, although in her case, it was more like a moth's attraction to the flame, but to work for him as we all did, well, it had to be more than professional. I've said it before and I'll say again the word "privilege" was overused back in those days, but what I'm asking from you now, Sol, is the privilege of putting my youth on display and you giving me the benefit of the doubt.

———◆———

Leaving David's apartment with dawn not far off, Marcel handed me off to Lance like a baton in a relay. These men were David's sentries, trusted with a most dangerous secret. In the climate of the day, a powerful man conducting a relationship with a younger woman was the kind of Clinton/Lewinsky scoop news outlets paid real money for. No matter the number of friends and admirers

David had, given the dynasty he'd created on sixty, there were many who wanted to see him fall.

In the absence of traffic, Lance drove south smoothly. The snow had stopped falling and the sky was lightening. I sat with what had just occurred, sinking into David's indentation in the back seat. His neatly folded pink Financial Times was tucked into the seat pocket, and I remember thinking it sweet that he still read physical newspapers.

As the car wound through the village, with its modest skyline, less kempt sidewalks, and vagrant street life, I worried I'd done something terribly stupid. I bit down on my lower lip and scratched my thigh. Would our sex be another cliché with the rising sun? I inhaled and exhaled deeply before pointing out to Lance where to pull over.

Out on the empty sidewalk, the sky a predawn light blue, my phone buzzed. It was David beginning what would become our infamous text thread, and its appearance on my screen at that surreal hour suddenly convinced me anything was possible. *I feel alive again*, he wrote. I knew that after losing Abigail, he had been fending off a somewhat slow crawl toward death, and it seemed making love to me had reversed that. I read the text again, this time with his voice echoing in my mind. I feel alive again. And it was exactly how I felt. Alive.

A few hours later, without any sleep but having showered and changed, I got a text from Grant on my way to the subway. *Want to Skype tonight?* Even as a trained actress there was no way. *I'll see if I can break free!* I replied, knowing that when the time came work would be an excuse he would have to accept.

Grant: *I miss you!*

Me: *What are you doing for Christmas?*

Grant: *My parents are meeting me in Thailand!*

Me: *Cool*

Grant: *We'll go someday. Hey, when do you leave for Miami?*

Me: *Two weeks! Talk later.*

I underestimated how hard it would be to get any work done with David's office just a few feet away. All I could think about was our night together and whether there would be a next time. I needed to maintain a cordial coexistence with Marnye and small talk with Lenore before heading to Florida in two weeks. Yaya and my mother represented a sort of home-base safety after which I'd return, hopefully, to some clarity on the eve of 2020.

I kept my head down and took orders diligently, afraid of giving something away, as if my feelings for David streamed across my forehead like a neon news ticker. Marnye was visibly satisfied David had reestablished her as our go-between, as if order had been restored to the universe. The fact he stopped walking the floor each afternoon led me to believe he worried about giving something away as well. There were times, however, when we passed in the hallway and our hands brushed accidentally, and he looked at me with an expression that made my heart race.

The AgriGlobal deal was heating up. A complication had arisen in that one of the seed breeders AgriGlobal hoped to purchase had put a poison pill in place, allowing existing shareholders to purchase shares at a discounted price thereby diluting AgriGlobal's ownership. David yelled in his office that we'd dump the stock and buy two smaller seed manufacturers that were privately held instead. He walked around with an intensity suited for the battlefield.

Marnye asked me to order dinner even though it was only four thirty. But the sky was dark, and food and hot beverages seemed to be her only physical comforts. I stood at my desk and yawned. She looked me up and down as if noticing something for the first time.

"What?" I asked, worried that I had some terrible ink stain on my elbow.

"Make sure you sit up straight. Otherwise your neckline is sort of plunging."

It's possible I was exuding something, not just in my choice of sweater, but my refusal to share in her misery. Whatever it was, she was looking for something to criticize. Maybe she sensed my happiness, a higher vibration I carried around the office. Not just because I hoped regenerative farming was something the merged company might latch onto, but because, despite all his intensity over the deal, I loved being close to David.

"Maybe you should stop worrying about my clothes," I said before she could assess my pants and boots. She raised an eyebrow as if she was about to accuse me of something worse than a plunging neckline but thought better of it. She pressed her lips together and ran a finger below her eyelids. It took me a moment to realize she was wiping away a tear. She turned and walked briskly toward the ladies' room. I followed a few seconds behind. She was standing at the sink, staring at her reflection in the mirror.

"Are you okay?" I asked.

"Do you think I like dressing like this?" She pointed to her loose-fitting blazer and pleated pants.

Tears were now streaming down her cheeks unfettered. She was operating on less sleep than I was, especially with Grant gone, as if this was her chance to prove something. "I'm just, I don't know. I'm wondering if it's worth it."

"What do you mean?"

"I mean, it's proving impossible to have both, you know?"

She had never opened up to me before. We stood side by side, looking into the mirror. She blew her nose into a tissue. "A woman can either have ambition or she can have love, but it isn't possible to have both."

"Really?" I asked. I was under the impression I'd been managing the balance pretty well, ambition and love. I had an important job and an important man who wanted more time with me, even if the details were a little fuzzy.

"Oh, believe me it's true." I gathered she was in the middle of a breakup. It was strange given the hours we kept, how little we knew about each other.

"I'm so sorry," I said. "Can I give you a hug?"

She scoffed at the absurdity. Even Marnye was aware she was not a huggable person. I wrapped my arms around her stiff frame and in so doing felt her insides quake. She had a million sobs in there that needed to be set free. Maybe all bankers were lonely, but I was increasingly certain the sixtieth floor had a unique way of hollowing us out.

"Maybe if you took some time off?"

"That's exactly what I mean. Nobody expects men to take time off."

"Not true. Everyone needs balance." I sounded like Yaya.

Marnye just shook her head. "Ah, Bets. You'll see. This 'having it all' myth will fucking kill you." She looked into the sink and I took in her sad posture in the mirror, her hunched shoulders and red cheeks. I felt sorry for her. She may have been in the workforce longer than me, but it felt like I was juggling what mattered.

"Want me to order sushi tonight?" It was her favorite.

"Sure," she said. But after she washed her face and we opened the door onto the floor, she switched gears abruptly. "You need to update the model for the new regulatory requirements."

That night, I fell onto my Murphy bed weary with few words passing between me and Rae. She had been attending holiday parties hosted by literary agencies. Well-fed on cheese and crackers and giggly from champagne. The last thing I heard her say before I dozed off was, "I made a new friend at the coffee shop."

The morning of my scheduled departure for Miami, I still wasn't packed. Marnye and I had been working around the clock and although I knew David would never ask me to cancel my trip, I was worried about hers. I pulled a carry-on out of the closet as I got dressed for work. I would stop by the office to put finishing touches on the AgriGlobal board presentation before heading to LaGuardia. My dirty laundry was spilling out of the closet and I was at a loss for what to bring to Florida. I texted Gloria: *Packing is rough, can I borrow some clothes when I get there?*

Gloria: *Of course, mija. Yaya can't wait to see you.*

A message appeared on my phone from Rae. *Stop by Café Jo to say goodbye?* I latched the Murphy bed back into the wall and stuffed my dirty clothes in a garbage bag beside it. Not exactly the best tidying-up job, but I hoped Rae would understand.

I'd passed by her morning haunt plenty of times on my way to the subway, spotting her through the front windows hunched over her notebook at a table in the corner. I'd rarely gone inside because I could get a free breakfast on sixty and Café Jo was the type of place that made you late with the scent of baking muffins and fresh brew wafting through the air, not to mention the sounds of frothing milk and cheerful conversation.

She was sitting with a young woman I took to be the new friend. The girl's hair was short, spiky, and dyed a cotton-candy pink, which paired with Rae's orange had me holding back a laugh.

"Morning," I said, inhaling sweet cinnamon sugar.

"Bets, meet Lucy."

"Hi Lucy," I said, smiling in her direction before turning to Rae.

"You got in late last night," said Rae.

I shrugged.

"The important investment banker," Lucy said.

I raised an eyebrow, as in "Where does your new friend get off ridiculing me?" Did my long hours away have her looking for a replacement? After all, I was her slob of a roommate who fell asleep mid-conversation and couldn't get her ass out of bed in the morning. The truth was Rae would never hold my personal habits or my morally bankrupt profession against me; however, I knew she'd never forgive my crossing the line with my boss. I could dismiss Marnye's attitude, but I didn't know what I'd do if Rae found out.

"What time is your flight?" she asked.

"After lunch," I said.

"Um, Lucy, would you mind grabbing me a refill?"

"You got it." When she left the table, Rae scooted closer.

"What's up?" I asked, concerned.

"Um. My mother." Her face filled with anxiety.

"Oh, jeez. What now?" I expected Sarah was tired of staying at Rachel's and had asked for my bed while I was in Florida.

"She wanted me to ask you. And I know this isn't going to sound right, but well, she was taking my great-grandmother's jewelry to the safe deposit box and one of the rings was missing. She wanted me to ask if you knew anything about that."

My stomach dropped. I thought back on that evening I'd tried a ring on in Rachel's bathroom. I had turned on the vanity lights, held my hand up, letting the sapphires and diamonds sparkle next to my face. I wanted to enjoy the ring in private without all their eyes on me, but I did put it back. The bedroom had been so dark, there was a chance it ended up in the wrong pouch.

"What are you talking about?" I asked.

"I knew it was silly, I just told her I'd ask you."

"What are you saying—your mother thinks I stole her ring?"

"No, it's just that she keeps bugging me to ask you and I'm going to be with her over the holidays, and I just wanted to be able to say that I had asked you."

"Well, you sure asked me." I stood up and spied Lucy at the counter watching us. I returned her benign stare with a vicious one of my own and stormed out of Café Jo without wishing either of them a Merry Christmas.

Minutes into my subway ride I regretted turning it around on Rae. I could have easily confessed what happened, but that would have meant confessing something way more humiliating than wanting to try on her stupid ring. It would have betrayed the envy I'd stomached every time I was around her family, and ever since that night with David, I no longer knew right from wrong. Putting on a charade for Marnye and Lenore was hard enough, but now Grant was asking when I'd fly to visit him. Half-truths and lies can do that, Sol, they can snowball. If this story imparts any wisdom, let it be the wisdom of living an honest life. During the final days of 2019, it was as if the ability to be honest, even honest with myself, had escaped me, and I was constructing whatever version of the truth might get me through the day.

CHAPTER FIFTEEN

The fading Florida sun amplified the peeling paint. I'd never before focused on the lopsided shutters, the rusty doorframe, torn screens, or the porch swing all off-kilter. My memory was unreliable when it came to what Yaya's casita had looked like the prior year, before I'd been spoiled by the sleek perfection of sixty.

It wasn't just the house, but the overgrown weeds in the yard, eyesores Gloria could have easily addressed. It's possible I was returning to Miami with higher standards and new financial savvy, but I couldn't understand why my mother didn't appreciate this home as our family's most valuable asset. I would use my new skills modeling cash flows to show her how it could throw off income as a rental property, how she might fix it up and eventually sell it for even more. I could point to all the recent development around Calle Ocho, how Little Havana was becoming a hot neighborhood, the next South Beach with prices on the rise. Sometimes Sol, it's easier to make a to-do list than face the real problems in your life.

The cab pulled away and I opened the front door.

"Aló?" I called into a dark room. Not exactly the homecoming I'd envisioned. My eyes adjusted, I dropped my bag and crossed the house toward the kitchen.

Yaya was sitting at the table, shrunken, her elbows resting on either side of the newspaper. Gone was the long silver braid, her hair was cut short and entirely white and with a flattened spot in the back where it rubbed against the pillow. The overhead lights were off, and the waning sunlight shone in from the window to where her trembling hand clutched a pencil. Underneath the table, one leg crossed over the other, a slipper hung from her big toe. Her skin was lighter than mine, and more leathery than I remembered. Her small voice, a murmur as she read aloud to herself, absent-mindedly scratching the fine white hairs on the back of her neck.

"Yaya," I whispered, not wanting to startle her.

"Yaya," I said a bit louder, standing over her shoulder. The kitchen still held the scents of my girlhood, cumin, cilantro, and rice. I squatted to meet her at eye level, my lower lip trembling and my eyes welling with tears as I watched her surprise slowly melt into recognition. A smile spread across her face as she braced her arms against the table to stand up.

"Ay, mija!" She teetered a bit before wrapping her thin arms around my waist. "You're home."

"Yaya, it is so good to be home." I hadn't been prepared for the well of emotion. I rested my cheek on top of her small fuzzy head. Maybe it was how thin she'd become, or the sad state of the house, or the fact that my mother wasn't there to greet me, but I was moved. I hadn't realized how much I missed Yaya and her kitchen. A year away from Miami had rendered it intangible and elusive, its details evaporating like steam rising from the sidewalk after an afternoon rain.

Rae complained about her family all the time, that swarm of women living a stone's throw from our apartment. But what I wouldn't have given to feel my yaya's embrace on a regular basis. Whereas Rae could access her mother or grandmother any day of the week, I didn't recognize myself in anyone's face in New York, nor did I interact with physical bodies who connected me to the planet.

If I'd had more proximity to my family, it might have changed everything. If there had been somebody in the city who knew me from the beginning, somebody who was acquainted with my clan's courageous history, regularly reminding me from whence I came, it might have all gone differently. Instead, I was caught up measuring myself on Wall Street's scale, that is to say by the hours I kept, the money I made, basically the tough skin I'd built up.

Miami served as a reminder that life wasn't constrained to that skyscraper-filled island. The smells of the kitchen, the sound of crowing roosters and barking dogs, as well as the tropical humidity were already having their effect. My core was regaining its pliability, a gradual thawing from the inside out. Yaya took me in with her cloudy eyes, her hands clapped together in her trademark expression of happiness, and I felt surrounded by her healing energy. She grasped my hand and we shuffled back to the bedroom I had shared on-again, off-again with my mother over the years. I sucked in a breath as she opened the door, expecting my belongings to be pushed aside or discarded, but everything was more or less as I had left it. The crucifix still hung on the wall next to a formal portrait of my parents, the only one of them together. Yaya had even placed a sprig of bougainvillea in a bud vase between the twin beds.

"You want to change clothes?" I was obviously sweltering in a black turtleneck and wool pants.

"Where's Mami?" I asked.

"Probably still at work."

I set my carry-on on my bed and rummaged a T-shirt from the chest of drawers. On my way back to the kitchen, I poked my head into Yaya's room. Her windows faced the street and were now shrouded in palm fronds, and I remembered the afternoon Mr. Levine came over to install bars on the glass. When he was done, Yaya invited him inside for a glass of lemonade. He took my small hands in his and said, "Betsabé, we are going to keep you safe," my fingers so small in his enormous grip.

I was curious about the years in which Yaya and Mr. Levine seemed especially close. She had been attractive in her fifties as was he, although a decade older. She made cookies and café Cubano so he'd have a reason to stick around after every repair. I recall Gloria scoffing in the kitchen, as if she was Abuelo's mouthpiece while he was away in Cuba.

For Yaya and Gloria, Fidel and the revolution were behind everything, most importantly the absence of their men. The void they left was a physical thing. Their photographs hung in places of prominence on the living room wall, not far from Yaya's shrine to the Orishas, which is probably why I held Abuelo in the same regard as one of her saints. Nothing like the portrayal of Bunny Meister with a golf club over his shoulder. No, Abuelo was formal and serious, no smiling. He wasn't tucked away in a nostalgic back stairwell either, rather saying to anyone who walked through our front door, even Mr. Levine, I am still here.

Thinking about it now, it was neither my father nor my grandfather, but Mr. Levine who made the greatest material impact on my childhood. He bequeathed the casita to Yaya upon his death, lending a stability to our day-to-day existence, something I'd never appreciated until I'd had to pay my own bills. Even if it wasn't as fancy as what Tía Julia and her husband eventually bought in Coral Gables, owning our pastel-pink home with its small front yard put Yaya on a different plane than our neighbors. It broke my heart to see the roof sagging. I wouldn't leave Miami without making sure to take care of a few things.

As I sat in the fading light, I thought about the terrible way in which I'd left things with Rae. In our New York apartment it was moonlight mixed with streetlights I traced across the ceiling while we talked in bed, and here it was the setting sunlight moving across the floor. That particular day was close to the winter solstice, the shortest of the year, and something about the light brought back memories of waiting after school for Yaya to get home from work. Gloria texted that she needed to spend some time with her boyfriend, Mateo, and wouldn't be home for dinner. It was just like her to create drama around my arrival. Little did she know the drama I left behind was going to be difficult to beat.

I asked Yaya if we might go sit on the porch. "Tell me about Mr. Levine," I said, pulling her closer to me on the swing.

"His father was our first landlord here in 1960."

"Was he handsome?"

"Qué guapo. He was something as a teenager. Very cool, you would say. He started coming around again after his wife died. Now he's my guardian on the other side." She nodded with a smile as if remembering sweeter days.

"Have you been alright?" I asked.

"Sí," she smiled, patting the top of my hand. Her parting lips exposed a gap where teeth were missing, but her eyes sparkled. "Tell me about New York. You are taking classes in acting and voice?" That had been my intention, and I lied to make her happy. How could I explain I worked seven days a week? "And you feel safe there? You are okay?"

I nodded. To give her an outright yes would not have been truthful. I didn't know if I was okay. I could never tell her about David, and I was ashamed of the tension I'd created with Rae not to mention the way I left Grant hanging.

"Sometimes, I don't know, Yaya."

"Shhh, mija. It's your journey." She squeezed my hand and I swallowed back tears. "Listen to your heart and pray. Mother Earth and Father Sky will light your path."

For some reason, it felt inauthentic to pray. I had never fully absorbed her faith. "What would you like for dinner, Yaya?"

"No Gloria?" It sounded like questioning my mother's where-abouts was something she did often.

"No."

"I made ropa vieja. It's in the refrigerator."

I put the beef stew on the stove. There would be plenty left over if my mother ever showed up. I turned on the flame and stirred as Yaya sat watching me from the kitchen table. "Betsabé," she said. "Your energy balance is off."

The wooden spoon almost slipped from my hand.

"What do you mean?" But I knew what she meant. Of course, it was.

"Mija, you are sending off a nervous vibration. Your light is fragmented." Yaya couldn't be fooled. She came up behind me and turned off the burner. Tears welled in my eyes as she guided me to her shrine in the living room. She anointed my forehead with a mixture of palm and lavender oil, placed seashells in a circle on the floor, then lit seven blue candles to evoke Yemayá's energy. She closed her eyes in prayer.

I shut my eyes as well, the darting flames still visible behind my lids. It reminded me of the atmosphere Rae created at bedtime. Yaya's incantations summoned Yemayá, the divine feminine, to look over me. I breathed deeply, my nasal passages noticeably clearer than they had been in months.

"Tomorrow, go to the ocean," she said, as if her living room shrine could only do so much. "The salt air will purify your lungs and the seawater will nourish your skin." But I knew I needed more than that, a deeper cleansing, a complete baptism. Unfortunately, Sol, I wouldn't submerge myself in the ocean as Yaya had prescribed until much later, until it was, in fact, too late.

I remained cross-legged in front of her shrine, my eyes closed, my breathing gradually slowing until my phone buzzed and skittered across the floor. The only reason I picked it up was because I thought it was Gloria. But it was a message from Marnye, a selfie taken at a long conference table, all thumbs-up. AgriGlobal closed, wires cleared. It seemed a world away, and the thing was I didn't care. The deal came with a three-billion-dollar price tag. A billion was a crazy number, I knew because I dealt with all those commas. Hell, a million had once seemed like a lot to me, a million of anything let alone dollars, but it had been drilled into me as peanuts. I wondered if all the poor employees who were deemed "redundant" would get the news before Christmas or after.

The closing meant Marnye could go home for the holidays, which would keep the peace. We had done lots of late-night speculating about how much time off we could expect. She explained it was one of those "propitious years," where both Christmas and

New Year's fell on Wednesdays and it was all very ambiguous as to whether people would work on Thursday and Friday or whether it was acceptable to take both weeks off. She never spoke about what she wanted or needed, or what she would take for herself, only what we might be lucky enough to get away with.

When I opened the *Miami Herald* the next morning over breakfast, the Coronavirus was front-page news. Thousands of people in China were being hospitalized for respiratory failure. The government was mandating whole populations quarantine, causing the Asian offices of multinational companies to close and sending expats back to their home countries. I wondered how Grant was faring in the midst of it, if he was still traveling with his parents.

Another headline caught my eye, "Citrus Greening is Killing the World's Orange Trees." Citrus was a mainstay of the local economy, and growers and scientists were in a rush to find an effective combatant against a devastating bacterial scourge called huanglongbing. In addition to pruning groves of diseased trees and planting bacterial-free saplings, the state's strategy included wildly spraying insecticides in an attempt to kill psyllids, the disease-carrying insects. The article went on to say that several large local citrus farms were spraying Fluoropluconin, made widely available by a recently acquired division of AgriGlobal industries, although several environmental groups had concerns it hadn't been properly tested and there could be residual damage to abutting populations and watersheds.

My heart sank even lower than it had reading about the Coronavirus. What if I had manipulated the model to show the AgriGlobal merger as too risky? David wouldn't have generated a $30 million fee, but I had more power than I gave myself credit over the outcome of that deal. The thing was, I hadn't dared use it. I mean, after Grant left nobody was checking the numbers that closely.

A local farmer was quoted in the paper as saying, "This is America and people expect orange juice at breakfast." The

AgriGlobal deal may have been announced in the *Wall Street Journal* but seeing that article about the citrus groves made its impact hit home. The more problems down the road for farmers, the more revenue for AgriGlobal. I left the paper on the kitchen table where Yaya did the crossword puzzle. I couldn't get that farmer's quote out of my head. What we wouldn't do to make sure everyone had their orange juice at breakfast.

CHAPTER SIXTEEN

One mistake I made was not placing enough value on having a foot in two worlds, one in the cold Northeast and the other in sunny Florida, not to mention I was bilingual. So, I should have seen myself as twice as likely to succeed; instead, all that Manhattan sophistication had me discounting the lessons of my childhood. That warm, slow week in Miami had me questioning everything I'd left up north as well. I tell you this because walking the streets of my neighborhood was comforting and disorienting at the same time. I was a confused jumble when Gloria finally showed up on Christmas Eve.

We exchanged a brief Qué tal? as I was in the bathroom applying mascara. She rushed past me with dry cleaning over her arm and closed herself in the bedroom. There would be no time to talk before leaving for the evening's festivities. We were expected at six o'clock to celebrate with my great-aunt and uncle's family as we had every year. I looked forward to seeing my cousins and took a little extra time blowing out my hair and choosing dangling earrings I hadn't worn since high school, knowing they would be looking for signs as to whether New York had changed me.

In our family, cooking was as much the religion on Christmas Eve as the midnight mass. The center of the party was a pig, no less than fifty pounds, roasting over a pit in my tío's backyard. He and my cousins would have picked it out on a farm for slaughter the previous day. One year I'd been invited for the cleaning and splitting its rib cage down the middle in the driveway. Our job was to shoo away the tiny lizards while Tía Julia made space for the animal to dry on top of newspapers in the kitchen. She mixed her famous mojo loaded with garlic, salt, herbs, and fresh orange juice in a large tray in which the pig would marinate overnight. Even though I'd clamored to be included in the prep, when it came to witnessing the removal of the pig's innards, once was enough.

Given Gloria's tardiness and the three of us doing shifts in the bathroom, it was a safe bet we'd be arriving once this year's pig was crispy red on the spit. When we drove into the driveway, smoke was rising from a heap of banana leaves with the men gathered around with beers and pokers to tend to the hot coals. There was laughing and cheering as the little kids raced barefoot around the outside of the cluster of men who protected them from the glowing sparks rising in the center.

Conversation always stopped when we arrived at Tía Julia's. My mother was once the infamous beauty of her generation, evoking parallels to her adopted namesake, Gloria Estefan. Dating an Olympic boxer had only furthered her reputation as a local celebrity, and her male cousins were admittedly shy around her until they were in their early thirties. I wondered if they looked at me in the same way now, as if I had stepped into her shoes, no longer that gangly teen who liked drama and spent most of her time in the library.

As the men and children approached our car, Gloria helped Yaya into the house where Tía Julia was presiding over pots of black beans and yucca, rice makers, and a sizzling sazón.

I took my place in the yard, standing around the pig like it was an idol to be worshipped. My cousin, Tomás, offered me a drink. "Wine?" he asked.

"Yes, please."

He pulled a wine cooler out of the tub by his feet and lifted off the cap with an opener.

"How is it to be home?"

"Ah, just what I needed." It was true.

Tío Luis came over and caressed my shoulder. "Our banking executive back from Nueva York," he said. "We are so proud of you, Betsabé."

"Gracias, Tío," I said, bowing my head, but not wanting to let First Provident or New York or anything about the cold, wintery world I'd left behind intrude on this special evening. Tomás dragged over a couple of aluminum lawn chairs with plastic webbing, offering one to his father and the other to me. Tío Luis took my hand in his while Tomás stood behind us, keeping the beer at his feet so the younger men couldn't go through it too quickly.

"You and Tía Julia are okay?" I asked.

"Bueno. You know, we are all getting older."

"Getting better, Papi," said Tomás. A cheer erupted from a neighboring yard. Many families were celebrating like we were. The sky was clear, and I searched for the moon. I inhaled deeply. The smell of the fire and the roast, even Tomás's cologne released whatever tension was binding my shoulders. There was a little girl's giggling behind me and then fingers running through my hair. It was Tomás's daughter, Ania, my youngest cousin. I pulled her around and up onto my lap.

"Ania, qué tal? You are getting so big!"

"You are pretty," she said in a quiet voice.

"Is Santa Clós going to bring you something tonight?"

Her eyes got wide and she smiled broadly enough for me to glimpse gaps where her front teeth had grown in crooked. "Maybe."

"Just maybe? Haven't you been a good girl?" And I caught myself about to blow raspberries into her neck, becoming the grown-up in the exchange, which sort of freaked me out.

"Do you like school?" I asked her.

"Yes," she said.

"Good," I said with a confident nod. I didn't want to get all serious on Christmas Eve, but it felt important to leave one of my few female relatives of impressionable age with a meaningful message. "Promise me you'll study hard?"

Ania nodded silently.

"Listen to your prima Betsabé," Tomás said, looking into his daughter's eyes. "She graduated from a fancy college and has an important job in New York City." It was no time to correct him or to explain the grunt work that filled my days. After my second wine cooler, Gloria leaned her head out the kitchen door asking if the pig was ready yet.

Tomás called back, "Sí," and the kids all cheered. As we carried in trays of meat, I got a promise from Tomás that he'd stop by Yaya's a few times a week after checking on his own parents.

"I can send money if you see anything she needs. Sometimes it's hard to live far away, you know? I worry about her."

He held my shoulder. "Don't be silly, Betsabé." He was a dentist downtown and ran errands for his parents all the time. "One more stop to see Yaya won't be a problem at all." Tomás had benefited from our clan's communal effort in the name of upward mobility. His wife, Linda, taught high school biology, and I could tell by the way he looked into my eyes he understood what it took for a woman to pursue a career.

"Go back to New York and make lots of money. Don't worry about a thing." It was understood I would repay his kindness someday. I kissed him on the cheek. "Thank you," I said, smoothing Ania's hair.

After Tía Julia's famous flan, my mother drove us back to Little Havana for mass. We went to St. Barbara's, a more modest structure than Sts. Peter & Paul's, the church associated with the school I'd attended. Yaya preferred St. Barbara's because instead of being hidden behind a façade of Catholicism, the religion was out in the open. Afro-Cuban traditions hadn't traveled from Havana with her upper-class family but took hold of her after Abuelo left and Tía Julia moved to Coral Gables. As a sought-after healer, Yaya had begun spending time with like-minded people and when I was little, she attended bembés, parties for the Orishas filled with dancing and thumping batá drums. She'd come home and tell me about her trilogía, Oyá, saint of death; Oshún, saint of love; and Yemayá, saint of sensuality. Bit by bit, she set up a shrine in the living room and incorporated gods with various powers and personalities into my bedtime stories.

St. Barbara's Christmas Eve service was lively and gleeful, the ceremonial rhythms and incantations raising the roof off the small building. Flanked by her daughter and granddaughter, Yaya's perspiring face was full of pride. After the service, as everyone was hugging and wishing one another a blessed Nochebuena, it was humbling to witness the reverence with which people of the congregation approached my yaya. She may have been a frail old lady to some, but here she was an elder for whom everyone had the utmost respect.

It was late when we returned home and Yaya went straight to bed, but Gloria spread out on the couch apparently ready to talk. "So, you look good," she said.

"Mami, where have you been?" I asked.

She shrugged, not at all apologetic. "I've been working double shifts at the nursing home. I haven't seen Mateo much and he was all out of sorts. He needed some extra attention for Christmas, you know? Besides, I wanted you to see for yourself what it's like taking care of Yaya."

"But you didn't have to stay away to make your point," I said.

"You left for college and got that fancy job and an apartment in New York City."

"Oh, Mami," I said. I had never gotten the sense she expected me to return to Miami after graduation. If anything, the theme of my childhood had been one where I was her burden.

"You're a woman now, Betsabé. Maybe you'll see what it's like to want, or maybe you won't. I have no idea what your life is like. It's hard for me to be a good daughter sometimes, just like it's hard to be a good mother."

"Oh, Mami. Stop it." I had no patience when she talked like that. "Look," I said. "I'm only here a few more days, and there's lots to do." I showed her the list of home repairs I considered most urgent. No longer concerned about her whereabouts, I was ready to flip into action, run errands, and enlist handymen to help, maybe take on some of the smaller projects side by side, but she snapped. "I have three days off. Can't I just put my feet up?"

Instead of reacting to her selfishness, I went into our bedroom and shut the door. Looking in the mirror hanging behind the door, I scratched away at the little rainbow and heart stickers adhered to the edges. In New York, nobody would expect their college-educated daughter to cash in a career on Wall Street to care for an aging relative, and here was Gloria trying to make me feel guilty for not spending enough time in Miami. She was the one who flipped out when my father disappeared, counting on Yaya to raise me, and now she couldn't even do what was right by her own mother.

Yaya would never hear of me staying in Florida, even if I wanted to. I would leave in two days as planned even if it made my heart ache. I refused to squeeze into that bedroom with Gloria any longer than I had to. I had thought Rae a bit of a brat when she complained about sharing a room with her mother at Eden, but now I totally got it. I returned to the living room to face her. "You are driving me to Home Depot tomorrow morning, right after breakfast," I said.

———

The next morning, I started water on the stove for espresso, spying Yaya's pencil and completed crossword puzzle on the table. I softened a little when my mother entered the room, purse and car keys in hand.

"Mami," I said. "If I send money every month, will you promise to keep Yaya comfortable at home?" Her face perked up a little.

"How much?"

"Not sure." Even though my gross salary was high, a lot was taken out each month for taxes. I was just keeping my head above water after rent and utilities, but I would be getting my bonus soon. "Let's go over what you need." If I stopped taking Ubers and ate only the free food at work, I thought I'd be able to send home meaningful amounts. I was sure that if she could stay in her own home, Yaya would be okay. She could walk to mass at St. Barbara's and to the grocery. She could visit with her friends in the park over cortaditos.

———

My mother drove me to the airport on New Year's Eve day. I received a text from David.

David: *When do you land?*

Me: *Seven*

David: *Come straight here*

I was taken by his insistence, the way he phrased it as a command. It made me feel wanted, even though nobody likes to be told what to do. I held off replying until I'd hugged my mother goodbye outside the car at departures. It was a slightly better farewell than the previous spring, but just barely. We were really bad at hellos and goodbyes. After I went through security and found my gate, I pulled out my phone.

Me: *I need to go home first*

David: *Please*

I had planned to write New Year's resolutions at the airport. Number one was to sign up for voice lessons, but the text exchange with David was distracting. I added a few more things to the list, "Get along better with Marnye. Ask Lenore to lunch. Take Rae to dinner and explain my real feelings about the ring. Apologize." My heart understood that shoring up a sisterhood was going to be extremely necessary.

But how to reply to David? I could hear his pleading voice. It reminded me of the loneliness Grant expressed on Thanksgiving. With Tamara at her mother's and the rest of his children off skiing in Zermatt or on yachts in the Virgin Islands, maybe he just needed a companion.

I wrote: *I'll text you when I land*

A three-hour flight with my phone in airplane mode gave me plenty of time to think. Being in Yaya's presence had grounded me, but David's text was already eating at my insides. When the plane touched down in New York and everyone started unbuckling their seat belts, I still wasn't sure whether I should rush over to his apartment.

I texted Rae: *What are you up to?*

Rae: *Home popcorn beer Lucy, maybe going out later with Ethan*

Me: *Ethan?*

Rae: *He reserved table service at a club, he invited you too, check your inbox*

Me: *Got it, well I'll see you in a minute*

I wondered how much Lucy would enjoy hanging out with Ethan & Co.

Rae: *Stopping by or staying?*

It was the first time her subtext was anything less than welcoming. I wrote back: *Not sure*

Being noncommittal, Sol, is just another form of denial. I was keeping everyone guessing, even myself. No matter how tempting it was to go straight to David, the most urgent thing was to have a moment with Rae to explain what happened to the ring. Her friendship was one of the few things that made everyday life not only possible, but fun. I would take her aside and clear the air, even if it meant crashing on her cozy evening with Lucy.

While my taxi crept away from the airport, David called. "Oh my God, I've missed you," he said. His voice filled me with some sense of duty, like I was the only person capable of returning his sense of equilibrium.

"I just need to stop at my apartment and then I'll come over."

"I'll send Lance to pick you up."

Rae was sitting on the futon with Lucy streaming a movie when I walked through the door. "Welcome home," she said, looking up only briefly from the screen and pointing to a small pile of mail on the kitchen table.

"Big New Year's plans?" she asked.

"I don't know," I said. "Hey, can I have a word?"

She let out a sigh, rising to her feet and joining me at the kitchen table where there were several postcards from Thailand signed with love from Grant. I began to speak, but the sight of his handwriting caught something in my throat.

"What is it?" she asked, her arms crossed over her chest.

"Um, during Thanksgiving dinner, when I used the bathroom, I tried on your great-grandmother's ring. I should have come clean when you asked. I'm sorry." I wiped my eye.

"Seriously?"

"I was embarrassed when you asked in the coffee shop. I'm really sorry."

She turned toward the darkened window and balled her fists. I sensed the matter had escalated while I was gone.

I said, "I must have returned it to the wrong pouch. Maybe Lee's?" I inhaled deeply and sucked in my cheeks. "I'm sorry I didn't tell you before." Lucy paused the movie and was looking down at her lap, and I hated having another tense exchange in front of her.

"Jesus, Bets," Rae said, shaking her head.

"Forgive me?" I'd ruined the whole sense of home we'd created just because I'd wanted some fantasy time with a ring. Lucy put in her ear buds.

"Ugh, if you could have heard my mother and grandmother bickering about it all week."

"I know. I'm really sorry."

"I know you are sorry, but if you had just told the truth this thing wouldn't have gotten all blown out of proportion."

She looked over her shoulder at Lucy and then looked back at me. "I know I don't always understand what gets you upset and certain things are hard to talk about, but please, Bets, I want our friendship to be based on honesty."

"I know," I said with tears in my eyes. We hugged. Obviously, being honest 100 percent of the time is challenging, Sol, but her words would echo through my mind for months to come.

She pulled away from our embrace with a grin, her eyes twinkling. "Okay, so I forgive you," she said. "Come out with us tonight? Ethan put our names on a list." I caught sight of Lucy rolling her eyes. They had probably rehearsed the way this conversation would go down and I imagined her coaching Rae to not let me off the hook so easily.

"We'll get dressed up," Rae said, her old bouncy self. And that's when I noticed the stuffed garbage bag of dirty laundry I'd left by the Murphy bed was gone and in its place two shrink-wrapped squares of clean clothes.

Pointing to them, I said, "You didn't have to do that."

"You expected me to live with your smelly clothes for two weeks? You owe me twenty bucks. Just say you'll come out with us."

It sounded like Ethan was planning to blow a wad of cash and I had never been to a club that swank. It was tempting, but then I pictured the guys he'd likely invited from our training program and caught a glimpse of Lucy with her arms crossed against her chest, and I knew exactly who I wanted to be kissing at midnight.

"Sorry," I said. "But I have a date."

CHAPTER SEVENTEEN

I strode into David's foyer wearing a black cocktail dress, all lips and hips, high heels, my hair blown out and wearing more makeup than I ever dared at work. It was provocative, I know, and maybe a little inspired by Miami, but I was curious what his reaction would be, whether he'd fallen for the whitewashed version of Betsabé Ruiz or whether he could handle some glitz.

"Wow," he said. He was more casual than I'd ever seen him, wearing jeans and a cashmere V-neck over a T-shirt, again, just wool socks, no shoes. A soft jazzy saxophone crooned over the sound system and the contemporary art on the walls was well-lit. The smoky scent of a crackling fire hung in the air.

"You look great," he said.

"Gracias," After a week with my family, sprinkling in Spanish was second nature. "My first New Year's Eve in New York."

"Looks like you have plans to paint the town," he said with a tinge of disappointment.

"Maybe," I said, letting him think this was my pregame. I followed him to the study, wondering if I'd ever see more of his apartment. Champagne was chilling in a crystal bucket. He popped the cork and poured two flutes.

"To 2020," he said, clinking my glass. As I tilted mine back to take a sip, we locked eyes. Maybe it was the break from First Provident, or maybe it was the desperation in his voice, but I was strangely feeling the upper hand. I walked around the room, perusing the artifacts of his life. Unlike his sterile office on sixty, his personality was on display here. There was a picture of Abigail with two golden retrievers and one with younger men I assumed were his sons on the deck of a big white boat holding fishing rods. There was a sampling of Tamara's childhood artwork as well as a curated selection of books, photographs, and diplomas rounding out the image of a family man. I got the sense, however, this fatherly chapter was ending and he was struggling with what came next.

A wooden card table in the corner of the room was covered with pieces of a jigsaw puzzle. Somebody had connected half a dozen border pieces but there was no great progress. I toyed with a few before turning back to face him.

"I brought you something," I said, retrieving my purse, and presented David with a gift every tourist carted home from Little Havana, but the humidor on his desk confirmed what Lenore had mentioned, that he appreciated a good cigar.

"Merry Christmas, or Happy Hanukkah I mean, and congratulations on closing AgriGlobal," I said, handing him two cylinders I'd tied with a bow.

He held them to his nose. "Ah, nothing I like more than a fine Cuban cigar."

"Cuban women?" Now I was being the flirt.

"I'm just developing my taste." He smiled, turning the aluminum cylinders toward the light to read their labels. "From the Little Havana Cigar Factory?"

His familiarity with my hometown made me smile. We both had grandparents who had sought refuge in Miami's pastel landscape. There was a growing population of Jewbans in South Florida as well, the offspring of Cuban and Jewish parents. Yaya had gone so far as to say Cubans were the Jews of the Caribbean, not just because of our exiled status but because of our work ethic, our industriousness, the impact we made on every community we landed upon. La Pequeña Habana was a ghetto existing to preserve the collective memory of our homeland which David said was the lifeblood of the Jews as well. Memory. The biggest difference between our cultures, as far as I could tell, was that I grew up glorifying pork and his diet forbade it.

He opened a desk drawer and pulled out a box tied with red ribbon.

"What?"

"Not for closing AgriGlobal, or Christmas for that matter, but because for ten days I couldn't stop thinking about you."

I blushed and opened the cardboard box to find another box of velvet. I snapped it open to reveal a pair of earrings, dropped balls of small diamonds. I caught my breath. They glistened as brilliantly against the dark velvet as one of Becca's rings. The envy I had confessed to Rae a few hours earlier was being tested, yet again. I could see Gloria hungrily snatching up such bling, but what would Yaya have done? Her voice in my head asked, "What kind of energy do they hold, Betsabé?"

Rae's great-grandmother stored most of her jewels inside their original boxes with corresponding note cards, as if warning future generations not to flaunt one's baubles.

"Tamara was fixated on these, but I thought they'd look better on you." Why did he have to mention daddy's little girl? I was grateful he didn't use his pet name for her, but I wondered if he'd given her a similar present. Registering the alarm on my face, he added, "I mean, left alone I'm not a very good shopper."

It was hard to imagine him afraid of making a mistake.

"Try them on?" he asked, and I pictured him as a modern-day Bunny Meister and me as Sadie resisting his generosity. And then JLo's voice was in my head, "Somebody's always throwing the money and somebody's always doing the dance." I closed the velvet box and searched his eyes.

"Don't you like them?"

"Oh David, they're beautiful. But I can't accept them." Although they could have financed a good deal of Yaya's bills.

"Of course, you can. Don't sell yourself short, love. Nobody ever got anywhere by selling themself short." His comment struck me as a dare, reminiscent of the way he convinced Roland to make an acquisition for AgriGlobal. Everyone knew diamonds were transactional. Accepting a diamond was the first step into turning yourself over. I took a sip of champagne. None of David's children likely ever declined a gift. I don't know, Sol, maybe that was my moment of no return.

I let David open the box and clip them on my ears. It was warped logic— as if my hands weren't getting dirty. Besides, his fingers against my neck were an added sensation. I went into his powder room to look in the mirror. They weighted down my ear-lobes so that even when I closed my eyes, it was impossible to forget I was wearing them. When I returned to his study, I held my hair on top of my head and spun around to show them off.

"Now, how about taking off that dress?" he said.

We would spend the next four days in a cocoon, leaving the master suite only for trips to the kitchen. My dress hung in his closet mocking the brazen entrance I'd made on New Year's Eve. It was one of those lazy holiday weekends when the world collectively agreed to pause, nothing expected besides nursing hangovers and exchanging gifts. David called out for food which Marcel sent up in the elevator, and we binged on noodles and Netflix, caught up on podcasts, and made love. I was lulled to sleep by the soft, soothing purr of his snores.

On the third morning, I was intentionally playful, increasingly comfortable with our nakedness in the light of day. I tickled his chest, and he placed his hands on my waist and smiled. "Well, good morning." Later on, we ate lo mein with chopsticks and I introduced him to A Star is Born, with Bradley Cooper and Lady Gaga, my favorite movie about a veteran musician and his protégée. He grinned then informed me there were older versions of the movie, one with Barbra Streisand, even one with Judy Garland from the 1950s.

"You are kidding!" That led us to watching more old movies, David introducing me to Woody Allen. For some reason he related to the neurosis of this small man. He cued up *Manhattan,* a movie he had loved in 1979 (!) starring a young Mariel Hemingway, but it hadn't aged well and the parallel felt a little weird, but possibly David's way of exploring how he felt about the May/December thing. I ignored the Lolita-esque theme and the fact that Woody Allen was now a confirmed sexual predator who had married his own daughter! Adopted daughter, but still. I shifted my focus to the setting alone. I loved movies staged in New York, and that weekend as we watched one after another, I felt like the starlet, padding around his extravagant boudoir in oversized slippers.

Gloria once told me a woman who was too good in bed could actually make a man insane, as in literally make him lose his mind. I took it as one of her humble brags, but with David I could see what she meant. It wasn't difficult to send him over the edge. He treated my body like the fountain of youth. Looking back, the wheels of his mind were spinning that weekend as we watched those movies and as he took me in. So, I think he was coming up with an explanation for what we were doing, one that he could live with.

For me, well, it felt like I was meeting the adult Betsabé that weekend, or maybe the adult I dreamed of being someday. In the bedroom, sex eventually became not a thing we did, but a place we went, our intimacy introducing new versions of ourselves.

I inhaled every bit of his pillow and even his walk-in closet with its rich combination of sweat and dry-cleaning starch. I ran my hands across the sleeves of the dozens of suits hanging there in black, blue, gray, and pinstripe. There must have been two dozen pairs of leather shoes gleaming on racks along the floor. The opposite side of the massive closet, however, was striking in its emptiness, large gaps of space spoke to where Abigail's hanging dresses, skirts, and blouses once lived. I imagined a row of ball gowns organized by color, once flowing from the highest rod.

Those barren shelves marked for lingerie, hosiery, and scarves made me feel young and inconsequential. David and Abigail had married the year I entered middle school. Even though I wanted to know more about her, it felt like the wrong time to ask. Instead, I entertained him with stories about Rae's family and the coywolf saga at Lyle College. I pulled up images on my phone to give him an accurate picture of the animals. They looked a lot like large undomesticated dogs. David found the talk naughty in a gossipy way because even though Rick Addington had once been a colleague at First Provident, they never got along. Tales of his woes, the wild animals, and now the activists' involvement was good theatre.

"Why did Rick Addington leave First Provident?" I asked.

"Probably had an idea about riding out his final days in a patrician manner."

"Patrician?"

"Snobbish noblesse oblige, giving back."

I laughed. "It's not as if that place needs his charity. There are few underprivileged kids at Lyle." We laughed even harder.

"I think he pictured sitting by a fire with his pipe, reading the classics. In the end, it was a graceful exit."

"I take it he wasn't successful at First Provident?"

"Not if you equate success with making money."

"Is that how you equate success?"

He wrapped his arms around me and sighed deeply, as if considering how to impart an important lesson, knowing that for somebody my age, there was a correct way to answer that question. It's easy for people with money to say things like "money doesn't buy happiness" or "there is more to life than money," but come on, you can't deny money lifts you up. I didn't want him to echo Rae's annoying ambivalence. He cleared his throat and I waited for an answer, hoping he knew who he was talking to.

"It's by no means the only way to measure success," he said. "But in our world," and he paused just long enough for me to digest the fact that he called it *our* world, "yes, money is how we keep score."

I'd done an accounting of the silver-framed portraits on his bookshelves and dresser, photos of Tamara and Abigail as well as women I didn't recognize, and I wondered if that wasn't another way he kept score. "You've been with a lot of women," I said. He sat up, then appeared amused, as if the silliest things had a way of slipping out of my mouth.

He traced my jawline with his index finger. "My mother died when I was a boy and I grew up in a household of men. Maybe that's why I seek women in my life." He had no mother and I had no father. Besides the fact that our bodies fit together like the jigsaw pieces in his study, I was beginning to see the psychic ways in which we completed each other.

"And since Abigail?"

"Just you."

Abigail wasn't just in photos but in the stacks of coffee-table books, the paintings, the chandeliers. Her kitchen and pantry were orderly yet overflowing with china and crystal goblets that stood in sparkling rows behind glass-fronted cupboards. I was reminded of Eden, each staple of gracious entertaining conveniently on hand as if dinner for sixteen might be pulled together at a moment's notice.

Out in the world, David could cast a long shadow, but at home, I got the feeling he'd been obediently conditioned by her. He never wore shoes past the foyer and wouldn't snack outside the kitchen. So, when he and I snuck ice cream before dinner, his face lit up with a mischievous grin, as if we were getting away with something. We acted young together, breaking the rules—not just Abigail's rules, not just First Provident's rules, but society's rules. Well aware our family and friends would be appalled, we behaved like coconspirators, which further collapsed the years between us. I was drawn to his sage soul, sure, but I was also attracted to the naughty boy he wanted to be.

The irony was that our age gap may have even strengthened our attraction. Considering himself an athlete, David reveled in rising to the challenge, accessing virility he'd feared no longer possible. He said most men his age, take Nathan, for example, were servants to gravity and the passage of time, while he planned on defying all that. In the light of day, the sight of my taut bronze skin up against his wrinkles may have had us closing our eyes, still we lavished love on one another like it might stop time. I was equally drawn to his passion beyond the bedroom, for wine, food, music, art. His appetite was expansive in a way I could relate to—not that he was gluttonous, but that he had a need to eke every last drop out of life.

During those four days, I fielded texts from Rae. Other than sending succinct replies that all was okay and mysterious heart emojis, I remained physically and mentally in the present, David and I gorging on each other in the unspoken knowledge that Sunday, January 5, was just around the corner, and we'd be thrown back into our lives on sixty where we would have to maintain a suitable distance.

Our last night before the holiday ended, I rummaged through the kitchen cabinets in search of popping kernels and a pot so I could make a snack to go with the movie. When I called into the bedroom for help with where to look, he referred to a "Melanie" and how she'd be the one to know where things were located. I walked into the study where he was stoking a fire. "Another daughter?"

"No, Melanie is the maid."

I became self-conscious as to what she might think upon returning from her time off. I scanned the place with alert eyes, picturing the way Yaya shook her head with stories of her employers, and was extra careful not to let oil spatter all over the stovetop.

CHAPTER EIGHTEEN

Walking into our apartment Sunday morning, I was met with
Rae's frowning face as if she were the mom and I broke
curfew. At least she was alone, sitting at the kitchen table instead
of perched on the futon with her new best friend.

"No Lucy?"

She turned her attention back to her laptop, the screen lighting
her face a blueish white. I dropped my bag and hung up my coat,
revealing the sweatsuit David had lent me from Tamara's closet.

"Nice outfit."

Besides being familiar with every stitch of clothing I owned,
the last time Rae had seen me I was dressed to the nines for New
Year's. She raised a second eyebrow, making no attempt to conceal
the conclusions to which she was jumping. Pulling all-nighters at
First Provident was one thing, but four days with only perfunctory
texting was entirely different.

"How was your New Year's with Lucy and Ethan?" I asked in a
preemptive strike, emphasizing the oil and water quality of her two
companions. Despite the catty jab, I'd returned to her with hopes
of sharing a pizza and falling back into the comfort of our bedtime
routine. But she was out of sorts, and I guess I was too. Miami left
me with the realization I could never go home again, and now there
was this intensity with David. It was like I'd been hurtled into an

161

adult future, the cosmos hitting fast-forward on the video of my life while I scrambled for the pause button or at least the slow-mo.

Despite Rae becoming the closest friend I'd ever had, daresay a surrogate sister, we were at a juncture in our friendship where we could either honestly share what was going on in our love lives or say nothing, assuming the other person could never understand. I was afraid to tell Rae where I'd been all weekend, afraid of what her reaction might be, and I sensed she was holding back too.

"It was fine," she said, eyes back on the screen. "Oh, and also, Grant keeps calling me because you weren't answering your phone. I think he was expecting to wish you a Happy New Year."

"Right, thanks." The postcard he sent was still sitting on the kitchen table. It was a picture of a beautiful gray elephant guarding her baby with her legs and trunk. I turned it over to see his familiar handwriting.

My parents and I are having an amazing holiday in Thailand. We even rode elephants (not mamas in the wild like this). Sitting so high up and rocking from side to side on their backs is a beautiful perspective. I want to bring you here someday.
Love,
Grant

Declaring his love on the back of a postcard for all the world to see. No wonder Rae was forming opinions.

"If the missing ring is still causing tension, I can call your mom tomorrow," I said.

"That would be a start."

"Then I'll call Lee." Rae shared her contact information with me. "And?"

"And then I'll call Rachel." Ticking it all off sounded exhausting, but it would give me something besides David to focus on at work in the morning.

"Thank you. I'd appreciate getting out of the middle." She closed her laptop with a smile. It was not in her nature to lie even if it meant covering up for a friend.

"Have you eaten?" I asked.

"Yeah, but I'm still hungry."

"Pizza?"

"Mexican?"

Once again it was Uber eats. Rae made tea, and I grabbed a spiked seltzer from the fridge.

"I don't want to go to work tomorrow," I moaned. I'd just taken the longest break since senior year spring vacation. It didn't take long to get used to waking up without an alarm and going barefoot.

"Me neither."

"But really. How was your New Year's?"

"Okay. We went to that club where Ethan had table service. He was bummed you didn't show. Oh, and your friend Sandra was there, asking about you." It had been ages since I'd joined Sandra on the sidewalk for one of her smoking breaks.

Ethan had told me he was going to spend the holidays in Vermont with his family, but for some reason the analysts in my class felt the need to rush back to the city for New Year's, claiming front row seats to the spectacle previously only watched on television. Then again, maybe I wasn't the only one who had a hard time spending more than a week in my childhood home.

"Seems like you're hanging out a lot with Lucy," I said.

"Yeah, she really gets me," she said with a smile in her voice.

We cleaned up our wrappers and took turns in the bathroom. It felt good to take a long shower, letting the hot water turn my skin a purplish red and filling the bathroom with steam. Rae hated when condensation streamed down the walls and the mirror, but it was nice not to worry about David wanting to join me or ribbing me for taking too much time.

When I emerged with a towel wrapped around my head, Rae had already folded down our beds and was lighting her candle. The flame darted about in the draft while I bundled up in flannel pj's, insulating the warmth from the shower against my skin.

"So, how was your break?" I asked, clutching my quilt to my chin.

"Okay, spent a lot of time helping my mom move. I went to Lyle with her to close on the condo."

"Fun?"

"Seriously?"

I laughed. "Any coywolf sightings?"

"No, but we had an encounter with mom's old colleague, Ann Campbell, who was shoveling out her car in the driveway. Mom asked how her cockapoo was doing after its run-in with a coywolf and then Ann made this expression *as if you even care.* And Mom was like, 'OMG, Ann, don't buy this narrative Addington's created. There is no need to cast blame. It's not possible to control nature.'"

"Go, Sarah."

"Yeah, moving back to the city has given her perspective. Small-town life is quaint, but it can crush you too."

"Did you know President Addington used to work at First Provident?"

"The asshole."

"Did you hang out with Lucy much over break?"

"A little bit. She went home to spend time with her sister. New Year's Eve was like the first time we were together."

"And you took her to a club with Ethan?"

"I know, stupid."

"Well, yeah."

"I'm feeling a little inept. You know, matching my actions with my feelings."

"I get it." It was amazing how I could see Lucy was interested in more than friendship and she couldn't. I yawned and rolled over. "Ugh," I whined. "Marnye just texted about our check-in tomorrow morning." Having typically worked seven days a week, I'd never experienced "Sunday Scaries" before, but the image of Marnye's scowling face had my heart racing.

"Wait, you have to tell me about Miami and where you've been since you got back."

"Everything is really good. Yaya and Gloria are doing well. I'm happy. I'll fill you in another time, I'm wiped."

"You can't just disappear for four days and not tell me where you went."

"New love interest. Early days."

"And what about Grant?"

"Hmmm," I murmured sleepily. "Great guy, but halfway around the world. And if I had to describe the difference, I'd say there were no fireworks with Grant."

"And now?"

"The epitome of passion. The definition of the word."

"What?! Tell me!"

"I can't do it justice right now. G'night Rae."

She blew out the candle on the coffee table. "Bets?"

"Yeah?"

"I'm glad you're home. I missed you."

"I missed you too."

During my Monday morning check-in with Marnye, she told me how the teams on sixty were being reshuffled, which David already prepared me for. Alan had never been a member of David's team but Marnye pulled him in to replace me. I was assigned to a refinancing team and would be building the model in conjunction with an analyst in private finance. It was a guy who hadn't given me the time of day during the summer training, and I was looking forward to impressing him.

"Also, Bets," Marnye said. "The AgriGlobal closing dinner is on you."

"What?"

"David wants to host it in January and Roland is asking about the date to make travel plans. Lenore can help you with the restaurant choices. Don't forget the deal toys; they can take three to four weeks to arrive."

That first week back was hard, as if my staying-up-late muscle had atrophied. I was dragging by four or five in the afternoon, enlisting the espresso machine in the private dining room to work overtime. Grant messaged, asking where I'd been, whether we could Skype later that night. The idea made me nervous but figured I could use Marnye as an excuse to keep it short.

So later that evening I took my dinner to an empty conference room, closed the door, and accepted Grant's call with my earbuds in. When the video came to life, he sat in a bare apartment, dimly lit and not a picture on the wall. He wore a dress shirt with the collar unbuttoned and his necktie draped around his neck. His hair was wet from a morning shower.

"Good morning," I said.

"Good evening to you, beautiful. What's for dinner?" I was glad he didn't come right out with jealous questioning, but the more he talked to me like a girlfriend, the lousier I felt.

"Pasta, my stomach is queasy."

I tried to steer the conversation toward work, the fact I would soon be lording status over an analyst in private finance.

"How's it going over there?" I asked.

"Pacificorp is hanging by a thread. And well, I'm sure you've heard about this virus." When Grant arrived in Hong Kong at the end of November, it was still a bustling outpost of Western business, but because of an outbreak of a pneumonia-like virus, expats were being sent home. It only made sense that First Provident would be next.

"Jeez," I yawned. I should have been more concerned, Sol, but at that point it all sounded so far away.

Grant looked at his watch. "Awfully early to be yawning."

"I am exhausted," I said, wondering how I might ease out of the call.

"How was Miami?"

I updated him on how Yaya was faring and that my mother was coming around to making repairs on the house. I told him the latest in the coywolf drama at Lyle College, that reporting to Marnye was a drag. The one person I did not mention was David, and I prayed he wouldn't ask how I spent New Year's. "Hey, got your postcards. Your trip looked amazing."

"Yeah, but my parents were begging me to return with them to the US."

"They must be worried."

"Well," he screwed up his lips. Poor Grant, how could he do an about-face and return home? "I'm sure it will be fine. If they close the office, I'll just work from this lovely corporate apartment." He gave me a virtual tour of the living room where there was one couch, one chair, one table, one lamp.

"Oh Grant." I lost my appetite completely, the buttery sauce congealing on top of my pasta.

"It's okay, don't worry. Things will settle down and I'll get you over here as soon as it's safe."

"I'm not worried," I said, summoning an expression I hoped would pass as a smile. I disconnected before he could offer a loving farewell. I threw my food container into a blue recycle bin and walked back to my desk. David had his coat and scarf on and was talking to Lenore as if he was on his way out. When he saw me, his eyes lit up like he had been biding time at her desk.

"Betsabé," he said in an assertive tone. "Can I have a word?"

"Sure," I said, putting my laptop on my desk.

"In my office?" I followed him inside and he shut the door. "Come over tonight?" He whispered instructions into a bound presentation, as if he were the catcher coming out to the mound to have a word with the pitcher. Despite feeling rundown and rather nauseous, in that moment I was beautiful again.

"Really?"

"I'll send Lance."

"Sure," I said.

———◆———

At ten o'clock I went to the sidewalk where a long row of town cars idled. I spotted the Mercedes and opened the door to the back seat. I placed my oversized bag inside, but before I could get into the car myself, there was a tap on my shoulder.

It was Sandra. "Hey," she said. "Want to share?"

"Oh hi, actually no, I can't," I said, trying to smooth out the panic in my voice. I had no idea if she recognized the car as David's.

"Okay, whatever. Was just thinking we could grab a drink?"

"Darn, wish I could. Sorry." And in a rather ungraceful move, I slammed the door. Lance must have felt a similar dread because he sped away from the curb immediately, leaving my friend blank-faced on the sidewalk.

CHAPTER NINETEEN

By now, Sol, I hope I've conveyed the physical strain that came with being an analyst, denying my body sleep and healthy food, even holding my bladder beyond what was normal. Toward the end of January, however, my physical condition became more worrisome. As I already mentioned, the first thing that hit was the fatigue, and although I'd heard stress could mess with your menstrual cycle, I was late and getting alarmed. Sitting in the cold stillness of my tiny bathroom one Saturday morning, I had to stop pretending. Having a head full of dreams wasn't going to make this go away.

I perched above the toilet seat, balancing on the balls of my feet, and held the plastic test stick between my thighs. The tile floor was cold, and I was noticing for the first time just how dirty it was, dust and hair gathered around the claw feet of the tub. There was the added indignity of spraying piss all over my fingers. I placed the test on the edge of the pedestal sink, washed my hands, and sat on the rim of the tub for the "three to five" excruciating minutes prescribed in the instructions. Elbows on knees, I cradled my forehead in my hands. It was a little late to start praying, but what were the chances of a single pink line?

As I waited for the test results, my head flooded with memories of a less complicated time, back when I was Ania's age, before sprouting breasts and hips and becoming a woman in the eyes of the world. My father was still on the scene, doing this fancy rope-skipping on Yaya's porch, his face chiseled in concentration while I tried hard to win one of his smiles. His image was all the reminder I needed that not everyone's prepared to become a parent.

When the timer on my phone sounded, the extra line was undeniably there. My gut hadn't needed a test, I'd been feeling different all around. It was my brain that demanded verification. I hunched over the sink with its cracked porcelain and rusty drain and splashed cold water on my face. Staring at my reflection in the mirror, I barely recognized the trembling lip and the rash spreading across my collarbones. After everything I'd accomplished, I didn't want this to be my story. My cohort at First Provident would remember me as *Betsabé, the good-looking one, the one who barely made it a year before getting pregnant! Can't say I didn't see it coming.* Despite my determination to be different, to make the most of the opportunities my generation had to offer, I'd succumbed to my mother's biological undoing.

There was the looming question of what to do. Counting back on my fingers, I must have conceived eight weeks prior, in front of the fire, on the floor of David's study, despite the fact he'd worn a condom! *First things first.* Literally. There was the imminent task of leaving the bathroom and facing Rae. She'd been puttering about the apartment all morning, making breakfast, folding laundry, and having to open the door to her cheerful order would be one more affront to my internal chaos. She turned and stared as I walked into the room.

"What?" I asked.

"Nothing," she said and went back to spritzing antiseptic cleaner and wiping down the kitchen counter. I stood aimlessly in the middle of the floor. She looked up, a wet paper towel still in her rubber-gloved hand. "Are you okay?"

"No, I—" I wasn't ready to say the words aloud. Besides, I was still convinced she would never understand. Rachel, on the other hand, might and she'd be happy to dole out advice. She had volunteered at Planned Parenthood, the one named for Margaret Sanger on the corner of Bleecker and Mott in the West Village, escorting women inside the clinic.

"Can you ask Rachel to come over?"

"Huh?" she said with a tinge of possessiveness at the mention of her grandmother.

"I don't know, I feel like I could use an adult point of view." In the minutes since those pink lines appeared, I had regressed into a child who wanted to be told what to do.

I was wrapped in an afghan, my thick hair wet from a shower when Rachel rang our buzzer. The security monitor lit up with a distorted black-and-white image, and I hoisted myself up to let her in while Rae kept on dusting the sill like this was a social call and not her grandmother on emergency business.

"Oh, Bets, you're pale," Rachel said when she reached the top of the stairs. She was holding a pastry box tied in string in one hand and a large Styrofoam coffee cup in the other. She was used to seeing me made-up, my long brown hair, glossy and straight down my back. Rae once pointed out that picking out physical flaws was Rachel's way of tuning in. I'd seen firsthand how the women in her family were prone to "catastrophize" situations, however in this case, I thought it might be warranted.

"I know. I look terrible. I feel terrible."

"You're not still kerfuffled over that ring business, I hope."

"Oh, no. That's not it," I said, the idea of jewelry now totally trivial.

She took off her hat and unzipped her long down coat. Rachel walked everywhere, even in the January cold. She ridiculed all the fitness studios popping up. "Walking is the best way to stay in shape," she'd once said. "Plus, it's a bargain! Don't ride elevators and don't take cabs." She was full of prescriptions that were easier said than done, which I attributed to the fact that she'd never worked eighty-hour weeks and was seldom in a hurry.

She made herself comfortable at our kitchen table and opened the box of pastries. Rae and I pulled up chairs across from her.

"So, what is it, doll?" She patted my hand. The answer hovered in the air, but before I could speak the kettle whistled, and Rae stood to make tea. For some reason her getting up and turning around made it easier.

"I'm pregnant," I said.

There it was, suddenly real. Rae's hand landed on my back, and Rachel's on my arm as if I were a balloon and a strong gust of wind was coming through.

"Okay," Rachel said after a few seconds. "There's a lot you need to consider. Betsabé, I know you're Catholic. Is abortion an option? Depending how far along you are, I can get you some pills. You wouldn't even need to go to the clinic."

To be honest, Sol, for a moment back in the bathroom I had assumed that was what I would choose. Today as I write this, I can't tell you how dismayed I am that reproductive medical attention has been rendered a privilege for the resourceful well-to-do. Back on that Saturday, sitting at the kitchen table, I took it for granted that I had a choice.

Tears welled in my lower lids as I considered all I had surrendered to this city, to my job, to the reinvention of Betsabé Ruiz. It wasn't so much Catholicism as it was Yaya and her convictions. Over Christmas, she'd seen I was off balance and was probably sensing my pregnancy a thousand miles away. I had assumed working my ass off in banking and making loads of money would make her proud, but that wasn't the way to make my yaya proud. Regardless of how I proceeded, she would know, and suddenly confiding in Rachel felt like a betrayal.

"I don't know," I said, sniffling into the back of my hand. Rae put a box of Kleenex in front of me. Maybe if I hadn't been a college graduate or a competent member of the workforce, it would have been an easier decision. Becoming a mother at twenty-three hadn't been the plan, but I could learn what needed to be learned, make it work somehow. My parents had me when they were even younger and on a whole lot less. A future in investment banking might be out of the picture, but that was fine with me.

And then an ugly idea began rising to the surface. It was an insecurity I'd kept at bay, Sol, but in that moment, it demanded recognition. It arose with the same cynical tone Gloria used the day I told her about my job offer. *Who do you think you are? Getting a college scholarship was one thing, Betsabé. Becoming a big-city, independent woman was asking too much.* It was the same voice that accused me of not remembering my place in the world. *You played with fire, Betsabé, and this is what happens. This is what you deserve.*

I wiped my eyes. "I'll have the baby."

Rae did a double take. "What about your job?" she asked, as if keeping First Provident happy was my greatest concern.

"Oh please," Rachel said, swatting a hand in the air. We sat quietly, letting my decision sink in.

"No matter what you decide, you'll need to let the father know," Rachel said.

"There's no chance it's Grant's?" Rae asked, full of hope.

I glared at her. It was a hateful expression she absolutely didn't deserve, but the question added a whole new layer of shame to the equation. And given the heavy period I got the day after having sex with Grant, there was no doubt who the father was.

"Grant's not the father,"

"Oh." Rae washed a bite of pastry down with some tea.

"His name is David."

"Wait, as in the guy who heads up M&A?"

I nodded.

"Oh, sweetheart," Rachel said. "Aren't there rules at that company?"

"What about Grant?" Rae couldn't disguise her disappointment.

Again, I shot her a death stare.

"You'll need to let this David character know right away," said Rachel.

"Wait," interjected Rae. "If she tells him, would that be like soliciting support? Won't that make it hard to press charges?"

"What are you talking about?" I asked.

"Sexual assault," Rae said.

I shook my head. "It wasn't like that."

"Of course, it was," said Rae. "The power dynamic was totally imbalanced."

"Just shut up, okay?" Rae had taken all those women's studies courses in college: The Politics of Rape, Rape as a Weapon of War, Rape as Power. As far as I was concerned all sex involved an imbalance of power. Somebody was on top and somebody was on the bottom.

Rae pushed her chair back from the table, the leg scraping against the hardwood floor. It was easy back in college watching the cases on television, Christine Blasey Ford testifying against Brett Kavanaugh, but how could I explain that wasn't what happened to me, that I was not a victim? Although it was not the predominant thinking at the time, I saw myself as an agent of my own desire, its danger even adding to the fun.

"David's not like that," I said. "You'll see." To them, the capitalist system was a breeding ground for misogyny. The world loves to typecast and generalize, Sol, but you must understand I'd seen something in David they couldn't, call it splendor or grace or imagination. I wasn't going to let them simplify what we had to fit the outrage of the moment.

Still, I couldn't let Rachel leave our apartment without getting more practical advice. First off, I needed the name of a doctor. Rae shook her head when I asked because she'd shared the name of her gynecologist months ago, but given my lifestyle, doctor's appointments had a way of falling to the bottom of my list.

"First things first, call the father," Rachel said.

"I don't think that will go over too well." I winced.

"It never does, but you have to do it."

I was silent, searching for some alternative. Leaving New York under cover of darkness?

"Look," Rachel said. "Not telling him is just as bad as lying, and lying shouldn't be your first instinct in touchy situations." It appeared my faulty character had been a topic of conversation in their family. How could I prove to them I'd rarely lied before coming to New York?

"I will. I'll call him today," I said, sitting up straight. "Absolutely, I will."

"Good," Rachel said. "Most men come around over time." She smiled at Rae while saying this, as that had been the case with her father.

I poured myself some tea and the three of us bellied up to the table, collecting the last bits of confectioners' sugar on our fingers. I rinsed our mugs at the sink and placed them in the drying rack in an attempt to maintain Rae's domestic order.

"Thanks for helping me think this through," I said.

"Don't put off calling him," Rachel said.

"I won't."

"Good girl," she said, "I should get going before it gets dark." That time of year the sun set by five o'clock. "Call me anytime." She hugged me before zipping up her down coat and making her way out the door.

Saturday afternoons were generally good for catching David. I collapsed on the futon and noticed a missed call and message from Gloria: *Mija, que tal? Call me. When will you send $$ yaya has bills due 2/1. besos, mami XOXO*

I buried my face in a throw pillow and muffled a groan. *Ugh.*

"What now?" Rae asked as if our apartment was too small for any more of my problems.

"Nothing." In Rae's family, money, furniture, and jewelry flowed from eldest to youngest, and I didn't want to explain that my mother and grandmother needed things from me.

I'd been disciplined with my finances since returning from Miami, because, Sol, if you weren't careful, that city just swallowed twenty-dollar bills. A coffee, drinks, an Uber, poof. I twisted a strand of my hair in a coil, figuring out how much I could spare for Gloria. I Venmoed and messaged that I'd call her soon.

I could have let my mother distract me, but Rachel's words were still sounding in my head. I opened my text thread with David and typed: *Need to talk.* He replied right away.

David: *At work then dinner with Nathan*

Me: *Breakfast in the morning?*

David: *Can it wait?*

A bubble with three dots indicated he was still typing, and then there it was:

David: *Promised princess I'd take her shopping.*

If he had just written "Tamara" or left out "Can it wait?" But it read like a dismissal, impatience at having to juggle the young women in his life. He was blowing me off for a daddy–daughter day with sales ladies pouring him sparkling water or steaming milk for his cappuccino while Tamara twirled about in one outfit after another.

The bad timing of his fatherly devotion stoked my fury, and I imagined my future as a real-life Fantine, begging for scraps on the streets of Paris, desperate to feed my infant, Cosette. It wasn't too different from a memory of Gloria pushing me in a metal shopping cart and breaking into tears at the checkout when she didn't have enough money to pay for the items on the conveyor belt.

I'd admired David's relationship with Tamara but becoming pregnant meant giving up all the things she took for granted: a career, a social life, walking down the aisle unblemished someday. She not only had the steady arm of a father, she had brothers who adored her as well. I sat frozen on the futon for several moments, gripping my phone. David may have been able to walk through life like some sort of king but let him figure this one out. I reread his text, my cheeks burning hot with humiliation, and that's when I punched out those three fateful words.

A subject, a verb, and an adjective that would go off like a stick of dynamite. *I AM PREGNANT.* I'll admit, it was a chicken-shit way of letting him know, but in those days, Sol, text was how we did things. The problem, however, was that a written message left too much up to interpretation. I made matters worse by using all caps, but it was only for emphasis, as in, "Houston, we've got a problem . . . Now what?" I should have paused before hitting send. I should have heeded that old adage, "It's not what you say, but how you say it."

I threw my phone across the floor.

It nicked Rae's ankle and she jumped. "Oh, Bets, I'm so sorry about this whole affair."

"No."

"What?"

"Don't be sorry, this is not a sorry. I refuse to be a sorry and I was not a victim. If you are going to walk around here pitying me, I'm going to move out." And I didn't want her to use the word affair either, it sounded like a booty call. As far as I was concerned, my connection with David was remarkable, and even if it might not turn out to be permanent, I was permanently changed. Being with him had been like putting on glass slippers.

"I'm so . . . I mean I get it. I won't say it again."

"Look, you act like this was something that *happened* to me. Maybe it wasn't, okay? Maybe I had some say in the matter."

She held her hands up in a gesture of surrender, like okay, back off, I'm just trying to help. Again, the peacemaker.

"Can you just act normal?" I asked. I had to pull it together too. I had already taken Saturday off and needed to figure out how I was ever going to return to the sixtieth floor.

CHAPTER TWENTY

I used to think there was nothing better than those few seconds before waking up, snuggled under the warm covers and clinging to the floating sensation of a dream. The morning after the pregnancy test, however, those seconds before lucidity included the shocking remembrance I was pregnant, as if my brain was slow to process the new reality.

There was the added anxiety of David not having responded to my text. I buried my face in my pillow, wondering if I went back to sleep and wished really hard, if I could make it all go away. Rae's footsteps on our hardwood floor rendered that idea impossible. I sat up in bed to see her standing by the door in a winter coat.

"Where are you going?" I asked.

"Ethan set up this brunch," she said. "I'm sure he invited you too. And then Lucy and I are going to the movies. Want to join?"

"What's the movie?"

"No, I meant for the brunch with Ethan. Some of his old friends from prep school are in town."

"Seriously?"

"I know, right?"

"Um, no thanks." I crossed the floor and pulled out clean underwear, a bra, and yoga pants from my dresser. "I want to be alone when David calls." I pulled a large gray sweatshirt over my head and walked toward the kitchen counter, thinking something bland, maybe bread or crackers, might settle my stomach. My phone sat in its charger where Rae had placed it the night before. When I picked it up, the home screen lit with notifications, Instagram, Snapchat, a text from Ethan about brunch. I scrolled through the texts to find the whopper I'd sent to David still unanswered.

Rae waited by the door. "Really, I'm fine," I said.

"I know, but if you change your mind just text me. Lucy might want to get dinner, but I could also come home." I nodded and smiled at Rae, who seemed oblivious to the fact she was dating Lucy while Ethan was supposedly her boyfriend.

"Nah, I should take it easy. Big week coming up."

Fifteen minutes after she left, my phone rang. I assumed it was David, even remarked to myself how thoughtful he was to wait until a decent hour to call, but my stomach dropped when I saw Ethan's name on the screen. I could barely get past "Hello" before he started haranguing. "C'mon Bets. I don't know what's going on with you but get your ass down here." His breathing was labored and there were sirens in the background.

"Where's here?" His carefree life was propelling forward while I had crossed into a time warp where things would never be the same. I resented his ability to prioritize Bloody Marys and smoked salmon.

"Le Coucou, my treat. Rae is coming and I really want you to meet Sam."

"Le Coucou?" The restaurant had been on my wish list despite Grant's sneering I'd never be able to get a reservation. A glossy spread in New York Magazine had featured its food, its art, its beautiful people. I'd never splurged on brunch like the rest of our class and his offer to pick up the check was kind.

Maybe hanging out with Ethan and Rae, not to mention their out-of-town friends, would take my mind off things. Maybe by the time we were done eating, there would be a message from David and I'd be adequately buoyed by the outing that I could speak to him from a place of confidence and not from the sad-sack space of this Murphy bed and apartment with its walls closing in on me. Besides, my stomach was growling, and our cupboards were bare.

I planted my feet on the floor. "Give me fifteen minutes."

The maître d' led me to a table covered in white linens where the four of them were already sipping drinks. It was Ethan and Rae along with a couple from San Francisco, Sam and Nathalie. Ethan and Sam had roomed together at Dunning Academy, and Rae reminded Sam they'd crossed paths one summer in Long Harbor, Rhode Island.

Rae beamed when I sat down. "Lipstick and everything. I'm proud of you."

Ethan made introductions. "Sam and I have known each other since we were pimply-faced fourteen-year-olds."

I raised an eyebrow as if not much had changed.

"People are still talking about him," Ethan said. It was my cue to ask what Sam had done to earn such notoriety, but his girlfriend, Nathalie, inserted herself with a little wave.

"Hey guys, I went to Dunning too, remember?"

"That girl is the one with the brains," Ethan said, tilting his champagne flute her way.

After the waitress took our order, it didn't take long for the three Dunning grads to start rehashing news from their alma mater. Rae rolled her eyes, but I paid attention. Nathalie said she had been pleased the new head of school was a woman, the first in Dunning history.

"Alas, it was too good to be true," Sam lamented.

"She left after a short time in office." Nathalie explained she succeeded Headmaster Williams, a seemingly sinister character, the one apparently responsible for Sam's downfall. Even though much of the Dunning community took the woman's appointment as a public relations ploy in light of all the scandal at the school, Nathalie had been optimistic it signaled real change. At the end of the day, the shining ray of hope must have found more skeletons in the closet than the board of trustees had prepared her for because she had already hightailed it back to her teaching post at the state university.

"You've probably heard of the glass ceiling," Nathalie said. Rae and I nodded. "But there is also a glass cliff."

"What's that?" I asked.

"When women are brought in to clean up a mess, basically positioned to fail, then dumped over the edge with all the shit they uncover."

Rae and I locked eyes. It sounded very similar to what happened to her mother at Lyle. The fact that I was now a card-carrying woman in the workforce, in a male-dominated industry, no less, made me sympathize deeply. Maybe Marnye was right. We were all in this together. And then I remembered I was pregnant with my boss's child and felt like a living, breathing embarrassment to my gender. I was extremely grateful for the arrival of the food so that I could bury my self-loathing underneath a cheese omelet.

Ethan asked if I wanted another drink. He was so busy playing the ebullient host, he hadn't noticed I'd been sipping tea the whole time.

"I'm fine," I said.

As we finished up, I excused myself to the ladies' room. After reapplying lipstick, I brushed my hair. Only then did I allow myself to check my phone.

Nothing. Oh. My. God.

The others had gathered around the exit. Ethan opened the door for me, and we all spilled out onto the sidewalk. Rae said she was meeting "a friend" whom I knew to be Lucy. Ethan was going to First Provident tower, and Sam and Nathalie were heading to Penn Station to catch a train to Boston for a visit with Sam's mother. "What are you up to this afternoon?" Rae asked, smiling in my direction.

"Heading home," I said, putting on my sunglasses. It was a mild day for January, mid-forties with splashes of sunshine. Maybe there'd be a church on my route where I could light a candle, maybe say confession. Something like that.

"They're giving you the whole day off?" Ethan questioned.

"Yeah and I don't want to squander it," I said, leaning over to kiss his cheek. "Thank you so much for brunch. It was delicious."

———

Heading east from the restaurant, I passed through several trendy neighborhoods and I couldn't believe I hadn't explored the city more, a new whimsical storefront around every corner. I'd double back, taking circuitous routes, hoping to get lost to make up for all the time I spent at work. There was a cute boutique in Greenwich Village that sold faux-fur vests and jackets, boots as well, and as I was studying the window, debating whether to splurge on retail therapy, I noticed three teenage girls crossing the street in a gangly pack. No older than sixteen, they were long-limbed and chic. They could have been models or maybe dancers, with hair pulled severely high, perfect makeup, and boots and handbags that cost more than my monthly paycheck. Not only that, they were well-groomed, and I felt the sudden need to get my eyebrows done.

They stopped next to me on the sidewalk and I was able to assess them not only out of the corner of my eye, but through their reflection in the store's window. I was startled to realize the tallest and loudest, the presumable ringleader of the group, was David's daughter.

"Tamara?"

She looked up from her giggling posse, surprised. "Yeah?"

I removed my sunglasses, anticipating some recognition. How many weekends had she come into the office, making small talk? She just cocked her head in confusion, and I shook my head too, confused that she was confused.

"It's Betsabé. From First Provident? I work with your dad?" It was a matter of semantics to say you worked "with" someone at First Provident not worked "for" someone, but Tamara long possessed the knowledge there wasn't a soul at First Provident on equal footing with her father.

"Oh, right, hi." She smiled. "I'm sorry."

"Out of context, I know."

"Totally."

"Nice boots," I said, pointing to the window display.

"Yeah, I love them. They are so it." Wasn't David supposed to be shopping with her? She turned back to her friends, poised to move on, but I wouldn't let her go so quickly.

"So, are these your friends? Do you all go to school together?"

"Um, no not really school. We take French lessons."

"Really?"

"Didn't Daddy tell you? I'm going to boarding school in Switzerland. Supposedly need to speak French."

"Oh, no he didn't," I lied, not wanting to reveal David had shared with me intimate knowledge of her life. Of course, I knew about the boarding school saga, the strife with her mother. I knew all that and a whole lot more. I had listened to David brag about Tamara on the one hand, while wishing she wasn't so flighty on the other. "It's a good thing she's gorgeous," he once said. "I'm going to have to keep the boys away with a shotgun." It was always her looks, her looks, her looks, both a source of pride and a cause for worry. The irony was that I ached for Tamara when David characterized her as one-dimensional, and here she was, regarding me as no more than a stranger on the sidewalk.

"By the way, do you know where he flew off to this morning? He had to cancel our plans." She put on a pouty face, but there she stood, surrounded by friends, laden with shopping bags that had likely been bank-rolled by David's guilt.

"No idea," I said with a pang of worry. Flew off to? What was going on?

"I just assumed it was like, work related, and you'd know," she said.

If it was work, I would have known. No, the reason he disappeared was definitely personal and the catalyst was definitely my text. I worried David might be trying to be in touch with me in some old-fashioned way. Maybe in person? Maybe on my First

Provident–issued phone? Maybe over email? Shit, I knew I should have stayed put and waited for him. "No, sorry. I took the day off. Friends in town."

I rushed home but there was no sign of him. No handwritten note, no email, no voicemail, no text, no Lance behind the wheel. I plopped on the futon and began jotting down the things I would say to him when given the chance. A speech had been forming in my mind the entire way home and I didn't want to forget it.

Not long after I arrived at the apartment, however, a text did come through that shook me. *Guess who'll be in NYC Monday? I'll call when I land.* It was from Grant. He signed off with a heart emoji.

I texted him back with a pit in my stomach. *Really, why?*

Weird, last minute, David wants my eyes on Marnye's due diligence, and he invited me to the AgriGlobal closing dinner.

The omelet almost came up. How would I manage Monday morning in the office with both of them? I crawled over to my unmade bed and hugged the pillow. Even if I was guilty of lies of omission, I told myself I'd been good to Grant. Rachel's words still played through my head, "Not telling him is just as bad as lying, and lying shouldn't be your first instinct in a touchy situation." I stared at the postcard he had sent me. I had propped it on the windowsill. Maybe his sudden return would be a blessing in disguise, giving me the opportunity to come clean. I turned the postcard over in my hands telling myself he had a mother and a father who loved him, a bedroom back in Ohio, and best of all, he'd gotten to ride an elephant.

It's sort of remarkable I was able to fall asleep after the stress of that text and in the middle of the day no less. It could have been the big meal or the walk home, but that's what started happening back then. Sleeping a lot and oh, the dreaming. Gloria once told me I was born having dreams, that as a baby I could wake up with a fright, crying uncontrollably. That afternoon, I had visions of coywolves in their dens, camouflaged by debris and branches, the trees barren of leaves and the ground covered in a thin coating of snow. The male wolves disappeared into the mist, scouting for food. They crossed the Lyle campus without fear, oblivious of protocol. The mothers stayed behind, guarding their pups, regurgitating food into their throats and protecting them from an inhospitable world.

Off in the distance, a door opened and shut, and somebody began shaking my shoulder, but I held onto the image of the woods, and Grant's voice calling from the depths of the forest. I spun around, looking for him. "Bets, I'm coming. Bets, I'm coming. Bets, I'm coming."

CHAPTER TWENTY-ONE

I woke Monday morning with barely enough time to make it to the bathroom. Pregnancy and all its side effects, even the throwing up, was changing me. My body was no longer a mere container for walking through life, a frame to adorn with clothing or through which I received pleasure; it was on a mission of its own. An organ inside my abdomen had dropped eggs and was creating a new human. The more I thought about what was taking place inside me, I was like, *holy shit*.

Rae had already left for Café Jo, so after my shower, I stood naked in front of the full-length mirror. I might not have had the build for gymnastics or ballet dancing, but I sensed I had the build for this. My breasts were substantial. My hips and thighs, proportioned to elicit catcalls, were strong and stable. All the better to birth you with, my sweet.

I wondered if petite women like Rae and Sandra, either naturally thin or the self-inflicted variety, could say the same. Sandra's pelvic bones were visible through her slacks, and she had no chest. Even if I'd been avoiding her since she caught me getting into David's car, it was clear she'd been shrinking away since the summer. How her life might have been different if she'd grown up in a culture that valued a woman with curves. Who knows, but looking at my strong body in the mirror gave me a plug of confidence.

Pulling a plain blue shift dress over my head, I recalled sitting cross-legged on my bed while Gloria and Yaya put on uniforms chosen by their employers. There had been a time when I only bought bright clothes that expressed my personality, but now I was squeezing into a uniform too. No more pink or orange. I gravitated toward conservative colors that didn't require immediate dry cleaning, comfortable, warm, easy to walk in. Lenore taught me to wear running shoes for the commute and keep a pair of leather shoes under my desk. It hadn't taken long to figure out those women who crossed the First Provident lobby in expensive shoes certainly hadn't ridden the subway.

Thinking I might be sick, I made one more trip to the bathroom then ran a brush through my hair. This was not going to be an easy day. I pictured David hunched over his desk in a do-not-disturb posture and Grant hanging around with those searching eyes, that smile. Please God, give me strength. I grabbed my coat and buttoned the front as I hurried down the stairs.

———

I'd been missing in action the entire weekend and Marnye raised an eyebrow when I sat at my desk. She approached the bullpen like she expected an apology or at a minimum, an explanation. Subtlety was not her strong suit, and for someone who professed wanting to bust the patriarchy, she was pretty fond of the chain of command. However, I'd learned nothing much happened in M&A before lunch. Analysts were expected to be on hand by nine but all we did was drink coffee and read the news. By the time VPs or MDs arrived and their requests filtered through associates, my workday was destined to extend past midnight. Funny how morning sickness made me intolerant of all the inefficient bullshit, including Marnye's attitude.

The one thing that did worry me was that David's office was dark. I searched around for Lenore, needing an ally who could fill me in. She wasn't at her post, however, and a cardigan draped over the back of her chair was a telltale sign she'd stepped away.

"Nice of you to show up," Marnye said. I started toward the dining room. Appropriately or not, I was still assuming the immunity that came with being David's favorite.

"Sorry, I was sick."

I brought a sesame bagel back to my desk, feeling a little better with each small bite that dissolved on my tongue.

"David's in Cleveland," she said.

"Okay," I said, faking indifference and turning my attention to my monitor.

"Did you know?"

"What?"

"That Grant is coming back today?"

I shrugged. "He texted me."

"Of course, he did." She looked around to see who else might be within earshot. "What do you think is going on?"

"I wish I knew." I tore off a larger bite of bagel and chewed on it. "It's not like I don't have things under control."

She wanted me to agree with her. I stretched my arms and let out a yawn instead.

"Okay," she said, turning back toward her desk. "Check your inbox, you have a lot to do."

When I glanced down at my keyboard, my pencil drawer was ajar, and the corner of a white envelope was sticking out. That familiar stationery associated with life-altering messages. I tore it open and read what ended up being cursory instructions. *Go to the lobby, anyplace off sixty where you won't be overheard, and call this number.*

I stashed the note in my purse, grabbed my sweater, and dashed to the stairwell. Lenore had taught me to take the emergency exit and go down to the fifty-ninth floor to call the elevator when I couldn't afford to be sidelined. In the lobby, I bought a pack of Mentos and a ginger ale at the kiosk and proceeded to a glass and marble corner behind a row of giant potted palms. My hand shook as I punched out the number.

David answered immediately. "Betsabé."

"David?"

"Well." He cleared his throat. "Okay, then."

"Why didn't you call me over the weekend?"

"I need to know. You're sure?" he asked.

"Yes, I'm sure. Those tests are never wrong, besides I've got morning sickness."

"No, I meant, are you sure the baby's mine?" It was a kick in the stomach and I almost dropped the phone.

"Yes, I am one hundred percent sure." I was perspiring and on the verge of tears.

"It would be so much more natural if this happened with Grant."

"But it didn't happen with Grant. It happened with you."

"I've asked him to come back for the closing dinner."

"I know."

"Good."

"What the hell does Grant coming to the dinner have to do with the fact I'm pregnant with your child?"

"Don't you see? It's the perfect solution."

"What are you talking about?"

"Everyone knows how much he loves you, that he would do anything for you."

"I'm not sure what you're suggesting."

"You're a smart girl. Don't make me spell it out." He was becoming exasperated. "I would help. The two of you would have everything. Watching you together would be devastating, but I'd do anything for you."

"David?"

"Bets, while he's here, you might, I don't know, rekindle the flame?"

I flashed back to the night in Grant's bed, the adoration in his eyes, and again when he took me to dinner to explain what he hoped for after returning from Hong Kong. What David was suggesting was so manipulative. I couldn't understand why he wouldn't take responsibility for this situation in a normal way, but my silence on the line seemed to worry him. "It can't be known I fathered the child. Think of our age difference, of my position."

"Think of you?"

"And your reputation, of course."

"And the baby?"

I was perfectly aware Grant would do anything for me, but then I thought of the VP's wife parked out in suburban Connecticut and I felt sick to my stomach. The idea was terrifying. Did he expect me to be one more woman hanging up her dreams? The phone was far from my ear, but I heard his voice ringing with desperation.

"Betsabé? Betsabé?"

I leaned over a potted palm, holding my hair behind my neck, and vomited up the bagel. My head spun. What he was proposing seemed more like an outlandish script from one of Gloria's soap operas than something I'd expect an intelligent adult to suggest. He was asking me to lure Grant into my bed and then lie, to make it all legitimate. Legitimate, hah. That word was my perpetual thorn.

I felt like telling David that if I wanted a life with Grant, I could have a life with Grant. He was the type of guy who would come around and forgive me, the type of guy who would raise a bastard child as his own. A life with Grant would be safe and secure and what a million women dreamed of. I didn't need to execute David's lying scheme to have a life with Grant. I hung up.

Back at my desk, I popped another Mento. Marnye sent a message asking if her revisions were done yet. I brushed lint from my lap and got back to work, but before I could get anything accomplished, Grant texted: *I'll be there in ten. Come down to the sidewalk? I can't see you for the first time in front of everyone.*

Inhaling deeply, I responded with a thumbs-up emoji. I took several deep breaths, trying to get my heart rate under control. I put on my coat, eliciting another evil stare from Marnye, and grabbed my purse. Downstairs, I turned right out of the massive turnstiles onto 53rd Street. The delivery ramp where I'd sweated in the hot sun six months earlier now served as protection from the biting wind. There was Sandra, standing in the freezing cold, taking a long drag from her cigarette and blowing smoke overhead.

"You never ask me to join you anymore," I said.

"Yeah, I don't want you knowing how batshit I am."

I laughed. "Be careful, you're sucking the life out of those things."

"I should be the one telling you to be careful." I was stunned by her forthrightness. She must have registered the fear on my face. "Don't worry, your secret's safe."

"Sandra, I'd die if anyone found out."

"I think I'd rather be dead than work here much longer," she said.

"Those aren't the only two choices, you know."

"We've got like four hundred eighty-seven days of the two-year commitment left."

"Ouch, you're counting?"

"Like you're not?" I wasn't going to tell her my days numbered far fewer.

I shrugged. "Maybe a little. Hey, suck on one of these." I offered her a Mento and shuffled toward the entrance to the building.

The town car pulled up with Grant smiling from the rear window, and I stuffed the pack into my pocket. Sweat broke out on my neck like it was ninety degrees instead of nineteen. I backed against the building, waiting for him to collect his luggage and thank the driver. "You must have really screwed something up for him to call me back from Hong Kong." It was just like him to joke, to make me laugh.

I walked across the sidewalk and wrapped my arms around him. "This is a nice surprise," I said, trying to gauge what he knew. The red rims around his eyes indicated he hadn't gotten much sleep on the plane, but everything else about him buzzed with excitement.

"God, I missed you." He leaned into the hug and snuck a wet kiss on my neck.

Sandra passed us on her way back inside, raising an eyebrow. *Oh God.*

"Hey, easy," I said, pulling away from him with a laugh. "Let's get you upstairs out of this wind."

"Wait." Grant held my wrist and pulled me back toward the street. He just stood there with that stare. "You look great."

"You look jet-lagged." My attempt at humor was lost on him. He was so damned earnest. "Oh, Grant, I missed you too." It was true, and facing him in the flesh, I was realizing how much. It seemed an eternity since he left, and I was not the same person who met him for drinks on Thanksgiving. He squinted, possibly sensing how his sudden appearance had caught me by surprise.

He looked toward the sky, taking in the sheer face of the building. "HQ. I didn't think I'd be back so soon."

"Crazy, right?" I swallowed hard and forced a smile.

"Hey, but I am craving some Cuban food." It had been an inside joke at the height of our flirting, but also gave me hope we might have a chance to hang out, make some time for me to tell him what was going on.

"Behave yourself," I said, poking his shoulder.

"Don't worry. I'll keep my distance. Marnye is going to have her eyes on us."

"Why do you say that?"

"I think she figured out we went to Rhode Island for the weekend and reported it to Helen in HR."

"What?" She could be abrasive, but I never thought of her as a backstabber.

"Yeah, I got a notice from Helen right after the transfer. Said a memo was going in my personnel file."

"That's ridiculous. You've always been the good Midwestern boy." I wondered if he'd connected the dots with regard to the timing of his transfer. The consequences of loving me were mounting.

"Yeah, and I get the sense that whatever investigation she's conducting isn't over yet. But, hey, the timing of David's big emergency couldn't be better. I really needed to get back to New York."

"Really?" I was startled.

"It's gotten bad over there. The combination of the virus and the political climate," he said.

"I'm so sorry, Grant."

"Who saw that coming?" He shrugged as if life had dealt him a bad hand, but I knew why he'd been sent to the other side of the globe. Even though I recoiled at David's plan, it was a way to help Grant return to New York. It would mean taking on a life I didn't want, not to mention pulling off the biggest theatrical stunt of my life, but then I remembered Grant leaning over the edge of the pool with that gigantic towel and how kind he had been to me.

I gripped the railing inside the elevator and an uncontrollable tremor started in my right leg. When the doors slid open, and we emerged onto the sixtieth floor, Grant shook his head as if encountering a distant memory. David's dark office, however, stopped him in his tracks. "Wait, where is he?"

"Marnye said something about Cleveland."

"What? He told me to station myself in your bullpen and await further instructions." David once told me how watching Grant perched behind my desk drove him crazy. Everything about this situation was making me increasingly anxious, but it was hard to separate my emotions from the heat flashing through my body and the need to be sick. I made it into a stall in the ladies' room just in time to retch the ginger ale.

CHAPTER TWENTY-TWO

D ear Sol, if hatching such a plan represented a low point in David's life, then the next twenty-four hours represented a low point in mine as well. I cannot pretend to be more righteous than David. Keeping Grant's get-out-of-jail-free card in my back pocket was one thing, but the fact I considered redeeming it, in the state I was in, well that was another thing altogether.

———

Returning from the ladies' room, I took in the sight of him, so fair and innocent, setting up his laptop at David's conference table. Lenore was leaning against the doorway, asking about life in Hong Kong, basically whether or not he felt scared, as Marnye shuttled folders back and forth, her face filled with fury. She began to take him through her work when he dismissed her, saying, "It's okay, Marnyc. I can figure it out."

Once Lenore returned to her desk and Marnye was out of sight, I went in to see him. I feared he might be able to sense my betrayal just sitting at that table, but he looked at me with a genuine smile. His eyes softened. "You alright?"

"No. I didn't feel well when I woke up, but I didn't want to miss you."

"Well, I'm going to camp out here and wait for David."

"The closing dinner is tomorrow night, so why don't you come to my place tonight, and we'll order in?" I ran my fingers across the top of his hand.

"I should probably stay here. There's no time to waste if I want to make that transfer happen."

"Well, I'm going home. So, text me." I could feel Marnye's eyes through the glass.

"Okay," he said. "I'll let you know. Feel better." He let out a monster yawn.

"You should get some sleep too. Isn't it like midnight your time?"

"Don't worry about me. I'll be fine," he said.

It would be my first weekday afternoon alone in our apartment. I sat on Rae's futon, reading the news and sipping her tea. Two things grabbed my attention: highlights from President Trump's impeachment hearings and the stock market's reaction to the spreading Coronavirus.

When Rae got home from work, she jumped a little at the sight of me. "What are you doing home?" she asked, pulling off her hat and gloves. "Are you okay?"

"I feel gross," I said, looking down at my screen, although we both knew it took a hell of a lot more than that to excuse my absence from work.

"Did you talk to David?"

"Yeah," I said, but I couldn't tell her what he wanted me to do. "Um, so Grant is back from Hong Kong for the AgriGlobal closing dinner and might come over later, so it would be really cool if you could give us a minute."

"What? He's in New York?" Rae asked happily, but her expression quickly shifted to one of suspicion. "Weird timing, don't you think?"

"I guess."

"Seriously, Bets?" She stared as if I was clueless, giving the big bad wolf directions to my grandmother's cottage. "Grant, who loves you, is back from Hong Kong, working with David, the father of your unborn child, and you're here reading? What is going on?"

"Except David's not here, he's in Cleveland."

She scrunched up her face and I shrugged in reply, hoping to convey that it was just too complicated, and I was not in the mood to discuss it any further. "So, yeah, it would be awesome if you could clear out, maybe for the night so Grant and I can work some things out."

She raised an eyebrow. Neither of us had ever made such a request before, but I knew that wasn't why she was indignant. "Are you going to tell him?"

"Who?"

"Tell Grant that you're pregnant!"

I looked at her with an expression that said mind your own business.

"Okay, I was planning on having dinner with Lucy anyway."

"And why, by the way, are you still stringing Ethan along while you're dating Lucy?"

"What?" Now she was the one staring me down.

"So, would you mind spending the night at her place?"

"Seriously?"

"Believe me, she'll be thrilled." A snarky jab to deflect what was going on with me.

"I'm just going to say it, Bets. You are being a complete bitch."

"Yeah, I know, but this is getting messy."

"Fine," she said with tightened lips, slamming the door to the bathroom. As she was leaving, Grant texted that he was on his way downtown. I buzzed him up and listened for his footsteps on the stairs. There was a lengthy pause before he knocked, and when I opened the door, instead of beaming his signature smile, he rubbed puffy eyes.

"Hey," I said, pulling him inside.

"Hey."

"You look beat. Want me to order some food?" I went for my phone.

"Nah." He looked pale and a little shell-shocked.

"Something to drink?"

"Shit, Bets, I have no idea what is going on. David never showed up."

"Really?"

He walked across the room, gesturing with his hands. "He called, but it was so strange," Grant said. I sat down at the kitchen table while he paced. "I told him I wanted to transfer back, but he kept asking me about you."

"Me?"

"He said, 'No need to be modest, I know about you and Bets. Don't you want to spend time with her while you're in town?' I kept trying to steer the conversation back to the future of the Hong Kong office, but he wouldn't listen. 'I'm sure you don't have time to date in Hong Kong. Why don't you go downtown to see Bets?' I mean, what was he getting at? And how did he know you were home and not at work?"

"Marnye?" I was trembling but had been working up the courage all afternoon for this very moment. Seducing him seemed like it would be easier than telling him the truth. How could I tell a talented guy on the road to a lucrative career he was somebody's puppet?

I wondered if I should kiss him.

"David couldn't focus at all," he said. "I mean, my flight back to Hong Kong is in forty-eight hours, and I want to get whatever he needs done, but he can't even explain it clearly." Grant was accustomed to his work ethic opening doors. He assumed his single-mindedness would result in David making a call so he wouldn't have to board the fifteen-hour flight back. "It was as if by mentioning your name, David was testing me. And I figured if I abstained from temptation, I'd pass. Maybe after our weekend in Rhode Island he needs to make sure M&A doesn't get mired in scandal."

"Yeah, that's probably it." Beads of sweat collected at the back of my neck. I had never seen Grant so unsure of himself.

"It was just such a weird conversation, but given the jet lag and everything, I must have missed something. He's the one who always preached the deal before the woman."

"Why don't I order us some food and then we can just relax?" I took his hand in mine, coaxing him toward a chair. If I could only get him off his feet maybe he'd be open to a wacky scenario that would get him home.

"Hmm, I don't know if I should be here." He turned his gaze toward the wall of windows like it was just dawning on him he had never been in my apartment before. Under normal circumstances he'd be taking in all the details, pointing happily to the postcard from Thailand sitting next to my pillow.

"Why?"

"I don't know. It's not that I don't want to be here." And he turned on his laser beam stare. "Something is telling me I should be at the office." I ran my hand through his soft hair, but he stepped backward.

He was unreachable. Even if I threw myself at him, it was obvious he would recoil. If I told him the truth, he wouldn't believe me. A wall was already going up, a defense mechanism to protect his psyche from a blow he wasn't prepared to take. He had been one of the most promising associates at First Provident, had put his life in David's hands long before I showed up, and for me to tell him David didn't have his best interests at heart, that marrying me was his best option for survival, well, who wouldn't have resisted that? I didn't want Grant to feel wronged, like his well-plotted life was unraveling. Or at least that's what I told myself. I told myself that by saying nothing, I was protecting him. Oh, Sol, what was wrong with me?

"Bets, you know how much I want to be with you, don't you?"

"Yes," I said, hugging him, but the fact that he hadn't even taken off his overcoat spoke volumes. His skin was clammy and his eyes were bloodshot. He was rigid in my arms. As he headed toward the door, Rae's voice rang in my head pleading for me to tell the truth. I only had a split second before he'd be down on the street. But the world expected a lot from people like Grant, and he expected a lot from himself in return, and it all hinged on the delusion that he controlled his own destiny. Even Rae had to understand nobody likes to feel the fool.

I kissed him on the cheek and said, "Go back to the office. I'm sure David will be back soon."

"I know you were looking forward to me staying over, but thanks for understanding."

"Oh yeah, I mean, I wanted you to stay if you wanted to stay. It's not a big deal."

"Okay." He squeezed my hand. "People will be getting to work in Asia soon, I need to log in to what's going on with Pacificorp. I can take a nap on the cot in the copier room."

"Get some sleep, Grant," I said. "Maybe we can hang out after the closing dinner."

I was glad to wake the next morning alone in my apartment. I didn't know what the day would bring, but in the morning light I was relieved I hadn't gone through with David's awful idea. I still wanted to find an opportunity to tell Grant the truth, but I wasn't filled with the shame of being a complete asshole. Not yet, at least.

I went to the office late only to leave before five to make sure all was in order for the dinner. Lenore had reserved a private room at a French restaurant on the east side named after a frog. We would be a party of twelve and I arranged the place cards so that David and I were at opposite sides of the round table. I put a gift-wrapped memento at each place setting. Lenore helped with the menu as she knew exactly what David liked at each course.

I was busying myself with my phone when Roland arrived with his CFO and lawyers. I led them into our mirrored and gold-leafed private room where servers brought out canapés on silver trays and took drink orders. Roland took me for a hostess at first, not appreciating that I was the analyst who ran the numbers on his deal until I cited the acquisition price as well as the divisions he needed to sell off in order to make the returns work. "Well, what do you know?" he said, and I made a mental note that a career in agriculture might not be a good fit either.

David and Grant arrived together and got right to work celebrating Roland as the man of the hour. Despite the names on the place cards, David kept Grant on his left and Roland on his right as if pouring on the charm was all that mattered. Marnye wedged herself between two lawyers, and about halfway into the entrée course, David made a toast to Roland's foresight and courage, and everyone clapped while they shook hands.

I stared over the floral centerpiece in David's direction for what seemed like minutes. He had to feel it but withheld his eyes from mine. All the while, he cut into his meat and tore at his bread in a way I'd never seen. He didn't wait for the server to pour the wine either but kept filling Grant's glass and then his own. I had a momentary desire to get good and drunk myself, but I was already internalizing the responsibilities of motherhood, that it would be me and me alone raising my child. This is as good a place as any, Sol, for me to remind you how unattractive overindulging can be and that it only clouds your judgment and has you forgetting your responsibilities.

When dinner was over and everyone was saying their goodbyes in front of the coat check, David approached me, dragging Grant by the elbow, their faces both red from the alcohol. He said, "Isn't it great to have this guy back?" He actually slapped Grant on the shoulder, causing him to stumble.

"Lovely toast, David," I said. "Thank you for dinner."

"I should be thanking you for pulling it all together." We finally locked eyes for a beat. He smiled somberly.

"It was nothing."

"That's not true, it was everything." We both knew he wasn't talking about the dinner. He held my shoulder and looked into my eyes with a painful expression. "We'll talk."

"Not tonight," I said as Grant teetered between us. After all the wine consumed, honest conversation wasn't going to be possible, with either of them. I telegraphed my disappointment and hurt with a frown and downcast eyes.

"No, not now," David agreed. "I'll drop this guy off at his hotel."

"I'm going home. My car is waiting," I said. I left quickly, breathing a little bit easier at the sight of David propping up Grant.

———

The next morning, I arrived on sixty at about ten thirty, relieved to see the lights on in David's office. His head tilted at a familiar angle, cradling a phone against his shoulder. But there was no sign of Grant, not in any of the conference rooms nor at the back of the bullpen. All his files were cleared off the conference table. I slinked over to Lenore's desk.

"Somebody slept in," she said.

"Yeah, I think I might be coming down with something," I said, flattening out the creases in my blouse. "So, is Grant around?"

"Ooh, sorry love. You just missed him."

"Really?" I was worried she could see my heart pounding through my blouse.

"I booked him on a flight back to Hong Kong this morning, with a layover in San Francisco. David wants him to meet with someone on the West Coast who is holding up Pacificorp."

My heart went from pounding wildly to practically stopping. I had to change the subject before she detected my shock. "Ah Lenore, I need to thank you. Last night's dinner went off very well."

"Of course. It did," she said. I looked over her shoulder to David in his office, not a strand of jet-black hair out of place. And then, as if sensing me there, he stood abruptly and began pulling the Venetian blinds in his office, turning his glass box opaque. "Oh dear," said Lenore. "He hasn't done that since Abigail passed. I wonder what's happened." I shrugged and raised an eyebrow as if I had no idea.

———

I spent an hour trying to proofread a document but kept heating up. I was mad at David for closing himself in and not making time to speak to me, but I was particularly mad at myself for not standing up to him when I had the chance. David was obviously grappling over what to do next. At the time, I discounted his worries. I was beating myself up for not telling Grant the truth no matter how brutal it would have been. I was a coward. I grabbed my coat and purse under the pretense of going to lunch. I took the elevator to the lobby and walked to the subway station. On my way downtown I received a text from Grant saying he'd just landed in San Francisco.

Me: *Be safe*

Grant: *Have to take care of some legal snags, then HK tomorrow*

Me: *Get some sleep*

I was equating rest with his overall well-being. His next text said he would be working from his apartment because the office had closed through the end of January for Chinese New Year (aptly the Year of the Rat). Local authorities had canceled the fireworks, street parade, and carnival because of the virus and many of his expat colleagues weren't returning to Hong Kong from their holidays.

CHAPTER TWENTY-THREE

I stepped out of my clothes, leaving them in a pile on the floor. I pulled down the Murphy bed, curled under my comforter, and closed my eyes. I woke up when Rae got home from work. It was dark and I was confused. "What time is it?" I asked.

"Almost six." She sat on my bed. "This is becoming a habit."

"Oh, wow, I'm really hungry." I sat up, swinging my legs out from under the comforter.

She went to the kitchen and peered in the refrigerator, its interior light illuminating the apartment. "Did Grant come over the other night?"

"Yeah, but then he went back to the office."

"Did you tell him?" She pointed to my stomach as if the word pregnancy was too hard to pronounce.

"No. And at last night's dinner he drank too much. He's on his way back to Hong Kong and David's avoiding me." I blurted out a brief synopsis of the past two days before starting to cry. It was the first time I'd shed tears in the presence of someone besides Yaya. Despite the fact I had been treating her terribly, Rae hugged me around the waist. I rested my cheek on her shoulder.

"Rachel predicted this," she said. "She said it was your responsibility to let him know and you've done that. So, let's move on and worry about you." It was so ironic. We'd embarked on this rooming relationship assuming I'd bring the fun and the friends. Who would have imagined she'd be the one taking care of me?

I stood up and wiped my eyes. "Yeah, you're right." It was time to worry about me. I'd been good at that in the past, but there I was, pregnant and not having eaten anything all day. "Let's get some dinner. I'm ravenous."

I agreed to a Mexican dive a few blocks away where I proceeded to devour a huge burrito and all the rice and beans that came with it.

"Did you go to the office at all?" she asked.

"Please, I do not want to talk about work." I wasn't sure I could count on David's protection at First Provident anymore, and I had missed calls from both Marnye and Helen in HR.

"Well, I had a good day."

"Nice."

"A senior editor singled me out."

"She liked your edits?"

"No, she actually knew my name, as in 'Rae, there's some leftover Danish in the conference room.'"

I laughed.

Rae was a proofreader at a publishing house that was located on the fifth floor of a prewar office building near Hell's Kitchen with painted moldings and strips of decorative copper artifice heralding back to an earlier era. Even though it couldn't have been more different from sixty, we both had nitpicking jobs, and in her case, one requiring good grammar. We had a good laugh over the absurdity of the most junior employees being the ones to uphold their firms' standards of excellence. We developed this game when ordering food, to see which of us could locate the most typos on the menu. Since I read Spanish, I had an advantage in a Mexican restaurant.

I may have joked about Rae being OCD but having to work in a messy office must have been the worst kind of torture for her. At first, she called it quaint, but each successive anecdote was coated in sarcasm. She was also discouraged by the manuscripts the editors selected for publication. "God," she moaned. "I don't know if working there was such a great idea. Depressing if you aspire to be an author someday."

Somewhere along the line I stopped listening and, despite all that was wrong at First Provident, mourned that I'd be leaving my analyst program prematurely. Compared to her description of the publishing industry, at least banking was transparent. There was also the magnitude of dollars we dealt with, and an urgency to the work that made it seem important.

Our waitress filled our water glasses with a vacant stare. She was about our age. I wondered if waiting tables was supporting her way to bigger things and if she considered quitting after every shift.

"Hey," Rae said. "Earth to Bets."

"Oh, sorry." I took a sip of my ginger ale. She just reached across the table and held my hand the same way Rachel had done the previous Saturday.

———

Later that night, as I stared at the ceiling, Rae asked, "What if it's a boy?"

"Excuse me?" My condition still felt tenuous and private, like she needed to be invited to speak about the baby in such specific terms.

"It's just we won't know what to do with a boy."

"What makes you think it's a boy?" We certainly were more in touch with the female realm, but it would always be easier to be the VP than the VP's wife.

"I don't know."

Rae's candle cast a dancing shadow on the ceiling. She sighed in the dark and even though I couldn't see her face, I thought she may have actually been giggling into the palm of her hand, as if sharing the apartment with not only me, but a crying infant wasn't totally out of the picture.

"I'm sorry," she said, reading my silence correctly. "I shouldn't have brought it up."

"It's fine."

"Hey, do you think I should cut bangs?"

"Always a bad idea," I said.

Months earlier it had been easy to pretend we were two girls on the threshold of adulthood, playing house and sharing our innermost thoughts before falling asleep and descending into dream worlds. She told me she never remembered her nocturnal dreams, but her days immersed in fiction provided an even better dreamworld because she could always pick up where she left off.

Even though our conversations were making us closer than I had ever imagined possible, I didn't expect Rae to wallow through this unsavory predicament with me. However, she leaned in, flirting aloud with the idea of playing auntie.

"We could definitely fit a crib in here," she said. And although I didn't respond, her loyalty filled my insides with warmth.

Overnight, the wind kicked up. I woke in the cold dark, my nose red and dripping. I reached for my phone before the sleep was even out of my eyes. Nothing from David. I dreaded the prospect of going back to the office, and I panicked at the idea of not going back to the office. My job was at risk, but what would happen if he and I had a confrontation and I broke down in front of Lenore and Marnye?

The silhouette of Rae's sleeping form across the room was almost angelic, her creamy skin radiating the light glowing through the window. At the restaurant she had shared that she wasn't sure how to break up with Ethan.

"It's hard to tell guys something they don't want to hear," I said.

"And also because he's been a nice boyfriend."

"Yeah, he's a nice guy." I'd once assumed David was a nice guy too. Now I was confused about who he really was, incredibly angry while sort of missing him at the same time. It was hard to distinguish the trembling in my chest from the hole in my heart.

Falling in love with Lucy was probably confusing too, but it wasn't keeping Rae from sleeping soundly. I envied her peaceful face. It was five thirty. I needed to pee, and I needed to gird myself for how cold it was going to be outside the covers. On my way through the kitchenette, I grabbed a sleeve of Saltines to stave off morning sickness. But it was more than nausea that morning, it was anxiety set off by Grant going back to Asia and David's sudden unrecognizability. I sucked the salt off the crackers and sipped a glass of water as the pit in my stomach grew.

I remembered Rae's words: "It's time to look out for you." I would devise a plan. Not a plan that depended on somebody texting or calling or swooping in to help. Something I could act on independently. I checked flights on my phone. I would ask Helen in HR for an extended leave, explaining there was a family emergency in Miami. I sent her an email with the subject line: *I need to talk.* Once the sun rose, I would call my mother to tell her I was coming home. No matter how hastily devised, a plan had me feeling better immediately.

Sol, I understood in that moment that if David wasn't willing to accept the truth, then I was better off without him. Gloria would be frustrated when the flow of money stopped, but I'd be there in person to pitch in with Yaya's care. She'd likely shake her head, implying she had expected as much, and then there would be Yaya's confusion and disappointment. My little cousin Ania, Tía Julia's sons, they'd all look away embarrassed, saying what a shame, I was turning into my mother after all.

I got back under the covers, holding my phone against the waistband of my flannel pajamas, so that when it buzzed, my entire abdomen vibrated. I fumbled to see the screen. *Oh God. It was him.*

My heart beat wildly.

David: *Please come downstairs*

I froze before sitting up to peek over the windowsill. The Mercedes was parked in front of our building, its headlights shining in the dark. I searched the kitchen table for my scribbled script and did an abbreviated run-through. I'd tell him what

DAUGHTER OF A PROMISE

a disappointment he was, ask him how he could be so cruel to Grant. With all the consumer DNA testing on the market, he was an idiot to think his lie wouldn't come out sooner or later. Most of all I would tell him: I was determined my child not enter the world an imposter.

Bets?

Coming, I wrote, fishing my slippers out from under the bed. I pulled a winter coat over my pajamas, repeating my lines as I descended the stairwell. I was going to tell him he was a terrible person. He needn't worry about me or his unborn child because I'd just booked a ticket to Miami and was leaving later that day. My heart was once again pounding in my chest.

Raindrops shone in the glare of the car's headlights, giving the street the aura of a movie set. Its engine was running, its wipers swooshing back and forth, clearing beads of water from the windshield. When I stepped under a streetlight, Lance emerged from the driver's side, opening an umbrella. He escorted me to the rear passenger door. I peered into the dark interior, not entirely sure which version of David I'd find, the hard-nosed, negotiating David prepared to give me a dressing down or the predawn David who liked to laugh and cuddle.

I slid across the leather seat as Lance shut the door. He remained outside under the umbrella. I shook out my hair, letting it land in front of my eyes, and remained silent. When David and I eventually looked at each other, his face was full of contrition, embarrassment even, and the ball of fury I had planned to unleash began to shrink.

"I'm so sorry," he said.

I crossed my arms against my chest.

"First, I was shocked. And then I just panicked. I panicked." He rubbed his eyes. I frowned.

"I was also concerned, sure for both of us, but most of all for you." I shook my head, unconvinced my welfare had been his concern.

"Have you seen a doctor yet?" He took my hands, trying to pull me closer.

"I am so mad at you!" I was fighting back tears. I hated to cry, but similar to anger, it was a default reaction I could seldom control.

"I know," he said. "That was a stupid solution."

"A solution? This isn't like work where you call on Grant to solve your problems. Pregnancy is not a problem to be solved."

"Your reputation," he said, shaking his head. "Grant is your age . . . it would have been so much more natural."

"You have been so dishonest, and you were expecting me to be dishonest!" My thoughts flashed to AgriGlobal and all the variations of the deal he had come up with. There were a dozen scenarios we could have offered Roland to solve his year-end earnings problem. Maybe playing both sides against the middle was David's approach to everything.

"I know, I'm sorry. It was terrible."

"You know how unstable Hong Kong is. You need to bring him home."

"Look," he said. "Give me some time. If I keep moving Grant around, it will only draw attention. I'll find him a place. If not within First Provident, then somewhere else."

While David tried to convince me Grant hadn't been sent off carrying his own death warrant, I tried to remind him he had the power to make whatever he wanted happen. "Please Bets, we have something more important to discuss," he said, pressing a palm against my stomach. Of course, we did. It's all I wanted to talk about, but my stewing anger made it hard to know where to begin. Returning to Miami and living with Yaya would be good for the baby, but deep down I wanted my child to have a father, even worse than I wanted a father for myself.

———◆———

Sol, there's something else I need to point out about that early-morning interaction. You see, sitting in that plush back seat, whether I fully comprehended it or not, I wielded a lot of power. Harvey Weinstein's trial had begun days before, and the climate in New

York was one of zero tolerance around sexual impropriety in the workplace. The jury had been selected and the prosecution made graphic statements. And although his defense team argued all the sex was consensual, even part of a "loving relationship," the prosecutor painted him as a seasoned sexual predator. God knows David was aware the media would jump all over the parallels. I've said it before, taking David down was the last thing on my mind. I did truly care for him, and from what I'd already seen of the world, attempting to ruin men like David came with a price.

"Do you want to keep the baby?" he asked, breaking our silence.

Quietly, I said, "Yes." He nodded as if he thought as much.

He said, "I care about you, Bets. A lot. But honestly, what's been keeping me up these past several nights is . . . well, I know this sounds terrible, but it's just I've created so much at First Provident. And then there's my relationships with my children. I want to do the right thing by you, but I'm scared to death."

That he could acknowledge his self-centeredness gave me a glimmer of hope. It was as if he'd taken the first step on the road to recovery. Ridding himself of his "Master of the Universe" syndrome was going to take a lot of work, and in the back of the car his narcissism was still reducing everything back to its effect on him.

"You have to get over yourself," I said. "My first concern is my health and that of the baby. I'm going to Miami."

"No, wait," he said. "I look at you and on the one hand I feel ashamed, and on the other, I hear Abigail's voice assuring me from her deathbed that everything happens for a reason." His back shuddered as he caught his breath. "I think of how she would want me to behave. Her memory sent me here this morning. I am not proud to say it, but if left to my own devices, I would opt for self-preservation every time."

I was immediately grateful for each one of her photographs gracing his bookshelves. He sniffled into the back of his hand and wiped his tears with his sleeve. "Please don't go," he said. "Please don't leave. I want . . . I want to take care of you."

Boom. Not I love you, I want you, I need you, but I want to take care of you. Until he spoke those words, I had no idea what their impact would be. I understand now that nobody can do such a thing, Sol, nobody can take care of you, anticipate your every need, not really. Protection begins with good intentions but eventually becomes superficial, or suffocating, or controlling, or patronizing, and then all you can do is get angry at the person you've become dependent on. Remember this, Sol, only you can take care of you. But dear God in that moment, in the back seat of that car, after the week I'd just had, with life getting harder by the minute, "I want to take care of you" was exactly what I needed to hear.

"And I don't just mean financially, I've been through this birthing thing a time or two. You'll want a partner," he said.

Rachel may have gone on about the power imbalance, the impossibility of consent. "Yes, you willingly crossed the threshold," she'd said. "But turning down an invitation to his apartment would have come with professional consequences." She told me the patriarchy had made me sick in the head and I'd never be able to see how much I'd bought into the system, but she couldn't understand what it was like in the back of that car with the sun rising and David wrapping me in his protective embrace. No Rachel, I will never see it as rape, my baby will not be the product of a rape.

I leaned into him and pinched the thin skin on the back of my hand to make sure I wasn't still asleep under my covers with Rae a few feet away, having one of those realistic dreams that can happen between getting up early to pee and when the alarm wakes you up again.

CHAPTER TWENTY-FOUR

You obviously know, Sol, I wouldn't board the flight home. Yaya and Gloria would be none the wiser when it came to my pregnancy, until much later at least. Instead, I'd go to work and meet with Helen. Since Marnye had evidently filed a report about the Rhode Island weekend, I assumed Helen had already formed an opinion about me. I sat across from her glossy, pinched face.

"Will our conversation be confidential?" I asked.

"Of course." I doubted that was true, but David agreed telling her would throw her off our scent. "Lenore said you've been in and out all week. What's going on?"

"I'm pregnant. Due in August."

"Oh. I see." She peered across the desk, as if searching for physical confirmation. "And is there anything else you would like to report?"

My acting background came in handy. "Like what?"

"As in, how you came to find yourself in the situation."

"I had sex, Helen."

"What I'm asking is whether a coworker put you in this situation."

"I didn't come here to discuss the baby's paternity," I said. "I want to talk about my last day and my health coverage afterward."

"As you can imagine, I don't run into this kind of thing with analysts very often. Most young people value the opportunity, show up ready to make the most of their two-year contract." I wanted to say, "Go to hell, Helen," but swallowed hard. I heard the sound of doors closing, and all I could think about was my mother after my father left, going to nursing school while Yaya took care of me.

"But my coverage?"

"You'll have a year under COBRA."

"Alright."

"Do you want to work up until your due date?" she asked as if the idea was very distasteful.

"I'd like my last day to be May first," I said, hoping for close to a year's tenure on my résumé. Given my build, people wouldn't remark if I gained weight. They would assume the lifestyle was catching up with me.

I may have worn a strong face in Helen's office, but I got teary as I rose to leave. She really took the human out of human resources. This was life and shit happened, but I guess shit didn't happen to type-A Ivy League overachievers. I had to keep telling myself I didn't care what she thought. I inhaled deeply, remembering David's promise to be there for me. I would work at First Provident until the first of May and then figure out what to do.

The rumor mill must have been working because bagels with cream cheese started showing up on my desk along with casual offers to bring me tea. Lenore offered me candied ginger each time I stopped to chat. Other admins searched my eyes with maternal affection in the ladies' room, their expressions saying, *I've been there.* Or, *my daughter's been there.*

Alan expressed roguish satisfaction at my diminishing role on deals. Marnye tried to explain it away. "David's punishing you for being out sick."

"Well, I got seriously burned out. The doctor said I need to pace myself and get more sleep."

"Good luck with that," she said, but just as Cubans enjoyed a protected status under US immigration law, I was impervious to her criticism. Grant's surprise visit from Hong Kong had her acting all competitive again, albeit with his ghost. I didn't tell her she needn't worry about Grant, that when he landed in Hong Kong, he'd been ushered directly into government-supervised quarantine.

———

Despite feeling bad about Grant's predicament, I gradually adjusted to my new reality. It didn't hurt that I was rested and flush with cash for the first time in my life. My bonus landed in my checking account the day after I met with Helen. I Venmoed Gloria an unexpected amount with the message, *Take Yaya out to eat!!*

Although David would send thoughtful messages from time to time, he would never raise the shades in his office 100 percent. In my mind, it was his way of flying the flag at half-mast, just enough to warn anyone who came near he had no patience for trivial matters. Or maybe he kept them lowered to block the view, knowing he couldn't be caught with his eyes on me.

I left work when the others were ordering dinner and joined Rae one evening at her grandmother's for pasta. Rachel was delighted when I helped myself to a second bowl of Bolognese. "Maybe someday Rae will have an appetite," she laughed. "It's no fun cooking for a girl who eats like a bird."

Rae and I walked home that evening, the street life especially colorful. The city was gradually becoming my own as the number and variety of experiences I was having downtown, midtown, and uptown enlarged the size of my bubble. Soon, I wouldn't be just another college grad in a training program, but a woman visiting doctors, a dinner guest, a mother pushing a baby carriage up and over curbs. I knew my way around by subway and bus, not to mention in the back of chauffeur-driven sedans. My baby and I would stroll through Central Park, breathing in the scent of blossoming trees. Maybe I'd even cross the Brooklyn Bridge, something that had been on my wish list since seeing people post their own traverse on Instagram.

That night, after Rae lit her candle, she talked about Lucy and how their relationship was definitely more than a friendship. I was glad she was trusting me with that insight since I'd begun confiding in her about everything David. She mentioned her family's plans to spend Easter at Eden with Joseph and Constance, and that of course I was invited to join.

Just before falling asleep our conversation turned to Sarah, who had been conspicuously absent at dinner. "She's thinking about suing Lyle for wrongful termination," Rae said.

"Seriously?" Even though it was an important development, I was already on the edge of sleep and a dream that would become particularly psychedelic, one of watery worlds where I floated on my back and was showered under waterfalls. I met up with David in coral caves with sandy bottoms. He was younger, but I still knew it was him.

———

The next day, I arrived on sixty to find Nathan sitting at the back of the bullpen. Even though I was used to him hanging around, waiting for David, he made me uneasy.

"Hi Nathan," I said, straightening a pile of graphs on my desk.

"Hello to you."

"Looking forward to spring training?"

"Still a little ways off."

"Can I help you with something?"

"No," he said. "I just came up to see for myself."

"See what?"

"To see you," he said. "To see how it's going."

"Oh, it's going okay," I said with mock cheer which, thinking back, I'm sure came across as childish.

David popped his head through his door. "Nathan? Nothing's on my calendar, did I miss something?"

Nathan stood up "No, no. Just thought we might grab a cup of coffee."

There must have been something in his tone because David grabbed his coat without protest. "Bets, why don't you join us?" Nathan asked.

"Are you sure?" I replied, sensing David's confusion.

"Absolutely," said Nathan.

I feigned a casual reaction to the most unusual of invitations, hoping we weren't being watched. We stood silently in the elevator, and out on the sidewalk, Nathan led the way to Ground Central Coffee on Madison. There was not enough room for us to walk three-abreast, so David kept astride with Nathan as I followed. I listened for normalcy in their small talk, something about the ups and downs of the market, even though I couldn't shake the feeling David and I were walking the plank.

Nathan found a corner table in a quiet back room and surprised me by mentioning President Addington at Lyle College. Ah, I thought. That's why he invited me. Lyle College. "Rick's in hot water. Didn't expect the life of a college president to be so fraught with controversy. First there were those stories in the news about PETA demonstrators and now Black Lives Matter have spotlighted the fact no people of color sit on the board of trustees and only two people of color are on the faculty. I think the headline was 'More than Snow is White at Lyle.'"

"Well, Bets has the inside scoop," David said. "Her friend's mother is the dean who's been keeping Rick's bed warm."

"Was," I said.

"Huh?" David turned.

"Was the dean and was keeping his bed warm. She's since been terminated and has moved back to the city."

"Right but tell Nathan the story."

I was embarrassed by his flippant betrayal of our pillow talk but went on, nevertheless, beginning with the vivid details of Ann Campbell and her cockapoo being attacked on the cross-country trail. I explained how President Addington expected Dean Stern to "take care of things" and the terrible incident of a coywolf dragging a child from his backyard by the hood of his sweatshirt. David looked at Nathan's face expectantly, anticipating delight at a well-told story, a drama replete with violence and illicit sex.

"Addington made Dean Stern the scapegoat," I said. "It was convenient too, since he had no further use for her. It was all very sad. I think she plans to sue."

"I'm sure old Johnstone will love having to rescue Rick yet again," said David.

Nathan raised an eyebrow while stirring creamer into his coffee. "A coywolf?" he asked.

"Yes, they're a hybrid species undeterred by human boundaries." I sounded like a biologist.

"Stalking vulnerable prey?" Why was he dwelling on the inane details?

I nodded. He bore his eyes into David, who looked around the café and toward the door, anywhere but in Nathan's direction. Finally, after a long silence, David ran out of distractions and had to stop avoiding the conversation at our table. He said, "Terrible, isn't it? He let the sharpshooters loose."

"Yeah," I said, the conversation feeling surreal. "President Addington paid vigilantes to raid the dens."

"But get this, Nate," David said, grinning. "This is the best part." He pointed to me as if I'd forgotten to deliver the punch line.

I said, "President Addington advertised one hundred dollars per coywolf pelt, so hunters were coming in from all over New York State, some even passing off the skins of large dogs, lining up to get paid."

"Now the town's pets are in even greater danger." David laughed. "The guy never did understand market incentives."

"But it sounds like the wolves are having the last laugh," Nathan said.

"Exactly!" David slapped his hand on the table.

"Just like you," Nathan said.

I froze, although looking back, who couldn't see it coming?

"You, David, are a coywolf."

"Me?"

"While Helen was busy investigating Betsabé and Grant Schafer, I put the pieces together. You dispatched him to Asia then lured Betsabé into your den. I just received word he's tested positive with the Coronavirus. And is it true? Betsabé is with child?"

David was silent.

"Forget sharpshooters, you're killing yourself," Nathan said. "What the hell were you thinking? Don't you watch the news?"

David pressed his lips together and his knee began to shake under the table.

"How would you feel if a man your age preyed on Tamara?"

"Nathan, I . . ."

"Don't play the innocent with me."

"Nathan," David said vehemently, looking around to make sure nobody was listening.

"Enough." Nathan's tone carried the weight of a club. "Speaking as your counsel and your oldest friend, please listen when I say there will be consequences. For both of you."

I shivered at the word "consequences."

"The problem is you've always considered yourself above the law."

"Nathan, not here."

"You'll have to resign."

That last word was hurled like a cannonball he knew would injure David the most, but what struck me was the way he accused David with absolutely no regard for the role I played. It was insulting, but as Rachel and Rae had suggested, victimhood was the popular narrative, mine for the taking.

"Nathan, wait," I said. "It wasn't like that. I wanted to be with David." He pushed back from the table. Maybe it was Nathan's legal mindset that had him considering the worst case, but he couldn't get beyond one party trying to get the other to do something against their will.

"Who's to say you won't change your tune after calculating the payday you could have coming?" he said. "Besides, if the press gets wind of it, they'll turn this into whatever they want." He painted an arid, toxic landscape with no love in the equation at all.

I never dreamt of going that route even if it would have been satisfying to sit across the negotiating table from Nathan and Helen in HR and stick it to them. Forget pawning the diamond earrings, I could have laughed all the way to a bank in Miami telling Gloria she could quit her job. But that's not who I was. That's not who I was and not who I am. Even though David gave me plenty of reason to be angry, I would remain loyal to that truth.

"Stop," David hissed. "I admit it. I'm guilty. But leave her alone."

"I'm sorry but keeping you out of the papers is what I get paid to do."

"Nathan." David was seething.

"Please tell me you've seen this movie before—Roger Ailes, Geraldo Rivera, Charlie Rose?" Nathan asked. "Retire, resign, however you'd like to phrase it. I need to protect First Provident."

David grit his teeth. "I'm not having this conversation now, and I don't need to have it with you."

He stood up, punching a message into his phone and knocking a chair aside. "We have work to do. Lest you forget who generates the fees that keep this gig afloat." I was overcome with an instinct to protect my protector and followed David out of the coffee shop, unsure of what would happen next. When we turned the corner, his car was waiting with Lance behind the wheel.

He held the door open for me and before he could completely shut it behind him, Lance pulled away.

"I'm sorry about that," I said.

David cradled his head in his hands. Nathan's dressing down had not only sounded alarms but triggered some inner wound. After all the acrimony with his father-in-law and brothers, Nathan was the one male friend David could count on. I'd witnessed their backslapping, ribbing over their squash rivalry, the contentment on David's face when he returned each evening from the club. I trembled, picking at some loose stitching on the hem of my skirt while I waited for him to say something. "I mean I don't think either of us want there to be a scandal," he said, pulling the handkerchief from his breast pocket.

"I don't plan on creating a scandal," I said.

"What about your friends? What about Grant?" Paranoia rose in his voice.

"Grant knows nothing. He's in some communist government lockdown in the midst of that goddamned virus."

David looked at me with fear in his eyes and I sat back against the leather seat. I took a deep breath and held his stare. I recalled Marnye's crumpled frame in the ladies' room telling me you couldn't have ambition and love, and the emails implying working mothers at First Provident needed a support group. I took David's twitching hand in mine and summoned a confidence I didn't realize I possessed. "Look, just because Nathan knows I'm pregnant, nothing's changed. You have my word. I'll work at First Provident until May first and then I'll be gone."

He chewed his lower lip, unable to meet my eyes.

"I won't come near you," I said, determined to see this through my way. "I'll spend every night in my own bed with Rae as my witness."

He picked at a fingernail and looked toward the street while Lance inched the car through stop-and-go traffic. He could have been thinking about asking Lance to keep driving until they found a spot to dump me, but I took his chin in my hand and made him look me in the eyes. "Hey," I said in my silkiest voice. "Nathan still loves you, he just totally freaked out." It was an oversimplification for sure, but that's how you talk someone off a ledge.

"Loves me," he grunted.

"Come on, you guys have so much history. He'll always be there for you. Now I am going to get out of this car and go back to work. By the time this baby is born, nobody will even remember who I am."

He shook his head like what he was agreeing to was completely insane. "Okay, but no chitchat. May first and not a day longer."

PART III

CHAPTER TWENTY-FIVE

When I replay that scene in the coffee shop or even in the back of David's car, I'm struck by the strength I showed. Sure, I was of consenting age, day in and day out playing the role of investment banker, but it's clear to me now that I was an unformed adult making things up on the fly. In the parlance of the theatre, pure improvisation. The funny thing is David claims he never saw me as anything but smart and self-assured. He said it would have been an insult to suggest I wasn't capable of making important life decisions on my own. I understand now that he needed to see me as strong and mature beyond my years, that my agency in our relationship was critical to the story he kept telling himself.

My memory, however, is shifting. It stings to describe myself as naïve, but remember, Sol, I'm writing this to explain what it was like to be me, because even the most wavering of voices deserves to be heard. I was in over my head, but not so much that I couldn't appreciate the sensitivity of the situation. I was under the impression, however, that if I stayed in the shadows and resigned from First Provident in a few months, everything would blow over. There was no way I could have known things were about to become even more complicated.

David said that if he hadn't been so damned preoccupied by Nathan's ultimatum, he would have seen it coming. After all, he credited his success to keeping his ear to the ground and sensing the winds of change. Anticipating breaking news, he said, was how you made money.

I felt sort of stupid too, having assumed that any event of significance would be first known on sixty. David did a good job of convincing us that because we made the lion's share of the firm's profits, we were smarter than everyone else. It wasn't until much later I'd understand his success was due to him being a white male, born at a certain time, and, of course, marrying well, and not because people in M&A belonged to a brain trust.

My desk may not have been surrounded by news tickers, but I read the paper every morning and had been texting with Grant as he went through the gruesome stages of his illness. *Oh GOD Bets, I am sweating from the palms of my hands.* I thought it was incredibly bad luck, as in what were the chances of knowing someone who actually came down with it? The virus was shutting down what was left of Hong Kong, but there was a time I refused to believe it would ever migrate to New York, as if germs needed passports.

But of course, as you know, it came.

On March first, the first confirmed case was reported in New York and the World Health Organization issued "the highest level of alert." Lenore said that N-95 masks were no longer available on Amazon and hand-sanitizer supplies were depleted. I didn't even know what an N-95 mask was.

"But seriously, stocking up wouldn't be such a bad idea," she said.

"On what?" Rae and I kept barely anything in our little refrigerator.

"Um, like food. I don't know, drinking water?"

A travel advisory came out from Nathan's office with a missive to "wrap things up" and return safely to the home office, but with the end of the first quarter thirty days away, people were by and large deleting that message. Marnye was going on about good numbers in the first quarter boding well for our bonuses.

That night, settling into bed, all Rae could talk about was keeping our apartment germ free. I tried to put her worries in perspective as she was certifiably OCD, but as you now know, I had a way of going into denial. I'd been in crisis mode for over a month, and with the spreading of the virus, it felt like everyone else was just catching up. There were even moments I considered the public health emergency a welcome subterfuge, something that might make a surprise pregnancy no big deal.

———————

That Wednesday I sat at my desk, reading about the CDC's lack of testing capacity and ill-preparedness in general. I spent a lot of time refreshing Twitter and doom scrolling. I texted Grant, *Are you feeling better?* My heart raced waiting for him to reply but then I remembered the twelve-hour time difference and hoped he was sleeping.

I stopped by Lenore's desk on my way to the ladies' room. "Does he seem concerned?" I asked, nodding in the direction of David's office.

"As wound up as ever."

"But like, are *you* concerned? What do you think is going to happen?" I yearned for a veteran New Yorker's perspective. How was this epicenter of commerce in which we all lived and worked in tight proximity going to survive wild contagion?

She looked up from her screen with an expression that said, "Do you really want to know?" It hadn't sunk in all she was living with, raising children as a single parent while keeping up with David's incessant demands, searching for ways to get Tamara home from Switzerland and having to act happy about it.

On Thursday David sent me a text: *Are you being careful? Are you still riding the subway?*

I looked up from my phone and caught him staring from his office door. It felt important to appear tough, to throw off a sarcastic smile and give him a thumbs-up. Of course, I was nervous, but yes, I was riding the subway. Even though my bonus had been a lift, daily cab fare would eat away at what I was saving for Yaya.

Ethan called later that day. "What the fuck, Bets. Insanity. I had a trip to the Bahamas planned, but now I don't know if I should go." He and a slew of other analysts were hoping to blow their bonuses on an upscale spring break–like trip. It was their reward for turning their lives over to First Provident and they needed amazing Instagram posts to show to the rest of the world it had been worth it.

"I don't know what to tell you." I knew Rae was counting on him leaving town, maybe having a fling while he was away to make breaking up easier.

"So, how's the air on sixty?"

"Same shit you're breathing down there."

"Oh hey, gotta jump." I wondered how much time it took to keep up the image of being everyone's best friend. His bursts of social mania only contributed to the ream of notifications coming over my phone. The ever-evolving news cycle was seriously messing with any sense of equilibrium I'd achieved over the past month. There was also the political news. I'd grown up under the impression there were adults in charge, and the scariest realization was that there was no coordinated effort facing down these problems. I desperately needed someone to tell me things were going to be alright.

The following Monday, Lenore met my reflection in the ladies' room mirror with an eye roll. "What is it?" I asked.

"His ex-wife's hosting a Purim Party and I guess it's a command performance."

"Purim?"

"I know, right? With everything that's going on! He's in quite a mood but Tamara's beside herself about returning early from Geneva and she put her foot down. Told me she baked those special cookies. It's not even nine o'clock and she's already called three times. Wants me to book a private jet back to Switzerland for the summer term. I'm like, hello? The border is closed."

"She bakes?"

"Supposedly."

"Hard to imagine."

"You said it, not me." I held the door open and we shared a laugh over David, the king of Wall Street, a man who declined five invitations for every one he accepted, having to attend his ex-wife's Purim Party while the world fell to pieces. Besides his schedule being co-opted, I assumed his distress was the result of being in the most vulnerable demographic. Men only slightly older than him were being hooked up to ventilators.

When I got home, Rae was spraying and wiping. When her publishing house closed its office, I considered it an overreaction, but Friday morning, a blast email came through from Nathan saying all First Provident employees should work from home until further notice.

"Shit," I said, sitting up in bed, scanning group texts to see how my fellow analysts were reacting. There was a follow-up text from Marnye: *Call me at ten.*

"About time," Rae said. For the past four days, she had the windows open despite the winter temps as if the deadly germ was all over me.

"My mom and Rachel and I are going to stay at Eden with Constance and Joseph," she said. "There's probably room for you too."

I smiled politely, but if she was leaving, I'd have the apartment to myself.

In movies and documentaries, New Yorkers were united in the face of a crisis. Many of the older bankers at First Provident had survived 9/11 and I figured the coronavirus would go down as a similar albeit less severe legend, striking the city in a unique way, instilling more grit, the price we paid to live here.

When my phone rang, it was David. "Did you see Nathan's email?"

"I just read it." I swung my legs out from under the covers.

"Pack a bag. I want you up here."

I looked at Rae, who was drying her coffee mug, not even trying to conceal her eavesdropping. "David wants me to go to his apartment," I whispered, covering the phone with one hand.

She shrugged as if it not only made sense but would ease the burden on Eden's guest rooms. I returned to the phone. "Um, okay, but will it just be the two of us? Where is Tamara?" She was the only one of his children with a bedroom there.

"On Long Island with her mother. I'm sending Lance for you now."

"Give me some time," I said. It felt like the house was on fire and I needed to decide what to save. My heart raced as I scanned the room. I wanted to shower and quell that end-of-the-world feeling by checking in with Yaya. Would she quarantine at home with Gloria or with Tía Julia? I wondered who would buy their groceries. Knowing Yaya, she'd look no further than her altar, her candles, and her oils for protection, but I needed her to take this seriously. Gloria answered Yaya's landline hanging in the kitchen.

"Thanks for the Venmo, mija."

"Sure, but hey, I just wanted to make sure you weren't letting Yaya go out."

"What are you talking about?" Sometimes Florida was a different planet.

"We've been ordered to work from home because of the virus."

"Can you still send money?" Heat surged across my chest—it's all she cared about.

"For now. Look, older people are very vulnerable, and you're working at a nursing home! You should both be very careful."

"Okay, okay. I got it." Gloria would say whatever it took to keep me quiet. I called Tía Julia next.

"Oh, Betsabé. I have been watching the news. Are you okay in New York?"

"Yes, T, I'll be okay. But I'm worried about you all."

"Us? There's no problem down here. Don't you think you should come home?" Home. Where was home? Even if I could call

Miami home, the last thing I wanted to do was show up with a swollen stomach. Yaya's definition of home involved water, energy, family spirit. She bowed every morning to Mother Earth, and I could picture her shaking her head over the virus the same way she did over the rising waters, the violent hurricanes that had her boarding up windows each September. For me, it seemed home was going to be New York, a penthouse on Park Avenue no less.

At the time I thought of it as snow day, borrowed-time fun, and hoped the forced togetherness might get our relationship back on track. David's despondency after our coffee with Nathan hung over us like a dark cloud. So, I dumped a mug of water on our little Christmas cactus, hoping it was sufficient for the length of this craziness, and hugged Rae goodbye, assuming it could be as long as two weeks before we'd see each other again.

CHAPTER TWENTY-SIX

A s I'd spent the better part of four days at David's over New Year's, he hadn't felt the need to play host when I arrived. The elevator door slid open and I stepped into his empty foyer. I was a little shaken after watching two separate families with young children downstairs tossing luggage into black Escalades and leaving for "the country." While David assured me his building was the perfect stronghold in an emergency, it appeared many of his neighbors were hightailing it for safer ground.

I followed the sound of televisions and found him in his study, staring at various news channels. He looked at me with a passing smile, but remained otherwise glued to the screen, on and off the phone with fellow higher-ups at First Provident, gray old men, spectacled and with paunches. It was unappealing to imagine David as part of the old boys' network. I liked to think of him as renegade, but those old men were on nonstop conference calls, in disbelief about the country's escalating paralysis. Colleges were sending students home. Businesses were closing.

I poked my head in the kitchen to see if there was any sign of this yet-to-be-met Melanie but there was no one. I opened the refrigerator, one of those mammoth ones camouflaged behind cabinetry, and helped myself to a seltzer. I set my laptop up at the kitchen counter, preparing to dial in with Marnye. David had been dispensing orders from his study, and she'd go on to delegate my piece a few minutes later with a little editorializing. If it hadn't been so strange, it would have been amusing.

Later that afternoon, David found me at the kitchen counter, and I muted my audio abruptly to make sure she wouldn't pick up his voice.

"Don't just barge in here, she'll hear you."

"Log off," he whispered, pointing to my computer.

"Why?"

"I got you a doctor's appointment. I want you to be seen before everything shuts down."

"I'm going to see Rae's doctor next week."

He shook his head. "Len Anderson is a few blocks from here. He's the best." Another Marcel or Lance, somebody David trusted with our secret.

"Okay." Ever since I'd arrived, he'd been ignoring me, but suddenly I was his top priority. I'd come to learn how David could do only one thing at a time, carving out specific hours for business and time for well, for lack of a better word, family. When he appeared in the kitchen, focusing on me, my heart lifted. Gone was the crazy man who schemed and gone was the intimidating dealmaker. The David who came to find me in his kitchen, who made me a doctor's appointment before the world fell apart, was the polar opposite of all that.

We walked up Park to 83rd Street where he made a sharp turn around a wrought iron railing and down a couple of stairs, like it was some sort of speakeasy. I felt better, spotting the bronze plaque mounted by the ground-level door with Dr. L Anderson's name in a clean black font. David pressed the glowing doorbell and we were buzzed in, however, the office looked deserted and the waiting room was dark. The only lights shone from the end of a long narrow hallway.

"Len?" David called out.

"Hello?" a young woman replied, wearing pink scrubs.

"Uh, its Robert David." It was second nature for him to extend a hand, but the woman just stared at it. "This is Betsabé Ruiz. Len said he'd make time for her?"

"Right," she said. "He asked me to get all your information and to get films. You're in your fourth month?"

"Um," I said. "About seventeen weeks?"

I completed a health history, peed in a cup, and received a prescription for prenatal vitamins stronger than the off-the-shelf brand I'd been taking. As the nurse took down routine information, I remember the appointment feeling uneventful yet monumental at the same time. Creating a record of my pregnancy in her computer made it feel real.

"This way," she said, leading me to a room with a large monitor at one side and an examination table covered in clean white paper. She handed me a cotton gown. "Take everything off and put this on, ties in the front."

David stayed by my side, his expression turning from one of concern to one of pride. He helped me onto the examination table. The nurse covered my stomach with a cold gel and swirled a large wand over my stretched skin. A staticky black-and-white image appeared on the monitor and I realized I was having an ultrasound. There had been so much written about this milestone in *What to Expect When You're Expecting*, but there I was, like everything about this day, totally unprepared. Given what was going on in the world and in the city, I should have been grateful I was getting one at all.

"The heartbeat," she said. "Looks good."

She turned up the volume and we heard it too, like an underwater whooshing. David squeezed my hand. Yaya's face and her altar to Yemayá in our living room flashed through my mind.

"Oh, and there you go," she said. "It's a boy."

"What?" I screeched. Wasn't she supposed to ask if I wanted to know the sex? I mean, wasn't the gender reveal supposed to follow some sort of big drum roll?

"A boy?" David was elated, which surprised me. Not because it was a boy, of course, what man doesn't get excited at the prospect of a boy to carry on his tradition, but because a pregnancy that had upended his life seemed to be making him happy. Hearing his excitement made me happy, his green eyes sparkling with even more tenderness as he gripped my hand and kissed me.

"Are congratulations in order?" asked a gray-haired man in a white coat who closed the door to the examination room.

"Len, we're having a boy!" David said.

"Such a blessing." He crossed his arms at his chest. And maybe for a few seconds, the four of us were able to think about something more hopeful than the plague casting a pall over the city. "Sorry to be doing all this out of order, but I want to send Marie home. We'll be closing the office and I'll be taking care of patients remotely for the foreseeable future."

"Thanks for fitting me in," I said. "Does everything look alright?"

Dr. Anderson turned toward his nurse, who was already removing her lab coat and digging a set of keys out of her purse. "It does," she said.

"And why wouldn't it, Betsabé?" said Dr. Anderson. "You appear to be a healthy young woman. Eat well and get plenty of rest. Let Mr. David here wait on you and call my service next week to schedule an appointment in four weeks." I was buoyed by his confidence in me.

"Wonderful," David said with relief on his face, as if the likelihood of some imperfection had been weighing heavily on his mind. Maybe he wasn't entirely convinced that at his age, he had what it took to seed a healthy life.

That evening David opened a bottle of champagne with the same orange label I remembered from New Year's Eve. Since I was off alcohol, he poured only one glass, offering me a tiny sip.

"The circumstances are unfortunate, but I'm grateful you're here. This celebration is long overdue." Before reading Nathan's email, I'd been preparing for another day of us avoiding each other.

Next thing I knew, I was discussing quarantine plans with Rae, and poof, David reached in and plucked me out of my life. Sitting with him in his study and sipping champagne felt miraculous.

"But we would have been together eventually, right?"

"I was worried about what our relationship looked like to others, but we don't need to think about that now," he said. "I wasn't expecting us to be together until after your last day of work." In addition to his words, the heat from his body was as soothing as the Florida sun.

"So, how long do you think we'll be working from home?" I asked. How long will I be staying here with you, is what I really wanted to know.

"One day at a time. A toast to you, my pregnant goddess." He raised his champagne. It was true that my skin glistened and my hair was fuller than it had ever been. What's more, I finally felt permission to be happy. No more doom and gloom, at least as far as my pregnancy was concerned. I gazed at his satisfied face, his strong jaw, and the softness around his eyes. He'd been down this road many times and his wisdom was comforting. He knew what to do and who to call, had people like Dr. Anderson on speed dial, for example.

Over New Year's I'd crashed here without luggage, but this time I unpacked my small bag. Facing Abigail's empty side of the walk-in closet, it felt wrong to use her hangers, so I stashed what I brought out of sight, in drawers. I put my makeup and toiletries away in what I assumed had once been her vanity in the large master bath.

The bathroom. I know I had seen it before, but it had the same effect on me as the first time riding the express elevator or ascending the driveway to Eden. Floor tiles radiated heat and there was a steam spicket in the shower, a stand-alone soaking tub, a fancy Japanese toilet with warming controls for the seat and spritzing functions to clean yourself, an adjoining dressing room. More than Abigail's art collection or the contents of Tamara's walk-in closet, the luxury of David's bathroom was eye-opening, and at the same time a little cruel.

I moved about the apartment studying Abigail's taste as if it might accelerate my education. Her photographs, oil portraits, even the perfumes on her dresser spoke of a woman with abundant grace. One evening, David caught me in the living room, staring at a Rothko that hung over a fireplace. "Our worlds are just so different," I said, not sure how to fully express the ways in which I didn't belong.

He hugged me from behind with his chin on my shoulder. "You and I are both from humble beginnings. Remember, Miami was a shtetl of Jews before the Cubans arrived. My Bubbe and Zayde followed their friends down to South Beach and passed their days a few miles from where you grew up."

"Your money," I said, again shorthand for so much more. Because being there didn't automatically mean more cash in my wallet or access to one of the credit cards Lenore paid off every month. His abundance didn't change the fact I still worried about paying my bills, especially since my paychecks from First Provident would stop coming soon. I calculated my bank balance in my head each time I used my debit card the same way friends counted calories before every meal. "You've never been without," I said. "You don't understand how different this is for me."

"Of course, I've been without," he said, but I doubted it. "Bets, you have to stop dwelling on money. Don't be so enamored by it. It's easy come, easy go. I was in the right place at the right time." David could downplay it, but I knew bigwigs on Wall Street identified with "their number," as if it equated to their value as a human and whoever died with the largest net worth won.

I stopped trying to explain it to him, like that part of his life was in a language I couldn't speak. Instead I meditated on my safety, the health and safety of my child. I justified my uneasiness with it all "for the sake of the baby." I imagined the penthouse was a stage set, my life a piece of performance art, made necessary because we were "living in unprecedented times."

In those early days, my worries and desires blended together in rapid interplay, depending on whether I was alone in the kitchen on Zoom with Marnye, or lying against David's warm chest in bed. When I felt overwhelmed, I put myself in his hands. If truth be told, I would rather have put myself in Abigail's hands. She may have been dead and gone, but I attributed her with extraordinary power on the other side. I stood in front of her oil portrait in the living room, just as I had done with the photograph of Bunny Meister at Eden, as if it was part of Yaya's shrine to saints and Orishas, and meditated on her likeness. I prayed she would show me how to do this, how to be a woman in David's world.

CHAPTER TWENTY-SEVEN

While lockdown, sequestration, sheltering in place, quarantine, social distancing—whatever you want to call it—was strange, it did allow us to be together, avoiding scrutiny as my belly got rounder. People couldn't gossip when we entered a room, whispering about which one of us was the bigger conquest. And while you will undoubtedly run into some who will comment on your father's age, Sol, the virus meant I didn't have to be called a trophy wife, a gold digger, or arm candy. I didn't have to be his baby mama and he didn't have to be my sugar daddy.

I began kidding he'd triggered world events in order to lock me up in his apartment. However, every morning when we woke and checked the news it became more and more evident the only thing in control was the virus. And because First Provident had so much to deal with, Nathan's directive to resign seemed to have fallen by the wayside. I also used the worldwide emergency as an excuse to stop answering Grant's messages and decline his phone calls. I hoped he would chalk it up to the stress of the moment, the anxiety we all were dealing with, that he would move on and just forget about me. It was a terrible thing to do, but if I couldn't tell him the truth about my life, I didn't want to talk to him at all.

One evening, David and I were carrying our dinner dishes into the kitchen when Tamara called. After hanging up with her, he got on with one of the sons, then an ex-wife, then circling back with another son who reported on some of the others. They touched base as if David's sagacity kept them one step ahead of the danger. I didn't think it was fair that I should do the dishes while he talked on the phone, so I quietly placed everything in the sink. The way he showed equal concern for all of them gave me confidence our son would always have a place in his clan.

He eventually joined me in the study.

"That was quite the daisy chain," I said.

"It's what we did after the towers fell," he said without apology. "The family was smaller, but I still took responsibility for everyone." The office had been downtown then, close to the World Trade Center. After making sure all his employees were accounted for, David fled on foot through the ash. The way he described the city infused with a sense of duty and sacrifice, a military code of ethics, gave me goosebumps.

I never brought that trauma up again, finding it easier to talk about things like groceries and the internet. His broadband made the transition to work from home seamless, everybody suddenly using Zoom. The rest of our time, however, involved medieval foraging to meet basic needs. David tracked down pasta, rice, and canned vegetables and when deliveries arrived, I wiped them clean. Lentils, peanut butter, bread, mayonnaise, ketchup, cans of soup and chili. The randomness of what he ordered spoke of a man who'd never followed a recipe. It reminded me of those times a big hurricane was headed toward Miami and after boarding up the windows, we were happy to have cans of tuna and some mustard in the cupboard while we waited for the electricity to go out.

David let Lance, Melanie, and all the doormen stay home with their families. They needn't worry about getting laid off, he told them with the pretense of generosity, but I suspected it was to keep germs from being carried in from the outer boroughs. David made a list of who was still in residence and their phone numbers. He studied how the air circulated through the heating ducts and even took a flashlight to the basement to assess the systems and see what supplies might be down there.

While he was gone, I walked across the living room carpet, scuffing the tracks from Melanie's last vacuum, and made myself comfortable on an overstuffed couch. I poured over Abigail's art books under a reading lamp, covering my legs with a fuzzy throw blanket.

When David returned up the service stairs, he regarded me there with a look of surprise.

"Well?"

"The furnace is archaic. To tell the truth I had no idea what I was looking at." Everyone who served on the co-op board had left town and when David phoned the president, he had no advice, having never toured the basement.

———

One of my favorite things was lingering in the bathroom, watching him shave. Even if he had stopped with the meticulous dress, morning after morning he recreated that soft layer of skin with even swipes through white shaving cream, infusing the entire bathroom with his clean scent. To kiss and smell him just as he finished ignited my brain in the same way a first cup of coffee once had.

Despite the cold, we bundled up and ate our lunch on his roof deck. The city had taken on an eerie quiet. The pulsing energy that I'd once identified with Manhattan was gone. My hair blew wildly as I leaned over the crenellated edge, and I saw no moving traffic on Park Avenue in either direction. Not one horn, not even a siren. The city that never slept was in a coma.

"Rapunzel, Rapunzel," he said, and I laughed at the parallel although it was painful. He claimed we New Yorkers who stayed behind were a class unto ourselves. Obviously, most people had no choice, but I wondered if it hadn't been for me whether he would have fled to Long Island like the rest of his family. He denied it, even becoming self-righteous. "You can't just take, take, take and then leave her when she needs you the most." It was the same devotion he'd shown toward Abigail as she withered away from cancer. It was as if he'd made a vow, in sickness and in health, to New York, refusing to turn his back while the dead bodies piled up in refrigerated trailers.

One evening, while David was on the phone with one of his sons, I called Rae.

"So, how's it going?" I asked.

"Given all the people in the house, Eden's starting to feel like tight quarters." *Oh please.*

I told her about the precautions David was taking. "You should see the mask and gloves he puts on to go down to check the mail."

"See how Boomers finally get serious when they're feeling threatened?" Rae said.

"I wish they worried as much about the environment."

"Hey, guess what? Coywolves have shown up in Long Harbor."

"Seriously?"

"Yeah, our neighbor took a picture of one in her yard. He invited my mother into a Facebook group." I could picture Sarah Stern pacing about that big kitchen, aware of the kind of screwballs that populate a Facebook group. "Speaking of my mother, you might be hearing from her."

"Really?" I couldn't imagine why.

"She's filing that wrongful termination lawsuit against Lyle. Wants to salvage her reputation. It's a tough enough job market without Rick Addington casting her as incompetent."

"Okay?" I said, impressed Sarah was standing up for herself. "But what does that have to do with me?" I asked.

"Well, given how closely the two of you worked on the Sustainable Food Initiative, she was hoping you'd give a deposition. Her lawyer is trying to paint a picture of her well-roundedness on the job and he wants a strong student perspective."

"A deposition?"

"Yeah, you know. Just explain how my mom was your advisor and how closely you worked together."

"Sure, have her call me." I may have been agreeable on the outside, but inside I was nervous. Getting involved in a suit against President Addington certainly wouldn't sit well at First Provident. Even though David didn't like the man, he'd advise me to steer clear of the whole mess, that I didn't need to get involved in a legal battle or do anything that might find its way back to him.

I hoped Sarah wouldn't end up needing me. I didn't want to have to explain it to David. He had enough to worry about. Pacificorp was going south, and Tamara was calling twice a day. She was finishing the school year on Zoom from her mother's house and couldn't understand why he wasn't also in the Hamptons. "What are you still doing in the city? You shouldn't be alone." From my end, all I heard him say was, "I'm fine. I'm comfortable. How is your mother? And your brother?" But he never said, "I'm not alone, I'm with Bets. And we're good. We have some happy news."

Sometimes he'd laugh and say to her, "That's my girl," and I couldn't shake the envy at her ranking above the rest of the women in his orbit, most notably me. When I asked him why he hadn't told Tamara about me or the baby, he winced. "I just don't think she'd take it well."

"Really? I guess I see her differently." I had hoped at some point I'd have my own friendship with his daughter, not yet understanding how men created the whole evil-stepmother trope in the first place, their egos enjoying the idea of women fighting over them. It was ironic because when Grant and David both wanted me, it made me feel horrible.

"This whole Swiss boarding school idea has fallen apart, and now she's in lockdown with her mother. I really don't think it's a good time to spring this on her," he said. "And what about you? Have you told your mother and grandmother about me? Have you told them about the baby?" Over New Year's we'd laughed our families would be stunned into silence if they ever knew what we were up to, but we never dreamed a day would come when we'd have to tell them.

"No," I murmured.

"Look, let's wait until things calm down with the infection rate. It would be nice to do it in person," he said, caressing my cheek. "We'll fly down there. I'd love to meet your family." I pictured him in a white linen suit, dark sunglasses, maybe a straw hat, greeting Yaya and my mother, winning them over with his easy smile.

CHAPTER TWENTY-EIGHT

One morning, I was sitting in the kitchen, spinning about on a barstool at the big granite island scrolling through the *Wall Street Journal* while eating cereal. I dribbled some on my robe and was wiping it clean when a strange sound echoed from the service stairwell. It was the frantic barking of a dog. I cinched the tie across my middle and opened the heavy metal door.

I'd never ventured beyond the trash bin and recycling chute before but was five flights down in my bare feet when I saw a small whiskered snout poking from a doorway wedged open with a roll of newspaper. It had been Marcel's practice to use the service stairs to check on elderly residents, delivering groceries or prescriptions, and to help with pets.

"Hello?" I called through the narrow opening. When there was no response, I pushed the door farther and the little dog jumped onto my legs, its barking now a whimper. I squatted down to pet his wiry fur. The air coming from the apartment smelled like pee and there were a couple of turds by the door. "Hey, little guy. It's okay." He had pointy triangular ears with pink skin on the inside, a moist black nose, and big watery eyes that met mine right away.

I held my breath against the stench, passing through the outdated kitchen and into a dark living room. There was an old man slumped in an armchair, a blanket across his lap, his hair all askew.

The television was on but with no volume. Yaya's voice was in my ears, "Don't be afraid, Betsabé. Death is a part of life."

I took the dog's leash from a hook in the kitchen and led him back up the stairs to David's as quickly as possible. I was out of breath when I reached the top and burst into the kitchen where David stood, wide-eyed at the sink.

"Where did you go?"

"This guy was going crazy downstairs." The dog and I both were shivering. "Your neighbor on the fourth floor. I think you need to call an ambulance."

"Mr. Jensen?"

"He could just be sleeping, but given the smell, I don't think so."

"Oh," David searched his pockets for his phone.

"I'm going to put on some clothes and take him for a walk."

"I think his name is Wallace."

"Huh?"

"I remember Marcel saying, 'Morning, Mr. Jensen, Morning, Wallace.'" David didn't look too sure about letting me outside with the dog. "Bets, put on a mask and gloves."

When I returned, I rummaged some soup bowls in the pantry. I filled one with cool water and the other with half a hamburger I was saving for lunch.

"Here you go. Poor doggy," I said, crumbling the ground beef into the bowl.

It took most of that day for the ambulance to arrive. We more or less put work on hold and sat quietly in David's study, me fiddling with the jigsaw puzzle and the dog curling into himself on the carpet next to David's desk. He looked up at us from time to time, his face sad and knowing.

"I think he understands," David said. "He's been living with old Jensen since Abigail and I first moved in."

"Where's the puzzle box? I want to look at the picture."

"But knowing the answer takes away all the fun."

I'd never tackled a jigsaw puzzle without looking at the picture and chalked David's challenge up to how things were supposed to be done, one more thing he had to teach me. I'd become obsessed with the mystery behind those wooden pieces, happy for the daily accomplishment of connecting two or three.

When the ambulance eventually arrived, its siren senselessly screaming, David put on his protective gear and went downstairs. He returned about half an hour later confirming Jensen had passed. But he'd found a bag of dry dog food in the apartment and put some in Wally's empty bowl.

We stood watching the dog sniff at the food when David noticed the sink overflowing with dishes. "Oh, Melanie," he sighed. "Where are you when we need you? This place was always immaculate, and now that there's an actual mess, I have no housekeeper." His reliance on other people was irritating. It had me remembering the way I shared Yaya with families I'd never met, families who counted her as indispensable.

"You can do something about it, you know," I said.

"But where to begin?"

"We could start here," I said, opening the trash and discarding some of the takeout containers. I pictured Rae washing, drying, and putting away every dish before we went to bed. It was ridiculous how overwhelmed David was by mugs and glasses, scattered sets of chopsticks, and the green packets of soy sauce strewn about. He rolled up his sleeves and searched for dishwashing liquid and a sponge as I lined up the dirty glasses.

It was a refreshing visual, David up to his elbows in hot water. And it reminded me of a story Rae told about Bunny Meister and his neighbors in Long Harbor after the 1938 hurricane, seeking refuge from the storm in a huge mansion. They stayed for several days but took their chances leaving when the last dish was dirty. It seemed like captains of industry were happy to saw down felled power lines and rebuild homes, but when it came to dirty dishes, they were helpless.

When I suggested we load all we could into the dishwasher, David looked at me sheepishly. Seemed all the custom cabinetry in that fancy kitchen of his made the whereabouts of certain appliances not immediately obvious.

"You have got to be kidding."

"Bets, please."

"You've never opened your dishwasher?"

He wouldn't admit it aloud, but from that point on any discussion about our differences included "the time you couldn't find your dishwasher, let alone turn it on." I'd discover he had not one but two dishwashers.

Standing at the sink side by side, making our mess disappear while Wally padded about our feet felt, I daresay, warmly domestic. Until then, the richness of David's world had left me uncertain as to how to behave. But that night, restocking the shelves with clean plates and glasses infused me with hope. Even David was adaptable.

As we got ready for bed, we deliberated where Wally should sleep.

"With us?"

"No way," he said, pulling a fleece blanket out of the closet and folding it in a square on top of the chaise. "How's that?"

"But he just lost his master."

"In a few months we'll have a baby in here. The last thing you're going to want is a dog in the bed. Trust me." He spoke as if from personal experience, like he had to keep reminding me that we had a baby on the way. His wisdom in big matters could be reassuring, but when it came to a dog snuggling in the bed, well those were mistakes I wished he'd let me make for myself.

The implication he knew better wore on me, and I'd turn my back on him. It would be like that with me, on and off, hot and cold, tossing about between gratitude for his support and a corresponding aversion to it. I could melt from his attention one minute and then fly into a rage the next. One could argue it was the hormones but suggesting anything of the sort got me more irate.

———◆———

First Provident had never respected the boundary between our personal and professional lives and working from home blurred the distinction even further. All the analysts were complaining on group chats. VPs and associates expected reduced turnaround time on projects because we were locked in our apartments with nothing to do, no commutes, no distractions. I would never again be pulled in as a full-fledged member of a deal team, but Marnye sent me messages at all hours requesting target lists or research.

During a very long and boring workday, I got a phone call from Sarah Stern. My stomach sank and I considered not answering, but I'd have to talk to her eventually. "Hello?"

"Bets, it's Sarah." After some small talk, reporting on the goings-on at Eden, she made the request I knew was coming. However, she implied that it wasn't exactly a favor, that I could be served a subpoena and forced to testify, but she would never want that, of course. I assumed she knew it was complicated while I lived in David's apartment, pregnant with his child. She had to know First Provident had ties to Lyle College and Rick Addington, and I wondered if she took all that into the equation before she asked me to testify.

"I really want to help you. I do, but . . ."

"Bets, I understand the position you're in. I do. But you are the student I worked most closely with on SUFI. You were there from day one with the coywolves too. Your testimony would go a long way toward helping me make my case." What she didn't say was that having my name on her witness list would also raise red flags with Lyle's biggest benefactor. I wished she'd at least acknowledge I was her secret weapon.

"When will this be happening? I mean, I could use a little time."

"The virus has set everything back, but my lawyer will be in touch."

I rose from the kitchen table and stretched my arms overhead, trying to relieve the ache in my neck from leaning over my laptop. I wandered down to David's study, planning to tell him about Sarah's call, but he was mesmerized by cable news. I dove onto the loveseat across from his desk. "How about we make milkshakes?" I asked, an attempt at spontaneity, a chance to butter him up before telling him about the lawsuit. But he was numb from the data streaming across the bottom of the screen—numbers of positive cases; hospitalizations; deaths, locally, statewide, nationwide, worldwide. This was not the time.

The way he could ignore me back then signaled our age difference more than anything. He seemed stodgy, resisting any attempts at breaking up the workday. Once I suggested we sit in the pretty living room for a change, but he said "no." He was lucky there were no theatres, restaurants, or museums, no charity galas to which I'd pester him to attend.

While he stared at the screen, I fixated on the one window in his study shrouded in heavy drapery. Letting in the light suddenly seemed terribly important. I stood up and pulled the curtain aside and pressed my face to the cool glass streaked with soot. I crossed my arms as a new headline came across the screen. The virus was killing members of the Black and Latin community at a higher percentage than whites. The same feeling arose in my gut that I'd had during brunch with Rae and Ethan and his prep school friend who described the demise of the first woman headmaster in Dunning history. I wanted to share the outrage with people of color, but how could I rail against society's inequities and enjoy David's protection at the same time?

My mind traveled to Yaya, and how she never went to the doctor. I wondered whether Café Habana had closed and about the guys who worked in the kitchen. The overrun hospitals and ICUs, doctors playing God, having to decide who would get the ventilators. Whereas I had grown up identifying more with the people on the front lines, my life was now sheltered at the other extreme.

———

The first of May came and went and with it, the loss of my identity as a First Provident analyst. I hadn't been a meaningful part of any project for months, so it was pretty anticlimactic. Ethan, however, made a big deal of organizing a Zoom happy hour from his parents' home in Vermont. Zoom socializing was like watching a depressing episode of reality TV from which you were unable to change the channel or tear your eyes away. Sandra logged in, although with her video off. I worried she had turned into an X-ray with lung cancer. God I was a terrible friend. I sent her a private message: *How are you?*

Sandra: *Okay. You?*

Me: *Where r u?*

Sandra: *A retreat of sorts*

Me: *Me too*

Sandra: *Haha*

Me: *Hang in there*

Sandra: *Somebody told me you're pregnant. True?*

Her question jolted me. I suddenly didn't care if she knew. It was my last day at the firm, after all.

Me: *Yes*

Sandra: *Why didnt i think of that?*

Me: *Haha*

I studied Ethan's image. Any strength from his lacrosse days had dissolved into fleshy softness. His neck was thick around the collar. The swath he cut was like a flash forward to a man twenty years his senior, a well-worn posture of defeat that made me want to scream "No!" and pull him back nine months to the day we sat at the training table together, ready to leap into a limitless future.

My phone buzzed with a text from Ethan, and I imagined all the side conversations going on while we took turns speaking on the screen.

newsflash: Rae and I broke up last night.

I'm sorry, hard to keep love alive during isolation. I left it at that. In the same way I spared Grant's feelings by not telling him he was David's pawn, I spared Ethan's ego by keeping what I knew about Rae and Lucy's relationship to myself.

Facing all those lives suspended in time, a sadness swept over me. There was no forward progress on the horizon, or at least not what we'd always thought of as forward progress. We once took it for granted that college grads would be arriving in the city to apartments full of roommates and work in turnstile training programs like ours. Their arrival would mean moving on to the next waypoint on our journeys. What we wouldn't have given to be sipping nasty beer at a soulless midtown bar with Ethan.

The irony was that the Zoom happy hour had me feeling better about my situation. I put whatever embarrassment I may have felt around my relationship with David on a shelf. The formula for propriety that I'd always heard was that men could date women of an age no less than half their age plus seven, or the age of their oldest offspring, whichever was greater. However, half David's age plus seven would have put me in my thirties, and I was several years younger than two of his sons. I wondered if there was a corresponding formula for older women dating younger men, or if that phenomenon was just too uncommon. Our thirty-year age gap would confuse people, having them wonder what we had to talk about, or by the image of our naked bodies lying together. What nobody would ever understand was that we complemented each other in emotional ways that were quite extraordinary.

Maybe my life hadn't veered off course. I had jumped off the stalled-out train my fellow analysts still waited to board and was moving forward to a different station. There was a human growing inside me, and the intense grow light of 24/7 togetherness was fostering a bond between me and a caring man that defied anything I'd thought possible.

The thing is, Sol, I've never possessed the precise vocabulary to describe what David and I had. Whatever words exist in the English language, or Spanish language as far as I am aware, are inadequate, or entirely absent. And there's something about the lack of a linguistic precedent that made it feel shameful. If there had been an easier way to describe us, I think I would have called Gloria and Yaya and told them sooner.

I spent a lot of time wondering if I could tell my grandmother that I loved him. Obviously, love is not sex. People tell you that love is a verb, not a noun, that love is the act of loving. Talk about inadequate vocabulary. David gave me pleasure in many ways, not to mention feeding me a healthy breakfast every morning. He also figured out how to make a decaf cortado with the fancy espresso maker we uncovered in the kitchen. As for me, I rubbed his shoulders and pulled him away from his desk in the evening. I sat him down in front of a meal and tried to entertain him with funny videos. Those were certainly small acts of love but back then, I continued to carry around the notion that love meant being in a state of bliss, and well, that year was not conducive to blissfulness. Sol, whether you are living through a global pandemic or experiencing relative tranquility, never expect love to solve your problems or erase your pain.

CHAPTER TWENTY-NINE

David sat in his study with Wally on his lap. He was wearing headphones, and I could tell by his side of the conversation, scheduling meetings and forwarding DocuSigns, he was on with Lenore. He dropped the call, however, when another came in.

"Hey, Nate," he said, and my ears perked up. There was a lengthy silence which was uncomfortable to sit through. Impatience rose on David's face, but he continued stroking the length of Wally's back. I wondered if I should leave, but David's drooping lids said he needed me there. After a few minutes of "No, I don't agree. I just don't, we'll have to agree to disagree," he hung up and looked at me. "Helen in HR is still digging."

"Really?"

"Somebody has raised suspicion about us, and Helen called Nathan about it."

"Who?" I would never suspect Sandra. It had to be Marnye.

"He won't say. But he's adamant I step down. Accused me of retirement neurosis."

"Oh, David. It might be for the best." I still hadn't told him about Sarah's lawsuit. Her lawyer had sent me an email requesting my testimony in June, and I figured he'd take it better after cutting ties with First Provident. I softened my voice and said, "You may not see it this way, but maybe Nathan's looking out for you."

"He's a pain in my ass."

"C'mon, you've been friends forever."

"Goddamn it, I want to decide when I retire." I wanted to ask him why he felt entitled to such a luxury. I hadn't asked for a pregnancy forcing me out of the workforce, but shit happens. Look at what was going on in the world. Life's not fair, David. Of course, that's not what I said. I walked behind his desk chair and massaged his neck.

"Everything is virtual. Work's not even fun anymore," I said, lowering my voice into his ear. "No office, no lunches with clients. You're sitting here in sweatpants. Seems like the perfect time to ride off into the sunset."

"I don't want to give them the satisfaction."

"Who's them?"

"There are people out there who'd take great pleasure."

He had risen in business during an era when being a rain-maker meant being above the law. Throughout history, movies and television had portrayed powerful men doing whatever they wanted. From the time he was a motherless boy, he was taught to be tough, never to cry or express hurt. Abigail's sending him into battle every day only reinforced that. I was realizing how keeping up the façade of a warrior had harmed him. I shouldn't have been surprised that it was asking the impossible for him to surrender.

Wally jumped on the floor. "I'll take him out for a walk before dinner," I said.

"Be careful."

"Don't worry about us," I said, patting my stomach, although I still thought about what Nathan had warned that day in the coffee shop: "There will be consequences." I couldn't shake the feeling of danger on the horizon. I wasn't sure if it would come from Helen's investigation or my testifying on behalf of Sarah Stern, but something told me David needed to obey Nathan and step down soon.

I was starting to think he was too old to change but that night after dinner, he surprised me by pulling an acoustic guitar out of the hall closet. "What is that?" I laughed.

"I've been wanting to dust this thing off." He strummed "Peaceful Easy Feeling" by the Eagles and acted surprised when I joined in on vocals.

"Musical theatre," I reminded him.

He played "Hallelujah," pulling off a good baritone impression of Leonard Cohen.

We sipped wine, made music, connected a few pieces of the jigsaw puzzle, and walked Wally before slipping into bed. It was wonderful when he held me tight, encasing my womb with an extra blanket of protection. He put his arms around my growing middle as if it was a life-giving force with any hope for the future beating inside me.

I was just about to fall into a peaceful sleep when he whispered in my ear, "I love you, Bets." He had already told me that he'd fallen in love with me that first day in his office, but this was different. You'd have thought I'd have a response ready. It's not that his confession of love didn't elicit happiness, it certainly did, but it also caught me off guard. My eyes opened wide and my breath stuck in my throat just like the first time I'd entered his apartment, unsure whether I should step all the way out of the elevator.

Sol, I can't emphasize enough how scary those times were and to be in his care was a salve my being craved. And even though I still wasn't convinced it was love, it had to be close. It was possible his sentiment had been induced by the wine, or the moonlight, or the music; as for me, I tried to see our future, a glimmer of David's potential and who I might become under his influence. "I love you too," I said. He squeezed me tight and I began to understand love wasn't a feeling but a decision, a commitment to jump in the pool instead of getting thrown in.

The next morning after wiping his face with a warm cloth at the sink, he came around behind me and, again, circled his arms about my stomach. With our declaration of love still hanging in the air, my bulbous middle and distended belly button served as our altar. Our eyes met in the mirror. "Your dimples," he said, kissing my cheek. David may have said he loved me, but he also worshipped the life I was carrying. There was something about my paramount state of fruitfulness that drew him close, as if I possessed a rare and regenerative ingredient. Life continued to bring challenging moments, Sol, but the way David embraced me that morning will forever be seared in my mind as a picture of love.

———◆———

As time went on, our bodies exhibited the effects of lockdown. David grew more sinewy and I grew fatter. Maybe it was a sense of security in our relationship that had us overly comfortable, leaving the bathroom door open and not brushing our teeth right away. I told David he was too old to pull off a ponytail, that he looked ridiculous. He eventually let me cut his precious hair, concern written on his face as I stood behind him with scissors. I'd stopped waxing and shaving the places Gloria once stressed as matters of life or death, even gave up on my legs, mostly because it was getting hard to bend over.

One morning I was poking around David's sink looking for toothpaste and began reading the labels on his pill bottles. I was stunned to find a vial of Viagra. Maybe I shouldn't have been surprised, he was closing in on sixty after all, but those blue pills were like a punch.

I wondered if he took one the night in December I'd accepted his invitation for "a drink." He was not the type of man to risk poor performance, and I got a sinking feeling in my stomach that what I had told myself was spontaneous, organic, and beautiful was premeditated. The night we came together and conceived our child suddenly seemed a chemically induced violation. I stood in the bathroom holding the vial and, even though I knew it was bad for the environment, flushed the few remaining pills down the toilet.

He came to bed that evening with a book.

"Missing something?" I asked.

He was silent.

"Be less concerned with your sexual performance and more concerned with me." He couldn't meet my eyes and I began to feel bad. He wore the face of a boy who'd been caught red-handed. If the definition of love is hard to pinpoint, Sol, so is the definition of masculinity.

"Look David," I said. "Love means being honest."

"Right," he said, staring over his reading glasses. "Speaking of which, is there something you need to tell me?"

"I don't know what you're talking about."

"Ted Johnstone called. He's been advising Rick Addington on your friend's lawsuit. He's irate your name is on the witness list."

Fever flashed across my forehead. "I was going to tell you."

"You must know how awkward this is. All the parallels and then the conflict of interest? Believe me Nathan had a lot to say on the subject."

"I don't work there anymore."

"Bets," he said with reproach.

"I was afraid to tell you because I didn't want to have this argument. Sarah Stern did not deserve to get fired and I am going to stand up for her. Besides it's not for months."

"It doesn't matter. Johnstone and Nathan flagged your name." Sarah Stern was one smart woman.

"Did you take one of those pills the night you invited me here?"

"I did not. I swear," he said. "There was only one lie I told you back then." My stomach dropped.

"What?"

"Tamara never asked me to buy those Hamilton tickets. I got them for you."

———◆———

Despite a superficial makeup before going to sleep, we were both cranky in the morning. He remained irritated by the lawsuit and I was in a pique over the pills. We stood at our respective sinks, brushing our teeth, avoiding each other in the morning light. The friction only compounded when Tamara called that evening, interrupting our dinner. His family's nightly calls were becoming less about checking in and more like negotiations over who needed support, who would sequester in which of his homes, who would receive loans for their businesses. Money, it seemed, was not only how he kept score, but how he showed love. He'd hang up with his kids nonplussed, but I wondered if they felt diminished. As for Tamara, it certainly seemed she and David were reverting back into that strange daddy-princess dynamic.

"What the hell has her so unhappy?" he asked one evening after they disconnected.

"Tamara is sixteen years old. Do you have any idea how hard that is? Especially in this day and age? Cut her some slack."

"She's beautiful, she has everything she wants. What's so difficult?"

"Um, a pandemic? You act like her beauty and your money solve every problem. You act like she's a fine car or boat you're keeping in mint condition to get the best price at auction. She is a person dying to live her life. She is not an extension of you."

He raised an eyebrow, and I thought back to the times Grant and Marnye speculated about David taking Tamara on his arm for black-tie events, as if she was a surrogate wife after Abigail's passing.

"It's sort of weird, right?" Grant had asked.

"Maybe it's how he justifies her clothing budget," said Marnye.

"Maybe he's just not ready to date yet," I'd said, defending him.

But three months into quarantine and six months pregnant, I could see what they meant. It was strange.

"I'm just glad we're having a boy," David said. "One daughter is enough."

I punched him in the arm. For someone who loved women so much, he certainly didn't understand us.

———

That was about the time I began fantasizing, while out walking with Wally, of never returning. But my stomach would growl, or I'd feel thirsty and remind myself not to get all crazy. It helped to text Ethan.

Hey whatup? I wrote.

Same old, hey did you hear FP closed all Asian offices? Also Grant no longer in directory, have you been in touch?

The last time I'd heard from Grant, he was sweating through his palms in a corporate apartment, suffering all alone because of me. It was easy to be critical of David, but I needed to come clean with the shitty things I'd done. After Ethan and I signed off, I stationed myself on Abigail's chaise, the one that doubled as Wally's bed. He looked at me with his big brown watery eyes.

My breath quickened as I listened to the ring tone. I held Wally against my ribs.

"Hey." Grant sounded surprised, not happy surprised, more like when you haven't heard from someone in a long time and your first instinct is that something terrible has happened. I was just grateful he answered.

"Hey, where are you?"

"Chicago. You?"

"New York."

"Is everything okay?"

"Yeah, I just wanted to talk to you."

"I heard you left First Provident," he said, in a way that insinuated he'd heard it all.

"Yeah, I did. And what are you up to these days?"

"Trading crypto. Found an antiestablishment, go-fuck-yourself crowd. I'm extremely rich on paper."

I laughed and then just blurted it out. I told him about being attracted to David and what that led to, why I was so freaked out when he showed up in January. I told him about my pregnancy, and how that had led to me moving in with David during quarantine.

"When did you know?"

"Know what?" But I knew exactly what he was getting at. I began picking the piping on the edge of a velvet cushion.

"When did you know you were pregnant with David's baby?"

I hadn't planned on him getting hung up on the timeline. "I figured it out in January just before David sent for you."

"Fucking hell." There was a long silence on the line.

"I'm sorry."

"You asked me downtown that night for a reason, didn't you?"

"Grant, listen. I wanted to tell you everything that night, but it was hard. I'm sorry. I'm calling to apologize." I couldn't remind him what a wreck he'd been, and I'd been afraid his ego was too fragile to handle it.

He was silent, which I took to mean my apology was not accepted.

"It's not that I expect you to forgive me, but I've been thinking about you. I miss our friendship and I just wanted to say I'm sorry. Losing your job and getting hung out to dry in Hong Kong, well it was because of me."

There was silence on the line, then he said, "You miss our *friendship?* Wow," and then he hung up on me, which I pretty much deserved.

CHAPTER THIRTY

No longer having to report to work, I went back to bed after walking Wally in the mornings. David would be in his study, on
the phone or glued to his screens, and instead of reading the paper
or eating breakfast, I'd huddle under the darkness of the covers. I
expected to feel freedom after my last day at First Provident, but with
no urgent requests from Marnye, no more spreadsheets, nothing connecting me to sixty, it was hard not to feel reduced and unimportant.

Sometimes I'd sneak Wally into bed. I wondered what he was
dreaming about as he whimpered and ran in place. Was he being
chased or reliving youthful days of glory maybe off the leash in
Central Park, a squirrel in the distance? Either way, we both got lost
in dreams. *What to Expect When You're Expecting* said pregnancy
intensified them and on top of that, Twitter confirmed COVID was
making them universally more intense.

Mine were most vivid early in the morning and had begun
including vicious wolves and huntsmen, Little Red Riding Hood,
David shriveling up and blowing away, giving birth to a poodle,
Bunny Meister stockpiling beans and rice, and Yaya dancing with
Mr. Levine in her living room.

After reading a listicle online, I diagnosed myself with depres-
sion. It didn't help that my conversation with Grant was on a loop
in my head. One morning, I dreamt of him, eating lo mein in a
conference room and his chopsticks kept breaking inside the piles

of noodles. My phone began to ring. It took a while for me to realize it was real life. I answered, hoping it was Marnye or Alan with an urgent question only I could answer, but when I held the screen to my face, I saw it was Rae.

"Hello?" I answered, my voice a little groggy and dispirited.

"Hey, how are you feeling?"

I curled on my side, holding my stomach with one hand. "I don't recognize who I am anymore."

"Oh, dear."

She began filling me in on the goings-on at Eden. "Nothing changes," she said. "A house full of women who can't share the kitchen. Rachel is going back to the city."

"Well, I don't work at First Provident any longer," I said, as if I'd been expecting a condolence card. "So, how's your nitpicking—I mean proofreading—going?"

"Haha, fine I guess," she said. "I actually prefer working from home." Of course, she did. Everything worked out for Rae.

"Hmm."

"Oh, and I wanted to thank you for agreeing to testify," she said.

"I'll do my best. But it's sort of created a thing between me and David."

"I don't see why. You'll just be telling the truth."

"Yeah, no, I get that. Never mind." What was the point of explaining to Rae that telling the truth wasn't always rewarded.

"I mean she really appreciates it, and I guess I do too," Rae said. "I never knew how much she relied on her job for self-esteem." I got it. Without work, I'd lost some self-esteem too.

"It's no problem," I said, even though I resented the tension it had created in the apartment. After hanging up, I hauled my laptop onto the messy covers. Google unearthed an article in the Albany Times Union about a lawsuit pending by ousted Dean of Students, Sarah Stern. The college had obviously hired a PR firm to craft its statement, but there was little else online, likely due to the fact that proceedings were ongoing.

The Concerned Citizens of Lyle Facebook page still contained posts about the coywolf invasion; however, they were outnumbered by posts about the virus and classes going virtual. I did uncover one article in the *Union* called, "Not Crying Wolf: They Are Here to Stay," which included a photograph of a mother with her litter spread out on the grass in an otherwise empty quadrangle. "Spring has turned an abandoned college campus into a home for predators."

It was a haunting, albeit grainy, black-and-white image of the animal staring dead into a photographer's lens while her four small pups played in the grass. Her stance was upright as if to say *this is our home now,* her direct stare a warning to stay away. Besides wolves roaming campus, the article reported other wildlife venturing into town including deer and moose. "It didn't take long," it said, "after all the students left." It got me wondering what might be filling the void down on the streets below now that most of the office workers and residents had fled.

David and I sat in horror, one morning in late May, watching a YouTube video of George Floyd. He was being held in a chokehold. Three police officers stood by and watched as he begged for mercy. "I can't breathe," he pleaded. Tears rolled down my cheeks and I coughed up my cereal in the sink. I wet a paper towel and wiped my eyes and mouth before returning to my kitchen stool.

The powerlessness was overwhelming. David's eyes penetrated my phone's small screen, but there was no way he saw the video in the same way I did. I tapped "play" on the screen and watched it again, recalling the way Helen in HR singled me out for check-ins, the way other analysts looked down at me, whether it was because I was a "Lyle-hire" or because I had dark skin, I'd never be sure. I thought about all these investment bankers recruiting from the same schools year after year, looking for athletes who played the same sports they played, where the college president and the firm's chairman had a handshake. Not to mention having to endure the humiliation of being thrown in the pool, of being an against-the-odds investment banker, someone who should have been grateful to be there in the first place.

David hit pause on the video.

"Wait, why did you do that?" I asked.

"How many times can you watch it?" I didn't know, but it felt like I should have decided when we stopped watching. Up until that point, our relationship had never ventured into the arena of race. We had enough pressure with our age difference and his money. Maybe our subconscious selves had been careful to avoid ethnicity. He liked to describe Jews and Cubans as more alike than different, but his ability to decide what we should get upset about was a luxury of being white. David's closing down the video felt like his way of saying, "I don't want to go there." My getting angry was recognition that we were going to have to.

I locked myself in the bathroom and stared at my reflection. That ugly voice popped up in my head again. You can resent David, but you are living under his roof. Privilege, as I've said, was becoming another overused and indefinable word, but after that video you couldn't help but take stock. Before I moved into his Park Avenue penthouse, I enjoyed the privilege of an education. I benefited from Rae's privilege. Even my morning naps were a privilege in a world where people didn't get enough sleep.

When David popped his head in the bedroom to see what I wanted for lunch, I told him to go away. I was busy painting on Abigail's thousand thread count Italian sheets "Black Lives Matter." I draped it off the roof deck, making my statement to whomever might walk down Park Avenue.

When I came downstairs, David was holding Wally in his arms. "Hey, do you mind taking him out? I have to get on a call."

I grabbed the leash from the hook by the elevator where we kept the keys. "No problem," I said. "Also, there's a protest downtown tonight and I want to go."

"What?"

"I want to go to the protest."

"Let's discuss it later."

People were home and paying attention, and supporters of Black Lives Matter had been gathering in large numbers. "I'm going," I shouted as he walked toward his study.

Wally and I stepped inside the elevator. The sidewalk was empty, and I stared into my phone, refreshing my Twitter feed. We walked to Central Park where I sat down on the first bench I saw. New grass was sprouting as were the dandelions, trees were covered with a youthful emerald green, and clumps of yellow daffodils were scattered about, reminders that life went on, even if I was paralyzed. I began listening to a podcast about Broadway talent and where people went after the theatre shut down. I closed my eyes and turned my face toward the sun.

Being outside helped clear my head. So much was beyond my control, but I could think of a few ways to make a difference. I wish I'd had a pad on which to draw a Venn diagram. The virus and the world closing down were out of my control, but living with David was under my control, and then there were all these cases of racial injustice that seemed to reside in the overlap.

I returned to the apartment to find David pacing. "Where have you been?" he asked, his face ashen.

"Sitting on a park bench."

"You can't just wander the streets with your phone turned off." This time the fear on his face had nothing to do with the virus, but with the idea of me not coming back.

"Didn't you hear me? I wasn't wandering the streets."

"You have to think about the baby." Instead of articulating some desire to never lose me, he played the baby's safety card. "I just worry so much about you."

"How long do you plan on avoiding the real world? Hiding up here in your bubble?" I unclipped Wally's leash and draped it over the hook.

"You'll see what it's like to be a parent," he said. He was trying to be nice, but I wasn't in the mood for David knows best.

"Um. You are not my parent."

"That's not what I meant."

"Everything is just such a mess."

"I know."

I shook my head. "Please, how can you know?"

"You don't think I can feel for that man? Look, I just don't want you to go out to a protest."

"Why, because I might bring the virus back and infect you? Or because somebody might see me on the news and then God forbid, what a scandal that would set off at First Provident?"

"No, because protests can turn dangerous. They can get heated and out of control."

"I'm not asking for your permission." I started toward the bedroom.

"Wait, what about dinner?" he asked.

How the hell could he think about food? "I'm not hungry."

He leaned against the doorsill. "Ah, Bets. C'mon, I'm sorry. You need to eat."

"I'll get around to it eventually." I looked at his tired, wrinkled face and saw his age. It had been there all the time, obviously, but I had been avoiding the paradigm of the once powerful man whose mortality was making him insecure and scrambling to retain control even if it was just over me.

"You are being crazy." The accusation rolled off his tongue too easily.

"Would I be here with you if I wasn't crazy?" I yelled back.

"Look, the isolation, well, it's making us all a little crazy." It was the soft preamble to an apology, but I wanted none of it. I grabbed a carton of yogurt and a banana out of the fridge and held it up to his face. "Dinner," I said, walking into the bedroom and locking the door. I filled the bathtub with hot water, and dumped in all of Abigail's Florentine bath salts.

CHAPTER THIRTY-ONE

The phone buzzed next to the pillow and woke me from a nap. I glanced at the screen and smiled. "Rachel?"

"Where are you?"

"Uptown," I said, guarding the full truth.

"Well, I came back to the city."

"I heard."

"Anyway, I know it's playing with fire, but I'm dying to protest." Rachel was over seventy, overweight, and had high blood pressure, matching perfectly the CDC profile of people at risk.

"Me too."

"Can I break you out of there?" The implication I was being held hostage made me bristle.

"I'm getting a little stir crazy."

"Health-wise, how are you feeling?"

"Fine."

"Really, can you come down to my place?" I liked the idea of taking a few actions on my own, actions I could be proud of. "Bring a face mask and a water bottle and meet me at my apartment," she said.

"I just need to . . ."

"Please don't tell me you need his permission."

I vacillated for a second or two. Hadn't I already given him fair warning? "I'll be there around five." I took a deep breath, inching my way toward his study, the volume of his voice rising with each step. I stood in the doorway, waiting for him to look up from his screen, sensing his harried demeanor might work in my favor. He glanced over and put his audio on mute. "Do you need something?"

"Rachel needs help and I told her I'd go downtown."

David knit his brow in confusion then glanced back at his screen, his body language suggesting I'd interrupted at a terrible time. He frowned and just as I turned to leave, he stood up at his desk. "No, Bets. I don't want you to leave."

"David, I know you don't, but I told Rachel I'd be there." I hoped he wouldn't make me spell out all the reasons why.

"You can't."

"What?" Ever since I was a little girl those two words sent me into an uproar.

"You can't go."

I raised my voice. "I can do whatever I want. Don't you dare talk to me like that!"

"Bets!" he called as I hurried down the hall. He didn't chase after me but rejoined his call instead, and although that was irritating in its own right, it would give me the chance to get out the door.

I pulled a formless sundress over my head and grabbed a sweatshirt. I threw sunglasses, a mask, hand sanitizer, and a water bottle into a bag and made for the service stairs, not risking even the hum of the elevator to alert him of my departure. Wally trailed at my feet. I bent down to scratch his head. "Don't worry mister, I'll only be gone a few hours."

I grabbed a Yankees cap that hung by the back door and pulled my ponytail through the hole in the back. It whipped about as I bounced down the stairs. Turning south on Park, I slowed down and it was then I was blasted by the warm weather. David's climate control had made me soft and I began perspiring almost immediately.

I made my way over to Madison and faced more passersby, everyone masking their faces. Even though I'd seen pictures on the news, the boarded-up storefronts were shocking firsthand. It was hard to tell which ones had gone out of business with the pandemic and which ones were protecting their windows from rioters. What's more, I was used to exchanging smiles, turning heads, having an outward personality. Wearing a mask with the figure of a pregnant woman was like wearing a costume and a billboard at the same time.

Passing through midtown, I paused in front of the First Provident tower just to make sure it hadn't been another one of my dreams. My hands against the glass, I peered into the massive lobby, fixating on the corner where I'd heard David's stupid idea, the planter into which I'd vomited. No more newsstand, no coffee kiosk. I took a sip from my water bottle and inhaled the hot, wet smell of garbage on the streets. The city that had once blessed me now felt like it was cursing me, indeed an entire country that had once blessed my family had become a mockery. I was devastated and angry and scared and sad.

I stood in the very spot I'd once taken breaks with Sandra. How I missed my friends. But poor Sandra. I may have been larger than her and the other women in our analyst class, but we all shared the same burden, the expectation to have a small waist and a cute butt, to wear push-up bras, totter around on heels to elongate our legs. We could be accused of being cold like Marnye if we weren't flirty enough and we could be accused of being sluts if we took it too far. The challenge was finding the sweet spot between sensual and modest, approachable and restrained, vulnerable and feisty.

All those mornings I dressed for work, I was reconciling the way Gloria taught me to show off my shape with Marnye's suggestion to hide behind pleated fabric. It was difficult to find a compromise that felt authentic because most conventional fashion put my curves on display. The same dress rendered me confident or shameful depending on the angle of the mirror. But quarantine had freed me from all that. In fact, alone with David at his sink in the morning, I had never felt more at home in my body. Despite walking farther and farther away from him, I had to acknowledge he made me feel beautiful.

I decided it best to avoid public transportation and walked the rest of the way to Rachel's. By the time I reached her building, I was red in the face with sweat pooling in my bra.

"My God, get in here," she said as she opened the door.

"I'm so out of shape."

"You walked the entire way? That's got to be five or six miles!"

I wiped the sweat from my forehead.

"Drink." She brought me a glass of water and guided me into the living room.

"Everyone's gathering at the District Attorney's office."

"This will be good but first, let's get you something to eat. I haven't marched since the fucker got inaugurated in 2017, then I marched in DC, I marched in New York. I still have some signs in the closet." I was embarrassed to tell Rachel I'd never marched, never protested a thing.

The last time I'd been over there for dinner, she'd accused Rae and me of being "hashtag feminists." Feminism is another word, Sol, like love and masculinity for which I struggled to find a definition. I would like to think that in some form all those words have to do with caring deeply about our shared humanity, but Rachel said Millennials and Gen Z were leaving all the advancements feminist Boomers had gained by the wayside. And watch out, she said, we were taking Roe v. Wade for granted. "You'll see," she said. "The fucker is packing the court with conservatives." And Sol, don't you know how she loves to tell us now, "I told you so."

Back then, I could never admit to my extended family's politics down in Miami. I was fairly certain all of them, including Gloria and Yaya, had voted for Trump. Our neighborhood was staunchly against Hilary Clinton's "socialist agenda." Yaya and her friends talked like she was an ally of Fidel Castro himself. They cared about democracy, freedom, and prosperity and not necessarily in that order. And even though most of them were political refugees from Cuba, they felt no association with today's immigrants. Republicans were a safeguard against socialism and kept taxes low. It didn't matter that Trump was vile and misogynist, as far as my mother and grandmother were concerned, men had always been pigs, so they accepted his hideous personality as part of the package.

"How is he treating you?" Rachel asked, and for a second I thought she was referring to Trump as his pussy-grabbing comment was still trotting through my mind.

She must have seen the confusion on my face. "It's David, right?"

"Oh, David." I paused, searching for the best adjective. "He's being attentive." I could have substituted paranoid or controlling, but I didn't want to get her going.

"Sweetheart," Rachel said, staring into my eyes. "I'm sure life up there is pretty swank. But it might not be a bad idea to go back to your own apartment."

I had been thinking the same thing that afternoon while walking through the old neighborhood. It had felt so nice to be out, to be independent, but Dr. Anderson was near David's apartment and there was Wally, and of course, David. Besides, living with him was keeping my expenses low, which made it possible to send money to Gloria every week even though I'd stopped getting a paycheck.

"Maybe, but he's expecting me back tonight."

"Ever heard of Stockholm syndrome?"

"You act like he's dangerous."

"He's a wolf in sheep's clothing." I bristled at yet another wolf analogy.

"Rachel, please. I didn't come down here to get lectured." I shot her a look that said don't push it.

"The shelter-in-place order has provided very convenient cover."

"You could put it that way, or you could call him caring for my well-being and our baby."

"Look, every woman deals with a certain amount of fear when embarking on adulthood and being pregnant only makes it worse. I know. I've been there. The patriarchy keeps us insecure, and then tells us men are the only ones who can provide security. It's royally fucked up."

It was like she'd been reading my mind as I hid under the covers that morning. The narrative I had to keep reminding myself of was that I was bold and a disrupter. I'd attended a college for rich kids and embarked on a career invented by white men for white men. I tried to think of living with David as another personal protest, infiltrating a foreign land and conquering a piece of it.

"What's more," Rachel continued. "COVID is going to set women's rights back decades. Women are finding it hard to manage their careers without childcare, without their kids going to school. Women are dropping out of the workforce at high rates."

If my feet weren't blistered and aching, I might have run all those blocks back to David. I wasn't sure how long I'd last into the protest. Rachel must have sensed this because she stopped scolding and got busy putting food on the table.

"Drink some more water," she said. "Are your ankles always that swollen?"

"As if I didn't already feel like an elephant." There was no longer any definition between my calves and my ankles.

"You should mention it to your doctor," she said before returning to the kitchen. I wished my appointments with Dr. Anderson hadn't been virtual. "Anyway, I just read they're removing Margaret Sanger's name from the Planned Parenthood where I used to work. From all the street signs too."

I was only half paying attention. "What's that?"

"It was in the Times." She raised her voice so I could hear her from the kitchen. "Something about eugenics, and a reckoning with her causing harm to reproductive health within communities of color." All the while David secured one of Dr. Anderson's last appointments for me and spoke to his concierge doctor almost daily. Shit may have been coming from all sides, but I was living above it all.

By the time we arrived outside Manhattan's District Attorney's office, there were several hundred people gathered and many more spilling down into the street and into Columbus Park. They carried signs and chanted, "Black Lives Matter." There was a woman with a bullhorn as well as constant directives coming out over Twitter. Rachel and I wore our face masks, making it hard to take a full breath, an apropos reminder of George Floyd's asphyxiation. I was briefly heartened by the crowd, people of all races, ages, and genders. Even though Black people had suffered the most, there was an acknowledgment in the air, that we were all suffering. People were calling it a national reckoning. Dear son, I want you to know that even though it was my first protest and I probably shouldn't have attended, the passion of the crowd infused me with a desire to speak up for the voiceless. I hope you'll feel the same way someday. Look out for the unfortunate, judge righteously, and be an advocate for the poor.

I hope we might partner in just causes in the future, but on that evening, all I did was some faint chanting. Rachel was much more energetic. "Justice for George Floyd!" she yelled. I was thirsty but afraid to remove my mask to drink. I wanted Rachel to take me by the hand and lead me home, but she was enrapt by the organizers and there was no way to break from the crowd.

I focused on taking calm, measured breaths. I hugged my arms across my stomach; for the first time I considered the word womb. A pregnant woman at a protest on a hot summer night in the midst of a pandemic. This was a terribly stupid decision and I hated that David was right. When the crowd started marching, I got carried along. Rachel grabbed my wrist before we could get separated. "We're heading over the Brooklyn Bridge!" Pure exhilaration shone on her face, and I shuddered at the irony of the route being on my wish list. Cramps made their way from my stomach down my thighs, but I kept walking, focusing on my breath. With each wave, I seized up.

"What's the matter?" Rachel screamed.

"I think I've walked too much today."

"Sit down," she said, pulling me out of the sea of bodies and onto an empty sliver of sidewalk.

She grabbed a water bottle out of her fanny pack. "Drink." Concern shone in her eyes, and as I swallowed, the cramping hurt so much I choked on the water.

"What is it?"

"I keep getting these pains," I said.

And that's when true fear appeared on her face. "Oh shit," Rachel said, looking up at the protesters swarming around us. "I've got to get you out of here."

CHAPTER THIRTY-TWO

"But my doctor is uptown," I said through gripping pain.

"Sweetheart," Rachel said. "We need a closer option. C'mon." And with the help of two extremely kind men who had been hovering nearby, I rose to my feet. They each took a shoulder, and we continued to New York Presbyterian's lower Manhattan campus. Yellow caution tape was strung outside the emergency entrance and staff dressed in hazmat suits and Plexiglas face shields approached as we got close.

"Is she hurt?" one of the staff members asked from a safe distance, her voice muffled by all the layers.

"I think she's going into labor," Rachel shouted. And that's when it dawned on me what the waves of pain were. God was I stupid.

"What?" I gasped.

"You're dehydrated." She squeezed my arm. "They'll get some fluids into you and we'll be out of here in no time."

The men seemed anxious to escape the emergency room entrance, not to mention a woman's pending labor. They wished me well once I was sitting in a wheelchair. "God bless you," said Rachel. "I'd hug you if I could."

"We'll get her admitted," the woman said. Rachel held my hand as a second staff member began to push the wheelchair.

"I'm sorry ma'am," the nurse said to Rachel. "You can't come any farther."

"Just give me a minute," Rachel said, grabbing my phone and going through my contacts.

"What are you doing?"

"Getting a few phone numbers. I should make some calls." She returned the phone to my bag, placing the bundle on my lap.

I was just glad to be sitting down. The nurse took my temperature in the driveway, then tilted my head back and inserted a long cotton swab up my nose.

"Have you experienced fever, sore throat, a dry cough?"

"No."

"Have you traveled outside the state in the last month?"

"No." I pictured Wally and David keeping dinner warm.

She read the thermometer and softened her tone a bit. "How far along are you?"

"Almost seven months," I said.

I was wheeled to a corner of the emergency room where I dug out my phone. I read a text from Rae that said: *Hope you had a good afternoon with Rachel, BTW landlord sent me the lease renewal.*

My God, Rae. I don't have a job or a trust fund. And, in case you forgot, I'm about to have a baby. She was from a different world. The mayhem in the emergency room sent a rush of anxiety through my chest and I cursed myself for ever leaving the serenity of Abigail's white living room.

A text came through from Rachel: *I called your mother to let her know.*

What on earth made her think that was a good idea? Gloria didn't even know I was pregnant. I had planned on this damned pandemic ending and flying down to Miami with David to explain about us and tell her about the baby. Within seconds my phone began to buzz with calls from my mother. I held my breath, sending her to voicemail. I just wasn't in any state of mind to have a coherent conversation. I was dehydrated, that's all. The IV was already helping and while the cramps or contractions or whatever they were still came, they weren't as severe. This little episode would be over soon, and I could call her back from the apartment. Maybe I'd even pass the phone over to David and let him talk to her too.

The emergency room was so much cooler than it had been outdoors with linoleum floors, fluorescent lighting, and stainless steel. Doctors, nurses, and orderlies all in different-colored scrubs, double masked, and wearing Plexiglas shields walked quickly, almost jogging. I shivered, clasping my hands inside the front pocket of my sweatshirt. I declined a call from Rachel. The person I needed to call was David. It would be hard to hear with all the noise in the background, but I mustered my courage.

"Where are you?" he hissed in a tone I'd heard him use with his children. A siren wailed outside and I swallowed hard, not wanting to fight.

"I walked downtown to Rachel's and I must have gotten dehydrated."

"I'll send a car."

"No, David, Rachel brought me to the hospital because I was having cramps."

"What? Where?"

As soon as I gave him the details, omitting the part about attending the protest, he hung up. Within fifteen minutes, my name was being called by a nurse and attention was being heaped all over me. I was taken to a private room in the maternity ward that, while spacious, was equally cold and antiseptic. I may have once envied those who jumped to the head of the line but doing it felt shitty. My default line of thinking was "put the baby first," which seemed to spare my conscience all sorts of stickiness.

David called as I was getting into bed. "Dr. Anderson can't care for you there."

"Oh," I said. "That's okay. They just need to pump me with some fluids. That's what Rachel said."

"Rachel?"

"The doctor on call will examine me."

He didn't respond.

"Look, I'm sorry." I cringed a little saying those words, but it felt like he was expecting an apology. Even I couldn't help feeling that this predicament was my fault.

"Well," he said, then clearing his throat, possibly taking back whatever scolding he had in mind. "Look, despite being able to get you into a private room, it seems neither Dr. Anderson nor I are able to get inside that building. I can't be with you."

"Oh."

"So, you're on your own, but I expect you to keep me posted. I will be in constant touch with Dr. Anderson, who will be in touch with the doctor on call."

Nurses were now entering at a steady clip, taking my blood pressure and my temperature and wanting to listen to my heart. "Okay, David. I'll call you later. I need to get off the phone."

"Any spotting?" a nurse asked.

"No."

"Are you able to pee?" She had laser beam focus on my abdomen, which may have been her style or just fear that meeting my eyes would give too much away.

"I can try."

I sat up in bed gingerly, but as I swung my legs over the side and stood up a rush of warm liquid poured down my legs and across the linoleum. I let out a whimper and clutched my side.

"Okay, let's get you back in the bed," she said, taking me by the elbow. She must have simultaneously sounded an alarm because things kicked into high gear. I had read far enough along in *What to Expect When You're Expecting* to know water breaking was a precursor to labor and this baby was still too young to be born.

"Am I miscarrying?" I asked nobody in particular.

"Ah, doll. Let's not think that way. Plenty of preterm births are viable. Stay positive." But it was the first week of June and the baby wasn't supposed to come until the beginning of August. You didn't need to go to medical school to know that was bad. I lay back on the bed and shut my eyes, surrendering to the monitors and equipment they hooked me up to. I was actually grateful David wasn't there to see it. I couldn't bear the questions: "What happened? What did you do?"

The same question was racing through my mind. Had all that walking caused this? Had I caught the virus? I pictured every shot of espresso I snuck in the kitchen, each sip of wine or champagne, even the lackadaisical way I wore my mask while walking Wally. Despite being surrounded by COVID, I had assumed being young and healthy meant my baby and I could survive anything.

One of the nurses helped me into a clean, dry gown and I tried to wish my way back to the day before, before our fight. When I opened my eyes, a doctor with long brown hair showing through her protective wear stood at the foot of my bed, my chart in her hand as she spoke with somebody who appeared to be the nurse in charge.

She turned toward me and introduced herself. "I'm Dr. Hernandez."

"Dr. Hernandez, hello," I whispered.

She parted my legs for a brief examination, then turned toward the monitor. She moved around to the head of the bed and asked me several questions. "There is no way for me to know, but since this is your first pregnancy, I'm going to assume you have an incompetent cervix. We'll administer two doses of betamethasone over the next two days. It's a steroid that speeds up the development of the baby's lungs. Our first hurdle is to keep baby inside for the next forty-eight hours."

Forty-eight hours? It didn't sound long enough. She continued, "And the IV drip will deliver antibiotics to fight off any infection."

"What kind of infection?"

"It's hard to know. But we can be grateful your water waited to break in the hospital, and we got you on meds right away." Her smile filled me with optimism.

"Okay." I tried to match her sentiment. I wanted so badly for her to say next, "You have nothing to worry about." It was the year 2020, after all, and doctors worked miracles all the time.

"Ms. Ruiz, we need to put off labor as long as possible, let the baby's organs develop. I am going to put you on magnesium sulfate to stall your contractions, but it will also affect your muscular and neurological activity."

"How?"

"You'll feel lethargic, heavy, sedated."

"Oh, okay."

She let me take in her answer and waited patiently for more questions. I inhaled deeply, and for the first time since this whole thing started all I could think about was how I had failed my baby boy. My body was his incubator, why hadn't I taken the job more seriously?

"Was it the virus?" I asked.

"It could have been any number of things. You may have been asymptomatic with COVID in the spring, and we're certainly seeing a lot of health complications due to stress these days. I know expectant mothers, all parents for that matter, blame themselves for everything, but we can't have you falling prey to that now. You need to relax."

"David expects a steady stream of updates." I'd already forgotten the names of the drugs she was putting me on.

"Who is David?"

"The father."

"Do I have your permission?"

"Yes."

"The nursing staff is extremely busy, but they'll do their best. What I'd really like is for you to get some sleep. I'll be able to get a better sense of the situation once you've absorbed the betamethasone. Can you do that for me? Rest peacefully for the next forty-eight hours?"

"Yes," I replied and placed my phone into her rubber-gloved hand.

I had been good at sleeping mornings away in David's master bedroom, but there was something about being told to relax that made it difficult, especially with the lights on, the beeping monitor, the nurses coming and going. The wires required me to lie on my back whereas up until then I'd been sleeping on my side with one pillow between my legs, one supporting my belly, one propped up against my lower back.

I took long inhales and exhales as if meditating, wondering if I could slow down my own heart rate along with the baby's. I wanted the sedation to take me to the brink of coma, to take me out the entire two days. I thought about all the women who had visited Yaya when they were trying to become pregnant or upon just learning that they were pregnant. I recall them lying on our living room couch, Yaya cutting a pomegranate in half and spreading honey on both sides. She lit candles and rubbed oils on their feet, their temples, and their abdomens. She petitioned Yemayá, also goddess of fertility, to bless them and their unborn children.

All those weeks I was preoccupied with David's money, how I stacked up against Tamara, or mourning my identity as a banker, I had not been paying attention to my baby's kicks. Yaya used to tell women pregnancy takes all one's attention. I should have been invoking her prayers before now. She wasn't around to remind me that there are few things more magical than carrying a child, that I was experiencing a time of abundant blessing and fortune. A child is a gift, she would have said. She would have told me to channel every ounce of energy into that, not David, not on salvaging my career, not on the news. Her treatment would have been totally different than what I was receiving in this sterile, freezing cold hospital room. However, the one thing she and Dr. Hernandez would have agreed upon was that I needed to sleep.

CHAPTER THIRTY-THREE

When I fell asleep, it was just that, a continual delirious falling. Falling and eventually floating, buoyant on ocean waves. I was carried along by a gentle, flowing current, with a mild ease I interpreted as Yemayá's presence. She reminded me infants already know how to swim, that they float in sacks of amniotic fluid just like saltwater. My child may have lived in his own private ocean, but he also resembled a tiny astronaut floating about in space, an umbilical cord tethering him to his mothership.

In another dream I was that same mermaid I'd dreamt about at Eden, half woman half fish with a powerful tail I pumped to propel myself up and down through the waves. I surfed among a school of dolphins parallel to a white sand beach. I was playful and happy, conscious of my ability to arc through the air as well as surge to the ocean's depth. When my face broke the surface, I caught glimpses of the empty beach. At one point, a pack of coywolves emerged from the woods, meandering across the sand. On the ocean's floor, I found a baby dolphin not strong enough to rise and scooped him into my arms, bringing him up for air while his family played. After taking a breath, he wriggled from my grasp, swimming by my side instead. Although I tried to focus my attention on the little dolphin, I couldn't help noticing the coywolves, spread out as if expecting one of us to wash ashore.

I tossed fitfully, between deep dreams and light sleep. When consciousness pulled me, I tried to sink again into the turquoise ocean. Being catheterized meant I didn't need to use the bathroom, but I eventually woke up thirsty.

"What would you like to drink?" a nurse asked.

"Do you have pomegranate juice?" I whispered.

"Cranberry?"

"Sure."

I was anxious to return to the floating sensation, resisting the light. Like Rip Van Winkle, I wanted to succumb to sleep that would extend until my due date, until my baby could safely enter the world.

The disorienting passage of time was nothing new after sheltering in place. Days felt like weeks which felt like months. I hoped if I kept sleeping and didn't ask what time it was, time might accelerate, my tiny boy maturing, his tail strengthening into a powerful muscle.

In my dreams, Yaya came with her birthing stool, extolling the benefits of squatting, the most natural, intuitive position in which a woman should labor. She floated into my hospital room and pulled me out of bed. "Do not lie on your back, Betsabé," she said. "It might be more convenient for the doctor, but you strain less sitting up." Turn over, turn over.

"Oh, Yaya." I breathed heavily between the strong currents of contractions. "He is not ready to come. We need to hold it off."

"Waves are the primordial force of the planet. They crash on the shore whether you want them to or not," she whispered.

"I'm scared. We need to make them stop."

"Don't be afraid, mija. Just listen to what they have to say."

"I need you to show me."

"No, you don't."

Yaya disappeared, an elegantly adorned goddess taking her place. It was Yemayá again. "Drink," she said, holding a warm mug of tea to my lips. She smelled of rosewater and coconut, and I yearned for her hands to remain on my skin because without them

I was covered in goosebumps. I slowly opened my eyes to bright sunlight illuminating the perimeter of the window shade. At first, I thought it was the radiant glow of Yemayá's crown, but when the figure came into focus, it was a nurse, turning the knobs on a monitor.

"What time is it?" I asked.

"Five o'clock."

"What day?"

"You made it two days. It is June second."

"That's good, right?" It wasn't thirty days, but it was what the kind doctor had asked for.

"Yes, that is very good. Dr. Hernandez is pleased, but we are keeping you on a steady drip of meds. Do you need anything while you're awake? The bedpan?"

"No, thank you," I said with a smile. A few minutes later I was back in the fog with Grant's voice over my shoulder. "All these variables should be in one table, and all of these cells should be formulas."

"Grant, where are you?" I kept swiveling around in my desk chair, but I could not see him, could not spin around fast enough to catch him over my shoulder. He laughed teasingly.

"Haha, you can't catch me."

"Stop, I'm getting dizzy," I said. And then he was gone and Marnye was standing in front of me, her face as stern as I'd ever seen it. "What's the matter?" I asked.

"You know what you did."

"What?"

"You know."

I flushed with heat. There were any number of things she could have been referring to. "Why do I need to apologize to you?" I asked.

"I stood up for you."

"No, you didn't."

I looked toward Lenore's desk for an ally, but she was walking down the hall. "Lenore!" I called out, but she passed me by without saying a word, and then, following in measured intervals were Ethan, Nathan, Sandra, and at the very end of the parade, David.

"David!" I called out. "David!" But he, too, was an expression-less zombie. I woke with a start, my heart racing. "David," I said to the nurse in the room.

"The guy who's been calling to check on you like a million times a day?"

I strained my neck toward the calendar. "Probably."

"Now that you're awake, let's just shift you around a bit and get the blood circulating." Otherwise, all the medical staff cared about was my uterus.

"I also think your mother would like to hear from you," she said as she hoisted me into a different position. "How about I bring you your phone?"

How could I tell this soft-spoken woman the last thing I wanted to do was call the baby's father or my own mother for that matter? But she read my mind. "I know you're tired but do it for them."

———

Before dialing, I caught up on the backlog of messages. Just as I was figuring out what to say, my phone rang, and I answered.

"Mija! Dios mío! Yaya and I have been so worried."

"I know, I'm sorry."

"When were you going to tell us?"

"We wanted to tell you in person, but everything got so complicated."

Gloria wasn't aiming to lecture like Rachel or David. No, my mother got very quiet, and I faced the fact that keeping my pregnancy from her was a pretty terrible thing to do. I strained to hear her words. "I'm coming up there."

"No, Mami. It's dangerous."

"Do you forget I'm a nurse? I know how to be safe."

"They won't let you in the hospital."

"I need to be close to you. Maybe I could stay in your apartment?"

I wanted to tell her absolutely not to come, but I was now able to relate to worrying over an offspring's well-being, empathizing with my mother in a way I never had before.

"Okay, Mami. But no need to rush. I could be in here for a month."

"Yaya insists I leave right away. She has oils and remedies for you."

"They won't let you inside," I said, sensing my mother liked her chances of sweet-talking the oils up to my room. "How is Yaya doing? Who will stay with her if you come up here?"

"She'll stay with Tía Julia. Mateo and I will start driving in the morning."

"Okay." My voice was small.

"Hang on, mija. I'll be there as soon as I can."

The next time I woke, it was the middle of the night. I decided it was a good time to call David. I didn't care if I woke him. I didn't tell him that my mother and her boyfriend were on their way either, that I had another source of support, my family.

My instinct was to keep that to myself, sensing he would see them as rivals for my affection. For several months he and I had been all each other had and telling him others were now firmly planted in my corner somehow sounded disloyal. I know, because that's how I felt when he told me he was now staying at his ex-wife's house in Long Island.

"I came out here to be with Tamara," he said, "for Father's Day."

"Oh," was all I could say, although I was thinking, *I'm lying prone in a hospital bed for the unforeseeable future, can't you at least stay put in your apartment?*

"Don't worry, I brought Wallace and he loves the beach." Clearing his throat, he said, "Hey, I just wanted to spend the weekend with my kids." Mention of his already born and fully developed kids stung, and it felt like Wally was a traitor too.

"Have you told them about us? About the baby?"

He was silent. "If there is an appropriate moment, I will." But what I heard was, *If the baby lives, I will.*

285

"David, I'm tired. I'm going to hang up now."

"Bets, please can we talk a little bit longer? I really miss you."

I stared at the ceiling. There were twelve light fixtures interspersed across fifty-seven ceiling tiles. The big hand on the clock ticked and then leapt forward one minute.

"Okay." I wanted him to hear the weakness in my voice.

"I'm praying for him, fasting too, as a sacrifice."

Oh God, David. Why do you have to make everything about you? "I have to go," I said, tipping back a plastic cup and biting down on the few slivers of ice at the bottom. Sol, I've worried about making you bear witness to the way we behaved, but I think it's important you never worship your parents. It isn't healthy. Your father was no hero and I was no woman of valor. We were, and continue to be, flawed human beings.

I stared at the neon green lines bleeping across the monitor, cannily reminiscent of the stock portfolio graphs David checked on nightly. I couldn't get worked up. I needed my green line to remain as steady and even as possible. "Happy Father's Day," I said before disconnecting.

With the tips of my fingers, I searched for a section of abdomen free of leads and wires. I tickled a tiny patch of skin with my fingernails. I spoke to my baby. Mijo, this is your mami speaking. Please hang on. I will lie here as long as you need me to.

I imagined him the size of a mango, his weak, little lungs preparing to emerge into a world where even full-grown lungs were under attack. I was in no hurry to bring him into a world where police officers put their knees on people's necks. I thought about my own lungs, my own breath and how I had taken it for granted. I was determined to sustain my son. I was all he had—my body, my strength, my spirit. I willed those steroids to travel through my bloodstream and permeate his. I imagined Dr. Hernandez standing over my bedside, a surprised expression on her face, exclaiming she had never witnessed such an extraordinary reversal of fortune. "A miracle," she would say, bragging to her colleagues about what she witnessed during the terrible plague while Yemayá whispered in my ear, "Your son will thank you someday."

I made it another week. And although I was feeling increasingly uncomfortable, I was never lonely. I was no longer that girl who suffered FOMO while working late into the night, despondently checking Instagram. Sol, in the hospital I migrated from someone seeking the validation of outsiders to someone who could appreciate peaceful solitude. That transformation, coincidentally, would be central to me eventually being able to love completely. I have written in these pages of friendship and romantic relationships, but people rarely speak about the relationship you must develop with yourself. It is the most important relationship you will ever have, Sol, and one I probably wouldn't have nurtured adequately if it hadn't been for all that time in the hospital.

———

Dr. Hernandez stopped in several times a day. One evening she seemed particularly worried. "There is still some vaginal bleeding. I'm concerned about placental abruption. Are you feeling any pain?"

It was hard to know what I felt, what had to do with the pregnancy and what had to do with being an inert, drugged-up blob.

"And the monitor shows contractions, although slight, are continuing."

I'd been trying to ignore those too.

"Let's increase the magnesium sulfate," she told the nurse, but what she didn't say was that I was at a critical juncture, twenty-eight weeks. At twenty-nine the baby had a much better chance of survival outside the womb. Still severely premature, he'd be at risk for all sorts of health issues, nothing like the brilliant shot of life David had been counting on.

The nurse was extremely kind, bringing me a red Gatorade with a sippy straw. I pretended it was pomegranate juice. How funny that I had never thought of my mother performing these thoughtful gestures even though she was also a nurse. It wasn't until my second week in the hospital that I understood how selfless her job was. When I was little, I had viewed it as something that took her away from me. Even though there was all sorts of talk about the courage of frontline workers, I hadn't considered what it meant until then. My Lyle education left me thinking that jobs like nursing and teaching were not what young women in this day and age should strive for, as if you were not a real success unless you made it in a man's world.

———

Rae was still at Eden, and my mother was staying at our apartment. I pictured her snooping for clues about this strange life I'd created. Somehow Yaya's oils arrived and I rubbed a dab of lavender inside each wrist and on my abdomen. I felt surprisingly awake, enough to put on some music. I chose a soothing playlist that kicked off with John Mayer. I took long, even inhales, extending the exhales in hopes of sending wavelengths of energy through every cell of my body. Slow down, everybody, slow down. There will be no coming out until I say so. I laughed, as if that would be the first of a million times I would say to my son, "Because I say so."

I was halfway between sleep and consciousness when a stabbing sensation ripped across my low back. I let out a half-scream, not so much from the pain but because it took me by surprise. At about the same time a whining alarm sounded on the monitor by my bed.

The nurse rushed in and pulled back my covers. "More bleeding," she said to Dr. Hernandez, who entered right behind her. "The placenta seems to be lifting off of your uterine wall," she said.

"Should I prep the OR?" the nurse asked.

"Baby is tolerating the bleeding at present. We may need to do a C-section but let's head to delivery now."

The medical staff was taking direction and conversing as if I was no longer there. We'd all been praying to hold the day off a little while longer. My heart rate sped up and the nurse squeezed my hand in her rubber glove. It was more of an expression of tenderness than she'd ever be able to manage from behind her Plexi-shielded face. "Don't worry love," she said. "He'll grow nice and strong in the NICU."

But how could machinery do a better job than me? It was crushing to think of my muscles contracting to expel my son, that I was no longer the optimal container for his life. Yaya would have clucked her tongue at their not putting me in a tub with rose oil. I should have insisted. At least the virus meant I was alone in this terrible moment, spared everyone's disappointment.

CHAPTER THIRTY-FOUR

Dr. Hernandez offered an epidural to block the pain, but I turned it down. I wanted to feel something, even if it was acute discomfort. "Are you sure?" she asked. But I was tired of being out of it. No more denial.

"Given baby's size and your dilation," she said, "this could go fast." I anticipated one of her reassuring smiles but caught her sharing a serious expression with a nurse from behind their masks. "I'm going to get scrubbed."

Inside the delivery room, new nurses took over and I missed the room in which I'd spent the past several weeks. Every mark on the ceiling, every monitor button and dial, even the blinds on the windows had been seared into my memory. It was a quarantine within a quarantine, a place where I was waiting between two existences. The nurses offered daily expressions of sympathy, as if it was such a hardship, but they had no idea how grateful I had become for the solitude. About to face yet another point of no return, I wanted to go back to that room where I could hold onto hope.

The delivery room was not designed for an adult patient but first and foremost for a baby, with blankets, bassinet, sink, and spotlights. This was the main stage where it would all go down, and when I was wheeled out of there, nothing would ever be the same. Being pregnant should have triggered that sentiment months earlier, but lifting my heels into the metal stirrups, scooting my ass to the edge of the gurney while Dr. Hernandez spread my knees apart . . . well, that sparked an anxiety I had never experienced before.

———

Whereas getting pregnant took David and me together, birthing our son and the placenta he'd been feeding on would be my solitary labor. I thought back on the evening in the back of the Mercedes when David said we'd be in this together and what comfort that had given me once upon a time. Why hadn't I realized that was impossible? There are things in this world, Yaya once said, that are a woman's business alone. I'd considered her old-fashioned, ignorant of the equity women were achieving every day, that is until I lay there all by myself, with a nurse in a hazmat suit gripping my hand.

The pain intensified and I wished I'd agreed to the epidural. It was unbearable. I could tell the bleeding was getting worse as well. Warm liquid ran down my thighs and the nurse was replacing towels quickly. I could see the exchange of looks between her and Dr. Hernandez, begging the question as to why they hadn't gone right ahead and performed the C-section. I may be remembering it wrong but it's possible Dr. Hernandez said as much under her breath. I sensed her regret, as if it was too late to move me.

I screamed, the urge to push uncontrollable. Every muscle in my body wanted to get the baby out. One nurse was positioned by my head, holding my hand, speaking in my ear. This kind stranger was the only person I had but because of her protective garb, all I could see were her eyes. I zeroed in on them as she encouraged me to stay focused. With one final push, the baby emerged between my legs and more warm fluid followed. The relief was almost immediate as was the desperation to see my son.

His entrance into the world was a resurrection of sorts and despite the relief, my heart sank at the fact there was no crying. Nobody was handing him to me. More nurses entered the delivery room and Dr. Hernandez passed my infant to a man I would later learn was a neonatologist. He took him in the palm of one hand and carried him to a nearby resuscitation bed. I sought out the eyes of the kind nurse who had been by my side through the delivery only to find despair.

I tried to pray for my baby, but other feelings began rushing through me. There was anguish, of course, but the word *penance* also came to mind. God, I am sorry. Please show mercy on me. Regret came spewing forth as well. For betraying Grant, for irresponsibly conceiving a child in a moment of lust, for envying Tamara, for sheltering in a penthouse while people suffered on the streets, for keeping the truth from my mother and Yaya, for disappointing my family and especially little Ania, for lying to David and walking downtown in a heat wave. For assuming I was immortal, and just in case there was any truth to it, for selling my soul to the devil by taking a job in investment banking instead of pursuing my dreams in the theatre. For all of it, I prayed for forgiveness. I looked toward the doctor bent over my son, but his broad back blocked my view of what was going on.

There had been times over the past two weeks I had dreamt the pesticides AgriGlobal traded in had seeped off the pages of its annual reports and onto my hands and into my bloodstream. Maybe they had contaminated my values as well. Nathan's condemning voice sounded in my head, "There will be consequences." I was guilty of perpetuating David's delusion that the new life I carried might regenerate his own. I had made that bargain, if not out loud then at least somewhere in the recesses of my brain, as if he could give me a pair of diamond earrings, but I could give him new life. David might have to resign, but I'd be the one to pay the real price for what we had done. My baby would forever be a child born of shame.

"Betsabé, I'm so sorry," Dr. Hernandez said. "We lost the heartbeat." She seemed unaccustomed to admitting defeat and left me to make the next leap of logic.

No heartbeat. No heartbeat equals not living. My baby boy had a heart that stopped beating. I looked to the nurse still clenching my hand. She nodded sadly. It was a terrible thought, one I would never admit aloud, but in addition to feeling shame and grief, there was also peace in knowing the outcome.

I closed my eyes as tears fell. "You should hold him," the nurse said, putting her hand on my shoulder. She had already washed and bundled him at the layette station by the sink. Without waiting for an answer, she placed him on my chest positioned so that our faces could meet, his so tiny I could practically breathe him in, swallow him whole if I wanted to. His skin was a grayish blue and his eyes and mouth were closed. I could almost pretend he was sleeping. The nurse dimmed the lights and all of a sudden, the room was empty with the exception of me and my son. I was still looking for somebody to explain what just happened, but the medical team left in silence, seeming to understand the sanctity of the moment.

I sat up against the pillows and held my warm bundle to my cheek. I took in his nose, his mouth, his jaw, recognizing something and needing to memorize everything.

Yaya never said a baby died, rather he'd been taken by the ocean.

I named him Edmundo for my father. Just as isolating with David had meant I didn't have to explain our love to anyone, holding Edmundo in private created a sacred bond between us. Forget what I'd learned in college, or on the job, forget my awakened passion with David, holding Edmundo was like tapping into the meaning of life. Holding him, I was overwhelmed by grief and sorrow that was intense and awful, but he also ignited something inside me.

Holding him made me aware we are all born with kernels of goodness that become concealed by layers of pain. It was that morning I began to see people in a different light, as the result of their circumstances. I relaxed my head to one side and everything I'd subconsciously learned from Yaya came rising to the surface. Growing up, I didn't understand why she took a turn sitting with bodies in the mortuary chamber at St. Barbara's church. When I was still fairly young, she had tried to explain it was important to ensure the deceased's soul departs peacefully without haunting the living. She spoke of the dead with reverence, the same way she spoke of new life. "Life and death, Betsabé. It is the natural order of the world." To only see death negatively is to lose sight of its power to enhance every moment.

I removed my gold chain and draped it across Edmundo's tiny body. The crucifix and pendant depicting Yemayá were ridiculously large against his chest, but I would bury him with them, nonetheless. I reached for the plastic cup of melting ice chips by my bedside and wet my fingers. I held Edmundo's small head in the palm of my hand and moistened his scalp. I kissed his temple and spoke to him aloud. "You were real. You existed. Even if for the briefest of moments and even if I was the only one to have laid eyes on you, your tiny life will make a difference. I promise."

With that vow, my heart lightened. Sol, I will never accept the narrative that your brother's death was my punishment. No, if anything it was a wake-up call. Something altogether new was floating through my chest, an emotion I can't name as it was way more complicated than any love I'd experienced. It was a combination of loss, regret, awe, and wonder, a mother's love. I was saying hello and goodbye at the same time. I was saying, "I see you," and in the act of seeing Edmundo, I also saw myself, or should I say I saw myself the way I would want my child to see me.

I took pictures with my mind's eye that would need to last a lifetime. Over the past four months so much life and love had been sucked out of the world and whatever portions intended for me were arriving in bizarre forms. First, in a lover over twice my age, and second in a tiny infant whose heart had stopped beating. Others might call it grotesque, but if this was my lot, I would call it beautiful.

The longer I held Edmundo, the more the world faded away. Even David became a minor character. I unwrapped my babe, needing to see all of him, those little feet that had been kicking me from the inside, his arms tucked up into his chest. I traced my fingertip over his tummy and the crease of his buttocks. There was no risk he'd catch a chill, still the need to safely wrap him back up was real.

I brushed the top of his head with my lips and my cheeks as dawn broke outside the window. The first hints of an orange and yellow sun crept across Edmundo's face as if the world's beauty was being shown to me for the first time.

The nurse returned quietly and asked, "Ms. Ruiz? May I take him now?"

"Yes," I said. "Thank you."

"I will ink his feet so you can take home his footprints."

"Thank you," I whispered. "I want him laid to rest in Miami."

She grimaced. "With COVID, it might be hard."

"Please." I closed my eyes, refusing her reaction. "My mother will come for him in the morning."

She cleaned me up further and wheeled my gurney from the delivery room back to my private room. Once my vitals returned to normal and I was able to go the bathroom, there was no more reason to remain in the hospital. In fact, the nurse said, given the infection rate, it was best if I masked up and went home as soon as possible. The question of home still haunted me. Where was my home? Miami? New York? My lease with Rae was lapsing, and now that there was no baby, David's apartment seemed an impossibility. Many people wrestle with the idea of home, Sol. It's inevitable if you choose a big, wandering life which I hope you will, but Yaya always said while we're all searching for a way to feel at home in the world, we forget that life is the journey taking us home. So, I like to think when I eventually do arrive home, your brother will be there, waiting.

After lying supine for so long, I was weak. My perspective was literally altered, and my legs had a hard time remembering how to hold me straight. I pulled the dress I wore on the day I was admitted over my head. The Yankee's cap was in my bag along with an empty plastic water bottle like artifacts from the day of the protest. I threw them in the trashcan. I brushed out my hair. It had gotten so long I had to clip it to the top of my head. I looked at my reflection in the small bathroom mirror for the first time since leaving David's apartment. I was so puffy, and there were dark circles under my eyes. My face didn't register as pretty, but I didn't care, it matched the way I felt. Being pretty was also a privilege, Sol. It's always been easier for good-looking people to get ahead, and I was coming to realize I probably would never have gotten into that situation if I hadn't been attractive. So yeah, I was okay with being puffy.

A nurse's aide pushed my wheelchair to the elevator and from there into the lobby. No baby in my arms, no bandages. What transpired over the past few weeks was invisible to everyone but me. Nobody could see the watery milk leaking from my nipples, or the thick maxi pad between my legs.

I spotted my mother in the driveway alongside a cab right away. It seemed David had been made aware of my discharge as well, because the Mercedes was also there, and he was waiting in the back seat with Lance behind the wheel reading the New York Post. I was no longer his obligation and the idea of indulging in physical pleasure seemed selfish.

I rushed straight into my mother's arms and hurried into the back of the cab. As I shut the door, I looked up to see David's face full of confusion.

I texted him as we pulled away: *Mami drove up from FL, I need to spend time with her. I'll be in touch.*

David: *But I need to see you too*

Me: *Soon*

David: *I'm distraught. I've missed you. Shouldn't we be going through this together?*

I figured he'd see this as an opportunity to be free of me, saving him from having to come clean with Tamara and the rest of his family. Besides, I doubted his mourning could match my own and I had no intention of molding my grief to fit his. Just as I had been alone giving birth and holding Edmundo, my instinct was the rest should be unique to me as well.

I wrote back: *I'll call you tonight.*

I stopped to catch my breath on each of the five landings leading up to my apartment. I reached across my middle each time, surprised by the softness where there had been a hard shell. My mother opened the door to an unmade Murphy bed and clothes scattered across the floor. She was a bigger slob than me. Rae would have been beside herself. "Where's Mateo?" I asked.

"I asked him to give us a minute. He's probably talking to his boss. We'll probably take off tomorrow."

On top of the emptiness I felt inside, stepping into my apartment for the first time in four months was an additional ache. Glimpsing reminders of a life I'd probably never reclaim was made worse by my mother's intrusion. The strange thing was I didn't want her to leave either. I sat on Rae's futon, curling up like she used to with her laptop.

"I need a shower," I said, too tired to make it happen.

"I'm sorry about the mess. I got the call early this morning and I didn't have time to straighten up before going to the hospital."

"It's okay," I said, stretching my neck from one side to the other.

"Was that him in the back of the Mercedes?"

"Yeah." Without having to say another word, she knew what I was thinking. That was the thing about my mother, she may have been loud, but she knew when to be silent. She sat next to me and rested her head on my shoulder as if everything I'd gone through ripped into her as well.

"You are a strong woman, Betsabé. You are my daughter. You don't need a man." It was an entirely different reaction than I'd expected.

"What if something's wrong with me?"

She wouldn't hear of that. "No digas eso. You'll have another child. When it's time. And watch, that one might grow up to be president."

"Mami, will you take me to the hospital tomorrow?"

"Of course, mija. But why?"

"To pick him up at the morgue."

"Oh."

"And I want to ride back to Miami with you. I want Yaya to bury him."

She was stunned silent, possibly because I wanted to transport a little bird of a body down I-95, or possibly because I was willing to spend twenty hours in a car with her and Mateo, or all of it.

"Please?"

"Yes, yes, of course," she said, shrugging like, anything you want.

———◆———

Mateo returned with food for the three of us and a six-pack. I was delighted he found Café Habana and that they had managed to stay open through the pandemic. After we ate roast pork burritos and drank a few beers, I was ready to fall asleep. I told Mateo to take the Murphy bed and that my mother and I would share the futon.

I brought my phone into the bathroom. After brushing my teeth, I called David. As soon as I heard his voice, tears began streaming down my cheeks. I reached for the roll of toilet paper from where I sat on the edge of the bathtub.

"I'm saying Kaddish," he said.

"David. I'm going to Miami in the morning. And I'm taking . . . him. I want to have a proper funeral."

He seemed to understand I needed my family; at times like these only a mother's love would do. Maybe he'd seen something in Gloria as they both waited outside the hospital, her maternal ferocity rivaling any wolf-like tendencies in him. She had arrived in New York prepared to guard my life and my spirit as if they were the only things that gave her life meaning, as if I was not only her future, but the future.

"I understand," he said.

I started to cry. "I wasn't expecting to love him so much."

"I know. Hey, call me when you get there?"

"Okay."

"And be safe."

"You're still taking care of Wally?"

"Of course."

I came out of the bathroom and curled up next to my mother and let her rub my back until I fell asleep.

CHAPTER THIRTY-FIVE

Sitting in the back seat of Mateo's Jeep with no luggage to speak of, I felt like a fugitive, stealing away as if I'd done something wrong. While he and my mother took turns behind the wheel, Yaya and Tía Julia were at home cooking. When we pulled up to the casita in our sweaty clothing stained with coffee, the savory smells of spices and onions greeted us. The yard was neat and new bushes had been planted on either side of the front stoop. The concrete steps and the porch were a fresh mint green and a new bench-seat swing had replaced the rusty one. The living room overflowed with cut flowers.

With a mask over my nose and mouth and after vigorously washing my hands, I held Yaya to my chest, breathing in the floral scent of her, her tiny body filling some of my emptiness. She pulled me over to the couch while Mateo silently unloaded the car. When he carried the container holding Edmundo's body into the living room, Yaya pointed to her bedroom. Tía said the vigil would begin the next day and plans for a funeral mass were still in the works. I was moved by so many things when we first arrived, but most of all Yaya. During the pandemic I had thought I might never again feel the softness of her cheek.

"Thank you," I said.

"Of course." To think, I'd once discounted these women as out-of-date, but their knowing how one begins to move on was exactly what I needed.

JEANNE McWILLIAMS BLASBERG

That night, Mateo returned to his apartment and my mother and I shared our bedroom. However, before going to sleep, we sat silently on the new porch swing, pushing through the thick summer air.

I received a text from David: *Did you make it to Miami?*

I replied: *Sorry, we just got home. A lot going on.*

David: *Your address? I'd like to send flowers*

I told him our little house couldn't hold any more flowers, but he insisted. Rae and her family had sent a basket of fruit and there was also a small arrangement of irises from Grant with a card that said, "With my deepest sympathy."

David: *I love you Bets, Sleep well.*

I put my phone on the swing and my mother smiled. We could read each other's minds, and no matter that my earliest motivation had been to leave home and grow up entirely different than her, we'd always be the same where it mattered. Hard work occupied our bodies by day, and dreams filled our minds at night. It was crazy how it took losing my baby to truly receive her love for the first time. She was a better mom in times of crisis than putting on birthday parties, surprising me at Christmas, or making a big deal of my graduation. By checking on me in the rearview mirror and buying me ginger ales and bananas at rest stops, that was how she showed love. Sharing this loss as well as the uncertainty of separation during the pandemic, well, it pushed us toward a fresh start.

She whispered in my ear, "Your son was an angel, too good for this world."

"I know," I said. "But I'm really mad at the world."

"Well, mija, welcome to motherhood."

I could no longer hold back the tears.

"Shhh, mija, you don't understand. Dead or alive, a birth begets a mother. *You are a mother now.*"

"I don't deserve to be."

She snapped her neck and looked straight into my eyes, "Don't ever say you don't deserve. Not on your abuelos's grave. Don't do that to us, Betsabé. Did that man make you weak?"

I wiped a tear. "No," I said.

"I saw him in the back of that car. He needs you more than you need him."

I smiled. She'd sized him up through a car window.

"Oh, Mami." She wrapped her arm around me and the story I'd been holding onto my entire life began to melt away. I forgave her ill-preparedness at parenting, becoming embittered when my father never returned. It was the first time I saw how brave she really was.

"I want you to know something," she said. "People who don't suffer can never truly grow up. And they never discover who they are. Adulthood means taking responsibility for what happens in your life while remaining open to a love that heals." I looked at her with wonder. She was spewing the type of wisdom I'd have expected from Yaya. Coming from my mother, it meant so much more.

"C'mon," she said. "Let's go to bed. We need to be rested for tomorrow."

The next morning, we put on dresses and Yaya lit a candle on her altar. Edmundo was laid to rest in an infant-sized white casket, surrounded by votive candles, flowers, and pictures of our ancestors. It made for a colorful tableau. I placed my necklace across his chest and gave his forehead one last kiss before closing the casket. Yaya looked me in the eyes and said, "Betsabé, it's the painful events that break you open, that allow you to bring healing to others. You have that power now. It was this baby's gift to you."

"Oh, Yaya."

"Tu sabiduría ha cobrado vuelo." My wisdom was set free and I pictured my soul a battered piñata at the end of a child's party. Sol, just as people say love is a verb, I like to think of wisdom as a verb as well. Wisdom is the process of gathering wisdom.

"Thank you, Yaya." It was then I considered the pain she must have experienced.

———

Family members began arriving by late morning. Florida was experiencing its surge of COVID and I was relieved people came in shifts. Tía Julia remained in the kitchen, sending out food, while Yaya and my mother sat on either side of me on the couch to receive visitors. My cousin Tomás and his wife and little Ania filled their plates and pulled up chairs to join me in the living room.

"Can I get you anything to drink?" Tomás asked before getting comfortable with his own plate. It was obvious his wife, Linda, was pregnant even though they avoided the topic of a new baby.

But I said, "Congratulations. When are you due?"

Linda smiled appreciatively, her long hair falling across her shoulders. "In the fall."

"Are you excited to be a big sister?" I asked Ania. She beamed and Tomás sat on the edge of his seat, looking nervously unsure over what might come out her mouth.

"We are having a brother," she said, her long, straight hair a younger version of her mother's.

"I am happy for you," I said to Linda, understanding what a blessing it was, but also the concern she must have been swallowing in light of what happened to me, what was happening to the world all around us.

"Thank you," she said. More cousins arrived and were helping themselves to the spread on the kitchen table. Small plates were handed to me, the flavors and scents almost as comforting as the familiar faces. Tío Luis once expressed his pride in my important job as a banker, but he now seemed relieved I'd come home for this sacred rite. Whereas I had once worried about my pregnancy disappointing everyone, I saw their relief at my coming home. The mystery surrounding the baby's father, however, was something about which they were too polite to ask.

Kids were back and forth onto the porch like it was just another room and it was easy to forget why we had all gathered, but a knock at the screen door got everyone's attention. I turned to see a bouquet so large you couldn't make out the delivery man. Tomás carried the arrangement safely into the house, but the messenger didn't leave. Was he so callous as to be waiting for a tip? He peeked his head into the living room with a teenage girl by his side and I froze. It was David and Tamara.

My eyes met his and I dropped my empty plastic plate. He was clean shaven with a fresh haircut and was wearing a dark suit. It had been such a long time since I'd seen him dressed like that. His face flooded with emotion and he crossed the room with his arms wide open. I stood to greet him and as he held me, we both shook with sobs, and so, as far as my family was concerned, mystery solved. It was our first embrace, our first physical touch since the day I'd left for the protest, and it seemed like he'd never let me go.

"David," I said, finally pulling away. "Let me introduce you to my family." There were so many things I wanted to say, but it was a small room and everyone's eyes were upon us. He took their hands in his, forgetting you weren't supposed to.

Tamara stood alone by the door, one foot inside and one still on the porch. When I walked toward her, she put her arms on my shoulders, pulling me in for an air-kiss. "I hope you don't mind that I came with my dad," she said. "I'm sorry for your loss."

———

Later that afternoon, a priest wearing all black and a white clerical collar arrived from St. Barbara's to discuss the mass. I looked around for Yaya, under the impression she would take care of the arrangements, but it appeared she had gone into her room to rest. The priest approached David and me while we were standing with Tomás and Linda.

"I am so sorry." I recognized him as the man on the pulpit on Christmas Eve.

"Thank you, Father."

"There are just a few things I need to ask before the mass tomorrow." David remained by my side.

"By all means."

"Was he baptized?"

Did a few droplets of melted ice on his scalp count? "No," I said. This is what I hated, all the rules around religion. In the case of our son, no natural laws had been followed. He died before he lived, everything was completely out of order.

"Okay," he said, and I wondered if it really was okay or whether he was more concerned with remaining in Yaya's good favor. "Did you name him?"

My cheeks burned. "Yes, I named him Edmundo."

David regarded me with surprise. "His surname is David. Edmundo David," he said. "And I'd like you to include the Twenty-Third Psalm in the liturgy."

"Of course," said the priest, and David seemed pleased.

My extended family may have come to the vigil, but Edmundo's funeral was just for us. David held my hand in the front pew. We were surrounded by my mother, Yaya, Tía Julia and Tío Luis, and Tamara. Instead of listening to the priest, I was mesmerized by the white lilies, inhaling their sweet scent. My grief was much larger than losing Edmundo. I cried over the whole damned year: Grant, COVID, George Floyd too.

I still couldn't believe I was standing in Yaya's church with David, saying goodbye to our son. Besides it being surreal, the moment also came with enlightenment. I reflected on my mother's words, that suffering was necessary in order to grow, and I realized something about love that day, about true love. It was a definition of love I could never have grasped in David's apartment. True love rarely leads to happily ever after, but it does strengthen under difficult circumstances. True love doesn't make troubles disappear, but it does gives one strength to cope with them.

After taking communion and reciting David's psalm, I offered one last prayer. I petitioned God, but also Yemayá, Mother Earth, even my dead abuelo, whomever might be listening: "Please forgive me."

The funeral home transported our son's little casket in an adult-sized hearse to the cemetery while David and I followed in a black sedan. Yaya, Gloria, Tamara, and the others returned home, sensing we needed some time alone. "We have to stop meeting like this," he said, as we climbed into yet another back seat. His ability to find humor, his smile, the smell of him filling the car all coated me with warmth.

"Thank you for being here," I said.

"Please."

"Really, your showing up has taught me something." It taught me what love means, is what I should have said.

"You've taught me something too," he said.

"What could I teach you?"

He looked like he might cry. "I resisted letting the grief truly wash over me when Abigail died. I think my ability to grieve has evolved with my ability to love."

"David," I said, kissing his cheek.

"Bets, I want you to know," he said, "I'm not the same man who lost his senses last January. Living with you made me better. I mean, I know I can continue to improve. I want to be an even better man, a better father."

And, Sol, I like to think he will keep his word. While your father isn't perfect, he strives, just as I do, to be better every day. I want you to be proud of him. Picture him holding my hand under the shade of a palm tree, watching in silence as your brother's casket descended into the ground. We laid baby Edmundo to rest beside Yaya's parents, while David wiped tears from his face.

The hole in the ground was not very wide, but it was still six feet deep. The soil was clay-like at the surface but sand-like at the bottom, and I imagined your brother dissolving into the sea from whence he came, a little baby dolphin swimming home after delivering a hazy message.

We traveled back to Yaya's casita, David and I still holding hands in the back of the sedan, that small physical connection meaning everything. "Also," he said, looking straight ahead. "I've retired from First Provident and I'm selling the apartment. It's time to move on."

He looked for my reaction. I said, "Big steps." It would take some time for him to abandon the strong, protective archetype, but just like me, he was evolving. Whereas Abigail had accompanied David while he amassed a kingdom, I would be the one to lead him down the mountain with grace. The way he was looking at me, I recalled the way he could plead in the early days for my company. This time, however, he was asking me to take his hand so that we might take on the changing world together. If making a king is to be in my future, Sol, let it be with you. I will impart to you the same lessons I tried to teach your father, that power isn't the same thing as brute strength and it's not about flexing muscles. The key is in humility, love, and forgiveness.

The car delivered us to Yaya's house but neither of us made a move to open the door, wanting to extend our last few moments alone. He looked at me with a serious face. "I love you, Bets," he said. "Missing you has proven how much. I want you to know it wasn't just because you were carrying our child or because we were thrown together during the pandemic. I loved you before all that, I love you regardless." He stepped out of the car before I could reply.

We said goodbye to Tía Julia and Tío Luis, who had cleaned Yaya's kitchen spotless. Yaya was resting in her bedroom and we found my mother and Mateo in the kitchen digging out wine glasses and a bottle. "Let me help you," David said, taking a corkscrew from her.

I went out on the porch where Tamara sat on the swing. I had been close to her age when I left Miami but never so overdressed or overstyled; however, she no longer made me self-conscious. I wasn't apologetic for my grandmother's modest home either, with lizards climbing the exterior walls and coconuts littering the yard. I was glad to have grown up in a house planted firmly on the ground that opened up to lush green bushes, not one that required elevators and windows that never opened. After all those months in a mono-chromatic environment of steel and concrete, and the pure white of the sixtieth floor and Abigail's living room, I was proud of my neighborhood's pinks, blues, greens, and yellows.

Tamara and Rae had given me unique insight into varying depths of wealth and what it could accomplish. Money tied gener-ations together in a way that was more complicated than I had ever imagined. While it bought organic groceries and kept landlords happy, it couldn't keep wives and babies from dying. It could buy top-notch health care and allowed for days off and more sleep, but it couldn't buy love or friendship. All that is true, Sol, but I don't ever want you to be so insensitive as to claim money doesn't buy happiness. Money makes day-to-day existence a hell of a lot easier, which has a direct impact on a person's happiness. Still, living one's life in pursuit of money isn't what I'm recommending you do either.

Tamara broke the silence. "That was a beautiful funeral," she said.

I'm not sure why, but my chin began to quiver. "Thank you."

"Dad was nervous about coming alone."

"David, nervous?"

She laughed. We both knew him well. "So, when are you coming back to New York?"

"I'm not sure what I'm going to do."

"Are you two getting back together?" The siblings back home were likely waiting for a report.

"Not sure," I said. "Hey, but there's something I've been want-ing to say, even if this is sort of a weird time." She tilted her head in curiosity, grazing her toes against the floor in one instant and pushing us higher the next. She may have been glamorous, but on the inside, she was still such a kid. "Your dad calls you princess, but I don't think of you that way." She frowned. "No, what I mean is that to me you're so much more than your father's daughter. I want to support you being whatever it is you want to be." Still, her expression suggested she didn't entirely understand.

"My dad and I are very close but that causes its own sort of problems."

"Family is important, but it's also important to find your own place in the world."

"If only," she said, obviously wanting precisely that while the world was having none of it. Inside, I knew she would benefit from leaving New York, disentangling from David, and discovering who she might become without him.

I attempted a sympathetic smile.

She said, "You know, I used to be really intimidated by you."

"What?"

"All the times I'd see you at my dad's office, I mean how can you be pretty and smart at the same time?"

"Ah, Tamara. We all are. You are too."

She shook her head as the screen door squeaked open and David came out on the porch balancing a tray with five glasses. Mateo held the door for my mother.

"We could all use a drink," said David. "And then Tamara and I should get going to the airport."

CHAPTER THIRTY-SIX

I spent a few days resting under Yaya's care, but the summer heat in the casita became too much for me. My mother had to go back to work and so it was Yaya and me sitting in the kitchen one morning drinking coffee and eating toast.

"I'm happy you came home, mija. But it's time."

I pretended not to understand, but we both knew there was a world out there waiting for me and staying too long would be a step backward.

"I'm glad you had the chance to meet David."

"Que vigor," she said, raising an eyebrow with a sneaky grin. It was neither approval nor disapproval, just an acknowledgment of his virility.

"Sí," I laughed, a little embarrassed.

Later that day, I was on my laptop checking into flights when Rae called. We went back and forth in our usual way, throwing in a few cutting remarks about living with moms and grandmothers, parallel lives at different latitudes, even though it went without saying we both felt blessed.

"Come to Eden?" she asked, sort of out of the blue. It was as if our banter unlocked something she missed and needed more of.

"Really?" I asked. "There's room?"

"It's a marvelous place to convalesce," she said with the snooty impersonation of a blue blood.

I laughed. "I still need to pack up my things in the apartment. I've blown through my savings and can't afford the rent."

"Don't worry, your stuff isn't in the way. I have no plans to move back to the city at least until the end of the summer. Anyway, I think I can find a new roommate." I was sure she meant Lucy, and I didn't want to come across as jealous.

"Really?"

"Yes, and I'm sorry that text about the lease renewal arrived when it did. Really bad timing."

"Sometimes you just don't get it."

"I know. But I appreciate you calling me out when I don't."

———

I flew to Boston, bypassing New York altogether, and took a train south to Kingston. Rae and Lucy were idling in the car outside the station. Lucy hopped out of the passenger seat to help with my bag as soon as she spotted me in the side-view mirror.

"She can't wait to see you," she said, insisting I sit up front.

"Bets! You look great!" she said, and I laughed at honest Rae lying through her teeth.

She looked no more an adult driver than she had the last time we were at this train station. Her hair was now its natural color and as she wrapped her arms around my neck, they were thicker than I remembered.

We drove toward the house, the sun high in the sky, the atmosphere in Long Harbor was different than the previous fall when I'd visited with Ethan and Grant. First of all, it was the height of summer, the leaves in the trees were green and despite the continuing pandemic, the seaside enclave was bursting with activity. The beach beyond the dunes was littered with blankets and families huddled in semicircles.

Sarah was standing in the driveway when we arrived, and suddenly I remembered her lawsuit and wondered whether it was still ongoing. She greeted me warmly and offered to help with my luggage. When the poodles came running to inspect the newcomer, I became wistful for little Wally.

Sarah assigned me a room of my own. Not as grand as where I'd slept the previous October, it was a little girl's room, all pinks and frills, and I couldn't help feeling like I'd regressed even further. The morning after my arrival, I was slow going down to breakfast. Unlike my mother and Yaya, the women at Eden seemed full of advice about my future and I wasn't in the mood for Rachel's prescriptions. Nor was I eager to face the portrait of Bunny Meister in the back stairs. He may have been a handsome icon of American enterprise, but now, all Bunny represented to me was the inequality with which the spoils had been split over the last century.

I was sitting in the guest room on the brightly upholstered window seat, brushing out my hair and staring at the ocean when there was a knock on my door.

"Yes?"

It was Sarah. "Have a minute?"

"Of course." She pulled up a chair beside me and I said, "I'm sorry I haven't responded to your lawyer's emails."

"Oh, gosh, with all you've been through," she said. "Anyway, Lyle College offered me a settlement, which I think I'm going to accept."

"Oh." I was surprised, not sure whether she considered it a victory or a compromise. But at least the power I'd wielded as an analyst pregnant with David's child hadn't been squandered. The prospect of my testimony and cross examination was enough to scare Nathan and Ted Johnstone. I hoped she got a big number.

"Betsabé, really. I just wanted to let you know how sorry I am." She put her hand on my thigh.

I pressed my lips into a smile. Very few people were aware of my son's death, and those who were never knew what to say. Given what was going on in the world, I'd begun to think my mourning was frivolous.

"Thanks," I said. "I appreciate that." I turned back toward the window.

"But yeah, on the Lyle front, did Rae tell you there have been a rash of coywolf sightings here this spring? Pets going missing and the like?"

"She did."

"My family served me up as the resident expert," she said with a shrug. "I've convened some town meetings like the ones we assembled for SUFI."

"Did you tell everyone the first step is eliminating a predator's food source?"

"And until then, keep your pets inside," she said. "But people won't be satisfied until the last coywolf is killed." We shared a resigned silence, having both accepted the inevitability of the predator–prey relationship and how all life relies on that balance.

"Hey, enough of that. I came up here for another reason." She opened her palm to reveal a gold band embedded with sapphires and diamonds, the same ring Rae had slipped on my finger before Thanksgiving dinner. "We all agreed it looked so nice on your long fingers. We want you to have it in memory of your son." As I stared at the gems, something stirred in my chest. It was as if Bunny had reached out from the other side himself, attempting to seduce me.

"Oh, Sarah, it's beautiful but I can't accept it."

"Of course, you can. Sapphires represent wisdom and royalty, and diamonds represent commitment and faithfulness." I wasn't sure what was more generous, the ring or the attributes she meant to bestow with it.

I looked into her eyes. "No, I can't. That ring belongs in your family. But thank you." Yaya and my mother would have more meaningful gifts to hand down, gifts meant just for me. Sarah looked disappointed, and I imagined the ring returning to the dark recesses of a safe deposit box, hoping for better luck with the next generation.

"But hey," I said. "Can I ask you something?"

"Sure."

"About your relationship with President Addington?" A flash of shock crossed her face. "I mean, I guess the rumors were true?"

"Yes, we were on-again, off-again for years."

"I only ask because, well, how did you handle his power? Like, the control?"

She chuckled. "You get right to the heart of a matter, don't you, Betsabé?" I had my mother to thank for that. "Well, there was a time he made me feel special. I came to Lyle as a young art history professor and when he invited me into his inner circle, it was like joining an important constellation in College Hall. The intimacy part, it was a sideshow to the professional attention. I guess I was lonely, and when a powerful man wants you, it's like a drug. Hindsight, you know?"

"Yeah." I related, I felt that intoxication. And maybe that's another reason I've written this all down, Sol, in case this book finds its way into the hands of a woman who's found herself in an unorthodox relationship, hooked on an indefinable rush and suddenly wonders, *What the hell just happened?* I want her to know she's not alone.

"Anyway," Sarah continued. "Rick was a narcissist and after a while it became clear he was only keeping me around, all of us around, for that matter, to feed his ego. And to take the blame when he made mistakes."

"I'm glad you sued."

"Me too," she said, gazing wistfully at the horizon. She patted my knee with a sigh that suggested our conversation was coming to an end. There might be support groups for working mothers, Sol, but I've yet to find a group for those of us who were seduced by the idea of a father. That brief conversation with Sarah was as close as I'd get. We are a bunch who tend to live in the shadows.

As I write toward my conclusion, you may still have questions. You may be wondering why I returned to him, because you know that's what happens, Sol. It has to, otherwise you would never exist. Even so, I'll bet you were rooting for a different outcome. You might be disappointed I didn't adhere more to "feminist" principles. But consider Sarah Stern's reasoning—perhaps David was a drug I couldn't kick, or more aptly put, maybe he was a medication I didn't want to stop taking. There is also the fact I began meditating every morning on what to do, and I heard a voice coaxing me in David's direction. It's hard to name, Sol, but I am pretty sure it was Abigail's.

So, with a compassion for the VP's wife I'd never been able to muster during my first year in the city, I accepted David's offer of partnership. Not right away, mind you, but we wound our way back together eventually. I was reminded of our first night and the way he described our coupling as "inevitable." I bristled when he'd used that word one cold December night in 2019, but looking back now, I agree. Our attraction was too intense to ignore. As for my part, returning to him was only possible once I realized I didn't need anything from him. Although our union would require compromise, I want you to understand that my marriage to David was in no way a sacrifice. If I learned anything that year, Sol, it was that to love and be loved, one must be able to bend.

———

One of my last nights in that frilly bedroom, the full moon pulled me from a sound sleep. I tiptoed into Rae and Lucy's room to find them snuggled under the covers side by side, heads on pillows likely having relayed the day's events before nodding off to sleep. A pang of jealousy shot through my heart, remembering the nighttime ritual I'd assumed she'd created with me.

I tapped her shoulder. She woke easily and was crossing the room quickly so as not to disturb Lucy. "What's wrong?" she asked.

"Nothing," I said, a little drunk on the moon and the stars. "Come with me?" I led her downstairs through the kitchen where I grabbed some fruit from the bowl on the table.

"What are you doing?" she asked.

"Shhh," I whispered, not wanting to jeopardize the magic of the moment. We left the house and crossed the dunes where I'd sat with Grant so many months earlier. As we approached the beach I stopped abruptly. I was so intent on getting to the ocean that I almost didn't notice what at first looked like dogs.

"Coywolves," Rae said in a high whisper. You couldn't miss the green glow of their pupils. There were three of them standing alert at the high point of the dunes, partially hidden by seagrass. They were statuesque, well-fed, and healthy, and although I felt certain they wouldn't harm us, that the moonlight on the water had been as much a magnet for these creatures as it was for me, we veered onto a different path. When we reached the hard sand and the foamy edge of the sea, the moon was hanging even larger over the swollen expanse of water. I pulled off my nightgown and walked in slowly up to my waist, tensing at the shock of the cold.

Rae gasped, but she didn't say a word, eventually pulling off her T-shirt and wading in to join me. There were no waves, only a calm lapping, as if the ocean understood all our human fragility. I gazed toward the filmy stardust surrounding the moon and closed my eyes, saying a silent prayer to Yemayá before releasing the apple, banana, and orange. The fruit bobbed on the glassy surface before drifting away. "It's an offering," I said, even though Rae hadn't asked. I didn't name the goddess Yemayá, nor did I tell her my grandmother had asked me to perform the rite the previous Christmas in Miami Beach.

Having Rae as my witness hadn't been necessary, but it felt important. After all, ours was a friendship that marked our transcendence from girlhood to womanhood. I needed her to see me as more than a working girl, more than her love-struck roommate. This is who I am now. I wanted to reclaim Yaya's teachings, to have her see me at one with the natural world. We walked back onto the sand arm in arm, our naked bodies shivering and glistening at the same time. "Rae," I said. "You are my best friend. And although we haven't had perfect role models, we'll always have each other."

We stood there, holding hands. There was a lot to balance, but eventually we'd get it right, we had to. The world needed us. "I love you, Bets," she said.

We walked back toward the house to find the coywolves standing in the same spot. "Don't be afraid," I said. "They won't hurt us; they are in awe of us."

I relaxed in that grand home for a week, charting my next move in the same way Yaya used to stare down tea leaves. Lucy tried to help. "It's New York. You can be anything you want." As if it was as easy as dying my hair a bright color. Nathan sent a note with his deepest sympathies, saying that since David had retired, First Provident could welcome me back for my second year as an analyst. I was surprised and flattered, but the image of a theatre's red velvet seats kept popping into my head. It was one I'd been storing at the back of my mind since the conclusion of Hamilton. Even though the idea was out of focus and I had to reel it back in from a dusty place, it filled me with warmth. Only a crazy woman would pursue a career in the theatre during a pandemic when every stage in the country was closed. The thought of it was laughable, but it also made my heart swell.

As you can imagine, David and I were hesitant to get pregnant again. But I'm prepared for your arrival, the wisdom I've gained surpassing anything I once thought only possible from elders. Gabriel García Márquez once said, "Human beings are not born once and for all on the day their mothers give birth to them, but . . . life obliges them over and over again to give birth to themselves." I like to think I will have ushered in several versions of Betsabé Ruiz by the time you sit down to read this.

We all encounter twists and turns on our paths, and as Yaya used to say, the more, the better. I traveled from childhood to adulthood, poverty to riches, lust to love, joy to pain, and birth to death all in a twelve-month period. Just as Helen in HR had said the summer's training program was going to be a four-year finance degree crammed into ten weeks, my twenty-third year was a concentrate of life's extremes. Perfect theatre, really.

And even though it etched scars into my skin, I have this dream where the scars have transformed into merit badges, far outnumbering what I'd ever earned in Girl Scouts. One badge for wisdom, one for honesty, one for love, one for courage, and one for patience. There is one in the shape of a lightning bolt stitched to my chest that glows the same iridescent green as a coywolf's eyes when I spin on the balls of my feet, twirling and twirling, as fast as a tornado. I gradually slow to a stop, and fear the dream is coming to an end, but I should know better by now, Sol, because it continues and I spin one more time through a revolving door, before strutting fearlessly down a white marble runway. I step into the spotlight, cloaked in a swath of red cape, with nail polish and lipstick to match.

ACKNOWLEDGMENTS

Writing a novel requires patience and surrender, qualities I don't come by naturally. For the motivation to keep going, I need to thank my writing communities: GrubStreet, She Writes Press, BookEnds, and the Wonderwriters slack channel. Thank you for your intolerance of negative self-talk and insisting that making art is essential even during the upheaval of a pandemic when I was often tempted to ask, "what's the point?"

Thank you to Rabbi Elaine Zecher and the Temple Israel Modern Midrash Class. We have studied Torah, Midrash, and wisdom literature for over twenty years now. Please accept this novel as a tribute to the marvelous community you have created.

This work would have never come to be without my year as a Southampton Writer's Conference BookEnds fellow. Thank you to Susie Merrell and Meg Wolitzer for helping me uncover the heart of the story. Thanks to all the "Fives," especially Jennifer Yeh and Sarah Haufrect. Access to your critical thinking was a gift, but to have your friendship, Dayenu. I hope we will always be three city girls with (possibly fewer) problems. To my mentor, Scott Cheshire, thank you for your enthusiasm and belief in my novel.

Thanks to Katherine Sherbrooke and Katrin Schumann, incredibly generous artists, for reading and commenting in ways that made this novel and my thinking infinitely better. To Jennifer Gilfond for introducing me to Mia Carbonell. Thank you, Mia, for helping me portray my beautiful and powerful protagonist with more accuracy.

Thank you to Dr. Donelle Laughlin, who advised for medical accuracy. To Cecilia de Havenon, for pressure testing the manuscript and challenging me to improve where she saw potential. To Stephanie Brownell for helping to keep the messiest of first drafts organized.

To Brooke Warner for her excitement about the novel and for coming up with a great title. To Shannon Green for extraordinary project management. To Crystal Patriarche for welcoming me back under the tent and championing my work as always.

Thank you to my three children. I am grateful you are avid readers and creative souls. The time you took with the manuscript as well as your intelligent feedback is deeply appreciated. More importantly, thank you for your unconditional love and encouragement.

To John, nothing would be possible without you. Your love has lifted me up since the day we met.

ABOUT THE AUTHOR

Jeanne Blasberg is an award-winning author and essayist. Her novel *The Nine* (She Writes Press, 2019) was honored with the 2019 Foreword Indies Gold Award in Thriller & Suspense, and the Gold Medal and Juror's Choice in the 2019 National Indic Excellence Awards. Her debut, *Eden* (She Writes Press, 2017), won the Benjamin Franklin Silver Award for Best New Voice in Fiction and was a finalist for the Sarton Women's Book Award for Historical Fiction.

Jeanne cochairs the board of the Boston Book Festival and serves on the Executive Committee of GrubStreet, one of the country's preeminent creative writing centers. When not in New England, she splits her time between Park City, UT, and growing organic vegetables in Verona, Wisconsin.

Author photo © Hunter Levitan

SELECTED TITLES FROM SHE WRITES PRESS

She Writes Press is an independent publishing company founded to serve women writers everywhere. Visit us at www.shewritespress.com.

Eden by Jeanne Blasberg. $16.95, 978-1-63152-188-1. As her children and grandchildren assemble for Fourth of July weekend at Eden, the Meister family's grand summer cottage on the Rhode Island shore, Becca decides it's time to introduce the daughter she gave up for adoption fifty years ago.

The Nine by Jeanne McWilliams Blasberg. $16.95, 978-1-63152-652-7. When well-meaning helicopter mom Hannah Webber enrolls her brilliant son and the center of her world, Sam, into the boarding school of her dreams, neither of them is prepared for what awaits: an illicit underworld where decades of privileged conspiracy threaten not only Sam but also his fragile family.

Royal Entertainment by Marni Fechter. $16.95, 978 1 93831-452-0. After being fired from her job for blowing the whistle on her boss, social worker Melody Frank has to adapt to her new life as the assistant to an elite New York party planner.

The T Room by Victoria Lilienthal. $16.95, 978-1-64742-383-4. Single mom Vera West's bodywork career is on fire, but her dynamic partnership with her charismatic and sexy married mentor turns out to be more like a deal with the Devil. Fraught with yearning, questionable decision-making, and fierce female competition, Vera's path to self-authority is a humorous and insightful tribute to the power of compassion.

Fish Heads and Duck Skin by Lindsey Salatka. $16.95, 978-1-64742-128-1. On the advice of a five-dollar psychic, Tina Martin, a zany, overworked mother of two, quits her high-powered job and moves her family to Shanghai—where it takes the friendship of an elderly tai chi instructor, a hot Mandarin tutor, and several mah-jongg-tile-slinging expats to help her find her way.

Mt. Moriah's Wake by Melissa Norton Carro. $16.95, 978-1-64742-138-0. A young woman returning home to her small southern town must face her past and the skeletons in her small community—and come to terms with her present life.